THE PREY

Also by Tony Park

Far Horizon
Ivory
Silent Predator
Zambezi
Safari
The Delta
African Dawn
African Sky
Dark Heart

Australian writer Tony Park fell in love with South Africa on
a short trip in 1995. He is a major in the Australian Army
Reserve and has worked in journalism and PR, including
six months in Afghanistan in 2002 as PR officer for the
Australian ground forces. Tony and his wife Nicola now
divide their time between Sydney and the African bush.

TONY PARK

THE PREY

Quercus

For Nicola

First published in Australia in 2013 by Pan Macmillan

First published in Great Britain in 2013 by

Quercus Editions Ltd
55 Baker Street
7th Floor, South Block
London W1U 8EW

A CIP catalogue record for this book is available
from the British Library

TPB ISBN 978 1 78206 161 8
EBOOK ISBN 978 1 78206 162 5

10 9 8 7 6 5 4 3 2 1

Printed and bound in Great Britain by Clays Ltd, St Ives plc

Typeset by Ellipsis Digital Limited, Glasgow

AUTHOR'S NOTE

At the time of writing this book, in 2013, there was minerals exploration occurring in several national parks and wildlife areas in Africa. Contrary to the story you are about to read, however, there were no plans to develop mines in or adjacent to the Sabi Sand Game Reserve in South Africa, or in the coastal region of Inhambane or Homoine in Mozambique. The proposed coalmines mentioned in this book are completely fictitious.

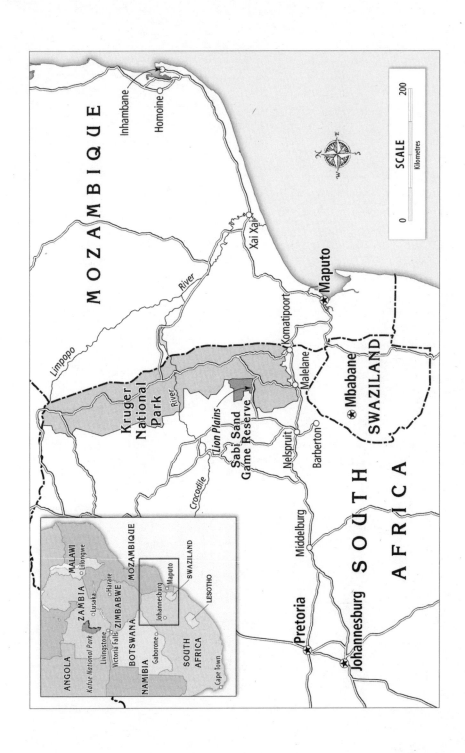

PROLOGUE

AUSTRALIAN FINANCIAL REVIEW ONLINE

MINING EXECUTIVES KILLED IN ZAMBIAN AIR CRASH
10 October 2013

Lusaka, Zambia: Troubled Australian mining giant Global Resources is mourning the loss of two of its brightest stars, second-in-charge Dr Kylie Hamilton, and a senior South African mine manager, Cameron McMurtrie, who died today in a light aircraft crash in Zambia.

Dr Hamilton, the company's director of health, safety, environment and community, had been widely tipped to take over the company if and when its besieged CEO, Jan Stein, departed. Dr Hamilton and Mr McMurtrie, who had been recently appointed to the position of director of new projects, were on their way to visit a mine in Zambia's copper belt region when their Cessna crashed.

A Zambian air force helicopter found the crash site yesterday in rugged bushland in the centre of the country's remote Kafue National Park. Reports said the badly burnt bodies of two men, one believed to be the pilot, and a woman were found at the scene of the crash.

Mr McMurtrie, from Barberton, South Africa, and Dr Hamilton, from Sydney, Australia, were the only two passengers on the flight.

'The pilot did not radio a distress call, and a ranger in Kafue National Park told us he saw the aircraft pass overhead and then heard a loud explosion a short time later,' Zambian military spokesman Colonel Oliver Mwanzi told the *Australian Financial Review*.

Mr Stein said in a statement issued last night that Dr Hamilton and Mr McMurtrie were irreplaceable members of the Global Resources family.

The news has sent Global Resources shares plummeting to an all-time low, continuing the trend of the last two weeks as the company has lurched from one crisis to another in its African operations.

PART ONE

1

SABI SAND GAME RESERVE, MPUMALANGA, SOUTH AFRICA

U nlike the rest of his kind, he was a catcher of fish, and unlike those of his relatives who also liked to fish, he did so at night. He didn't fear the darkness, populated as it was with the lion and the leopard on the hunt and countless smaller predators, such as the wild cat, the serval, the genet and the civet. Secrecy was part of his defence. He was a master of camouflage and, although he had a big voice when it was called for, he usually went about his business in silence.

He scanned the water of the Sabie River in front of him. It was the end of the long dry winter and the river, which had been a raging torrent that claimed trees and washed away banks in the summer, was now gurgling gently. Perfect.

His eyesight was good. In the light of the full moon he could see a fat barbel snaking its way along the bottom, its ugly black tadpole-shaped bulk and its cat's whiskers clearly silhouetted against the rich gold of the sandy bottom of the shallow river.

A crocodile cruised a little further upriver, its nostrils and eyes the only parts of it that sliced the glittering surface. A hippo honked its impatience at another in its pod as it wallowed and queued, waiting for its turn to wade ponderously out of the river and begin a night of foraging for grass.

The deep shade of the sycamore fig cloaked the fisherman in a dappled moon shadow, so the barbel wouldn't see him until the second he speared the water and struck. He watched the fish and thought of the feast to come.

From the home he shared with his mate he heard the cry of his baby. He turned his head three hundred and sixty degrees to face the sound.

His baby squawked again. A fiery-necked nightjar offered a prayer to the night: *good Lord, deliver us, good Lord, deliver us*, the bird called.

He was under pressure.

A blade of bright light suddenly slashed the darkness and played across the surface of the Sabie River. The barbel, as startled as the fisherman by the intrusion, flicked his tail and disappeared upriver at a speed surprising for his size. The crocodile dived, like a submarine preparing for action.

'Look, it's an owl,' a human voice called.

The fisherman took flight.

2

BARBERTON, SOUTH AFRICA

Chris Loubser hated the dark. He stole a last glimpse of daylight as he walked into the cage, and closed his eyes tight as the gate slid shut. The few people in his personal life who knew of his phobia – his sister and his parents – had been astounded when he'd taken the job working underground.

The cage bell rang. Immediately it felt to him as though the rock walls around him had started to move inwards, as if pushing the bodies of the other mine workers into him, so that he melded with them, a single multi-armed, multi-legged crush of flesh sandwiched between the pressing rock.

This was his nightmare, and his job. Themba, his newly recruited and freshly university-minted assistant, elbowed him in the ribs. Chris, startled, opened his eyes to see the young man grinning. He'd said something but Chris hadn't heard it over the screaming of the spooling cable.

'What?'

'It's faster than I thought. Hell of a ride, man.'

Chris nodded and took in the scene in front of him. Themba

seemed to be enjoying it. Two other men in the cage chatted and laughed casually, and another couple stared straight ahead, looking bored. Just another shift. Chris wished he could be like them.

'It's a job, Mom,' he'd said to his mother. 'And I'm a twenty-nine-year-old Afrikaner *oke* in a workforce where black women are at the top of the hiring list – even in the mines – and white men are at the bottom.'

'You could go to Australia, Chris, there's plenty of work for smart boys like you there.'

His mother hadn't looked into emigrating, but Chris had. He knew it wasn't nearly as easy for him to enter Australia as she thought, and besides, the only industry that would offer him a job and sponsor him into the country was mining. If he was going to have to work in an underground hell he would rather it be at home. He loved the bush and he loved his country, despite all of its faults.

'I can do more here in South Africa,' he had told his mother. 'In Australia safety is already the industry's priority, whereas here there's much more to be done on that front. I can achieve more here. I can save lives, Mom.'

His stomach lurched as the multi-deck cage he was riding hurtled into the black abyss. Suspended below the platform he stood on were two more decks, each with a further six people in them.

He knew the statistics, and they didn't make him feel better. The temperature rose by 0.4 of a degree for every hundred metres they descended. He'd checked the thermometer before entering the cage and worked out that the wet-bulb temperature would be 30 degrees – flipping hot – in the *madala* side they were heading to, one thousand, four hundred metres below ground level.

'You feeling OK, man?' asked his dreadlocked trainee.

Chris looked beyond the confines of the cage and saw the rock face rushing past. He wished he'd kept his eyes shut. 'Big night last night,' he responded weakly.

Themba threw back his head and laughed. 'I thought you were the quiet one in the office?'

Chris supposed he was. He hadn't been out drinking last night; he had been poring over the environmental impact assessment for a new mine, the one planned for the game reserve. He was one of six people in the South African office of Global Resources who'd been asked to contribute to the assessment when it was in draft form. Most of his comments had been included, some ignored.

Chris closed his eyes again. The truth was he spent very little time underground, but Themba had never been into a *madala* side and it was company policy that no one went into the disused tunnels, or an 'old' side or area as the name meant in English, alone. It was too risky. They were also being escorted by a mine security guard, an Angolan named Paulo Barrica, who carried an R5 assault rifle in addition to his lamp and the self-rescue pack they all wore underground.

The smell and heat of the bodies around him added to Chris's sense of unease, a feeling that was rising steadily with every additional level they plummeted. *Nearly a kilometre and a half*, he thought to himself. It would have been worse if he was working in one of the big goldmines in the Free State; some of them were more than three thousand metres deep. He clasped his hands together to stop them from shaking. He couldn't let Themba see just how frightened he was.

When the hoist driver stopped Chris and Themba's deck at level fourteen, bells rang to tell the onsetter controlling the cage it was safe to open the gate. The man nodded for them to get out. Barrica knew the way to the disused workings and he led off, his rifle cradled across his broad chest.

'Who were you out partying with last night – some of the boys from the office?' Themba asked him. 'Get in trouble from the wife?'

'No. I'm not married.'

'I am. We have a little girl, just turned six months. Do you have a girlfriend?'

'No,' Chris said.

Chris wondered if Themba was making small talk because he sensed that Chris was nervous and was trying to ease the tension.

If so, it wasn't working. He wanted to be alone with his thoughts and fears.

They left the parade of men and machinery behind them as the three of them turned into an unlit side tunnel. Barrica turned on his lamp and Chris and Themba followed suit.

'This leads to one of the *madala* sides,' Chris said. In front of them, in the light cast by Barrica's lamp, they could see where the tunnel had been bricked closed, and where a man-sized steel door had been fitted at the wall's centre. Barrica unclipped a key chain from his belt, set down his R5 against a wall and tried three keys before he found the one that opened the padlock on the latch.

'Although this part of the mine isn't being worked it still needs to be monitored,' Chris said, more to stop himself from turning and running back to the cage and begging to be hoisted back to the surface, than from any real need to explain to Themba why they were here.

'Because of the dead *zama zamas*?' Themba asked. 'Why do we even care about them?'

Chris didn't bother to hide his annoyance. 'Because our men work nearby. We know some of the bodies the *zama zamas* leave out for us to collect died of cholera and others from carbon monoxide poisoning. Cameron wants us to find out how close the contaminants are to our workers.' He risked adding, 'And because they're human beings.' The term meant 'try try' or to chance, and Chris despaired at the poverty or greed that would make men want to live likes a *zama zama*, slaving away for months on end underground, where death was a more likely outcome than riches.

'You sure we're safe down here then, man?'

Chris stopped and turned to Themba. The younger man took half a pace back. Chris saw he carried his own fears. 'You're worried about the *zama zamas*?'

'No.' He shrugged his shoulders. 'Well maybe.'

'That's why Paulo's here,' Chris said, nodding towards Barrica's broad back. The security guard now held his rifle at the ready, the tip of the barrel leading the way. He didn't bother looking back at them. Paulo had been hired because of his military skills – he was a veteran of years of fighting in the Angolan civil war – and because as a foreigner there was less risk of him being bribed or coerced into working for the local *zama zamas*. He would also have no qualms about killing them if he had to.

'Come on then,' Chris beckoned Themba with false bravado. 'We've got work to do.'

As they trudged behind Barrica in the subterranean heat, Chris was sweating and a little short of breath. He stumbled every now and then as his gumboots slipped on an irregular chunk of rock. As they rounded a bend, he smelled something.

Barrica stopped and held up a hand. Chris gave Barrica a nod, and the Angolan started moving forward again, at a careful pace, rifle at the ready.

'*Eish!* What is that *stink?*' Themba put a hand over his mouth and coughed.

The rank odour grew stronger as they moved down the tunnel. Chris forgot his fears of the roof of rock falling on him, or of the side walls closing in on him. There was something very real waiting for them in the blackness ahead. The stench reached out for them.

'What *is* that?' Themba asked again.

Barrica stopped and turned to fix the young man with the hard stare of a warrior. 'Ssssh. That smell, it is death.'

SYDNEY, AUSTRALIA

Kylie set down her takeaway latte on the boardroom table and looked into the lens of the video camera.

'OK, please tell us your name and position in the company as a tape identification and sound check,' said the thin man operating the camera. 'And look at me, not into the lens.'

She shifted her gaze. 'Doctor Kylie Hamilton, EGM, HSEC for GR.' She'd been interviewed a few times for real, for mining industry magazines, some country newspapers in the Hunter Valley where she had managed a coalmine for five years, and twice for regional television. Kylie wasn't nervous about the media training course she'd been volunteered for by corporate affairs, but given the choice she would have been back at her desk – she had a mountain of work to get through before her flight to South Africa the following morning.

'EGM HSEC?' The media trainer smiled condescendingly. 'GR?'

'Executive General Manager, Health, Safety, Environment and Community, Global Resources,' Kylie said with the patience of a teacher taking extra time for the slow learner.

'Window-dressing, in other words.'

Kylie sighed inwardly. So this was how it was going to be. There were three other people on the course, her CEO, Jan Stein; the human resources EGM, Jeff Curtis; and the new South African corporate affairs manager, Musa Mabunda, who was in Australia for four days of familiarisation with the business. Out of the corner of her eye she saw Musa put his hand over his mouth to hide his customary smile. Let him smile. 'I wouldn't say window-dressing, I'd say –'

'*Environment?*' the thin man said over the top of her. 'How *environmentally friendly* is a company that destroys the pristine bushland of the Kruger National Park, South Africa's flagship game reserve?'

'I'd say we're very friendly. The land we've been exploring on is hardly pristine and –'

'The land you've been exploring,' the trainer paused for a moment to check his notes and Kylie was about to jump back in and finish her sentence when he silenced her again, 'is home to a denning site of the endangered African painted dog, as well as black rhino, cheetah, lion, leopard, and a host of other threatened animals.'

'Actually, it's –'

'Why is Global Resources *raping* South Africa's iconic national park?'

Kylie was getting annoyed at the trainer. She knew it was only role-play and she had been in more stressful situations before – both in training and in real life – but she suspected he was going harder than was useful, possibly because she was the only woman in the room and on the exec team. 'We're not raping anything. If I could just finish what I was –'

'Yours is the same mining company that's recently been exploring in other parts of Africa, isn't it? How much does Global Resources expect to make off the backs of poorly paid African workers this year?'

'Our mines in South Africa were spared the strikes and violence that plagued other operations in that country last year because our workforce is treated with respect and we have negotiated mutually agreeable pay packages with our people.' Finally, she thought, she was getting it together. She added: 'Our financial position is particularly strong given the demand for resources in developing countries.'

The interviewer nodded. 'Yes, and China and India's hunger is going to cost South Africa one of its great wilderness areas.'

'You're putting words in my mouth,' she said. He smirked at her and she felt like punching him in the face. She could feel the sweat pricking at her armpits and beading on her top lip. She'd stared down unionists over enterprise agreements, green activists over open-cut mines, and politicians over the mining tax, but those were real negotiations, where Kylie had at least been treated with respect, even if her views weren't popular. Kylie was also conscious that her boss and the rest of the exec team were watching her, like Roman spectators at a one-sided gladiatorial contest.

'How safe are Global Resources' mines?' the trainer asked, changing tack just as she was formulating something to say about profits and demand for minerals worldwide.

She reached for a lifeline. 'I'm pleased you asked,' she said, smiling. 'Our mines are very safe. Safety is our number one priority.'

'In Australia perhaps, but what about Africa? Isn't it true, Ms Hamilton, that nine workers were killed in workplace accidents in South African mines last year?'

She stared at him.

'Well?'

He trotted out his make-believe questions like he was some hotshot investigative reporter, but the truth was he hadn't worked as a journalist for years. Kylie, on the other hand, had seen what was left of a man when his remains were dug from the cab of a truck that had just had five tonnes of coal dumped on it by mistake. This was bullshit.

'Ten,' she said.

'Sorry?' said the trainer.

'Regrettably, ten people were killed in our coal and goldmines last year, not nine, and that is ten too many.' She paused. 'And it's *Doctor* Hamilton, if you don't mind.'

The man glanced at his notes, then looked up at her, this time meeting her eyes for the first time. 'Thanks for your time.'

Kylie unclipped the microphone from the lapel of her jacket, picked up her now lukewarm coffee, stood up and went back to her seat.

The trainer rubbed his hands together. 'Next victim.'

Kylie had volunteered to go first but now Jan Stein and Jeff Curtis looked at each other. They'd just seen her demolished on camera by a one-man wrecking ball and neither wanted to go next. Kylie thought Jan would have had bigger balls. She opened the workbook the trainer had given each of them; as a senior member of the team she would be required to face the media more often and now that the shock of the pretend interview was over she was looking forward to mastering a new skill. If she had a chance at a second interview, and she suspected this would be part of the training, Kylie wanted to be able to nail it. She had not got to where she was in this male-dominated industry by backing down from confrontational situations.

'My turn,' said Musa. He was beaming. Kylie looked up from the course notes as Musa got up, adjusted his silk tie and buttoned his suit jacket. He was the smartest dressed man in a head office full of suits – some of them very expensive. By contrast, Kylie's approach to her wardrobe could be described as pragmatic at best. While she had an office in the company's Sydney headquarters, in Macquarie Street with a view out over the Botanic Gardens to the Heads, she spent most of her time on the road and on-site at the company's mines. There she wore steel-capped boots not stilettos, and the standard uniform of blue overalls with a yellow high-visibility vest ringed with reflective panels – a uniform she felt far more comfortable in than the navy A-line skirt suit she'd thrown on for today's training session.

Musa took a seat in front of the trainer, threaded the lapel microphone up under his jacket and carefully attached it to his perfectly tailored grey suit jacket. Kylie felt sorry for the man already, he was about to be eaten alive.

'OK,' said the trainer, 'we're rolling. If I could just start by getting your name and –'

'My name is Musa Mabunda,' he spelled in a clear, deep voice, his delivery slow and precise, yet not laborious. 'I am the Manager of Corporate Communications for Global Resources in South Africa.'

'Mr Mabunda, how can your company rape –'

'Perhaps I could start by giving you an overview of our plans for a new mine in South Africa – a mine that will uplift an impoverished community, provide valuable resources and income which will aid the development of the new South Africa and be a world-class model for safety and environmental protection.'

The trainer tried to interject, but Musa had the ball and he was running with it. Kylie smiled. The former journalist tried again to ask one of his barbed questions, but Musa raised his voice ever so slightly and continued his monologue.

'First, the site of the proposed new Global Resources coal extraction facility is *not,* I repeat, *not* in the Kruger National Park. It lies to the west of the park on a former game farm that was returned to its rightful owners, the Shangaan people, back in 2009. The traditional owners of this land own the mining rights, not the national parks board of South Africa.

'This proposal has been the subject of an exhaustive environmental impact statement and Global Resources has not only met, but in fact has exceeded the requirements placed on the company by government in terms of air and water quality management, economic upliftment of local communities and wildlife conservation conditions.'

'But –' tried the trainer.

'Further,' Musa continued, 'this project will employ nine hundred formerly disadvantaged South Africans.'

The trainer looked at his notes. 'There were ten fatalities in South African mines last year. What guarantees can you give that –'

'As a company, safety is our number one priority and I can assure you that Global Resources works tirelessly to educate our workforce and to continually review our operations in order to improve this part of our business and ensure our people go home from work at the end of each shift as fit and well as they started.'

Kylie was impressed by Musa's performance, but as the corporate PR man, this was his bread and butter. She had paid careful attention to the way he had steered the interview away from the trainer's inflammatory line of questioning and back to the company's key messages. She looked over to her CEO, Jan Stein, and saw that he was grinning broadly.

'Well, I think we're done here,' said the trainer.

Musa unclipped his microphone and stood up. Jan, the naturalised Australian from South Africa, started to applaud. Jeff and Kylie joined in. It was all bullshit, Kylie thought, but it was damn good bullshit. Musa winked at her as he took his seat beside her.

3

'*Zama zama*,' said Barrica, as his headlamp played over the body at his feet. Themba was dry-retching, having just thrown up his breakfast.

Chris held his hand over his mouth and played his lamp across the dead man. Decomposition accelerated underground, aided as it was by the heat. The corpse was so swollen that the dead man's tattered and threadbare overalls had started to split. His mouth was stretched in an obscene grin and his fingers were like plump black sausages.

Chris composed himself, then looked over to Barrica. '*Ja*. But odd they didn't leave him somewhere easier for us to find him like they usually do. They couldn't have known we'd be inspecting this site any time soon.'

Themba looked up. 'What do you mean?' he asked.

Chris explained that the *zama zamas*, the pirate miners who worked the *madala* side as industriously – sometimes more so – than Global Resources' legitimate employees, often suffered workplace fatalities, but usually the bodies were dragged to a working part of the mine, or even as far as the main shaft, so they could be found by the next GR shift and returned to the surface. No one wanted to work around decomposing corpses a kilometre and a half underground. Not even illegal miners.

'What do they die of?'

Chris shrugged. 'Everything. Accidents, exposure to harmful chemicals such as mercury in the extraction process, heat exhaustion, AIDS – and lately cholera and carbon monoxide poisoning. These guys live underground for weeks or even months at a time – many don't survive.'

'We need to get back and report this, *baas*,' Barrica said, yet even as he spoke the words he was stepping around the body and heading deeper into the darkness.

'What are you doing?'

Barrica held up a hand to silence Chris. He glanced back and put a finger on his lips and switched off his lamp. Chris immediately did the same, then reached out to Themba and switched his off too. 'Shush,' he said to the young man, and dragged him to the side wall of the tunnel and down to his knees.

'What's going on?' Themba whispered.

'Quiet.' Chris felt the fear rising in him. Now their lamps were extinguished he could see a pale flicker of light further down the tunnel. It wasn't as dark as it had seemed. There was someone down there. 'Stay here,' he whispered to Themba, and crawled towards Barrica.

He groped ahead of him and felt the big security guard start as his hand found his body. 'You said it yourself, we need to get out of here,' Chris whispered.

'They are close,' Barrica growled. 'Listen.'

Chris heard the voices now, speaking in Portuguese. Mozambicans. In recent years the South African government and the unions had insisted that seventy per cent of a mine's workers had to be South African citizens, and over time this had meant that many Mozambicans had lost their jobs and turned to illegal mining. Sometimes they returned as *zama zamas* to the same mines where they'd once held honest jobs.

Behind him, Chris heard footsteps, a stumble and a curse. Themba was making a run for it in the dark.

'*Ola!*' a voice called. Light flickered off the rock walls. The man was probably carrying a candle. *Shit*, he thought to himself, *this was not going well*.

His peripheral vision was suddenly lit up and Chris looked back to see that Themba had switched on his headlamp. It was bobbing away from them, the bright light bouncing off the side walls as he ran.

'*Fok*, no,' Chris cursed under his breath.

A series of explosions rang out, the crack and thump of passing bullets pounding Chris's eardrums. He flattened himself onto the floor as sparks bounced off the walls and a muzzle flash seared his eyes. Someone was shooting at them, with an automatic weapon by the sound of it.

'AK-47,' Barrica said, his summation punctuated by a three-round burst from his own assault rifle. 'Fall back!'

Chris needed no urging. He crawled on his hands and knees over the jagged floor of the tunnel, scrambling as fast as he could. The AK fired again and a stream of red-hot fireflies whizzed over his head. He was glad he'd stayed low. Themba, however, was still running, and Chris saw his lamp pitch to one side, then fall.

'Themba!' he screamed.

Barrica returned fire. 'Run, check the young one. I will cover you,' the security guard shouted out through the chaos.

Chris forced himself up and started to run on feet that felt encased in lead. He'd had a dream like this, where he was being chased by a man with a gun and he couldn't make himself move fast enough. He tensed his muscles, waiting for the spear of pain in his back that would pitch him into the abyss of death. 'Themba!'

His foot collided with something slightly yielding and he fell forward onto the rotting mass of the dead miner. He yelped as he scrambled to get up. Something popped and a hiss of foul-smelling gas jetted up into his face. He put his palm on an arm, or maybe it was a leg, and felt the putrid skin slide away from the body. Covered in slimy, stinking fluid he finally managed to stand. He stumbled a few more paces, got clear of the corpse and glanced back to see if Barrica was following him.

The guard's R5 chattered again, silhouetting Barrica in flashes from the muzzle.

'Grenade!' Barrica shouted. He turned to Chris and started to run towards him. The homemade bomb, a stick of dynamite with a burning fuse in a can packed with nuts and bolts and screws to act as shrapnel, bounced on the floor of the tunnel behind Barrica and erupted. Barrica was blown forward, arms outstretched, as Chris was knocked off his feet and thrown onto his side. His ears rang and he felt like he'd been kicked and punched all over. He crawled towards a shard of light – from the door where they'd entered the chamber – and saw the beam of Themba's light fixed horizontally across the floor from his helmet, which lay beside the young man. He covered a few more metres before he reached Themba, who was sprawled on the rock floor, face first, and placed his fingers on his neck. He couldn't find a pulse. Chris half-rolled the fallen man and gagged. A bullet had drilled a hole in the back of his head, and the exit wound had ruined his once handsome face. Chris had feared death underground for so long – virtually every time he ventured below the earth's surface – but it was not supposed to be like this.

'Bastards!' He tried to stand, but crumpled to one knee when his left ankle buckled. He started to hobble, but was knocked to the ground by something shoved into the small of his back.

Chris rolled over and squinted as a miner's lamp was turned on and shone in his face. A man in overalls stood over him, pointing an AK-47 down at him. He smiled. '*Bom dia*, mister.'

*

Kylie had started to take the media training seriously after her initial humiliation by the trainer. She still didn't like the man, nor the media, but she was fast gaining an appreciation of the skills she needed to master if she was going to be the public face of Global

Resources. And she also had to ensure that she wasn't perceived as the weak link in the management team. She'd fought too hard to get where she was to be defeated by a day-long PR course.

Jan had followed Musa into the trainer's hot seat and while he hadn't done nearly as good a job at getting his messages across and batting away difficult questions as Musa had, their chief executive had acquitted himself well. Certainly, Kylie knew, he'd done a better job than she had. Kylie was never happy coming second, not even to the boss. She would bring her A game when it was time for the second interview, which the trainer had told them would come at the end of the day.

As far as Kylie knew, no one had mentioned to the trainer that the reason she was here was because Jan had told her he wanted her to take over those media interviews he would normally handle. When Jan had poached her from a competitor five years earlier, he'd been full of promises about the amazing opportunities ahead of her. But in the first few years her career had stagnated and she had spent three years longer than she wanted to managing the sustainability division when she really wanted to be at the coalface – and to join the executive team. Finally, a month ago, Jan had given her the EGM position she should have gotten years earlier. She was glad she'd stuck with it, but now she knew the pressure was on – she had to prove to the others that Jan was right to promote her. She had to prove it to Jan, too. And she had to prove it to herself.

'Do you think the gender of the potential spokesperson has any bearing on how the journalist will conduct the interview?' she interjected.

The trainer swung in his chair to look at her, and gave a little smile. 'Since I don't work for Global Resources I don't feel the need to be particularly politically correct in answering this question. So I'll say yes, it does.'

'What do you mean by that?' Jan asked.

'I mean that Kylie here would be a perfect spokesperson for your company. She's female and attractive – definitely not what your average journalist or Joe Blow thinks of when they try to picture a miner.'

'OK,' Kylie said, 'but don't you think the journalist would see this for what it is – using a woman to try and soften the image of a company that's copping a lot of flak in the press?'

'Yes, they will, and it may make the tone and the line of questioning even harder, particularly if it's another woman interviewing you.'

Kylie folded her arms. 'So you *don't* think it's a good idea. You're saying a journalist may be straighter with a man representing a mining company.'

'What I'm *saying* is that there are some who will try their damnedest to expose your being wheeled out to face the cameras for the cynical tokenism that it probably is.' He paused. 'Just being honest,' he added.

Kylie looked at Jan. He was straight-faced. She'd just been utterly undermined by an outsider, yet Jan remained silent. Not for the first time, she wondered whether he truly believed in her, or if he had only wanted her to do more media work because she was a woman and he thought that might soften Global Resources' image during a tough time.

Jan put his fingertips together and rocked back in his chair. They all looked at him. 'Not that it's any of your business,' he said, looking first to the trainer and then to Kylie, 'but there were three people in line for the Executive General Manager role. When I interviewed all of them I told each of the candidates that part of the duties of the EGM would be to engage with the media and progressively take on more and more of the media interviews that I've been doing as a matter of course. I don't think I'm particularly adept at dealing with the media, and neither do some of our shareholders. The two *men* who were in line for the position – a significant promotion I might add – both said they wouldn't be comfortable dealing with the media on areas outside their direct area of expertise. In short, Kylie here was the only person with the gumption to take on this job.'

Kylie smiled at him. Jan had been put on the spot, and he'd done what he always did best – set everyone back on their butts and reminded them why he was the boss.

Kylie's BlackBerry was sitting on the boardroom table. It vibrated. From the corner of her eye she saw Jan and Musa both reach into their shirt pockets. She and Jan exchanged a glance. Group messages usually meant one thing. Trouble.

Jan scrolled through the message and looked at Kylie. She'd already read it. 'Two dead, one missing,' she said.

'This is the last thing we need right now in South Africa,' Musa said.

'It's the last thing we need any time, anywhere, Musa,' Jan said.

'Of course.' He looked chastised.

'You're right, though,' Jan nodded, 'it couldn't have come at a worse time with the South African press baying for our blood over the new mine.'

'Should we take a break now?' the trainer asked.

'No.' Jan fixed him with his grey eyes. 'You can really earn your money now by preparing Kylie and Musa to face the media on a real-time critical issue. We've just had a security guard and a graduate trainee environmental officer killed in a gunfight underground in our goldmine in South Africa. A third man is missing. The people responsible are what we call *zama zamas* – illegal miners, sometimes referred to as pirates. They've taken hostages before, so it's possible they'll ransom the missing man, Chris Loubser.'

'Shit, it doesn't get more critical than that,' the trainer said.

Musa looked at the ceiling. 'Welcome to my world.'

Jan picked up the phone on the boardroom table and called his personal assistant, Margaret Lamont. 'Mags, I need you to set up a video call with Cameron McMurtrie in South Africa.'

Jan hung up. 'So, Kylie, given you're halfway through your first media training session and only a few weeks into the job, what do we say to the media about this one?'

She'd been making notes while Jan had been on the phone. She'd flicked through the trainer's handbook and checked some other notes she'd taken while he'd been speaking. She took a deep breath. 'We need to give the immutable facts of the incident – who, what, where and when, if not why. We don't know why the *zama zamas* would have killed these guys. I'm assuming the security guard would have been armed, but if our environmental manager and his sidekick were down there it doesn't sound like our guys were looking for a fight. We need to express remorse for the loss of our people and condolences to their families and position Global Resources as the innocent victim of criminal activity. Our number one priority is getting this guy, Chris –'

'Loubser,' Musa prompted.

'Right, getting Chris Loubser back alive and making sure these pirates are brought to justice.'

Jan leaned back in his swivel chair again while he thought for three seconds. 'Mister media expert, what do you think?'

'I think Kylie's been paying attention during her training today,' the trainer said.

'I felt I had to after you humiliated me at the beginning of the session,' she said.

'Don't blame him,' Jan said. 'The real media are going to be a lot tougher on you, and it won't end with this terrible incident. Next, you're going to have to sell South Africa on the idea of a new mine being opened on the doorstep of the country's favourite national park.'

There was a knock on the door and Margaret came in. She nodded greetings to them all. Mags was twenty-five and looked a picture of innocence with her blonde curls, but Kylie knew from personal experience she guarded Jan and his diary like a Rottweiler.

Mags turned on the widescreen plasma TV monitor mounted on the wall and sat at the table and dialled on a desktop console.

The screen came to life and they saw a utilitarian meeting room. The decoration on the miners' wall consisted of whiteboards covered in targets and plans. The only man in the room sat at a circular timber laminate table and was leaning forward, fiddling with the monitor he was looking into.

'*Howzit*, boss,' Cameron McMurtrie said. He wore overalls with the Global Resources logo embroidered above the breast pocket.

'Fine thanks, Cameron. Sorry to be talking to you for this reason, and sorry for the loss of your men.'

'Thanks boss.' Cameron held out a personnel file at arm's length so he could read something and Kylie recognised the sign of someone who would soon need reading glasses. Men could be quite vain about such things, she knew. 'Themba Tshabalala was a new guy and I didn't know him well, but old Paulo Barrica was a good *oke* and straight as can be.'

Kylie had never met Cameron McMurtrie in person but had seen him in a couple of video conferences. His eyes were red-rimmed and his face and shirt were smeared with dirt. She guessed he'd already been down to the scene of the killings and hadn't yet taken the time to shower.

'Do you think that was a factor in what happened?'

'Barrica's honesty?' Cameron shrugged. 'Maybe. If I had more security guards like Paulo, these bloody *zama zamas* would find it a lot harder to stay in business. The truth is that some of my guards are directly involved in letting the pirates in and out, or getting food down the mine and gold out, and others would probably turn a blind eye to the smuggling. Barrica had the guts to come to me a couple of times and tell me when stuff was being moved down the mine, and we were able to confiscate a lot of contraband – food, drugs, booze, tools, the sorts of thing the pirates need to stay in business. He would have made some enemies so, yes, I guess it could have been a set-up to kill him, but I didn't think the *zama zamas* would be stupid enough to try and take out two environmental guys at the same time.'

Jan nodded, and looked at Kylie.

She'd made some more notes, and she looked up from them to the camera mounted at the top of the screen they were watching. 'Cameron, what do you know about Chris Loubser?'

Cameron rubbed his chin. '*Howzit*, Kylie. He's very good at his job; sometimes too good. He'll get me to stop operations if he sees something or his monitoring tells him something's not right. He's a stickler for the regulations and safety, which is how it should be, even if he can be a pain in the arse, you know?'

She nodded, although she wanted to tell him that safety really was a priority and not a pain the arse. She held her tongue, though, as an argument was not what any of them needed right now.

'Also, between us, Chris doesn't like being underground. He's never said anything but I've been down with him and I can tell when a man doesn't want to be there. It's not for everyone and it doesn't stop him doing his job, but I'm worried about him if he's alive and maybe hurt down there with those bastards.'

'So we need to act quickly,' Jan said.

'The guys are pissed off by this attack, boss.' Cameron's hands, visible on the tabletop, balled into fists. Kylie saw his eyes harden as he leaned closer to the camera. 'I'm putting together a team to go down there and get Chris out.'

'Shouldn't you wait for the police?' Kylie asked.

'I don't know what state Chris is in – there was blood all through the *madala* side. Besides, my guys know the mine and the *zama zamas* better than the police do. They're ready to *moer* the bastards.'

Kylie guessed *moer* meant something bad. 'I'm worried about more of our employees getting injured. Have you called the police?'

Cameron shook his head. 'Kylie, with respect, this is Africa. The police don't want to get involved because they're not experienced in working underground. Plus, we think the local commander is being paid off by the illegal miners. We have to do our own dirty work.'

'Global Resources can't be a party to vigilante action and –'

'Boss,' Cameron pointedly turned away from Kylie, 'you know what needs to be done and you know we can sort this out ourselves.'

Jan leaned back in his chair, bringing his hands together and to his lips as he always did when he was thinking. He nodded, but said: 'Kylie's right on this one, on both counts, Cameron. This isn't the old days. There's a crime scene underground and the police are going to have to be called in. I also agree that the last thing we want now is any more of our people hurt as a result of this thing. Let's all take a deep breath.'

Cameron rubbed his forehead with the thumb and forefinger of his right hand. '*Ja*, all right, boss, but the guys won't like us doing nothing. The union's going to *bliksem* us over this as well. COSATU's already gone on record as opposing the new coalmine in the game reserve, and there's the ongoing agitation over workplace deaths in the mines.'

'But it's not a game reserve,' Kylie said. 'If we're using incorrect terminology in private it will spill out into the open arena. That land is privately owned by the local people, it's no longer part of the Sabi Sand Game Reserve.'

Cameron snorted. 'Tell that to the animals that live there, Kylie.'

'Enough, Cameron,' Jan said. 'Kylie's right. We need to stick to the facts. Our priority now is to get this mess sorted, and that man out alive. Kylie, when are you due to fly out?'

'Tomorrow morning, boss. On the Sydney–Joburg direct flight.'

'You're still coming over here?' Cameron eyeballed her.

'Why wouldn't I?' Kylie said, quicker than she'd meant.

'You'll be walking into a shit storm,' Cameron said. 'If you thought pitching the new mine was going to be tough, then it just got a lot worse.'

'I'm not the sort of person who backs down from a challenge,' Kylie spat back.

'OK,' Jan placed his palms down on the table with enough force to silence Cameron and Kylie. 'Enough. Two of our men are dead and their families must be cared for, and another of our colleagues is missing. Kylie, change of plans – get Mags to book you on tonight's flight via Perth. That will put you on the ground a working day earlier. Use the time between now and when you arrive in South Africa to thoroughly ground yourself in our operations and business there. Cameron, if you lead some maverick rescue operation without my approval I'll have your balls as a paperweight. The South African media went into a frenzy last time a mine security contractor slotted a bunch of *zama zamas*. We don't need any more bad press. Understood?'

'All right, boss.' Cameron looked at his watch. 'If there's nothing more to discuss, I have to contact the dead men's families and call Chris Loubser's parents again.'

'Good luck,' Jan said, and indicated to Mags to terminate the video conference. He turned to the media trainer. 'Give Kylie the toughest time imaginable – it's going to be far worse for her in Africa.'

4

Tertia Venter zipped up her green polar fleece with the lion's head logo embroidered above the left breast. It was going to be another perfect sunny September day in the lowveld, but the mornings were still nippy.

'Morning, my boy,' she said to the old bull elephant they called Marula, who was peeling the bark from a tree with his left tusk, his remaining good one, fifty metres from her house. Tertia got into the old open-topped Land Rover Defender and turned the key. The vehicle, Old Smokey, was like her – not a creature of the morning. Eventually it started.

She drove along her gravel driveway out onto the rutted road that led from the deliveries gate to the back of the main lodge. It wasn't far, not even a kilometre, but hunting lions had been seen between her house and the lodge the night before, according to her head guide, Tumi Mabunda.

Tertia shifted down to first gear as she drove down the bank of the dry riverbed, then selected diff lock as she hit the sand. She gunned the diesel engine and looked left and right in case the resident leopard was in one of his favourite trees. No luck. It was cold in the riverbed, a few skerricks of early morning mist still visible in the air, but the temperature rose as soon as she climbed out of the low-lying area.

The grass on the plain that gave the lodge its name – Lion Plains – was golden yellow and she scanned it for the tuft of Big Boy's tail, but the old pride male was not out marking his territory this morning. Perhaps his lionesses had killed in the night and he was there now, muscling in for the good bits while his ladies and his cubs waited none too patiently. She hoped something was going right for someone or something this morning. Her time was running out.

She'd done this drive almost every day for the past eleven years. It had been her dream come true; hers and her ex-husband, Karl's.

Staying on had been worth it; she'd wanted to live here since she was a child. The property, now called Lion Plains, had been bought by her grandparents as marginal cattle-farming land, infested with remnant wildlife, in the forties. They had hunted game on the property, known then as Sunnydale, and their children and grandchildren had spent family holidays on this wild tract of bushveld and golden grass. In the early sixties, her grandparents had joined with other local landowners to create the Sabi Sand Game Reserve, dropping fences between their properties to allow wildlife the freedom to move. Unlike on many of the other farms, there hadn't been enough money in their family to develop a lodge or luxury camp for tourists or hunters. Tertia's grandfather had been a better farmer than he was investor and a series of his get-rich-quick schemes had gone belly up. When he died from a heart attack, Tertia's grandmother and parents had wanted to sell Sunnydale.

Tertia, however, had an eye on the future. It was the early nineties and change was coming to South Africa. Many whites feared a bloodbath if Nelson Mandela and the ANC eventually took power, but Tertia predicted – correctly, as it turned out – that Mandela would oversee a peaceful transition and that the foreign tourists who had boycotted her country during the years of apartheid, would one day be drawn to reserves such as Sabi Sand in droves.

Her father was doubtful and her siblings more interested in studying subjects that would lead to careers abroad, but Tertia's mother encouraged her to look further into the viability of the idea of building a luxury tented camp on Sunnydale.

She met Karl when she was at university and fell in love with him. When she graduated, her father begrudgingly agreed to invest in Tertia's plan to breathe new life into Sunnydale, which Tertia immediately renamed Lion Plains. Karl's work kept them apart in the first year, but he always maintained a strong interest in the game farm.

When Karl managed to get time off and make it to the farm, they had the place to themselves, living in a safari tent, with a caretaker to keep the donkey boiler stoked to provide hot water, and the man's wife to wash the clothes.

By the time change came to her troubled South Africa, with Nelson Mandela's election as president in 1994, Tertia found herself in an empty house, with no husband. Karl had left her for a new life in a new country.

After both her parents were killed in a car accident, she and her siblings sold the family home in upmarket Rosebank and Tertia invested her share of the inheritance in building the accommodation units on the farm and renovating the old farmhouse as the main lodge and dining and entertainment area. With her parents taken from her in tragic circumstances and her husband gone, Tertia had poured her fortune, her tears and her wounded heart into the lodge.

The building gleamed the colour of an elephant's ivory, newly washed in an African stream. Tertia pulled up to the office, located behind the souvenir shop, and got out of the Land Rover.

Tertia had had Lion Plains up and running in time to catch a wave of overseas tourist interest in South Africa. She'd put her business degree and her brains to their best use and created a camp that had won accolades in premier travel magazines around the world. The rich and the famous had stayed in her camp. It was her life's work, her legacy and she couldn't be more proud.

She let herself into the office and turned on the computer and the television. Portia, one of the waitresses from the dining room, knocked on the doorframe and entered with a tray of plunger coffee, low-fat milk, and two health rusks. Tertia bade her good morning and asked if she was well, and how her three year old was doing. When Portia left, Tertia sipped her coffee and reached for the remote. She was turning up the volume when she saw the crawler message on the bottom of the screen: *Two dead, one missing in goldmine battle.*

The phone rang.

'*Kak*,' she swore as she pressed mute. It was just after seven in the morning and the receptionist wouldn't be at work until eight. She wanted to watch the television news – anything about mining was of interest to her these days. 'Good morning, Lion Plains Lodge, Tertia speaking. How can I help?'

It was a New Zealander, a man with no concept of time differences, enquiring if they had a vacancy in three months' time. 'Just let me check, sir.'

Tertia minimised the window in which she had open a Global Resources media release – more spin and lies about their damned new mining project that would put her out of business – and clicked on the diary. She had a vacancy, and told the man on the phone, leaving out the fact that he might find his stay at Lion Plains, a 'tranquil, exclusive private game reserve', interrupted by the boom of explosives and the dust of an open-cut coalmine wafting over his luxury safari tent. He asked for a price and she gave him the standard rate. He said he'd get back to her.

Tertia hung up the phone and released the mute button on the television. The story on the mining incident was coming to an end. The reporter was doing a voice-over on some vision from an old story which included a shot of the entrance to the mine. It was Global Resources' Eureka mine at Barberton.

The reporter said: '*A company spokesman said the men were taking part in an environmental monitoring audit of a disused working. The men killed have been identified as Themba Tshabalala, aged twenty-two, a trainee environmental officer, and mine security guard Paulo Barrica, forty-one. The company said both men were valued employees who would be missed. The name of the third man, who is still reported as missing, has not been released.'*

Tertia took a breath and held it. She reached for the phone again and dialled the cellphone number she knew by heart.

The phone went straight to voicemail. '*Hi, this is Chris, leave a message.'*

*

Outside, the sun was on the horizon. Chris has been missing for nine hours and there was still no word. Cameron hit the hands-free button on his phone and dialled the extension of his secretary, Hannelie. 'Hann, please can you get me Themba Tshabalala's home address?'

He heard her sniff. '*Ja*, boss. You want me to read it to you or email?'

'Neither. I'm going out.' He ended the call and got up from behind his desk. The Australians from Global Resources thought they could micromanage a mine in South Africa from the other side of the Indian Ocean, but he preferred not to work by memo or email.

Cameron left his office and walked into Hannelie's smaller space, next door. She dabbed her eyes with a tissue and looked up at him. 'I've written the address here. Themba and his wife were renting a small house in town. Paulo's wife and children are in Angola, in Luanda. I've tried the cellphone but there's no answer, just a voicemail message in Portuguese. I've got some more correspondence for you to sign.'

Cameron took the piece of paper from her. 'I'll get one of the Mozambicans to come see you and leave a message in Portuguese.'

Cameron had called his head of human resources, Nandi Radebe, from underground when Themba's death had been confirmed. The gunfire from the ambush had been heard by some passing miners who'd called security. Nandi had notified Beauty Tshabalala of her husband's death by telephone, but Cameron had told Nandi that he would visit the widow in person.

Hannelie retrieved some letters from the printer. She was a matronly woman of fifty, old-school and very formal, but when she came over to him her body shuddered and tears rolled down her cheeks.

Cameron took the papers and put an arm around her shoulders. 'We'll get through this, Hann. We must be strong for Chris.'

Hannelie dried her eyes. 'I know we've lost men before, but to have them murdered in this way, and young Chris kidnapped. That poor Themba – he and his wife have a little one. I saw her at the gate on his first day.'

Cameron laid the letters on Hannelie's desk and signed them. He checked the address of Themba's widow and put the paper in his pocket. 'I'm going to see her now.'

'Roelf and Casper want to see you.'

On cue, his engineering manager and senior geologist appeared at Hannelie's door. 'I called head office again, but no news,' Cameron said. 'The Aussies say we can't organise a rescue mission to go get Chris.'

'*Fokken* wimps,' Casper spat.

Roelf shook his head. 'What are we going to do, boss?'

All three were looking at him, waiting for his decision. He had dealt with death and serious injury in the past, too often, although Eureka mine's safety record was enviable by South African standards. But Hannelie was right, this situation was different. These were his people and they had been ambushed. This was not a workplace accident; it was a declaration of war.

'I say we round up some Angolans, get us a couple of R5s and go flatten these bastards,' Casper said.

'We do no such thing.' Cameron held up a hand to silence Casper's objection before he could voice it. 'I've already told Hein to start posting the other Angolan security guards, the ones we can trust, in observation posts on level fourteen and at the points of entry above ground that we know the *zama zamas* have used in the past. We're going to bottle them up and deny them freedom of movement underground.' Hein Coetzee was Cameron's deputy mine manager and, like Cameron, Casper, Roelf and most other South African middle-aged men, he'd seen military service during the border war.

Casper shook his head. 'So we do nothing.'

Cameron understood the geologist's frustration but did not read his comment as an insult. He was saying what everyone above ground was thinking. He pointed at Casper. '*You* stay here and man my office. You, too, Roelf, in shifts with Casper and Hein. This is our crisis centre now and we don't stand down until Chris is rescued and whoever killed Themba and Paulo is dead. You call me if you hear anything from the *zama zamas* or if anything else happens underground. Understood?'

The two men nodded. Roelf said, 'But we feel helpless, and we all know the police won't do anything.'

Cameron moved his gaze from the two men to Hannelie and back again. 'The safety of Chris and the control of this mine are my responsibility, and no one else's. Understood?' They all nodded. 'The buck stops with me, and I am going to get him out. In the meantime, we watch, we wait, and we listen.'

Cameron left them and went outside to his mine *bakkie*. He started the engine and gripped the steering wheel so hard he fancied he could almost snap it. He exhaled and rolled his shoulders, forcing himself to think coolly and not let the emotion rule him.

It was a short drive from the mine to Barberton and he parked outside the facebrick house. It was larger than he expected, but when he walked up the stone-flagged path and knocked on the door a white woman, perhaps in her sixties, with her hair in curlers, answered. '*Ja?*'

'Excuse me, *mevrou*. I must have the wrong address. I'm looking for Beauty Tshabalala.'

'*Ag* she's in the flatlet, out the back. Up the driveway.' She looked at the logo above his breast pocket. 'You're from the mine. Is there trouble? I was having second thoughts about letting the flatlet to them. But money's short, so what can a widow do with the cost of things these days and –'

'I need to see Mrs Tshabalala. Her husband has been killed.'

The woman put her hand over her mouth. 'My lord!'

'Please.'

She drew her housecoat closed and came out onto the *stoep* in her slippers. 'I'll take you to her.'

Cameron followed the woman to the backyard and the modest, tired-looking flat. He wondered from its meagre size if it had been built as a domestic's quarters. The woman knocked on the door. 'Beauty?'

A child screamed inside. The door opened and a slight woman, with red-rimmed eyes and an infant in her arms, opened the door. Her lip started to tremble when she saw Cameron.

'Mrs Tshabalala, I'm Cameron McMurtrie, the general manager of Eureka Mine. I am so sorry for your loss.'

Beauty opened her mouth to say something, but seemed unable to form the words. At the same time she staggered. Cameron took one of her arms and the landlady stepped past Cameron and gently took the child from her arms. Beauty felt listless in Cameron's grasp. 'Can I come in? You should sit down.'

'There, there, my girl,' said the woman, cooing to the child.

Cameron took in the simplicity of the shack: a wooden table with two ageing aluminium-framed kitchen chairs, their upholstery cracked and oozing foam, and a double bed in the corner, neatly made. Cameron sat Beauty on the bed and took one of the chairs.

'I'll go to the house and make some *rooibos*, OK?' the landlady said.

'Thank you.'

Beauty watched the woman walk out with her child, but said nothing at first. She turned her big eyes on Cameron and blinked. 'He is truly dead?'

'Yes.'

Her bottom lip started to tremble, and she took a deep, rasping breath. 'We have been married less than a year. You know, this was his first job. He was so excited.'

Cameron nodded. 'I interviewed your husband and I was very impressed by his attitude and his skills. He was with us for such a short time, but he was one of us.'

She looked out the small window of the flatlet. 'He was with all of us for a short time. We both just graduated from university.'

'Do you have family? Is there someone who can care for you and the baby, Mrs Tshabalala?'

She looked back at him and blinked. 'Themba was an orphan. His parents died when he was in high school, yet he fended for himself and worked at nights and weekends to put himself through university. My mother is alive, but I am from Zambia. She lives in Ndola. She has nothing.'

The enormity of her situation seemed to poleaxe the young woman and Cameron had to reach out to her and again take her arm as she slumped sideways. 'How am I going to care for my baby?' She started to sob. 'My love is gone.'

Cameron took out his handkerchief and passed it to her. 'What did you study at university?'

She dabbed her eyes and sniffed. 'Marketing.'

'You'll be able to get a job, I'm sure.'

She blew her nose and looked up at him, her limpid eyes now cold. 'You know how bad the economy is. I have a baby and no family to take care of her and I am a Zambian. Who would hire me? If I take her home to Zambia it will be worse.'

Cameron thought about her situation and knew she was probably right. With no experience and no family to back her up, her prospects were not good. Around her neck Beauty wore a simple silver cross on a thin chain; it gave him an idea. 'There is a project here in Barberton the mine supports, a jewellery-making collective. They train women and unemployed people in basic metalwork skills.'

Beauty sniffed. 'I am not good with my hands. I can't even sew. I worked as a part-time maid to get through university. I will have to go back to that, I suppose, although I can't afford child care.'

'No, that's not what I was suggesting. The Imvoti Jewellers, that's the name of the project, do good work, but their products could be better marketed to tourists coming to Barberton, and further afield, in Nelspruit and even Johannesburg. They don't even have a website.'

Beauty wiped her eyes. 'I studied website design. And I love jewellery.'

'What would you say to, say, six months' work on contract, writing a marketing plan for Imvoti Jewellery and designing a website for them? If things work out and you can improve their sales I can put a case to our new head of environment and community to make the position permanent.'

'My baby?'

'We have a crèche at the mine. You must still consider yourself as part of our family, Mrs Tshabalala.'

There was the rattle of china behind him and Cameron turned to see the lady of the house standing in the doorway, carrying a tray with a teapot and three cups. Beauty's eyes widened in alarm. 'Don't worry, girl, your little one is asleep on my bed for now. I put pillows either side of her so she won't roll out.'

'I don't know,' Beauty said.

'Yes, you do,' said the woman as she set down the tray and started to pour. 'I couldn't help but overhear what *Meneer* McMurtrie is offering you. You must stay here in Barberton if you have nowhere else to go. I can look after your little one if you have to go to Nelspruit or Joburg or whatever outside of the crèche's opening hours.'

'You would, Mrs Van der Post?'

The older woman nodded. 'My Frikkie was killed down the mine twenty years ago and my boys are all grown up and living in Australia now. What else is an old woman going to do with herself? Like Mr McMurtrie says, you are part of the Eureka family.'

Beauty stood and took her hand. 'Thank you, Mrs Van der Post.' She turned to Cameron and started to thank him, but she dissolved into tears, her narrow shoulders shaking.

Cameron put his arms around her and she pressed her face to his chest, her tears soaking his shirt. After a while she looked up, eased herself from him and wiped her eyes. 'Thank you, Mr McMurtrie. I will not disappoint you. But I just need to ask one more thing of you, please.'

'Child,' the woman interrupted.

'No, Mrs Van der Post. Just one more thing.'

'What is it?' Cameron asked.

'The men who did this to Themba, to the father of my baby – you will kill them?'

There had been armed raids against the *zama zamas* in the past and lives had been lost in underground combat, and this had drawn the ire of the board of Global Resources over in safe, law-abiding Australia. He had been ordered not to take matters into his own hands and send in armed security to rescue Chris and avenge Themba and Paulo. Cameron himself had not fired a weapon at anyone since he left the army more than twenty years ago.

'Yes, I will.'

*

Chris Loubser wanted to scream into the hessian bag that covered his head, but he knew if he did so his mind would unravel like a ball of string. It was bad enough being underground, stripped of his headlamp and his rescue pack – which contained an emergency oxygen supply – but the weave of the hessian made the claustrophobia almost unbearable.

The man who was leading him through the darkness pushed him in the back with the barrel of his rifle and Chris stumbled and fell yet again. His knees were wet with blood and his ankle throbbed in pain. 'I can't *fokken* see, you *poes*,' he yelled into the hood.

The man obviously spoke Afrikaans because calling him a cunt earned Chris a rifle butt in his kidneys as he tried to stand. He groaned and staggered to his feet. His hands were unbound, but there was no point trying to disarm the man, as he would need to remove his head covering first and he doubted the man would have any hesitation about pulling the trigger, given that he'd just killed Paulo Barrica and Themba Tshabalala. Chris felt nauseous when he remembered the gore oozing from the back of Themba's head. Why had he agreed to come underground again?

He tried to picture where they were heading. He knew the *madala* side in this part of the mine stretched for a kilometre before it ended at the disused face. The *zama zamas* could be working the old face or they could be using this tunnel as a base.

Chris had read hundreds of reports about the shady activities of the *zama zamas* in this mine and others. Sometimes they reopened old workings, blasting with their own explosives when they could get them, but more often than not they piggybacked on a mine's legitimate operations.

During a shift in the legal mine the miners would drill holes in the stope face, where the gold was found, and charge them with up to two hundred kilograms of explosives. At the end of the shift, a fuse was lit and it burned slow enough to allow the workers time to return safely to the surface. The next shift would not start work to retrieve the dislodged ore until the workplace was clear of deadly gases, such as carbon monoxide, nitrous oxide, ammonia and methane.

The *zama zamas*, who cared nothing for safety, would either leave their underground hideouts to cut the fuses and steal the explosives for their own use, or wait for the blast and then go to the stope and steal chunks of ore with high-grade visible gold. As well as disregarding their own wellbeing, the *zama zamas* would also blast away pillars of rock that the legal miners would leave in place to stop the roof caving in, thus making the workings too dangerous ever to mine again.

Chris heard noises ahead of them, voices and the clang of tools striking ore. He smelled excrement and urine as he passed a hole in the rock the illegal miners used as a latrine. He gagged on the stench of it. The man behind him laughed and prodded him again. Chris could only imagine the litany of environmental health and safety breaches he would uncover in ten minutes, if he could see, and if he could stop his hands from shaking.

'Move,' the man said, and jabbed him again.

There were voices around him now and he heard shuffling feet. The language was a mix of Portuguese and Fanagolo, the lingua franca of the mines. Most of the legal miners at Eureka were South African Swazis from the local area, which bordered the Kingdom of Swaziland, an independent country bordering South Africa and Mozambique. The ranks of the *zama zamas* were filled with illegal immigrants from the poorer neighbouring countries of Zimbabwe and Mozambique, as well as local criminals.

'Boss?' the man behind Chris said.

'*Lapa,*' said a voice in front of him.

He was being taken to a boss of some kind. Chris knew the *zama zamas* operated an organisational structure similar to that of the legal mining world. There would be shift bosses and miners, and working crews, but no environmental safety people like himself. The risks were high for these pirate miners, but the rewards were great.

The hessian in front of his mouth was getting moist from his breath and he felt sweat running down his face in rivulets. His breathing was rapid and shallow and his legs started to feel like jelly. 'I need to sit down,' he said into the hood.

The man prodded him in the back again.

'I. Need. To. Sit. Down.'

The man loosed a stream of invective and turned the rifle broadside and pushed it into his back. Chris fell again. An order was barked in front of him and Chris heard his guard take a step back. Words were exchanged in Portuguese.

'Here, let me help you.'

Chris flinched as he felt fingers at his neck. The man who had just spoken English was untying the string that bound the hood to his neck. Chris forced himself to kneel still as the hessian was drawn up, the coarse weave scratching his nose so that he wanted to sneeze. He looked up, blinking. It was almost totally dark, but a candle was set in a carved-out alcove on the side wall. The man who had freed him from the bag was silhouetted, his face hidden in the darkness.

'Welcome to my mine.' The man laughed, then slapped Chris on the shoulder with a big hand and enough force to almost knock him sideways.

'The others, you . . .'

The man held up a hand. 'You were stupid to come into our mine with an armed guard who chose to shoot first and ask questions later. The body of Fernando should have been enough of a warning to you to come no further.'

Chris spat fibres from his mouth. 'You should have left him out by the shaft or somewhere where we could have found him.'

The man nodded, conceding the point. 'We would have moved him in time for the arrival of the next shift. You caught us by surprise; we knew you were coming, but not what time.'

'You knew? Themba Tshabalala, the man your pirate killed, wanted to finish work in time to go with his wife to the church, to organise his baby's christening. That's why we chose the early shift.'

The man nodded. 'Regrettable, but unavoidable, I am afraid. But I am being rude. I have not introduced myself. You may call me Wellington Shumba. Down here, I am the mine boss – not your Mister Cameron McMurtrie. And you are Christiaan Loubser, manager of environmental services.'

Chris blinked again. He didn't know how this man knew his name and his job. Chris looked around but could see no more than a few metres. He saw shadows moving and caught the occasional sweat-glistened arm or torso passing by. He smelled sweat and burning gas and heard the clang of tools on rock and the squeaking and grinding of ore being processed by hand.

He'd heard about how the *zama zamas* processed ore underground but had never witnessed it. As his eyes began to adjust to the dark, he could make out a man sitting in front of a homemade miniature ball mill. It was made from a steel camping gas cylinder that had a hole cut into it and a trap door fitted to the opening. The bottle was laid on its side and fitted with welded rods at either end that were then laid in a cradle. To one end was added a crank so that the operator could wind the cylinder, allowing heavy steel balls inside to crush the ore dropped into the cylinder. The ball mill above ground acted exactly the same way, except it was massive and driven by a motor. The man turning the mill glanced at Chris, the boredom plain on his face and his escape from it visible from his red eyes. The hot air was laden with the smell of marijuana.

'Keep working,' Wellington barked at the man operating the mill, before walking away a few metres, further down the tunnel. Chris squinted and saw Wellington had sat down behind what looked like a camping table. He was almost completely swallowed by the darkness now, just a voice. 'Stay where you are, Christiaan. But you may sit instead of kneeling if you wish. Make yourself comfortable.'

'What are you going to do with me?' Chris asked. He moved so he was sitting with his knees hugged to his chest. The man said nothing in reply and Chris's imagination filled the void with a dozen hellish scenarios. He thought of Themba and Paulo again – the blood and the brains. The silence stretched out; Chris could hear his own heart beating.

'I need your expertise,' the mine boss's voice reached through the quiet. 'I'm losing men – more than usual – and I want to find out why. You'll work for me until I negotiate with Global Resources to pay a ransom for your life.'

'As simple as that,' Chris said.

'As simple as that. I want you to work your magic with your monitors and your pumps, to find out what is making my men ill.'

'Since when have *zama zamas* cared about health and safety?'

'Since Cameron McMurtrie started bulldozing closed some of the old shafts we used to come and go by. I need to get the most out of my workforce. I can't afford to keep replacing men ad infinitum. As this mine goes deeper and my methods of ingress and egress are increasingly curtailed, I need to keep my men down here for longer periods than I have in the past. When Eureka was less deep we could come and go through old workings, but the new shaft is deeper than these. I need my men to stay fit to mine.'

Wellington's English was better than Chris's, whose mother tongue was Afrikaans. The man's diction was precise, which made his voice sound somehow crueller. Here was an educated man who was working men to death, but was greedy and rational enough to know that even in the world of the pirate mine he had to wring a few more months or years out of his labourers. Chris realised he'd been the target of a planned ambush and that, ironically, this Wellington wanted him to carry out a task similar to the one he and Themba had set out to do. 'Did you have to kill the others?'

'No.' A match flared and the man's face was illuminated for the briefest moment. The brow frowned for an instant, the head nodded a little. 'That was not part of the plan. If the guard had not opened fire first then we would have tried to take you all alive.'

'I . . . I can't stay down here.' Chris gripped his knees tighter to try to stop the shaking, but the harder he squeezed, the faster and harder he shuddered. 'Please . . .'

'Quiet. You will be fed. There is drink and some *dagga* if you wish it. You're not going anywhere for the time being; not until you have finished what I need you to do.'

'I . . . can't.'

'You can stay, and you will, Christiaan. I have plans for you, and you will help me make my mine safer and then you can go.'

Chris closed his eyes and tried to fight back the tide of panic. He couldn't stay down here. He would die. He opened his eyes again and saw the glowing orange tip of Wellington's cigarette. He needed to find a way out. He needed to outsmart this underground mine boss.

'You . . . you can start by putting out that cigarette. I was already picking up elevated traces of methane when we came through the safety door. You . . . you'll blow us all up if you and your men keep smoking this far into the site. We need to move closer to the main shaft where ventilation is better.'

The man laughed in the dark and drew again on the cigarette. He stood and walked to the alcove where the candle glowed weakly. He picked it up and blew it out. Chris was in total blackness again. He heard the man's footsteps. He wondered if he was going to reach out and help him to his feet. 'Don't try and outsmart me, Christiaan. I know there is no methane in this mine.' The steel-capped toe of his boot lashed out and drove the air from Chris's lungs.

*

Luis Domingues Correia worked by touch in the darkness while he listened to the Afrikaner being beaten. He had been bullied by white South African miners when he'd worked in legal mines, and he had been beaten by people of his own colour when he'd lived in the informal settlement on the outskirts of Barberton.

It had been this way for generations. His father and grandfather had worked for the mines, recruited from their beachside village near Inhambane on the Indian Ocean coast. In the old days, under the apartheid regime, the men of his country and others as far north as Zambia had been recruited by WENELA, the Witwatersrand Native Labour Association, to work in the mines in South Africa. They had been allowed into South Africa to provide cheap labour and at the same time they had followed their own dreams of wealth and peace at a time when their home country was poverty-stricken and war-ravaged.

Luis had ostensibly benefitted from the peace in Mozambique that followed the end of the civil war in 1992. He'd been educated in metallurgy and engineering in East Germany, but WENELA no longer trawled the villages of Mozambique and Zimbabwe looking for labour. The catchcry after Mandela came to power was South African jobs for South Africans. But there were still opportunities for those prepared to work hard and the minimum wage in South Africa was still a relative fortune in Mozambique.

So Luis had walked south and then west and crossed the Limpopo River and joined the *mahambane*, 'the walkers', who braved the wild dangerous expanse of the Kruger National Park to cross into South Africa and put their skills to use in a country that, despite its job creation rhetoric, had a pressing need for them. Others from his village had disappeared on the journey to *e-goli*, the place of gold. Some had been killed by lions in the national park, others became lost and died of thirst or starvation, while still more fell prey to criminals who stole what little they carried in their suitcases.

Luis, though, had made it to Johannesburg, where he had met a man from his village working on a mine near Benoni. It was a small mine, and not as diligent as the bigger companies at sticking to the letter of the law when it came to hiring policies. Luis had soon proved his worth to the shift boss as a labourer, and his metallurgy qualification meant he had hope of a job above ground. Luis moved in with his friend from the village, taking a corner of a jerry-built shack in an informal settlement, the new South Africa's euphemism for a shanty town.

Things were good for a while. As well as sending money home to his wife and two-year-old son in Inhambane, Luis managed to save enough to buy himself some sheets of plywood and corrugated iron to start building his own shack.

In 2008 trouble began brewing in the settlement. No one could remember what started it, but it spread like a bushfire through their community and others across the country. In what became known as the xenophobia riots, South Africans living in the informal settlements turned on their neighbours from other countries. Mozambicans, Zimbabweans, Malawians and other Africans who had lived peacefully alongside the locals for so long suddenly found themselves the targets of mob violence. Some were beaten, others stabbed and burned in a spontaneous orgy of hatred that claimed the lives of more than sixty migrants across the country.

Luis's shack was burned to the ground, along with his meagre possessions, and his friend's home was likewise razed. The mob had caught up with him as he'd tried to salvage his suitcase – they had dragged him into the dusty laneway and kicked him and beat him with sticks.

As Luis listened to the screams of the environmental manager, he felt again the thud of boots on flesh. Wellington Shumba, the man they called 'the Lion' after his surname and his predatory nature, was the devil who ruled this underground hell, but he had given Luis a job when the mine in Benoni had made him redundant for exceeding his sick leave entitlement. It didn't matter that Luis had spent weeks recovering from a broken arm and ribs and septicaemia in a church-run clinic and had been unable to get a sick note from a doctor sent to the mine. The mining company had heeded the call of the unions and the streets to employ fewer foreigners and more South Africans – even if they couldn't do the jobs they were paid to do.

Luis had used the last of his money to catch a bus to Barberton, and there he'd walked straight into the devil's arms.

5

Kylie declined the complimentary champagne as she arranged herself in her business class seat on the Qantas Boeing. She put on her headphones and selected the news channel.

She'd had barely enough time to get back to her flat and pack and make it to Sydney Airport in time, but flying to Perth tonight and connecting to the overnight SAA flight to Johannesburg would give her an extra working day in South Africa and a chance to get a handle on the situation with Loubser before the rest of her itinerary kicked in.

She had plenty of work to do on the flight. On her lap was a folder of printouts of press clippings, extracts from reports, and the executive summary of the environmental impact statement for the proposed new coalmine near the Kruger National Park.

Even though Global Resources had several interests in Africa, this was her first visit to the continent. It was also her first business trip in her new role. She wanted to hit the ground running.

She had received the standard email from the company's head of security about risks and dangers in Africa. Johannesburg seemed to have a justifiably bad reputation for violent crime and a couple of the South Africans in the office had put the frighteners on her by recounting tales of home invasions, carjackings, shootings and murders of friends of friends. Kylie wasn't scared by the stories, but nor was she particularly looking forward to this trip.

As well as getting to meet the people in the South African office who would now be reporting to her, she was going to get a full briefing on Global Resources' operations and a visit to the site of the proposed new coalmine. The Eureka mine in the historic gold-mining town of Barberton in Mpumalanga Province would have been a one-day stopover, but Jan had told her to spend as much time there as she felt necessary, particularly if the situation with the missing environmental manager wasn't resolved before she arrived. Jan wanted the men and women at the mine to know head office was concerned about their losses and the missing man.

Kylie had dealt with death in the past. When she was managing the coalmine in the Hunter Valley, two miners had been crushed to death when the hanging wall had collapsed. She'd had to front the local media to give a statement and deal with the workplace safety investigators and police. Most difficult of all, she'd had to contact the wives of the two men who'd been killed. Kylie had gone home that night and cried her eyes out and polished off a bottle of wine, but the next day she'd visited the widows in person and later helped organise a fundraising dinner with the mine employees and the local community to ensure there was enough money for the children of both families to get the education their mothers expected.

Mining was dangerous. Every man and woman who went underground knew that, and Kylie thought it wasn't a bad thing if every man and woman in head office at least once in their life had to look into the crying eyes of a grieving spouse or parent or child of a dead miner. It made the risks real and meant decisions were taken less lightly.

Kylie flicked through her folder to the latest figures on workplace accidents, injuries and fatalities in South Africa. She'd seen the figures before, but still exhaled through her teeth when she read them again. Numbers like this would be front page news in the *West Australian* or the *Sydney Morning Herald*, but the explanatory paragraph beneath the figures in the report pointed out that Global Resources had the lowest number and ratio of workplace fatalities per days worked of any mining company in South Africa. She wondered if the two deaths at Barberton two nights earlier would change that.

Whatever. It wasn't good enough being the best of a bad bunch. Kylie had her sights set on the top job and she wanted Global Resources to be a company where no one had to make the call to tell someone a loved one would not be coming home.

Kylie flipped back to the itinerary her personal assistant, Sandy Hyland, had prepared for her. She circled a couple of things. The schedule had been prepared long before the latest disaster and still had her spending a night at the Lion Plains Lodge. The plan was that she and Cameron, and Chris Loubser if he hadn't gone missing, would meet with the incumbent but strictly former owner, Tertia Venter.

From what she recalled of the press clippings from the South African newspapers Kylie doubted they would be able to silence the woman, but it might be worth a try. As important as the new mine was, however, she knew that her first priority, and Cameron's, would be the fate of Loubser; she didn't want to be taking happy snaps of lions and elephants while there was a man down. There was a note in the file from Sandy saying that when they got to the reserve they would also probably meet Tumi Mabunda, the cousin of Musa the corporate communications man. Ironically, Tumi was head ranger at the lodge; the briefing said female black rangers were still a rarity in the male-dominated safari business and much had been made of Tertia Venter's promotion of a woman from the local community to the head ranger position. Kylie didn't consider herself an animal person at all and wondered what it would be like driving around all day looking for wildlife for a job. *Musa advises his cousin is very much anti the GR mine proposal,* her PA had further noted.

Kylie shook her head as she leafed through the press clippings again. 'Great,' she said to herself, 'so is most of the country.'

Also in her folder was a printout of an email from Cameron McMurtrie that gave the latest on the investigation into the deaths of the security guard and trainee environmental officer, and efforts that had been made to find Chris Loubser. The police had been in attendance, but Cameron noted: *As with previous incidents involving* zama zamas *the police have not been of great assistance. Most arrests of illegal miners in Eureka – and the rest of South Africa – are effected by mine security personnel, not police. The police lack the experience and will to venture into an unfamiliar environment. Permission is again sought to launch a rescue operation of our own.*

No way, Kylie thought. She would have a word to the police officer in charge when she got to Barberton. She had met plenty of men and a few women like Cameron before. They were miners through and through who had been ambitious and smart enough to make it into senior positions in mine management, yet they still harboured an us-and-them attitude when it came to head office. Things were no doubt compounded by the fact that Eureka was one of a trio of mines which had been owned by a smallish South African mining company that had recently been bought out by Global Resources. Cameron would have been beholden to the old owners and probably chaffed at having to report to foreigners – especially Australians. He would be tired and stressed at the loss of his men, which was understandable; but on other occasions when she'd faced Cameron in video conference meetings, or exchanged emails with him, she had detected an undercurrent of surliness and, she thought, misogyny.

A flight attendant stopped and asked her if she wanted a drink and Kylie ordered an orange juice. Despite her gut feeling about Cameron, she would have to get used to working with him and he with her. She'd faced off with sexists before, and she wasn't afraid to do it again. Also, he was about to move up a corporate rung himself. By the time she arrived at Barberton Jan would have contacted Cameron to tell him he was being promoted to South African director of new projects. One of his first duties would be to oversee the implementation of the new coalmine, and he would be working even closer with Kylie on that project.

Kylie flipped through the file again to an article she wanted to read in full, an investigative piece on illegal mining from *Mining Monthly*. As controversial as her industry sometimes was in her native Australia she was learning the stakes in Africa were as high as the risks. She wanted more responsibility from Jan, but she had an uneasy feeling that the maelstrom she was about to walk into in South Africa could break her as easily as it could make her. She had fought all her working life to get to where she was and she savoured a challenge, but how many mining execs in Australia, she wondered, had ever had to deal with the fallout of lethal underground gun battles and a new mine in – on the verge of, she corrected herself – a national park? None, she reckoned. She would show them.

*

Luis sat with his back to the rock wall of the tunnel and sacrificed some of the precious power in the batteries in his cheap plastic torch to re-read the letter from his wife, Miriam. He wished he could call her, but he couldn't risk escaping to the surface. There was too much work for him to do.

He wanted to reach out to her, to touch her, and to tell her to stay right where she was.

I miss you, Luis. The words made him bring a knuckle to his mouth and he bit down on the blackened, dirt-encrusted skin, tasting the chemicals of his trade in the dust on his hand. He knew he was killing himself through exposure to dangerous substances and dust, poor nutrition and slavishly hard work; he was trying to make a life for his family, but what sort of a life was this?

I cannot bear not knowing where you are, or if you are safe. We read of accidents, of people killed in the work you are doing. She didn't know he was a *zama zama* now. *Why can't you tell me the name of the mine you are working on? At least then I could call the shift boss, or email you.*

He was too ashamed to tell his wife, who might one day tell his son, that he was a criminal. Luis knew he was running out of excuses. It was implausible that a man with an honest job in a real mine could supply his wife with nothing better than a nondescript Barberton post office box as a form of contact. If he was a legitimate metallurgist at Eureka he would have an email account, a cellphone, a shared room in a dorm, or even a small house in the village or a shack in an informal settlement. Instead, he lived like a rat in a hole in the ground for months on end. It was ninety-seven days since he'd last seen daylight.

I want to bring Jose to South Africa and be with you. Unless I hear from you by the end of this month, we are coming. All my love, Miriam.

No! He turned off the torch and put it in the pocket of his raggedy overalls. In the dark he folded the letter and brought it to his lips and kissed it. No! It would be madness for her to join the *mahambane* and walk to South Africa. If the thieves did not rob or rape her, then the lions might devour her and his son.

Luis rested his chin on his chest, the bristles soaking up a little of the sweat that slicked his skin. He tried to keep himself clean as best as he could with the limited water they could tap off from the mine's underground lines, but still the sour smell of his body offended him. Luis was trapped in this hot, stinking hell, and he only hoped he could live long enough to see his wife and child again.

Men were dying underground. Fatalities weren't unusual among the *zama zamas*, but the current numbers were. This past week six men had died of illness; Luis had helped carry the bodies of two of them to the shaft between shifts so that the legal miners would find them and get rid of them. Last week it was four and three before that. The victims he had seen had all been fouled with copious smelly diarrhoea; the eyes were sunken and the skin on their fingers had wrinkled as though they had reached old age within just a few days.

Luis had overheard Wellington scheming with his lieutenant to kidnap an environmental officer, the man they now held, to inspect the areas where the pirate miners worked and slept, and to test the air in case they were being poisoned. Luis thought the men might be suffering from cholera; a Zimbabwean he worked with claimed he had seen similar symptoms in outbreaks in his country. The man was too nervous to approach the boss with his suspicion; when Luis had tried, Wellington had dismissed him and told him to go back to his work and mind his own business. As a precaution, though, Luis had started boiling water to drink and had ordered his underlings to do the same.

Whatever was killing the *zama zamas*, Luis hoped the unfortunate man Wellington had taken could help them find a cause and a treatment, and that no more blood would be shed. Word had already spread that two men from above ground had been killed in the gunfight and that would surely bring retribution.

*

Cameron went back to the mine after seeing Beauty Tshabalala. There was no news from below ground and no ransom demand for Chris's life. The longer they went without hearing anything, the more worried Cameron became for the man's life.

The frustration grew within him like a fast-spreading tumour as he tried to busy himself with the day-to-day paperwork and a host of problems that were inconsequential compared to the deaths of two men and the life of a missing one. It was dark outside as he finished writing a proposal for funding for a contract marketing manager for the Imvoti Jewellery project, which he would hand to Kylie when she arrived from Australia; he would talk her into hiring Beauty. He tried snatching an hour or two's sleep when Casper, still pleading to be allowed to mount a rescue mission, relieved his vigil. At midnight he sent Casper and Roelf home, knowing there was nothing they could do, and that in the unlikely event he dozed off, the phone would wake him. At seven in the morning, when his deputy, Hein Coetzee, arrived, Cameron told him there had been no word from below ground overnight.

'I'm going home for an hour or two, Hein, to make breakfast for Jessica, and pack her lunch before she leaves for school.'

'Take a few hours, get some sleep, boss,' Hein said. 'I've got things under control here.'

'I'll be back at nine.'

He could have escaped the chores – Petty, their maid, could have made breakfast and Jessica would have happily told him that at seventeen she was perfectly capable of looking after herself – but Cameron knew his daughter needed something approaching stability in her life.

He parked his Hilux in the driveway, not bothering with the garage remote. He wouldn't be home long. He got out and unlaced his boots on the *stoep*. He didn't know why he was bothering. Tania, his wife, was gone and he didn't give a fuck if he traipsed dirt through the hallway. Petty would clean it up. Force of habit, he guessed.

'Dad, is that you?' his daughter called from the study down the hallway.

'*Howzit*, my girl, what are you doing up out of bed so early?'

He walked into the study just in time to see her closing the laptop. 'Nothing much.'

'Nothing much? Were you online?'

'*Dad*, it was only Facebook. Just some friends from school is all.'

'Facebook.' He knew of it, of course, but wasn't on it. Anything to do with the internet made him want to punch a hole in the wall.

Jessica shrugged. 'You can't hate it if you don't know how it works, Dad.'

'I'm not interested in the bloody internet. I get enough of computers at work,' he snapped, and instantly felt bad for doing so.

She glared at him, as though she was going to throw something smart back at him. She was a clever kid – took after her mother. And Cameron could see Tania in her face: the fierce set of the mouth, the cute turned-up nose; the eyes. He couldn't read his daughter any better than he'd been able to read his wife. Jessica seemed angry at him often and he couldn't blame her, though he was doing his best to be strong for them both.

Jessica got up off the chair, came to him and wrapped her arms around his waist, burying her face in his dusty uniform shirt. 'Dad, do I have to go to school today? I feel . . . sick.'

He held her out. 'Yes, my girl, I'm afraid you do. You can't hide from the world.' He felt himself choke up, so he coughed. 'Now, now, look at this. You've got mine dirt all over your pyjamas.' Maybe she wasn't angry, just sad. He didn't know.

'I don't *care* about my pyjamas. Why did she leave us, Dad? What did we do wrong?'

He looked her in the eyes. 'You didn't do anything wrong, Jessie. It was me. It was between me and your mother.'

Jessica nodded and looked down.

They'd been through this, or variations of it, countless times over the past two months since Tania had left. He knew it was tough on Jessica – dammit, he knew only too well how tough it was – but he had to lead by example, show her that she had to keep on getting on with life and couldn't wallow.

He drew her into him and held her tight. He couldn't imagine life without her, which was why he found it so hard to understand what Tania had done. He had seen a few marriages and relationships on the mine break up – plenty in fact. Usually, but not always, it was the man screwing around with some young *poppie*, or some other *oke's* wife. Or sometimes a miner's lonely wife or girlfriend looking for some action with someone from a different shift. It took two to tango, so they said, but normally the woman took the children in a split. Plenty of other men only saw their kids every second weekend, but Tania wouldn't even get that – she was in bloody America.

America.

It was almost inconceivable, but it had happened. Tania's timing, of course, had been impeccably terrible – he really didn't need to be dealing with all of this now, not with Loubser missing and the families in mourning and the unions clamouring for his head.

'Dad?'

He said nothing. He eyeballed the laptop, as though it was a murder weapon. It was small. An inconsequential jumble of processors and plastic and cheap components soldered and stuck together in some Asian sweatshop. They'd paid a small fortune for it three years ago and now it was probably worthless: obsolete, slow to process data, memory too full. Just like him.

To think such a small item could have been the cause of all of these problems. That it led to Tania getting on an aeroplane – the ticket paid for by that man – and flying away from her husband and her only daughter.

'I need more,' was all she'd said to him.

He felt Jess tug at his arms and he released her from his hold. 'Okay, Dad . . . I'll go to school.'

She was being reasonable and mature. It made him proud.

'That's the way, my girl.' He attempted a smile. 'It's probably about time we got a new one of those, eh?' He gestured towards the laptop.

She smiled up at him. 'It's a *vrot* old one. I wish she'd taken it with her when she left.'

He ran a hand through his hair, felt the grit from the mine. He needed to shower and change. Bloody Kylie Hamilton was arriving on the Seagull express in a few hours. 'I have to go to Nelspruit today to pick up someone from the airport. Things are a bit busy at work.'

'I know.' She laid a hand on his arm. 'I saw the news.'

He put his arm around her.

She looked up at him again. She was growing up so quickly, but she would always be his little girl. 'Dad?'

'Yes?'

'Even if we fight, like me and mum did,' she cuffed away a tear, 'please don't leave, OK?'

He squeezed her shoulder. 'Never, kiddo. Never.'

He led her to the doorway and watched as she disappeared up the corridor towards her room. He circled back to the desk and felt suddenly very angry. He brought a huge fist down onto the laptop and then swept it roughly across the desk, sending it crashing to the floor. He kicked it once, for good measure.

He looked up to see Petty in the doorway, looking at him apprehensively. She looked down at the computer on the floor. '*Eish*, can we fix it, boss?'

He shook his head. It wasn't the computer's fault his wife had left him, and Jessica's mother had abandoned her. He thought he'd been a good husband; he'd never cheated. Jess and Tania had fought like cats, but it wasn't the kid's fault and nor was Tania the only one to blame. Tania hated their life. The mine provided them a good wage, a good house, stability, a cocoon from some of the bigger problems people in South Africa had to face. And maybe that was the problem. It was another world, living and working on the mine, and it just wasn't for Tania.

'No, it's finished, Petty.'

6

Wellington looked down at the dishevelled figure at his feet. He felt no pity for the Afrikaner.

Wellington Shumba had worked the mines since he was seventeen and had risen to the position of shift boss in his native Zimbabwe, until the mine he worked for at Bindura closed. The owners had been negotiating to sell the mine to a Canadian company, but the imbecilic government had become greedy and insisted that all overseas companies wanting to invest in Zimbabwe had to be fifty-one per cent locally owned. The Canadians had got cold feet and walked away from the deal. The owners had had to sell their gold through the government's foreign exchange bureau and had been paid so little for it that the mine had stopped being viable. Wellington and hundreds of other miners had been laid off and he'd made his way south, joining the three million-strong Zimbabwean diaspora.

'On your feet,' Wellington barked at Loubser.

The man looked up at him and Wellington, who wore a miner's lantern, saw the streaks of tears that cut the grit on the man's face. *Pathetic*, he thought. He wouldn't last a week here as a *zama zama*. Wellington nodded to Phineas, his trusted lieutenant and, like

Wellington, a Shona from Zimbabwe. 'Keep an eye on this *mukiwa* while we walk. It's time for the scared little white boy to go to work.'

Wellington had expected more of the man. The Afrikaners he knew were tough men. This one, however, had the look of a frightened girl the moment before she was taken. Wellington reached out to pull Loubser to his feet. The man recoiled in terror. Wellington laughed, deep and loud. 'Come with me and I'll introduce you to the Professor.'

Wellington led, shining a path for them through his underground kingdom with the lamp on his hard hat. He may have been a shift boss when he'd still had a job in Zimbabwe, and a lowly miner again when he'd crossed the Limpopo illegally into South Africa from his homeland, but down here he was the mine captain, the ruler of this netherworld.

And he loved it.

He made more money in a month, leading his workforce of two hundred and twenty-three *zama zamas*, than he could in a year if he was working for Global Resources, or Anglo Gold Ashanti or Harmony. Above ground he kept a house and a shiny black BMW Z4 at a house in Emjindini township, near Barberton. When he travelled across the border to Mozambique to sell his gold he stayed at the best hotels in Maputo. He drank VSOP cognac when he partied and had women waiting for him in different countries whenever he surfaced.

He was due back in the daylight within the next few days, but he could not leave while they still held the Afrikaner captive. Loubser would have to prove his worth to them, and if he refused to play along, or if he had some kind of nervous breakdown, then Wellington would be faced with the choice of ransoming him sooner than expected, or killing him and dumping his body at the shaft before mine security came looking for him.

The deaths of the other two mine employees concerned him. They should not have happened, but he was ready to deal with the retaliation if and when it came.

'Phineas, have you prepared the defences?'

'Yes, boss,' Phineas said as they walked. He prodded Loubser with the barrel of his AK-47.

'Good.' Wellington had ordered booby traps set at the entrance to the old tunnel where the two mine employees had been killed. He'd had Phineas place hand grenades, with their pins removed, in old fruit cans to stop their detonation levers springing open. Trip wires had been tied around the ends of the grenades and then anchored to bolts in the side walls opposite the cans. Anyone walking into a wire would pull the grenade from its can, freeing the spring-loaded lever and detonating the explosives. As an added precaution they were moving their main operation. It was time for him to find a new location in any case as this one was fouled with waste and men were sick and dying. He had scores, if not hundreds of kilometres of abandoned workings to choose from, and he moved regularly to keep the mine security people confused.

'What are you going to do with me?' Loubser asked, but when he turned to look for an answer Phineas jabbed him harder.

'Eyes front,' Phineas said.

'That's a good question. It really depends on how much use you are to me. If you help me sort out some of my environmental problems I will let you live, let you return to the surface. Of course, I may extract a price from Global Resources for the privilege of having you back again. I know they'll pay.'

'Don't be so sure,' Loubser said. 'The Australians are running us now.'

Wellington laughed. 'It's good you can joke. That means you are feeling more comfortable, yes?'

Loubser shrugged.

'Give me the rifle,' Wellington said to Phineas.

Wellington took the AK and slid back the cocking handle a little with his left hand, checking there was a round chambered. 'Keep walking,' he said to Loubser.

Phineas called ahead of them into the gloom.

'*Mangwanani Baba*,' came a voice from the darkness.

'Professor, *bom dia*. At least I think it's *dia*, no?'

'I don't know if it's day or night, boss.'

'Luis, my professor, this is Christiaan Loubser, environmental manager for Global Resources, up where the sun still shines, or perhaps it's the moon at this time of day.'

Wellington played the light of his headlamp over both men and they gave small nods to each other. Wellington saw how the professor flinched when he'd used his real name. 'Luis Domingues Correia doesn't like me using his real name, Chris – you don't mind if I call you Chris, do you? Luis is worried that if you are released you will reveal his identity to the mine security people. However, I *want* you to remember his name, and to feel free to tell the authorities above ground when you get there who you've met working down here. I want Luis, Phineas and the rest of my happy band of brothers to be too scared to surface again for good. I want them to know that this is where they belong; this is the only place they can work from now on.'

Luis looked down at his scuffed boots. Wellington had learned a lot about men, working on the mines, both legally and illegally. He knew Luis hated being here, hated the fact that he'd had to become a criminal to survive. It would have gone against the grain of every-thing his Catholic, Portuguese-speaking parents had drummed into him. Wellington used that shame – compounded it – to keep Luis here. And, to be fair, he paid him well to keep him loyal. He knew that Luis, if pushed too far, might just find a way out of the mine for good, and walk back to the beach in Mozambique where he came from. Wellington couldn't afford that. Like a legitimate mine boss he had superiors, and he had production quotas to meet. He wouldn't have a hope of delivering what was required without the Professor's technical and scientific know-how.

The weak light of a battery-powered torch glowed briefly further down the tunnel. Luis took a box of matches from his overall pants pocket and lit a candle, then another. 'Sit, please, Chris,' Wellington said.

As the Afrikaner sat down, they were joined by three other men, their faces and overalls encrusted with dried sweat and dust. Two wore helmets, the other did not. Wellington had long since grown accustomed to the smell of unwashed men, but he noted with wry amusement that Loubser was swallowing hard, almost gagging. All the men took seats on hand-carved wooden stools.

'Nelson, Gideon, Wonderboy, meet Chris. These are my shift bosses. Gideon and Nelson are from Zimbabwe, while Wonderboy is from Lesotho. Welcome to our regular management meeting, Chris. Men, I will explain Chris's role with us soon, but first we need to talk about production levels. Professor?'

Luis picked up a school exercise book from the rockfall at his feet. Its cover was tattered and scuffed. He opened it and held it close to the nearest candle. Wellington made sure he sat out of the circle of light. It was fine for Loubser to take back the identities of the others, but not of him. None of the men who worked for him knew Wellington's real identity, and he wanted to keep it that way.

Luis coughed, then wiped his lips with the back of his hand. 'Production for this month is fourteen kilograms of gold. This is up three hundred grams on last month, but still short of our average of sixteen kilograms over the previous six months. I have done the calculations as you asked, boss.'

'Very good, Professor. Men, we have a problem, as you know. I have been working hard to recruit new blood for our organisation over the past eight months, not only to replace those of our brothers who have gone to God, but to increase production. And what do I find?'

He let the silence hang heavy in the darkness. Someone shifted a foot. Wellington had a good idea who.

'Professor, are you short of chemicals? Have your refining operations suffered in some way I am unaware of?'

'No, boss,' Luis said.

'Nelson, Gideon, Wonderboy . . . are your shifts slacking off?'

Wellington knew he was just a disembodied voice in the darkness. He smiled to himself as he saw Loubser peering into the blackness, trying to make him out.

'No, boss,' came the answers, almost in unison, but each strident, defensive.

'So why are we producing less gold?' He waited, imagining the nervous sweat rolling down one nose, falling between one pair of scuffed boots.

'There was the rockfall,' Nelson said, breaking the silence. 'That cost us three days last month. And we have lost, what, thirteen men in the last three weeks to this illness.'

'Ah, yes, the rockfall, and Chris is here to help us with the recent deaths. Hmmm.' Attack was the best form of defence, so some people said. Wellington disagreed. If he'd been in Nelson's shoes he would have maintained his silence, toughed it out. 'But how does that account for the drop in production the month *before* that, or the fact that I added three extra men to your crew after the fall, to replace the two who were killed and increase your numbers, Nelson, my friend?'

Nelson said nothing. *All very well*, Wellington thought, *to go on the attack, but it did you no good if you were stupid.* 'Phineas?'

Phineas emerged from the gloom and grabbed Nelson by the collar of his tattered overalls. The shift boss was bigger, a muscled, broad-shouldered man. He swung back his hand to cuff Phineas, but Wellington stilled him with the laser-like brightness of his miner's lamp, suddenly switching it on, illuminating an AK-47's barrel in the process.

'Put him on the ground,' Wellington said to them all.

Nelson stood and tried to run, but the two other shift bosses and Phineas were on him, punching and kicking him to the ground, eventually pinning him. Luis, the Professor, stood back, and Loubser had fallen backwards off his stool in a bid to escape the melee. Luis picked up a candle that had fallen and snuffed itself out, and relit it.

Wellington stood over Nelson now, the rifle pointed down at his face. 'You should have been more discreet, Nelson. Phineas talks to the girls in the whorehouses in Emjindini as well, you know. He listens and he reports back to me. He knows of the boasts you've made of jewellery for pretty girls and a new BMW X5 for yourself – the one you've already ordered from the dealer, Nelson. Tsk, tsk. I don't pay you that well, do I?'

'I saved, boss. You've been too good to me.'

'That I have,' Wellington said. Then pointed the AK between Nelson's eyes.

'No! I swear it, on the lives of my children. I've stolen nothing, boss.' His head thrashed from side to side. 'It was one of them, not me. I tell the girls lies to make them like me. Every man does. Please, boss.'

Wellington shook his head. 'You've lied to *me*, and that is what hurts my soul so much, Nelson. And you, a countryman of mine; I almost hate to do this.'

Wellington lowered his head, slowly moving the beam of light from his lamp down Nelson's body, until its brightness shone on the man's crotch, his face, hands and feet in the shadows. The barrel of the rifle tracked the same path. 'Hold him.'

'No!'

Loubser screamed as the shot reverberated through the tunnel and all their eardrums. Nelson bawled and writhed and yelled for his mother as the blood pumped from where his penis and testicles had been.

'Tie him,' Wellington said, 'and gag him.'

Wonderboy let go of a hand and Phineas passed him a coil of rope. Nelson reached instinctively for his groin but Wonderboy grabbed his hand away and he and Gideon tied the man's hands behind his back and stuffed a rag in his mouth. Nelson bucked and screamed with the pain as they moved to his legs.

'Finish him off, please, boss. Have mercy.' Luis crossed himself.

'No.'

*

65

Kylie woke as the SAA flight attendant was moving down the aisle preparing for the landing. Kylie checked her watch, which she had set to South African time. It was five-thirty in the morning so they were already about an hour behind schedule, but she reckoned she still had plenty of time to make her connection.

She looked out the window and caught her first sight of Africa as the sun came up. She thought it didn't look all that different to Australia, Western Australia in particular, and wondered if that was why so many South Africans had settled in that part of the country, because of its physical resemblance to their homeland.

The land was dry, and she knew from her reading this time of year was near the end of the long winter. Most rainfall fell in the summer months, from October through to March, yet still she'd expected Africa to be greener, more exotic. Instead the landscape was a camouflage patchwork of khakis and golds. She saw the ordered boundaries of farms, the circular tracks of giant irrigation pivots, and the vapour from a power station. Johannesburg itself looked like any other city from the air. As they banked Kylie could see the sun was emerging from a band of smoky haze that blanketed Johannesburg. The diffusion of light tinged the city gold.

She retrieved her folder of papers from the pocket beside her. She had drifted off to sleep about two in the morning, Perth time. Her brain was crammed full of South Africa and so she flicked through the documents to another report relating to Africa, though this one was about Zambia. Global Resources had a geological survey team there which had been granted an exploration licence on the border of yet another national park, this time Kafue in Zambia. What was it with Global Resources and national parks? she wondered. It was as though Jan had thought, in for a penny in for a pound with his aggressive expansion strategy. She knew he was no greeny, but she wondered whether they might not be setting themselves up as a bigger target than necessary. Still, according to the report, apart from some traffic on some African news and travel websites the Kafue project hadn't yet attracted as much interest as the planned coalmine near the Kruger Park in South Africa. Admittedly the Kruger mine – she admonished herself immediately for using what the media trainer would have called 'poison' words – admittedly the *Mpumalanga* mine, named after the province it would directly benefit, was far more advanced than the Zambia project. They might yet stir up a hornets' nest of environmental activism in that country once the South African plan came to fruition.

She and Cameron were due to fly to Zambia during this trip, to inspect a GR mine in the country's copper belt region, and they would meet with the exploration team there. She skimmed through the Zambian report to the conclusions.

The area currently subject to exploration is of marginal value to the Zambian Wildlife Authority (ZAWA). Poaching has severely depleted game in this sector of the park; local people have logged the area extensively for firewood and building materials; there are two illegal goldmines (that we know of), and the area is infested with tsetse flies, making it the least visited part of the park by tourists and tour operators.

Sounded like paradise, Kylie thought. Like the Mpumalanga project, this was marginal land that the government had legitimately identified as being worth exploiting for mineral resources for the greater good of the community. She read on.

Global Resources has negotiated with the government a contribution levy per tonne which will be quarantined for payment to ZAWA to aid in conservation programs and rehabilitation of the national park.

Kylie nodded to herself. People had to look past their own self-interest when it came to mines in controversial areas. Both of these projects, while unpopular with conservationists, would deliver jobs, income to the respective governments, economic spin-offs to local

communities through local purchasing and wages, and contribu-
tions to help conserve wildlife areas of true value. She shut the folder.

There was a bump as they touched down and Kylie saw dry grass
flashing by. The aircraft taxied to its air bridge and once the seatbelt
light was out Kylie filed out with the other business-class passengers.

Through a chink in the expanding vinyl curtain that linked the
air bridge to the aircraft came a beam of early morning light that
made a hundred thousand tiny dust particles dance before her eyes.
Then she smelled it. Rich earth, dried grass, the promise of rain,
perhaps something not quite right somewhere out on the tarmac. It
wasn't the spice that hung in the air in Asia or the bone-dry nothing-
ness of Australia, or the fossil fuels of America. It was something
else. Africa.

She was exhausted, and still had another flight to board, but the
people at the mine would be in worse shape, and that's where she
needed to be now.

7

Cameron watched the Airlink Embraer jet aircraft taxi up to the terminal at Kruger Mpumalanga International Airport as he sipped a coffee in the Wimpy, upstairs in the terminal. The airport was set in the picturesque hills near White River and served the Kruger Park and Nelspruit, the nearby provincial capital.

He shielded his eyes against the glare of the morning sun and searched the line of passengers emerging from the shimmering heat haze. Kylie strode across the tarmac. He drained his coffee cup, paid and walked downstairs to the arrivals area.

He was waiting when Kylie emerged through the swinging doors from the baggage collection area. He'd seen her on the widescreen plasma during video conferences plenty of times, but she looked different in the flesh. Taller. Thinner. Better looking.

'*Howzit*. Welcome to Nelspruit. Let me take your bags.'

'I'm fine. I can manage,' she said.

He shrugged. 'OK, let's go.'

He could have sent one of the drivers; he should have, probably, as he hated to be away from the mine in case word came through about Loubser. However, he knew it was important that she get the right impression about the mine and what was going on with the *zama zamas*. He didn't want some oaf telling her they should poison all the illegal miners, or some African blabbing about how easy it was to bribe the security guards to get contraband underground and gold out. Also, he knew he had to work with Kylie Hamilton, even if she did have a reputation for being a ball breaker.

He'd brought his mine *bakkie*, the Hilux. Juma, the Malawian gardener, had offered to wash it before he left, but Cameron had told him not to bother. He'd seen Jess off to school with a hug, then taken a long shower to drown his own tears. He couldn't dwell on his own problems right now. He was tired, and he had forgotten to shave, but he didn't care.

Cameron got into the truck while Kylie hefted her bags up into the load bin at the back. If she wanted to do it all herself, let her. She got in and he drove off. The road took them past citrus and macadamia farms, back to the R40, which led to Nelspruit then Barberton on the other side of the mountains.

Kylie shrugged out of the jacket she had been wearing on the aircraft and reached into the back seat to drape it over her daypack. 'Is it always this hot here in winter?'

'*Yes*. Except when it's cold. Hotter underground.'

'I've been underground.'

'Right.'

'Have you had any more news about the missing man?'

'Chris Loubser is his name. No, nothing. But he has to still be alive. If he was dead the *zama zamas* would have taken his body to the shaft, so that it wouldn't stink them out, and so that hopefully we wouldn't go looking for them.'

'I can't believe that you have standard operating procedures with these men. They're *criminals*.'

He heard the slight against him in her voice. It didn't matter to her that there were *zama zamas* in virtually every goldmine in South Africa. Because it didn't happen in Australia, she couldn't imagine it happening – or a manager allowing it to happen – in Africa. She would learn. Or maybe not. There was nothing he could say that wouldn't sound defensive or offensive to her. He kept his mouth shut. The drive was scenic enough, he thought, to occupy her for a while. They stayed on the R40, crossing the N4 motorway at Nelspruit then heading through the thickly vegetated ranges south of the city via a series of twisting passes that then led down into the De Kaap Valley.

'You've brought in the police?'

He clenched the wheel harder. That tone. It was like Tania criticising him for having to respond to a call-out at the mine and missing Jessica's piano recital or her dance or whatever. He took a deep breath. 'Yes.'

'And?'

The hell with it. 'And like I tried to tell you on the video conference the other day, the buggers are completely bloody useless. They're too scared to even investigate. Look, there's a reason most *zama zamas* are arrested by mine security and that's because the police don't want any part of it. Hell, they're probably being paid off by the gold dealers to look the other way as well.'

She stared at him. If there was a veneer of civilisation between them it had already begun to split and peel like the laminate on his kitchen cupboards. 'Yes, and there's also a reason people are killed in battles with illegal miners – because mine security in this country shoots first and asks questions later.'

'That's rubbish,' he said, glancing at her. He was tired and he knew he shouldn't be getting into a fight with her. He should just let her do her seagull thing – fly in and shit all over them and fly home – and then go back to running his mine and trying to run his life. But he couldn't keep quiet in the face of her know-it-all pontificating.

'Is it?' she said. 'Explain to me why the *zama zamas* would kill two of your people and, presumably, capture one of them. I've read plenty of reports about clashes between mine security and your *zama zamas*, and the casualties happen when security goes looking for a fight.'

Her eyes challenged him. They were a vivid emerald, something he hadn't noticed on the TV screen in the video conferences. The word was she was a machine, and had no man and no personal life whatsoever. 'So now you're saying we should do nothing about them – not go after them in case someone gets killed or wounded?'

'I'm saying that perhaps your security guard, Paulo Barrica, went looking for a fight when he should have been protecting your environmental officers.'

Cameron indicated right and turned onto the mine access road, but pulled over onto the dusty verge before they reached the perimeter gates.

'What? Why are we stopping?'

He pointed his finger at her. 'Paulo Barrica was a good man – one of the best security men I've ever employed. He never took a cent from the *zama zamas* and was helping me with an operation to catch some corrupt security guards at the mine. He was as honest as the day is long and, yes, he was a hard man, but if you're going to point the finger at him for what happened you can get out of this car and walk, because until we know what happened I'm not going to be blaming anyone except myself for the death of those two men, and whatever's happened to Chris.'

Even as he said the words he knew he was digging his own grave, although part of him didn't really care. Paulo was a hard man, which was why her words and her tone rankled so much – because she could be right. Ironically, if he'd sent Chris and Themba down with one of the lazier guards, one of the ones he and Paulo suspected of being corrupt, it was likely no one would have been killed or captured. A crooked guard would have avoided confrontation and perhaps even had a message delivered in advance to let the *zama zamas* know which *madala* side the environmental team would be visiting that day.

Christ, Cameron thought, he was tired.

'If you don't mind me saying,' she said in a softer voice, 'you look like you could use some sleep.'

He started the car again and pulled back onto the access road. 'Could you sleep if you were me? If one of your men was still down there?'

She looked at him, lips pursed. 'No. I suppose not.'

They drove to the checkpoint and the guard made Kylie get out of the car and sign in. Cameron could have just had the guard wave them through, but he'd made a point of telling the man on duty, on his way out to the airport to collect Kylie, to stop them on the way back in and have the white woman sign in. He wanted her to see that they took security seriously.

'Sorry for the delay,' he mumbled.

'No, not at all. Protocols are protocols. But how can a *zama zama* even get onto the site?'

Cameron drove the short distance to the mine office, gesturing to the perimeter fence. 'Take a look. It's a big area to secure and it's not a prison. Those big hills you can see behind the mine are covered in bush and stretch all the way to Swaziland. I've got armed response security patrols and two dog teams, but there are too many tracks leading to the mine to patrol. We concentrate on the perimeter but as fast as we find and repair cuts in the fences or burrows underneath them, the *zama zamas* find a new way onto the mine. If you want to double or quadruple my security budget I can put up searchlights and machine-gun towers.'

'I'll review it.'

'I was joking,' he said as he pulled into the manager's parking spot, adjacent to the single-storey administration building. 'You know, we could make this place like Polsmoor Prison but that wouldn't stop the *zama zamas*, it would only slow them down.'

'Why is that?' She got out of the car and he answered her as they walked to his office.

'Even if we stop them getting in and out of the mine site via the perimeter fence, they can still come and go underground. There are mines everywhere here, some dating back a century. Many of the mines are interconnected underground, sometimes because you had one mine taking over a neighbour and deliberately breaking through, and sometimes it just happens – we'll accidentally stumble on an old mine we didn't know about. You can walk for kilometres underground. We bulldoze old shafts shut if we can find them, but there's always a way into and out of a mine. Sometimes the guys use old escape ladders, and sometimes just ropes knotted together.'

'You're saying you can't do anything – that the situation's hopeless and we just have to live with the theft?'

He opened the door for her and the airconditioning beckoned them inside. Cameron said hello to the receptionist, Ilse, and introduced her to Kylie, which saved him from having to answer her barbed question, at least until after they'd asked for their drinks – black coffee for him, green tea for her. Cameron saw the perplexed look cross Ilse's face and wondered how long it would take her to get someone to drive to town to get green tea. If such a thing even existed in Barberton.

Cameron introduced Kylie to Hannelie, then showed her into his office and shut the door. He sat down behind his desk and she took a seat opposite him. He put his elbows on the blotter and clasped his hands together. 'Yes.'

'Yes? Just like that, you've admitted defeat?'

He sat back in his chair. 'We know the gold stolen from mines in South Africa finds its way overseas to Dubai and Athens mostly. You know how much gold is worth these days. We estimate Eureka alone is losing about half a million US dollars' worth of gold every *month*. We can't afford to pay our security guys and our miners who are supplying the *zama zamas* as much as the criminals can.'

'Yes, I read that some of your employees are involved as well. It's hard to believe.'

Cameron felt his face flush, but simply shook his head. 'Not really. Some of them are related to the criminal miners. Because we're going deeper with the new shaft our workings aren't as accessible from old mines, so the illegals are bribing our guys to take supplies down to them.'

'So what, we just accept it?' She looked incredulous.

Cameron sighed. 'We do what we can. We carry out spot checks; we run undercover operations like the one I'd organised with Paulo Barrica; and we used to send armed security down into the mine when we located a *zama zama* work site, until you risk-averse people in Australia halted our operations. Like I said, we close illegal access points when we find them, but as long as there's a demand there's going to be men who will take the risk to work down there.'

She folded her arms and looked at him, then around his office, her gaze stopping at an old painting Jessica had done when she was a little kid, which he'd framed.

'Cameron, we definitely need to review your security, but there's something else I need to talk to you about first.'

'Yes?'

'Jan wanted me to tell you in person – you're being promoted.'

He nodded. 'For having two men killed on my watch and another disappear, and for not being able to control security at my mine, as you've just inferred.'

She frowned and he knew she was probably thinking the same thing. 'We want to make you head of special projects for southern Africa. You'll be overseeing planning for all the new mines, and you'll be based in Johannesburg.'

Shuffling papers. He had known it was coming when Jan had asked him to oversee planning for the coalmine at Lion Plains and he'd told himself he was ready for it, but still it felt like a kick in his ribs while he was down after a punch that had nearly knocked him out. He'd probably have a secretary, he thought, but no staff. The environmental work and the real planning and development was done by others, and by consultants. His job would be to report to Jan – via this Kylie woman – on the progress of others. He would become a mail man. No, worse than that, a mailroom boy, putting things in electronic envelopes and posting them to others. There would be travel – to tsetse fly-ridden wastelands such as Kafue, and trips back to the lowveld to address public meetings full of irate farmers and game-park owners who hated everything he and Global Resources stood for.

'It's because of Tania, my wife,' he said.

Kylie shook her head. 'Cameron, your personal life is none of our business. This is –'

He held up a hand to silence her. He was beyond arguing with her, but it needed to be said, so that she knew the truth behind Jan's decision. 'Whether he's told you or not, Jan is right. He knows how the workers and the middle managers here are talking: they think my mind hasn't been on the job since my wife walked out on me They blame me for the deaths, and rightly so. Maybe you are right, with your outsider's simplistic view of things. Maybe there was more I could have done to stop the *zama zamas* and maybe I shouldn't have sent Paulo down the mine with those men.'

She folded her hands in her lap and looked down at them.

He didn't need to hear it from her. He'd been humiliated by a disembodied American on a computer who'd typed the words his wife wanted to hear in a cesspit of a chatroom. The man wouldn't have had to promise Tania much to get her to leave. She was sick of Barberton and sick of him. All he knew was mining. He had tried not to think about it, but he thought she had slept around. Not with people on his staff: probably men in town. Cameron clenched his fist.

'It *is* a promotion,' Kylie said, breaking into his thoughts. 'More money, a new start for you and your daughter. How old is she?'

He glared at her, then looked up at the ceiling. He didn't want her pity. He hated that he couldn't tell her and Jan to go fuck themselves, to stick their desk job up their arses. All he'd wanted from his career, since the day he'd started work underground, was to be the boss of a successful goldmine. He'd made it, and instead of bringing him happiness it had cost him his marriage.

Cameron looked out the window at the headgear of the mine, the tall concrete and steel tower that shielded the winder and the cables that lowered his workers down and brought ore up. He thought of the men as part of his family. And two had been killed and one was missing.

He looked at her again and saw she was smart enough not to push it further with him. He knew he'd sounded churlish and childish. He was losing all that made him who he was, but Cameron suddenly knew what he had to do, before he left Barberton for the new desk job. He could never come back, but he could leave it a better place.

'You come over here and you can't understand how I can turn a blind eye to the theft that goes on here,' he said.

'I'm not saying that.'

'No, but you're thinking that, and you're not all wrong. I've done what I can to improve security, but I've also walked a tightrope. I've compromised to try to keep the peace and save the company money. You think we're a bunch of vigilantes, but the truth is I could have done more. I could have sent more armed security guys down to the *madala* side workings, but there would have been more bloodshed – our people and theirs. I probably would have had a revolt of my own workers, as well. Plenty of them have a stake in the *zama zamas'* operations.'

She nodded. 'Well, it'll be someone else's problem now that you're being promoted.'

That cut him more than anything else she could have said. 'Someone else's problem' – like he was walking away from the years of theft and the deaths of good men, turning his back on them.

*

Chris forced himself to concentrate on his notes to keep his fear at bay.

He worked by the light of a torch whose batteries were nearly dead. He'd asked for his hard hat and lamp, which had been confiscated from him when he'd been taken captive, but Wellington had laughed, saying he didn't want him being able to find his way out. Chris wondered if he could have found his way out. He'd been led to more than half-a-dozen different work sites, sometimes with the terror-inducing sack tied over his head again.

Chris was now working for Wellington, whether he liked it or not, and it seemed his life depended on what he was able to come up with.

The chief pirate wanted to know what was poisoning so many of his men. It could have been a number of things, Chris thought. The men were going into the unmonitored stopes before the toxic gases had cleared, and those processing the ore were exposed to dangerous levels of mercury, but Chris already knew what had killed the men in the last three weeks: cholera and carbon monoxide poisoning. While he was here, though, he would conduct as many tests as he could to find out where the areas of greatest risk were for carbon monoxide, and how sanitation and dirty water supplies could be improved to halt the cholera outbreak. The work kept his fear at bay – just.

He was currently in a stope with Phineas and the Mozambican metallurgist they called 'the Professor'. He'd been given back the daypack he'd gone underground with, once it had been thoroughly searched. He knew it had been gone through, not only because everything he'd packed neatly had been rudely stuffed back in, but also because the spare Leatherman tool he kept in the front pocket was missing. He had no weapon to fight back with or to use in an escape bid. What was the point, anyway; these rats would be on him before he found his way back to the shaft.

'Luis?' Chris called out.

The Professor moved from the darkness into the cone of Chris's torch. '*Sim?* Yes?'

Chris followed Luis, who seemed at ease moving in the half-light and the shadows cast by Phineas's lamp behind them. Chris tried to calm himself by taking note of their progress – which way they turned when they came to junctions, and to make note of land-marks. These were precious few, but he noticed bits of abandoned machinery and tools lying where they had last functioned.

'Do you want to be down here?' he whispered to Luis.

Luis half glanced over his shoulder and shook his head.

'Hey, keep quiet. No talking unless I tell you,' Phineas barked.

There were two soft beeps. Luis held his watch, a cheap digital, close to his face and pressed a button which made it beep again, and the tiny screen lit up. 'Chris, cover your ears and open your mouth.'

'What?'

'Blasting,' Luis said.

Chris was about to ask what was going on when the whole tunnel around them shook. A wall of dust raced up the working and the following shockwave knocked Chris to his knees. His ears rang and he felt like he'd been punched in the chest. When he took a breath he sucked in a lungful of dust, then coughed. '*Jislaik!*'

Chris felt a hand under his arm, lifting him.

He was vaguely aware of someone whispering at him. Luis moved so he was face to face with Chris and mouthed the word 'blasting'. Chris got to his feet and patted his overalls. Clouds of dust erupted from his clothes and hung in the air. Luis held his watch up so Chris could see it and pressed the light button again.

It was the end of a shift of legitimate miners and the charges had just been detonated. Chris spat grit from his mouth and took out a multi-gas meter and a dust monitoring pump from his pack. The meter measured oxygen, carbon monoxide, nitrous oxide and methane, and the pump was normally worn by a random sample of miners during a legal operation's eight-hour shift. He knew already his instruments would confirm just how unsafe the air was around them.

Phineas put down his AK-47 and rested it against the side wall. He took out a box of matches and Chris drew a sharp breath and winced at the flare as Phineas struck a light and lit the ring on a gas cooktop attached to a Cadac bottle. Chris exhaled; it was almost suicidal to light a match so soon after a blast and so close to its origin. Phineas put a battered saucepan of water on the blue flame.

'Tea,' he said.

Chris shook his head. Work hadn't stopped because of him. It was to be expected. He wondered if that meant they thought he was dead. In all reality, the way these guys worked he probably would be before long.

8

Kylie adjusted the plastic strap at the back of her hard hat, then tested and attached her lamp. She had brought her own overalls and work boots, but not her hat as it was too bulky for her luggage. 'All set,' she said to Cameron.

He stared at her a moment and she thought she detected the slightest shake of his head. *Fuck him*, she thought. There were plenty of women working underground these days, even in South Africa. This was no longer a man's game.

They joined a line of mine workers shuffling through the gate into the steel cage. Below them were two more decks, with six men in each. It would take them four and a half minutes to descend the fourteen hundred metres to the lower workings of the Eureka goldmine.

All the men she passed nodded or said, 'Good afternoon, madam', which she thought was nice but faintly ridiculous. She wanted to say, 'Call me Kylie, that's what all the blokes on the mines do back home', but she thought it might be insulting in some way. In fact, when she rode a cage down into an Australian mine, most of the time the workers didn't even acknowledge her presence, such was the inverse snobbery of the workplace culture in Australia when someone from 'head office' visited a mine. Kylie missed the days when she, like Cameron, had run a mine of her own and the workers really were happy to see her and greet her on her regular underground visits.

She and Cameron moved to the edge of the cage and filed in with four other men. The miners seemed more slight and wiry than big and burly. Some looked painfully thin and she wondered how many of the Global Resources employees around her were HIV positive. From her briefing papers she had learned the infection rate in the general population in South Africa was around ten per cent. Among the mining workforce, in the fifteen to forty-nine year old demographic, it was estimated at double that. The company encouraged its employees in South Africa to get tested and to know their HIV status. Cameron, she knew, had instituted an incentive program whereby employees received a ticket in an internal lottery every time they had an AIDs test, and stood to win cellphones, televisions and cash prizes. At the end of each year one lucky worker won a pickup truck; lucky, that is, if he or she also tested negative.

The cage closed and Kylie felt the oddly familiar crush of muscled bodies against her. The banksman sent a signal to the hoist driver and the brakes were released. The floor dropped and Kylie experienced the same mix of excitement, trepidation and contentment she did every time she went underground. She loved it down here, as she watched the cut rock wall of the shaft flash past her eyes. She reckoned that if she hadn't been accepted into university to study engineering she might have been just as happy being an electrician or a welder or any other job that could have taken her to work in a mine. She had noticed four females getting into the cage. Yes, it could be a boorish, blokey, sexist and bigoted working environment, and it was hot and dusty and dangerous, but there was something cocooning, she thought – comforting even – about being in the embrace of the earth. And she liked the fact she had cut it in this hard world of men and machines.

The cage stopped abruptly, sending Kylie's tummy jarring up against her rib cage. Her flinch was instinctive; they were nowhere near deep enough yet. There was movement in the darkness all around her. Men were fidgeting and bending in the darkness. 'Hey!' An elbow dug into her back and she felt someone's bony butt press into her thigh. 'What's going on?'

Cameron snorted. 'You'll see.'

She didn't like surprises, or someone lauding it over her with knowledge of something. When she asked a subordinate a question she expected an answer, not 'You'll see'. There was the clang of things dropping on the steel floor of the cage. Men whispered to each other rapidly from the other cages below them. There was more movement and bustling in the blackness. A motor whirred and the cage jerked and started to rise.

'We're going back to the surface?' she asked.

'Yes.'

Kylie wanted to know what was going on but she couldn't demand an answer of Cameron with all these workers pressed around them. She didn't want him to lose their respect by being bullied by her, and she didn't want to display her own ignorance of procedures any more than she already had.

Kylie felt an elbow in her ribs as a man fussed next to her in the dark. 'Hey, watch out.' There was a muttered apology and more whispering as more men in the cage appeared to be fidgeting. When they returned to daylight Kylie was amazed to see glimpses of dark skin as the man two across from her zipped up his overall shirt. He looked away from her. A man next to her was trying, without much success, to fight the crush of bodies to bend down and put his boots back on. What the hell was going on here?

'All right, everyone out,' Cameron's voice boomed. There were more hushed words as the men filed back out of the cage and Kylie joined them on the bank.

Kylie saw the floor of the cage was littered with stuff – just about everything in life a man might need. Two uniformed security guards entered and retrieved the contraband before the cage was raised to allow the men in the one below to get out.

While they waited for the next batch of miners the guards sorted the abandoned goods into piles. There was food – packets of biscuits, bananas, oranges, plastic bags of what she guessed might be maize meal, three small bottles of cooking oil and two bags of rice. There was tobacco – packets of cigarettes, tobacco papers and loose leaf. There were two ziploc plastic bags of what looked to her like something she hadn't seen since her university days – marijuana – and another bag of small white pills. There were seven small half-litre bottles of various spirits, pornographic magazines, some unopened letters in envelopes, pens, CDs, an iPod and batteries scattered everywhere. The second cage revealed a similar hoard.

'This stuff is all for the *zama zamas?*' she asked.

'Yes.' Cameron surveyed the mounds of goods with his hands on his hips. 'This is part of the problem, why we're unable to stop the illegal miners. For the most part they're supplied by our guys.'

'Did you put this on for my benefit?' Kylie asked.

Cameron scoffed. 'Why would I show you how incapable I've been of stopping my own men from accepting bribes and perpetuating a crime that's costing their employers millions of rand per year? No, I knew there was going to be a spot check sometime today, but not exactly when. I imagine the head of security, Tobias, timed this one for your benefit, though.'

A rotund man in the paramilitary-looking blue uniform of a security company pushed his way through the throng of miners and greeted Cameron then introduced himself to her. 'Tobias Nombekana,' he said. 'Pleased to meet you, Dr Hamilton.'

Kylie shook the proffered hand and was impressed that someone, at least, had taken the time to read her CV on the company website or intranet.

'Welcome to South Africa. I'm sorry to delay your visit underground, but we take security very seriously here at Eureka and I have to conduct some questioning. Would you like some coffee, tea or a cold drink while you wait?' Tobias asked.

'You can use my office if you want to check emails,' Cameron said. 'I'll call you when we're done here.'

She wasn't about to be parked in a tearoom or fobbed off, and she was interested in how Cameron would deal with this situation. Clearly a number of employees had broken the rules, but how was he to conduct a thorough investigation and still get the shift underground in time to get some work done? 'No, I'm staying. I want to sit in on the investigation.'

He looked at her and shrugged, then walked to the steel staircase that led up a level.

Cameron started speaking in an African language. 'What's he speaking, and what's he saying?' Kylie asked Tobias.

'He's speaking Swazi. He learned it as a boy and he is very fluent. He's telling them the security officers are about to inspect the seals on their self-contained self-rescuers to see if they've been tampered with – opened. These packs contain an emergency breathing apparatus that –'

'I know what an SCSR is, Tobias.'

Tobias nodded then called instructions to four other uniformed security guards who started moving into the ranks of miners.

Kylie watched the men. Some held their SCSR containers immediately out for inspection and stood there, looking either bored or relieved. Others jostled about in the group and tried to move to the back or lose themselves among their peers. The security guards started tapping men on their shoulders and separating them from the rest of the shift.

'Those men have nothing in their SCSR containers,' she said to Tobias, faintly incredulous as one by one the containers with broken seals were opened. She couldn't believe men would go underground without their emergency breathing apparatus.

Tobias nodded and didn't look alarmed at all. 'It's what they sometimes use to carry the contraband in. They know we do spot checks – frisking some of the men, and the women, too – and they must carry their own food for the shift in those clear plastic bags you see most of them carrying. If they have too much food we know it's to be sold to the *zama zamas*.'

'But what if there's a carbon monoxide leak or a fire? They're gambling with their lives.' Kylie thought of Cameron's lottery. Perhaps day-to-day life was a gamble for these men.

Tobias shrugged. 'Cameron will not be happy. This has happened before, and all the men know that emptying their SCSR is an offence for which they will be dismissed.'

Cameron spoke some more to the men, his cadence and tone rising. She could see his knuckles were white on the steel handrail he gripped.

Tobias translated: 'He is asking them, "How can you men supply drugs and drink and food and tobacco to the men who murdered your colleagues?" He's saying, "The bodies of Themba Tshabalala and Paulo Barrica are not yet in the ground; their widows and families are grieving, and you men are profiteering from the criminals who were responsible." He asks how they can deal with those who have a good man, Christiaan Loubser, possibly held captive. Chris was well liked, Dr Hamilton, as is Cameron. These men must be feeling bad now.'

All bar seven men, those with the empty emergency packs, moved back into the cages.

The last gate was shut and the remainder of the shift were lowered away. They disappeared into the blackness. Cameron walked down the stairs, his heavy boots ringing on the steel. It was the only sound in the winding-gear room.

'I'll speak English now, so Dr Hamilton from head office can see what we do not tolerate here at Eureka. Anyone not understand me?' He repeated the question in Swazi and then, according to Tobias, in Fanagolo. There were no responses and no raised hands. 'Good. You all know the rules. They are given to you in written and verbal form by your shift boss each week. You are to check your SCSR packs before your shift starts and any man who does not have his emergency breathing apparatus with him underground is liable for dismissal. Understood?'

One man raised his hand. 'Boss, someone tampered with my SCSR. I didn't know it had food for the *zama zamas* in it until just now.'

Cameron shook his head. 'I say again, you know you are to check your pack before you start your shift, to ensure that doesn't happen, Gideon. Safety is my number one priority. My *number one* priority, and it should be yours, too. It's your life we're talking about. Now I know that some of the other men who just went down for their shift were also carrying gear for the *zama zamas* and they will be complaining because all that stuff in the bin bags, which they paid for and expected to make a profit on, is going into the furnace. But they still have their jobs. You seven do not.'

A few of the men looked at each other in silence as the words sunk in.

'I'm going to speak to each of you now, in the presence of Dr Hamilton, and with your union shop steward in attendance as well.'

Kylie looked to the door at the sound of footsteps. A man in jeans and a polo shirt walked in. She guessed this must be the union man. He folded muscled arms across his broad chest and stared at the men. They could expect little intervention from their representative this time. Cameron nodded to the man, who returned the gesture. This had either been done many times before, or Cameron had lied and it was choreographed for her benefit. It didn't really matter either way. Kylie was actually pleased to see him exhibiting some modicum of managerial skill. She had begun to wonder how the man had ever made it to mine boss in the first place.

'Tobias?'

The security guard stiffened. 'Sir?'

'Have these men escorted to my office. They are not to leave, unless they want to forfeit what pay they're owed from this month, and they are not to talk to each other.'

'Yes, sir.'

Cameron walked to Kylie, pointedly ignoring the beseeching stares of the men. 'Come, let's go.'

She resented his tone, but she was curious about what was going to happen next. Kylie replaced her lamp in its numbered spot, effectively registering that she was not underground. If there was an accident and her lamp was not in its place it could be assumed she was lost in the mine somewhere.

She quickened her step to catch up with Cameron as he strode back to the office block. 'So, what happens to the men who dumped the grass and the pills? Do they just get away with it? You can hide a bag of grass anywhere on your body, but bananas and oranges would have to be carried in the SCSR containers. Surely drug supply is a worse offence than supplying food?'

He waved a hand in the air. 'Yes, you're right, it's not a perfect system. The reality is that we can't really stop the contraband getting to the *zama zamas*, nor the gold coming out. If I investigated and prosecuted everyone who was involved in supplying the illegals I'd be hard-pressed putting together a shift.' Cameron looked over his shoulder then opened the door to the office block for her, not moving until she went ahead of him. He lowered his voice. 'And I'd have no head of security.'

'Tobias? Really?'

'Don't let his "yes Dr Hamilton, no Dr Hamilton, three bags full Dr Hamilton" fool you. I've changed my head of security three times in the last four years. He'll be next. Paulo was in the process of getting me proof that the bribery of the security men goes all the way to the top.'

She put her hands on her hips. 'Surely this is a matter for the police?'

'Like I said, they're not interested, or more likely they're being paid to look the other way. Besides, they have bigger problems on their hands, trying to keep a lid on the violent street crime in this country. What's it to them if a multibillion-rand goldmining company loses a few million here and there?'

'What about the men we lost?' she countered.

'On average, a policeman is killed every day in the line of duty here in South Africa and we have a higher murder rate than Iraq. The cops are drowning above ground, we're not a priority.'

'I give up,' Kylie said, throwing her hands in the air in exaspera-
tion. 'Is there nothing we can do?'

'In the past we worked with a specialist underground security
company and apprehended plenty of *zama zamas*. I know the board
in Australia thinks the security guys were a bunch of Rambos, but
losses on both sides were minimal. We worked with the local prosecutors to prepare dockets for court cases: in effect, we did the police
service's job for them. But that's all stopped,' Cameron said, unable
to hide his bitterness.

'Your idea of *minimal* losses and ours were different.'

He shook his head. 'Please go through to my office. I have to get
something out of my car. The union rep is on his way and Tobias's
men will bring the workers.' Cameron closed the main door to the
administration block behind her and walked over to his *bakkie*. She
went to his office and let herself in.

*

Chris sat on a pile of rock in the blackness, hugging his knees. The
claustrophobia came in waves; but funnily enough, the longer he
was entombed, the easier it became to deal with it. Wellington blew
a stream of cigarette smoke in his direction and Chris coughed. He'd
given up five years earlier and couldn't stand the smell now.

'How much are you worth?' the Zimbabwean asked from the dark,
his face momentarily illuminated as he drew on his cigarette again.
Chris doubted he would be able to recognise him in daylight – if he
ever saw daylight again.

'I don't understand. Do you want to know how much money I
have?'

'Hmm, not yet. I hope it won't come to me demanding payment
from your family. I know you're not married, and I don't imagine
your retired parents have much money.'

Chris shivered, despite the oppressive heat. It unnerved him how
much Wellington knew about him. He was no madman. He'd done
his research. 'Are you going to ransom me?'

'Very astute. How much do you think Global Resources will pay me to get you back alive?'

Chris thought it was a very good question. 'They won't negotiate with criminals.'

Wellington laughed, the peals echoing off the walls. 'We're not talking about the US government negotiating with the Taliban. There are no morals or ethics or public relations issues to consider here, Christiaan. This will be a commercial arrangement. They want you back alive, presumably, and Global Resources is a very powerful company. Besides, you know it's not without precedent. There was the strike last year.'

Chris remembered the incident well – a shift boss, an unpopular man whose management methods had not moved with the times, was taken hostage by his own workers at the time of a protracted pay claim being put to Global Resources by the union. The shift had gone on strike and sent a message above ground that they would stay underground, holding the shift boss hostage, until the company agreed to the union's demands. Cameron had been away in Mozambique on leave, uncontactable on the Island of Dreams where he was helping an old army buddy and his employer renovate a dilapidated hotel. Coetzee, Cameron's deputy manager who had been left in charge of the mine, was a friend of the kidnapped man, and he'd sent word on the second day that the company would agree to meet the workers' pay demands.

'The deputy mine manager nearly lost his job and the shift boss who was taken hostage was later made redundant,' Chris pointed out.

'So what?' Wellington said. 'The point is the company paid. Think how bad the press would be for the company if I sent them your head when they refused to pay, along with a short video to SABC 3 or eTV. No, on second thoughts I'd send it to a television station in Australia, then the company might really take notice.'

'They'd send the army in here to kill you.'

Wellington laughed at the empty threat, and Chris knew his captor was right. 'They don't scare me, Christiaan, and they could never catch me. But back to business. How is the testing coming along?'

It was Chris's turn to laugh, though he barely managed a snort of derision. 'The testing is underway . . . but noxious gas, mercury poisoning, unsafe work practices and elevated dust particle levels are only part of the problem in your mine. All those will bring slow death, but you've got a real killer on your hands, an immediate threat to you and your men.'

'I *know* that. So, find out what it is and how to stop it or you'll end up like Nelson, screaming in the dark.'

Chris was concerned by any avoidable loss of human life, but part of him couldn't care less if Wellington and his whole band of pirates all died of cholera. Chris felt something brush his head and he screamed. When he tried to flick it away he realised it was Wellington's fingers, now wrapped firmly around his neck.

'Christiaan.' He'd come to him silently in the dark, like a black cat, and his breath, which smelled of mint toothpaste, was warm on Chris's ear. He felt the panic rise in him again. 'You'll do the fucking job I need you to do. Or I will skin you alive.'

9

'**K**ylie, I wonder if you could give Tobias and me a moment alone, please,' Cameron said.

He hoped she wouldn't object, and undermine him, as she had been doing since she'd arrived in South Africa, and as she'd often done when they'd spoken on video conferences in the past.

To his surprise, and relief, she said, 'No worries. I'll just go get a coffee. Can I get you one?'

'I'm fine, thanks,' Cameron said.

'Tobias?'

'No thank you, Dr Hamilton, though thank you very much for asking. We have a girl who can get you coffee.'

'Where I come from we look after some things ourselves.' She looked at Cameron and excused herself. Perhaps she was smart enough to know that she didn't want to be in the room for what happened next.

They had interviewed the men who'd been caught with empty rescue kits. It had all been done by the book. All of the men except Gideon admitted their guilt and apologised for their actions. Cameron, with the accordance of the union man and Kylie, was inflexible, though. Gideon, however, had ranted and yelled, protesting he was innocent and that he had simply forgotten to check his emergency pack. He said he'd had no idea it had been tampered with. Cameron might have been tempted to believe him if he hadn't been aware of the man's track record – and if he hadn't noticed the way Gideon repeatedly looked to Tobias, rather than his union representative, for support. Tobias, in response, kept pointedly looking away.

'This man knew the consequences of not checking his emergency pack,' Tobias had said at one point.

It wasn't the security man's place to make any comment on Gideon's guilt or innocence, and Cameron had thought Gideon was going to get up and attack Tobias after the remark, such was the seething hatred in his jaundiced eyes.

Cameron had also smelled booze when he'd stood and moved to Gideon, on the pretext of getting him to sign an admission of guilt. Gideon had screwed the paper up and tossed it across the desk. Cameron suspected Gideon was still drunk at the start of his shift. He had been disciplined in the past for being caught with alcohol underground. He'd said it was for himself, but Cameron had suspected him of taking it for the *zama zamas* – and having a few nips by way of commission. Gideon had been adamant it had been for his own use and had volunteered to undergo alcohol counselling. The union had supported his request and his apparent contrition had saved his job.

But when Paulo had begun investigating the trail of corruption through the ranks of his own officers he had told Cameron that he had seen Gideon giving Tobias an envelope on returning above ground after a shift. It could have been a handover of something innocent, but Cameron couldn't think for the life of him what a miner would carry in an envelope for several sweat-drenched hours underground and then present to the head of security on emerging.

Kylie closed the door behind her.

Tobias rose from his chair. 'You did the right thing, Cameron. Now I should be getting back to work.' He extended a hand.

'Sit down.'

Tobias looked at him, then at the door, and realised it wasn't a request. He lowered himself back into his chair.

'Gideon will be waiting for you outside.'

Tobias seemed to visibly relax a little, as if he'd misjudged Cameron's intention. Cameron liked that. Maybe Tobias was thinking that his stupid, weak boss was simply concerned about his safety.

Cameron walked around Tobias so that he was standing behind him. He rested his hands on the seat back. Tobias swivelled his head to look up at him. 'I can look after myself, Cameron. I really can't imagine why Gideon was so angry at *me*. Did you see the way he kept glaring at me?'

Cameron vaguely remembered Tobias making some reference to being an ex-MK man. It was probably bullshit, but if Tobias had served in the ranks of the ANC's military wing, Umkonto we Sizwe, the Tip of the Spear, during the struggle against apartheid, then he *might* have had some resistance to interrogation training and there-fore known that the best defence was often attack. Cameron would have been throwing questions back at his interrogator as well, for he had been through the training himself.

'Oh, I saw it, all right.'

Cameron reached behind his back. When he had gone to his *bakkie*, after sending Kylie ahead of him inside to his office, he had opened the glove compartment and taken out the small lockable gun safe he kept there. Inside was his Sig Sauer nine-millimetre pistol. He drew it from the waistband of his overall trousers and placed the barrel up under Tobias's chin, ramming it hard.

'What –'

'Shut the fuck up. Listen to me, China, I know you're running the supply operation into the *zama zamas* and bringing the gold out.' Cameron reached down to Tobias's belt where, like the uniformed men in his charge, he carried a pair of handcuffs and a can of mace in leather pouches. He took out the handcuffs and opened one of the bracelets. 'Put that on your left wrist.'

Tobias took the bracelet but paused. Cameron dug the gun in deeper into his throat. Tobias snapped the cuff in place.

'Hands behind your back.'

'Cameron, please, be reasonable.'

'Do it.'

Tobias sighed, and did as he was told. Cameron tightened the first bracelet and fastened the other to Tobias's right wrist. This should have been the moment Tobias tried to knock him off balance and go for his gun, but he was going to play innocent.

'I have done nothing wrong, my friend,' Tobias said.

'Paulo Barrica had fingered you already, my *friend*.'

Tobias glared back at him. 'He's dead.'

'Yes. You assigned him the task of escorting Chris and the new guy underground. Why?'

'You agreed with my decision. You wanted to send Barrica because you knew he wouldn't take any shit if they bumped some *zama zamas*.'

The accusation hung between them. Cameron swallowed and hoped Tobias didn't see his bobbing Adam's apple – an admission of Cameron's uncertainty and his realisation that Tobias had played him. Cameron pushed the gun harder into Tobias's throat and had the pleasure of watching him squirm. 'What did they want with Chris?'

'I . . . don't . . . know . . . what . . . you're . . . talking . . . about.'

Cameron had already racked the pistol. Tobias blinked. With his free hand Cameron reached for the phone on the boardroom table and called Hannelie. She answered immediately. 'Hann, I'm going to be in a strategy meeting with Tobias for the next two hours, until after five. Please make sure we're not disturbed – by anyone. I won't be needing anything more from you this afternoon.'

'*Ja*, OK, Cameron. I wanted to take my grandson to get some new rugby boots some time, so I might go a bit early if that's OK.'

'That's fine. See you tomorrow.' Cameron hung up the phone. 'We've got all afternoon and all night if we need it.'

'My uncle is the provincial governor . . .'

'And mine was a dustman. It doesn't matter, Tobias, and don't try and scare me with your ANC credentials or your time in MK. I was a recce in Angola.'

Now it was Tobias's turn to swallow. 'You're crazy. Global Resources will fire you when they find out about this and I'm going to the police.'

Cameron shook his head. 'I'm finished here anyway. And I don't think you're that stupid. No, I've got a better idea. You tell me what I want to know and I'll let you live. You can resign from Global Resources and go and rip someone else off. All I want to know is who's in charge underground.'

'I don't know. I'm going to scream in three seconds. Three, two . . .'

Cameron had never tortured a prisoner during his time in the South African recce commandos, the army's elite special forces unit, but he'd been present while others had. The screams of those men were one of the things he'd tried to put behind him, but they still returned in his occasional nightmares. They always talked, in the end.

'Let me save you some time.' Cameron turned his hand and smashed the butt of his pistol into Tobias's nose. It shattered with a crack of cartilage and Tobias screamed. Blood spattered the desk and gushed from Tobias's nostrils. He moaned. 'Did you forget about the HIV AIDS awareness seminar that's on this afternoon, Tobias? Hannelie's the only person in the office and she's slipped out to Mr Price already for her son's new boots. *Ag*, shame, man, there's no one here to listen to your crying.'

Cameron gently touched Tobias's bloodied nose.

'Aaah! I'll tell you, I'll tell you all I know.'

Just as Cameron thought. Tobias was full of hot air; he was a bully and a coward who had caved in at the first sign of pain. Cameron was pleased. He didn't like what he had just done and didn't know if he could do much more to Tobias. 'Who's in charge down there?'

'A Zimbabwean. I don't know his real name. He calls himself Wellington, after the British general who defeated Napoleon, and

Shumba, which means lion in Shona.' Tobias coughed and spat blood on the carpet squares. 'It's what they called a *chimurenga* name during the bush war in Zimbabwe – not his real name.'

'Is he ex-military, a former Zimbabwean guerrilla?'

Tobias shrugged. 'All I know is that he used to be a shift boss in a goldmine in Zimbabwe. He knows what he's doing. He and his men are well armed.'

Cameron moved his face so that he was close enough to breathe on Tobias. The other man flinched away, his tears mixing with his blood and streaming down his chin. 'Tell me, did you set Paulo Barrica up to be killed?'

'On the lives of my children, I did not.'

'You *knew* those men were going to be attacked, didn't you?'

Tobias screwed his eyes shut.

Cameron lowered his voice to a whisper. 'I know this mine better than anyone, Tobias. I can find a *madala* side and finish you off down there and no one will ever find you – not your God, not your children.'

Tobias opened his eyes and Cameron saw the fear. 'No, please. Listen to me. Wellington wanted Chris – he told me no one would get hurt. He was going to capture them, disarm Barrica and release him, and then ransom Chris and Themba Tshabalala when he was finished with them.'

Cameron bought part of the story, but not all of it. The *zama zamas* stole Global Resources' water, power, machinery, tools and gold, so why not their expertise? There had been a significant increase in recent weeks in the number of dead *zama zamas* dumped by the main shaft. Perhaps this Wellington Shumba wanted a solution to this problem from Chris. But that still didn't explain Paulo's death.

'You recommended Paulo because you knew he wouldn't let himself be taken. You wanted him dead.'

'You agreed with me. You wanted a fighter down there,' Tobias reminded him.

Cameron wasn't buying that. 'You wanted him dead.'

Tobias drew a breath and coughed. Tears of pain rolled from his eyes, but there was a spark of his former defiance there. 'How are you going to explain how I came out of this strategy meeting looking like this?'

'That's easy. No one here is ever going to see you again. You're going to leave and you're going to email me your resignation letter.'

'You've got nothing on me.'

Cameron reached into the top pocket of his overall shirt. He pulled out a digital voice recorder – he'd never learned to type properly and dictated all his correspondence into it for Hannelie to transcribe. He hit the review button then pushed play at a random point. '*No, please, listen to me. Wellington wanted Chris . . .*' On hearing his own words, Tobias closed his eyes again.

Cameron reached for the stack of personnel folders that Hannelie had extracted for him before the disciplinary meeting. Gideon's was on the top. He opened it and found the man's cellphone number. He dialled while he kept his Sig trained on Tobias, even though the man had his head on his chest and looked utterly defeated. The phone rang four times, then Gideon answered.

'Gideon? It's Cameron McMurtrie. I've had a change of heart. You can have your job back. Meet me at the Wimpy in town, in an hour's time.'

*

Kylie had set up her laptop in the meeting room of the mine offices. She recognised the layout from the many video conferences she'd sat in on. The decor was older here than most of the mine offices she had worked in or visited in Australia. It was a bit like a seventies or eighties time warp with its carpet squares and timber panelling.

Hannelie, Cameron's personal assistant, had knocked and come in to check on her, announcing that Cameron had told her she could leave early to collect her son from school. Hannelie had explained that everyone else in the office was at a health seminar.

'And your hire car is here now,' Hannelie said. 'The man from the office in Barberton dropped it off. It's the silver Tiida just outside. Cameron thought you might like to have your own vehicle while you're here.' Hannelie put the keys down on the boardroom table beside Kylie's computer then said goodbye and left.

Kylie checked her watch. Cameron had been half an hour with Tobias. She could only guess at what was going on in the mine manager's office. Perhaps he was giving Tobias a written warning and although she had heard a muffled yelp she had resisted the urge to check on them. She shut down the laptop and closed it. She knew it was right to give Cameron some space, but she wasn't used to being kept waiting. Cameron could come and find her when he was finished. She packed her laptop in her small wheelie bag and went outside.

A stiff, hot breeze was blowing dust from nearby mine dumps over the car park and her rental car was sporting a fine coating of grit. When she opened the door Kylie saw a GPS unit on the passenger's seat. She attached it to the windscreen, turned it on, looked up 'accommodation', and found the address of the Diggers' Retreat Hotel.

She left the mine via the main gate and, although the GPS told her to turn right, decided she would drive around the mine's perimeter and check out the local area first. She turned the sat nav off. The wind trapped plastic bags against the diamond mesh of the fence and snagged on the coils of razor wire on top. Workers coming off shift turned to look at her as she cruised past. She waved and two waved back, although the third just stared at her. About a kilometre down the road she carried on past the corner of the Eureka property until she came to a settlement of what looked like about thirty or forty shacks. Some were made of sheets of rusted corrugated iron, others with odd bits of timber and sheets of plywood. Smoke curled from makeshift pipe chimneys in a couple of the shanties. A woman with a baby in her arms stared at her through listless eyes as she slowed. Kylie made a mental note to ask who lived in these huts.

Bush-covered hills rose steeply to her left and on her right a wide green valley patchworked with farms stretched across to the base of the next mountain range and Nelspruit beyond. It was stunning countryside.

Kylie made a U-turn and switched the GPS on again. Two hundred metres from the Eureka entrance gate she saw a ute – what the South Africans called a *bakkie* – pull out and turn towards her. All the mine's vehicles had the same livery, but as they closed on each other she thought the single male driver looked like Cameron, with his dark wavy hair. She reached over to her handbag on the passenger seat and took out her iPhone. Driving one-handed she scrolled through the recent calls and found Cameron's number. She dialled it. Kylie saw the oncoming driver look down and take something from his pocket and hold it out in his left hand, towards the windscreen. She could see, now, it definitely was Cameron and she waved at him through the windscreen. The phone continued to ring for two more seconds, then stopped.

He passed her and while he had missed seeing her because he was checking his phone and not the road, he had deliberately ended her call before answering it.

She was annoyed. Furious, in fact. She had been discreet and professionally deferential to him when she had agreed to leave him in peace with Tobias, even though she'd had every right to sit in on their discussions, and now he was snubbing her because he wanted to get home. She swung her car's steering wheel to the left, driving onto the verge, then wrenched it around hard to the right in a another U-turn. She changed down and stood on the accelerator.

Kylie bit her lower lip. Was it petty of her, she wondered, to be following him? Perhaps he was merely sticking to the letter of the law by not talking on his cellphone while driving. The GPS started badgering her again, telling her to turn around when possible, directing her to the hotel. Just as she was thinking of doing exactly that she saw Cameron raise his phone to his ear. He obviously had no qualms about talking while driving, even though she knew from her security briefing it was illegal in South Africa.

'*When possible, make a U-turn,*' the GPS lady said again as Kylie carried on through a cross-street, in pursuit.

'Shut up,' she said to the device.

From behind she saw the blur of Cameron's hand moving in the cab of the truck, as though he was putting his phone in his pocket. She stabbed his number from the recent calls list. It was hard to see him clearly, but his phone rang a couple of times before it cut to voicemail; she was sure he had killed the call deliberately.

'Bastard.'

She would tell him the truth when she caught up to him, that she had been out for a drive and had seen him on the road and wanted to talk to him. She would put him on the defensive and see what he had to say for himself about ignoring her calls. Kylie sometimes ignored calls when she was busy, but never from Jan, her immediate superior. With things in such a state at the mine and Loubser still missing, there was no excuse for Cameron snubbing her. She had been too soft, she realised, giving him his space with Tobias, and now he was riding roughshod over her. That would soon change.

Cameron indicated and accelerated to overtake a lorry. Kylie started to veer out but saw a line of traffic coming the other way. A horn blared as Cameron nipped in front of the lorry. The oncoming driver flashed his lights in annoyance. Not only was he disrespecting her, he was also a maniac driver. She wondered if his recent split from his wife was affecting his judgement.

The stream of oncoming traffic seemed never-ending. Kylie knew the sensible, mature thing to do would be to turn around, find her hotel and calm down over a glass of wine. She could deal with Cameron in the morning.

The truck in front of her pulled over to the left, over the yellow line that marked a half-lane. Even though there was still traffic coming towards her she had enough room to squeeze through. She hit the accelerator and sped past the truck.

She couldn't see Cameron's vehicle and she was coming into town now. Her phone rang and she indicated left and turned into a suburban side street.

Kylie exhaled, feeling relieved. This would be Cameron and he would be calling to say that he was sorry, and that he hadn't wanted to take her calls while driving. She picked up the phone from the centre console and saw that it was Jan.

'Shit.' Kylie hit the answer key. 'Jan, hi.'

'Kylie, *howzit?*'

'Fine,' she lied.

'You don't sound too sure. How are things going with Cameron?'

It was what made him such a good leader, she thought, the ability to read nuances, to cut through the bullshit and not waste time on trivialities. She was angry with Cameron right now and she wanted to vent, but that wouldn't solve her problems and she didn't want Jan to think that she needed him to sort out her problems. 'He's under a great deal of stress.'

'I'm sure he is. Any word about Loubser?'

'No, nothing, but I'm learning more and more about these *zama zamas* all the time. It's out of control here, Jan.' That wasn't venting, she told herself, that was the truth.

'It's out of control throughout South Africa in the entire gold-mining sector – and it's also a problem in the platinum mines. The question is what do we do about it?'

He was asking her for the solution to a multimillion-dollar problem after she had been in Africa for less than twenty-four hours. It was good to analyse and plan in business, and to make important decisions only once you had a full appreciation of the facts and had considered all possible courses of action. And sometimes it was fine to shoot from the hip. 'We can't stop the underground illegal miners without sending in a private army and causing casualties in the process. We need to go after the middlemen and use them to get to the heads of the syndicates.'

There was a brief pause on the other end of the line. 'Kylie, you were the one cautioning Cameron not to act like a vigilante. If you don't want him sending armed security underground to clear out the miners, and the police aren't interested in acting to help out foreign mining companies, then how do you suggest we catch these buyers and middlemen above ground?'

Kylie knew she had put her foot in it, but she wasn't one to back down from a point of view she knew was right, even if she didn't yet know how she would implement her plan. 'Intelligence.'

'You've got plenty of that, but how's it going to help you bust an international gold-buying syndicate?'

'We don't put our money into armed thugs, we put it into surveillance and intelligence gathering. We find out who the middlemen are, who the buyers are, and through them, who the principals are.'

There was a pause on the end of the line. 'You mean, we do the police's job for them and then hand them the intelligence so they can bust the big men?'

'Yes.'

'Hmmm. It'll cost money.'

Kylie knew she was right and that Jan was just testing her now. 'It will cost lives if Cameron sends down more armed security men to pick a fight with the *zama zamas*.'

'True. I'll give it some thought. Now, what's your plan for getting Chris Loubser back, or even finding out if he's still alive? We can't sit on our hands.'

'I'm working on that right now,' she said. 'By the way, do you know Cameron's home address?'

'Why?'

'He gave it to me. He has to go home and see his daughter and he told me to come to his place so we can discuss strategy, but I lost his address and directions and he's not answering his cellphone for some reason,' she lied.

'Strange. He wouldn't have given you a street address because he doesn't really have one.'

'That's right,' she said quickly. 'I meant I lost the directions.'

'You head out of town, towards the old Agnes mine, past the

prison, and he lives up in the hills, on a forestry road to the left. The turn-off's just after a trio of small identical houses.'

'Ah, yes, that sounds right.'

'What aren't you telling me, Kylie?'

She swallowed. He was too clever and she was no good at lying. 'My signal's dropping out, Jan. I have to go.'

'Are you two playing nicely?'

Kylie heard the smile in Jan's words. 'What do you think? Bye, boss.'

'Bye, Kylie.'

10

Cameron unzipped his overall top as he walked through his empty home. Jessica was still at school. The sight of her in her last school photo, on the wall, smiling back at him, snatched at his heart. He was being crazy, thinking about himself only, and not her.

He forced his eyes away from his daughter's, though his steps slowed as he made his way to his bedroom. Tania's pillow was plumped on her side of the bed, while his was indented from his last sleep – he could barely remember when that was. Seeing the emptiness of his room galvanised him again.

Whatever happened, Jessica would understand. She was a smart kid, and tough too. She'd weathered her mother leaving relatively well, given the circumstances. Cameron *was* doing this for himself, but in a way he was also doing it for Jess. She would learn, soon enough, of his move from mine management to the desk job in Johannesburg. Hell, Cameron thought, she might even prefer living in Jozi as she'd be closer to shopping malls and cinemas and all the stuff teenage girls liked. But she would remember the times he'd said to Tania he would fight a promotion if it meant him leaving the mine – any mine – and moving to the city. Jess would know he had been shifted sideways, against his will, and that he had been sold out.

What irked him, too, was that Kylie Hamilton was right about him. He hadn't done enough to stop the *zama zamas* and this Wellington Shumba was calling the shots from his black hole. Cameron would be damned if he sent mine security down to mount a rescue of Chris, and be damned if he did nothing. He tossed his shirt in the corner and went to the built-in wardrobe.

He reached up and pulled down the long green canvas bag and unzipped it. He pulled out the twelve-gauge pump-action shotgun and opened the breech. From a drawer he took the box of shells. He loaded five into the gun, gaining a small measure of confidence with every shell he slotted home. He laid the weapon on his bed and found a black long-sleeve T-shirt. He took off his boots and changed into black jeans, then re-laced his boots. He shifted an old suitcase and the cardboard box full of the photos of Tania that he'd taken down from the walls but hadn't yet had the heart or the balls to throw out. Jessica might still want them if something happened to him.

He dragged the green vinyl dive bag from the back of the closet and lifted it out. He unzipped the bag and took out the brown canvas and nylon combat vest. It smelled mouldy. He hadn't worn it in nearly twenty years. Cameron opened the right front pouch and poured in the remaining shotgun shells from their box. In the drawer there was a box of nine-millimetre bullets and a spare second magazine for his Sig. He loaded the magazine and put it in another pouch. He took his belt from his pants and rethreaded it, along with his Leatherman, onto his jeans.

Cameron stuffed the Sig in the waistband of his jeans, pulled his T-shirt down over it and then slid the shotgun back into its zip-up carrying bag. The last things he took from the cupboard were a big Maglite torch and a tin of black boot polish. Jessica watched him from a photograph as he walked down the hallway. He tried not to look back. If something happened to him, Jessica would end up with his sister and brother-in-law in Krugersdorp. They were good people.

He drove down his paved driveway and onto the winding gravel road that led down the mountain. The phone rang again and he held it out at arm's length to read the number, but he already knew who it would be. Kylie again. He didn't want to talk to her and there was no way he could tell her what he was going to do. He ignored the call, as he had done the previous two. At the bottom, where the dirt road met the tar, he turned right and drove past the prison into town. He reached into the back of the double-cab and tossed the dog's travelling blanket, covered in hair, over the shotgun and his combat vest.

Cameron turned left into Generaal Street and then right into the Jock of the Bushveld shopping centre, a low-rise laager of businesses arrayed around an open-air car park. He found a spot outside the Pick n' Pay, which was next to the Wimpy. Most of the seating was in front of the restaurant, under the cover of an awning roof. There were, predictably, a couple of faces he recognised, one of his miners and his wife and children, and the wife of the head of Jessica's school. The woman had been a friend of Tania's. She waved and smiled, and he nodded back to her. He opened the door of the restaurant. 'Table for one?' the waitress asked him as he entered. 'Inside or outside?'

He looked around the interior and saw Gideon sitting with his back to the far wall, his look of cocky disinterest not quite covering his uncertainty. 'No thanks. I'm just here to collect someone,' he said to the girl. Cameron pointed at Gideon, cocked his finger and turned and walked out.

Cameron stood outside on the pavement, in front of the outdoor seating area, and hoped Gideon's curiosity would get the better of him.

The miner walked out of the restaurant. 'You said I could have my job back.'

'Get in my *bakkie*. We'll talk about it there.'

Gideon shifted his weight from one foot to the other. 'Why? Where are we going? I thought we were going to the Wimpy.'

Cameron looked up and down the street, then lifted his T-shirt and wrapped his right hand around the grip of the Sig. 'Get in the car.'

Gideon's eyes widened and he, too, looked around, for a means of escape rather than potential witnesses. Cameron grabbed him around the bicep. The younger man tried to shrug him off, but Cameron's grip was iron. 'In the *bakkie*. You can come and listen to me, or we can go to the police.'

'You have nothing on me.'

'I have Tobias and he gave you up to save his own neck. I'll play you the digital voice recording if you like, or we can all listen to it together at the police station.'

Cameron nodded to the truck and Gideon reluctantly allowed himself to be led to it. He opened the passenger door and got in. Cameron went quickly around to the driver's side and slid into his seat, started the engine and reversed.

'Where are we going?'

Cameron turned left out of the car park and accelerated up Generaal Street. The brick bulk of the police station was on his right as he waited to turn left at the robot back into Crown Street. The building was ugly and incongruous with the rest of the town, a symbol of how things had changed in Barberton. The light went green and he turned back towards Eureka. 'We're going to work.'

'I don't understand.'

'You will soon.'

'What if I don't do what you want me to do?'

Cameron shrugged. 'Then I'll kill you.'

*

Kylie nosed into a spot in the corner of the shopping centre car park furthest from the Wimpy. She shifted in her seat so she could just see Cameron's truck. She made out his broad back at the entrance to the restaurant.

She had followed Jan's directions to Cameron's house, driving up the steep hill until she passed a driveway to a house near the peak.

Kylie carried on until she reached a forestry boom gate, restricting access to the pine plantations beyond. She did a three-point turn on the narrow track and headed back down, realising the earlier driveway – the only one she had seen – must be Cameron's. As she approached the home she could see, from the benefit of her uphill vantage point, Cameron's truck parked outside a garage. She stopped her car, wondering again at the merits of an angry confrontation.

Just then, Cameron had walked out of his house and loaded a long gun bag into the back of his pickup truck. The presence of what seemed to be a weapon checked her desire to confront him in his driveway. But she was curious. Surely he wasn't going on a hunting trip while one of his workers was still missing underground. She had decided to follow him some more, but gave him a couple of minutes' lead. Behind and above him, she had been able to keep him in view, just, and see him turn right off the access road, towards town. If he knew there was a car behind him he gave no indication.

Now, as she waited for him to leave the restaurant, she wondered again if she should just get out and march up to Cameron and ask him why he was continuing to ignore her. Cameron came out again just a minute or two later and stood outside the Wimpy. To her surprise, the next person who came out was Gideon, the man Cameron had fired that afternoon. Cameron had his back to her but he seemed to be talking to Gideon, so it was no coincidence. Next, he led Gideon to his pickup truck.

Kylie felt her heart beat faster. She slid down in her seat as Cameron reversed out of his parking spot, drove through the car park and turned left into Generaal Street. She put her car into gear and eased out of the car park. There were already two cars between her and Cameron, and she slowed as he pulled up at the traffic light just past the municipal offices, diagonally opposite the police station. His left indicator was on, so she was sure he was heading back towards the mine. She followed him, keeping the other cars between them. It was one thing to give him space to deal with his issues at the mine, but it was another thing entirely if he was in cahoots with a man who by rights should have hated him. Kylie was also worried about the presence of the gun. Jan had told her Cameron's wife had left him and she wondered, now, if he was suffering some kind of breakdown.

Kylie eased off the accelerator as she saw Cameron indicate to turn into the mine. She pulled over onto the side of the road and thought about her options. She could go to her hotel room and confront him in the morning, catch up to him now, or call Jan and report that Cameron was acting like a madman. A thought crossed her mind that made her shiver: what if Cameron was actually in business with Gideon and the *zama zamas*? She wondered if instead of grilling Tobias while she was out of the room Cameron had been plotting some new crime, or even just shooting the breeze. Maybe Gideon's firing had all been for show, to make it appear to her that Cameron was actually in control of the mine. It was possible Cameron was now going to let Gideon slip underground, between shifts, to continue working – for the *zama zamas*.

Kylie gave it two minutes then drove to the gate. She showed her company ID to the security guard. 'Did Mr McMurtrie say where he was going?'

'No madam,' the guard said. 'But he has not proceeded to the office. I saw him drive towards the headgear just now.'

'Thank you.'

She drove slowly along the access road. When she came to the headgear she saw Cameron's parked truck. Again she weighed up her options. The sensible one would be to do nothing for now, and to confront him later. She got out of her car and walked over to the Hilux. It was unlocked so she opened the passenger door and looked inside, scanning the cab. Next she unhooked the rubber bungy cord securing the vinyl cover of the load area. Nothing. The rifle case was missing.

Kylie knew she couldn't go to Tobias and she doubted she could mobilise mine security to go after Cameron and Gideon on the flimsy pretext that she now thought the mine boss might be in part-nership with the criminals below.

So she did the only thing she could do: she went back to her hire car and got her borrowed hard hat out of the boot. If Cameron was up to something, she needed to know about it.

*

Gideon had dredged up a little courage on the drive to the mine and had threatened to call the police and lodge a complaint against Cameron for abducting him and threatening him with a gun.

'All I want is Chris Loubser back above ground,' Cameron had said to him. 'If you help me get to where the *zama zamas* are holding him you can do whatever you want. You can come back to work if you want. I don't give a fuck. But if Loubser dies, then so do you.'

Once at the mine they had gone to the locked storage room where the seized contraband was being stored before being destroyed or, in the case of the drugs, being handed over to the police. Cameron unlocked the door and picked one of the emptied SCSR packs and told Gideon to fill it with a mix of food, alcohol and a bag of marijuana.

When they arrived at the cage at the bank, the top of the shaft, Cameron saw the mix of confusion and fear in banksman Cassius's face as Cameron told him to tell the hoist operator to send them to level fourteen. Cameron was sure Cassius was in the pay of the *zama zamas* and suddenly he was sick of it all – sick of turning a blind eye, sick of head office's non-confrontational approach, sick of Tobias's duplicity, and sick of thinking about what he could have done differently to keep his wife from running away from him. And as much as he hated to admit it, Kylie was right. They needed to go after the middle and upper management of the *zama zamas* rather than the illegal workers themselves. It was time to go find his subterranean counterpart. Cameron unzipped the gun case and pulled out the twelve-gauge. He tossed the bag on the floor and said to the operator as he motioned for Gideon to get into the cage: 'Call the police – not mine security – if I'm not back by the time the shift comes up.'

'You made sure that Cassius saw the gun and saw me. The *zama zamas* will know it was me who led you to them,' Gideon said.

Cameron nodded. 'Still want your job back?'

'There is nowhere I can run now. The Lion will find me and kill me and my family.'

Cassius signalled to the driver in the hoist room that the cage was bound for level fourteen. Ten seconds later the brakes were released and they began to drop. The black rock walls hurtled past them. Cameron switched on his headlamp, in case Gideon tried something in the dark. He shone it in the other man's eyes and saw the terror. Gideon was crooked, but perhaps no more so than half his employees. 'I will give you money for a bus ticket.'

Gideon closed his eyes. 'Even if you give me enough rand for an aeroplane ticket Wellington will find me. I cannot do this. Please.'

The cage juddered to a halt and Cameron opened the door. He hardened his heart. He raised the shotgun and pointed it at Gideon, motioning with a flick of the end of the barrel for him to get out.

Gideon stepped into the darkness and turned on his lamp.

'Just take me as far as where their workings begin, where you usually make your drop-offs and pickups. After that you can come back here and wait for the cage. You heard what I said to Cassius. They will come for you eventually if something happens to me.'

Gideon looked back at him and smiled. 'They will kill you, and Wellington the Lion will feed on your heart to make him strong. I have heard he does that.'

'We'll see who eats who.' Cameron's words belied his nerves. He knew what he was doing was stupid, perhaps suicidal, but at the same time he felt more alive than he had in years. The shotgun felt like a natural extension of his hands and he experienced the scarily familiar surges of adrenaline electrifying his nerve endings, just as he had in the moments before a contact in Angola.

When they had moved a hundred metres Cameron allowed himself to lag behind Gideon. He slung the shotgun and reached into a pocket for the tin of black boot polish he'd taken from his home. He quickly smeared the greasy substance on his hands and face. Next he opened the pouch slung across his body and pulled out a set of night-vision binoculars. He had bought them with his own money, online, from the United States. They had cost a small fortune. He'd put in a request for mine security operators to be issued with them, but Australia had turned him down. The reluctance to hire outside specialist mine security teams or properly equip his own men for offensive operations had prevented him from gaining the upper hand in the fight against the criminal miners.

He switched on the binoculars and Gideon appeared as a ghostly glowing green image. Gideon stopped and looked back. Cameron lowered his eyes as he knew a bright light, such as Gideon's head-lamp, would blind him and possibly damage the cathode tube inside the night-vision goggles.

'I am still here,' Cameron said. 'And I can see everything you do, even if you turn off your lamp. Carry on.'

Gideon moved off again. Cameron knew that the night-vision binoculars drew on ambient light and intensified it, but if there was no light at all he could switch on an infra-red beam that would cast an invisible light ahead of him.

As Gideon led him through a maze of tunnels and stopes, Cameron realised he had been right to think that it was not enough for him to know which level of the mine to get out on in order to find the *zama zamas*.

After a few minutes Gideon stopped and Cameron crept up behind him, the shotgun raised in case the other man was about to try something. 'It is here. In this old refuge chamber. This is where I drop the stuff off.'

'And pick up the gold?'

'I never smuggle gold.'

'Whatever,' Cameron said.

'No, it is the truth. They say Wellington trusts no one but himself. He used to use donkeys, fit young men, to carry out the gold, but one of them tried to rob the Lion by swallowing some gold in a condom. Wellington caught the boy and slit open his stomach. They say he pulled the gold from him while he was still alive, then let him bleed to death.'

Cameron nodded in the dark. If Gideon was telling the truth it was good intelligence. With luck he might stumble across this Wellington. He would try to take him alive, but if not, this whole underground operation might fold because of the paranoia of its leader.

'Who is there?' a voice from the darkness said in Swazi, then added in English: 'Freeze motherfucker.'

Cameron dropped to a crouch and backed up the tunnel. He melded his body with the side wall and hoped that if the man who had spoken turned on a lamp or a torch then his black clothing and blackened face would disguise him. He trained the shotgun on the sound of the voice.

'It is me, Gideon.'

A light appeared as a green sun in Cameron's field of vision, though it wasn't as bright as Gideon's miner's lamp; perhaps a torch with failing batteries, Cameron thought. The light played briefly on Gideon's face as the man confirmed his identity. 'You are late. What happened?'

'The mine boss, that white cunt McMurtrie, stopped the shift on the way down and searched everyone.'

Cameron smiled in the darkness.

'Then why are you here? Why were you not caught?'

'I had a doctor's appointment and I was only working a half-shift today. I came down with one of the artisans, an electrician, and they did not search us.'

'Hmm. What have you brought me?'

Gideon held out the SCSR container and the *zama zama* darted into the light of Gideon's headlamp, then back out again. It was as if, Cameron thought, he was scared of the light, or perhaps blinded by it after having lived so long in the dark. The glimpse had been brief, but long enough for Cameron to make out the distinctive banana-shaped magazine of an AK-47 in the man's hands. Cameron licked his lips.

The man checked the contents of the pack with the shielded light of his torch. The sound of his fingers greedily sifting through the contraband sounded like a rat's nocturnal foraging. 'This is all? What am I going to tell the Lion?'

Cameron strained to hear the conversation.

'Perhaps, my brother,' Gideon said after a pause, 'you tell him nothing. Word will filter to him eventually of the search of the shift. No doubt you have the money from all of the *zama zamas* to pay for the whole shipment of stuff the miners were smuggling down before they got caught. Maybe you can give me your little bit of money that you contributed for your share and you can keep what I have brought.'

Cameron smiled again. He had to give Gideon credit. He was a fast and devious thinker and he'd walk out of the mine with some bucks in his pocket.

'Maybe five hundred rand?' Gideon said, filling the silence while the other man considered betraying his boss.

'Maybe I'll take you to Wellington now and explain to the Lion how you suggested cheating him.'

'Four hundred?' Gideon replied.

'Three.'

'Three-fifty,' Gideon countered.

'All right.'

Cameron listened as the notes were peeled off and the deal sealed. Gideon and the man exchanged muted goodbyes and Cameron backed further down the tunnel as he saw the beam of Gideon's headlamp sweep towards him. Cameron stayed low as he moved, in case the *zama zama* decided to put a bullet in Gideon's back and retrieve his three hundred and fifty rand.

Cameron retreated ahead of Gideon until they were back at the shaft. 'Put your hands behind your back.'

'Why?' Gideon asked. 'I'm not going anywhere. You told me I could wait here until you were finished, or until the security guys come looking for you.'

'For some strange reason I just don't trust you, Gideon.' He brought the other man's hands together and bound them with a cable tie he pulled from a pouch on his vest. He told Gideon to sit down and then zip-tied his ankles.

'I'll be back,' Cameron said.

'I doubt it, Schwarzenegger.'

*

The cage juddered to a halt. Kylie switched on her lamp and opened the door and got out. Something moved in the shadows and she caught her breath. She saw the man sitting with his back against the rock wall. 'You're Gideon.'

He glared back at her, then raised his feet so that she could see they were bound.

'What happened?'

'Ah, he has gone mad, that one.'

'McMurtrie?'

'Yes. He threatened to kill me because I said I would go to the police and tell them he is the middleman in the gold-smuggling operation.'

'That's ridiculous,' Kylie said, even though the thought that Cameron might somehow be involved with the pirate miners had crossed her mind.

'He fired me because I was going to expose him.'

Kylie wasn't convinced. 'If he's involved with the *zama zamas* as you say, why did he bring you underground?'

'He is the big man above ground – he doesn't dirty himself with the work underground and he doesn't know how to get to where the *zama zamas* are working; he needed me as a guide. Wellington takes the gold up to him and McMurtrie negotiates with the Arabs, and the one they call Mohammed. People like me are the ones who keep the *zama zamas* supplied with all they need. You know how big the problem is. Why do you think Global Resources loses so much money from this mine? McMurtrie will tell you it happens everywhere, but no mine is as lucrative for the *zama zamas* as Eureka.'

Kylie didn't know what to believe. She still thought Gideon was lying to save his own skin, but what was Cameron up to, and why had he ignored her? He was acting like a guilty man. 'Where is he now?'

'Meeting with Wellington and discussing what they will do to me. McMurtrie wants to kill me, but he knows the Lion can use me underground as well. Either way I will be dead too soon. The *zama zamas* are dying down here in high numbers.'

'I don't believe you.'

Gideon shrugged. 'What are you going to do now?'

'I'm going to find McMurtrie and hear him out.'

'You'll never find him without a guide, or the *zama zamas* will find you first. We haven't been able to smuggle a whore down here for three months. Tobias stopped that traffic when the *zama zamas* moved too deep for them to be marched in via the old workings. You are in danger of being raped.'

She wondered if he was just playing her, making her think everything McMurtrie had told her was a fiction. But the suspicions still nagged at her. One thing Gideon was right about, however, was that she had no idea where this abandoned tunnel led to, or how to find Cameron. If Cameron was involved with the pirate miners she could bring down the syndicate if she could catch him colluding with this Wellington.

On the other hand, if Cameron was off on some one-man vigilante mission to bring down Wellington and rescue Chris Loubser, then he had deliberately ignored her wishes, and Jan's, and gone behind her back. He had signed his own dismissal letter. What concerned her, however, was that if this was the case then she felt as though she had goaded him into it.

Kylie unbuttoned the pouch of the Leatherman Wave multi-tool she always wore on her belt. It was a useful gadget. She had heard of miners who had been trapped in rockfalls and had had to amputate their own hand or foot to free themselves and escape. She dropped to one knee, unfolded the blade and sliced through the cable tie around Gideon's ankles. She grabbed his shirt by the collar and helped him get to his feet.

'My hands.'

She shook her head. 'I don't trust you, but take me to where I can find McMurtrie, and if you're telling the truth, then I'll see you get your job back and maybe even a reward.'

'All right. I will show you the way.'

11

Chris Loubser sat at Wellington's feet. The claustrophobia attacks were fewer and milder now, perhaps because he was so engrossed in his work.

So much of what he did for Global Resources was quality control – ensuring that the monitoring systems were employed correctly, and having water and air quality samples analysed to confirm what he usually already knew, that the company was in all cases sticking to the letter of the law in terms of environmental compliance and, in many cases, doing better than the legislation required. It was important work, but it was somewhat predictable and dull.

Occasionally he would pick up an errant reading and work with the operations people to find out how the contaminants had risen in the air in the mine or the water, and a plan would be made to fix whatever had caused the problem. Global Resources prided itself on its record of compliance, and its safety record.

But down here with the *zama zamas* it was different. Sure, they were criminals, but they were also human beings.

'I know what's killing your men,' Chris said, tilting his head up to Wellington, who sat as his desk, a fold-out camping table. Chris's back was against the side wall of the tunnel. He had also grown less afraid of Wellington, the Lion. He realised he was here for a reason, and as long as he did his job then Wellington would keep him alive. The realisation gave him a small measure of power.

'Then tell me, what is it?'

'Two things. The first is the silent killer, carbon monoxide. It's colourless, odourless and is a by-product of the blasting operations in the stopes. The simple fact is that your men go into the stopes too soon after the blasting's been done, and the unlucky ones are poisoned.'

Wellington nodded. 'I know about carbon monoxide. I suspect it's the same in the *madala* sides where I do my own blasting.'

Chris didn't want to think what safety breaches he would find if he watched the *zama zamas* working with explosives. 'You need to improve your ventilation to the *madala* side and to stop raiding the working stopes' faces.'

'It is an equation, Christiaan. I must balance the value of a worker with a guaranteed but risky haul from the working stopes, or putting more time into a safer operation in a disused working. Which would you choose?'

Chris rubbed his chin, wiping a trickle of sweat. He was acutely aware of his own body odour. Wellington, however, seemed not to smell. From the glimpses he caught in flickering candlelight or the occasional beam of a near-flat torch, Wellington's overalls appeared as clean as could be expected underground, a crease running up each sleeve. He wondered if Wellington had a boy to do his laundry here underground. Chris shivered. 'You know which I would choose.'

'Human life means far more above ground, you think.'

'I do.'

'Well, you're naive. It's all about money in the end, here or up there.'

'It won't be about money if I don't return to the surface. They will come looking for you. McMurtrie will take it personally.'

'Hah! I'm not afraid of McMurtrie. He is a clawless lion.'

Chris reckoned differently. Koos, who worked in accounts, said Cameron had been in the recce commandos during the war in Angola. Chris sensed a strength and perhaps an anger in him that was cloaked in the niceties of modern management practices. In the old days, Chris thought, Cameron might have been the type of boss who ruled with his fists as well as his words.

'What's the second killer?' Wellington asked.

'You have a cholera outbreak on your hands. Your men live in their own filth and your drinking water must be contaminated. You could all die down here unless you clean up your act, literally.'

*

Cameron smelled sickly sweet tendrils of marijuana smoke. It reminded him of matric; his life before the army, sex with Tania in the cramped back seat of his Cortina. Fun.

He used the night-vision goggles to defuse the booby trap. This reminded him of the war, dicing with death. Carefully he eased the hand grenade from the old tinned mango can, his other hand ready to keep the pressure on the arming lever as it emerged. Holding the explosive, he took the short length of wire he had snipped from a discarded length he had found on the footwall and slid it into the holes where the pin had once been. The grenade now safe, he placed it in one of the pouches on his vest. It was just like closing on a SWAPO camp in Angola: every sense was alert, nerves stretched to snapping point, trying not to think about home.

He and Tania had to marry when she fell pregnant, and he had gone off to the border war and left her. When he had returned he had taken her and Jess to live in a mining village. He remembered Tania saying she would have liked to have studied journalism. How much, he wondered, had she hated her life, and for how long? It was too late to worry about such things.

The tip of the marijuana cigarette glowed like a lime green firefly in the washed-out world of the night-vision goggles. Cameron saw the face, momentarily illuminated and temporarily transported from the hellish life of the *zama zama* by the weed. The man was sitting, smiling, with his back against the side wall of the tunnel and Cameron also saw the flash suppressor of an AK-47. Through the smoke he smelled the man's sweat. He crept forward.

Cameron slung his shotgun slowly and carefully across his back, and slid the hunting knife from the sheath tied upside down to the front of his combat vest. It was a long time since he'd drawn it. He knew he should have sharpened it before he left home, but hopefully it wouldn't come to that.

He guessed men such as this one, who spent their lives in the darkness, had more highly developed senses of hearing and smell. If this one was a good sentry he would hear Cameron coming long before he could use the knife.

Cameron knelt, carefully, and picked up a small rock half the size of a golf ball. He threw it so that it passed the man and landed on the far side.

Instantly the joint was dropped in a mini shower of sparks. He heard the man reach for the AK-47, then the metallic click of the selector being moved. With no ambient light Cameron switched on the infra-red beam on the goggles. He saw the man's back. He was looking down the tunnel.

Cameron picked up another rock and tossed it. It clattered in the area the man was looking.

'Who's there?' he asked in Portuguese.

Cameron continued to kneel, his right hand tight around the hilt of the knife. After a few taut seconds the sentry's shoulders relaxed and he lowered his AK a touch. The man turned back to where he had been waiting and started searching the ground, presumably for the cigarette he had abandoned.

Cameron moved in, as swift and silent as a predatory big cat. He reached around with his left hand, smothered the man's mouth and brought the blade to his neck.

'Lower your rifle, slowly, or I will gut you,' Cameron whispered in Portuguese. He had learned to speak the language prior to deploying to Angola which, like Mozambique where this *zama zama* probably came from, was a former Portuguese colony.

The man tried to speak and Cameron clamped harder, and pressed the blade tight enough to draw blood. The man lowered his weapon. 'Speak and it will be the last sound you make.'

'Please don't kill me,' the man whimpered as Cameron removed his hand from his mouth to take the AK-47 from him.

'I said be quiet. Down on your face.'

Cameron kneeled on the man's back and cable-tied his hands behind him. He kicked the man's legs apart and knelt between them. He brought his knife up to the man's genitals, pressing them through the sweaty fabric of his pants, and leaned close to the sentry's ear. 'Where is Wellington?'

'Please . . .'

Cameron pushed the knife harder.

'He has his office in an old refuge chamber.'

'Where?'

'Go two hundred paces then turn right. Then one hundred and turn left.'

'Any more sentries?'

'No.'

Cameron pushed harder.

'No!' he hissed.

'All right.'

'Where is the white man, Chris Loubser? Is he alive?'

'He is. He is often with the Lion. They talk,' the sentry said.

Cameron brought the man's ankles back together then cable-tied them. He reached into a pouch and brought out a roll of duct tape. He tore off a strip with his teeth and lifted the man's head.

'Wait.'

'What is it?' Cameron asked.

'If you find Wellington, kill him, please, *senhor*. Otherwise the Lion will kill me, and my family, for failing in my duty.'

Cameron gagged the man with tape and removed the magazine

from the AK-47 and put it in one of his pouches. He cocked the weapon and let the round in the chamber fly into the blackness. He couldn't carry two weapons so thirty metres along the tunnel he laid the rifle down and continued on. He thought about Jess, and what the sentry had just said.

*

Luis supervised a team of four *zama zamas* who were each cranking empty gas bottles that had been turned into mini ball mills, grinding gold-bearing ore that had already been crushed to a workable size with heavy hammers and an old lorry axle.

Luis thought about his wife, Miriam, and how he must find a way to get word to her, to stop her crossing the Kruger Park with their son Jose. He'd had a nightmare during his last period of sleep – he had no concept of day or night any more, only exhaustion and restless, hallucinatory snatches of semiconsciousness. She had been running to him, through long yellow grass, Jose at her heels. He had taken a step or two towards her, his arms wide to receive her and his child. There was a deep, guttural growl that resonated in his chest and in the next instant Miriam and Jose vanished from sight.

He knew that many of the *mahambane* never made it to South Africa. But as hard as Luis tried, he could see no way out of his predicament. If he was able to convince Wellington to let him go, just for a week or two, to visit his wife, then he knew she would never let him return to his criminal existence. Wellington would miss him, but he doubted the Lion would pursue him to Inhambane on the Indian Ocean. He might escape the man's wrath, but he would be back where he started, with no job and no money. If he stayed underground Miriam would risk her life and the life of his child to come and find him. Even if she did survive the journey, what would become of her once she was here?

Luis sighed, then coughed. Wellington would never let him go. He was the only qualified metallurgist below ground and the mine boss depended on him completely. He coughed again.

This place was killing him. Luis was the son of a Machope tribal chief but instead of sitting in the shade of a palm tree drinking beer, or casting a fishing net, he had pursued an education and it had all been for nothing. He would die underground in Barberton and he would never see his wife again. His life was like a mournful Portuguese *Fado* folk song: short and sad.

Behind him, something moved. Luis's ears had become sensitive to the slightest noise. Wellington had a habit of sneaking up on his workers in the dark to check on them.

Luis left his workers and took a few steps down the tunnel away from their candlelit workplace. He switched on his torch and stabbed the darkness. It was a man.

The man froze and looked at him. He was dressed in dark clothing and his face was black, but Luis could tell immediately he was not Swazi. Luis played the weak beam of his torch down over his body and stopped when he saw the barrel of the shotgun pointed at him. Luis switched off the torch and heard the man come towards him.

'Wait,' Luis whispered in English. 'You are heading in the right direction. Loubser is with the Lion. Be careful.'

A thought crossed Luis's mind. If this man killed Wellington in the process of rescuing Chris Loubser, then the *zama zamas* would be without a leader. Phineas Ncube was Wellington's second-in-command, but Phineas was little more than Wellington's enforcer and would never be a threat to Wellington's leadership. He had neither the brains nor the experience to run a mining operation. Luis had killed during his time in the civil war, and he wondered if he could kill Ncube.

No, he said to himself.

'Are you still there?' Luis whispered into the darkness.

There was no answer. The white man had carried on. Luis went back to his men. 'All of you, listen. Stop working. Go to the old stope face and wait there.'

'Why?' a Zimbabwean asked.

'Because I said so.'

'Yes, boss.'

Luis liked the sound of the man addressing him that way, but he knew he didn't really have it in him to take over this criminal enterprise. He just needed the impetus to get out and to try to go straight again, but he couldn't do that while Wellington was still alive. Luis crossed himself in the dark and said a silent prayer for the blackened ghost who had just left him. *Please God, let him kill Wellington.*

*

Cameron's heart was still thumping as he forced himself to move slower and with more care down the tunnel. He had been watching the workers cranking their rudimentary mills and not his footing and had dislodged a rock. He hadn't realised there was a fourth man, almost in his path. The man had let him pass, but he hoped he was not walking into a trap. Despite that risk, Cameron could do nothing other than continue moving.

All Cameron's senses were on high alert now as he made out the twists and turns ahead using his night-vision goggles. He silently covered another one hundred metres or so.

'What you need to do is tap into Eureka's ventilation system without them knowing about it.'

Cameron froze. It was Chris Loubser's voice, coming from around a bend in the tunnel. He reached into his left-hand ammunition pouch and pulled out a thunder flash, saved from his days in the army. It was a simulated explosive device that let out a hell of a flash and a loud bang.

'The alternative,' Chris said, 'is to install your own system and run it via an old shaft, away from here.'

'McMurtrie has sealed all of the shafts within easy reach of our workings,' said a deep voice.

Cameron stood rock still. The man knew his name. He and Wellington were, he thought, like mirror images of each other. Each had a job to do and each was accountable to more senior people. He was suddenly filled with hate for this man he had never met. He had

125

killed two of his employees and kidnapped another. Poor Chris had even been drawn in to helping the bastard. The way Wellington had operated with near impunity, thanks to Global Resources refusing to use armed security, enraged him, but at the same time he felt a sense of calm flow through him, tempering the adrenaline.

Cameron edged slowly along the side wall until he reached the bend. He pulled the cord on the thunder flash, waited a couple of seconds, looked around the corner and tossed it. He saw two figures in the green glow of his goggles, Chris Loubser sitting with his back to the side wall, and a bald black man seated, incongruously, at a camping table. There were lights on.

In the pause in the conversation between Chris and Wellington the clatter of the thunder flash bouncing on the ground sounded as loud as a bulldozer. Cameron raised his shotgun and closed his eyes as the explosion assaulted his eardrums.

Chris screamed and when Cameron opened his eyes again he saw the boss had fallen over backwards in his seat and was already rolling and trying to scramble away.

'Chris, stay down!'

Cameron fired, aiming high, and shotgun pellets ricocheted off rock. He charged forward, shotgun at the ready. Chris was trying to stand, groggy from the blast and possibly temporarily deafened by the magnified effects of the pyrotechnic in a confined space. Cameron placed a hand on his shoulder and forced him down. He saw the man – Wellington – crawling away and took aim with the shotgun. The temptation to shred his body with lead was overwhelming.

Cameron swallowed his rage. 'Stop! Stay where you are, Shumba!'

Bright flashes of orange seared Cameron's vision and the air around him was cleaved by bullets. He fired as he dropped to his knee, pumped the shotgun and pulled the trigger again. There was an AK-47 firing at him from further down the tunnel. Cameron grabbed Chris's shirt and dragged him back the way he'd come. 'Move it, Chris!'

Cameron ushered Chris around the bend in the tunnel. 'Run man, keep going!' Chris stared at him and Cameron understood his confusion. He could see nothing and his ears were probably still ringing. Cameron shoved him in the back and Chris stumbled away. Cameron pulled out his last trick from his combat vest, the hand grenade he had pocketed when he disarmed the booby trap. He pulled the wire from the pin holes with his teeth. He heard voices around the corner, shouted commands. A probing burst of gunfire pinged off the side walls, sending chips of rock and fireflies of sparks into the bend. Cameron ducked around the corner, tossed the grenade and ran.

*

Kylie heard the first explosion and the gunfire and knew instantly that Gideon had lied to her. Cameron was not collaborating with the *zama zamas*; he was here to rescue Chris and take on the pirates single-handedly. The bloody idiot. 'You lied to me.'

Gideon darted to the side wall and knocked his helmet against it. It fell from his head and clattered to the ground, the attached miner's lamp playing wildly along the walls. He came at her and Kylie raised her hands, but was too late to stop him. Gideon smashed his forehead into her nose and Kylie wailed with pain. She tasted blood in her mouth and felt woozy. Gideon crushed her against the side wall then backed off so that she slid to the ground. He was on top of her, on his back, before she could roll away. Every time the back of his head connected with her face and nose, a tactic he was using deliberately, she screamed. Kylie could feel his bound hands on her.

'Get off me!'

As she tried to shift him, and keep her nose out of his way, she could feel his fingers groping at her midsection. She screamed, trying to remember what she'd learned in a self-defence class years earlier.

Eyes. She hooked her fingers into claws and reached around to gouge at his eyeballs. She had the satisfaction of him letting out a howl, and heaved up against him with her pelvis. Too late she realised what he had been after, and found – the Leatherman in the pouch on her belt.

Gideon elbowed her in the stomach and she convulsed and relaxed her grip on his face. Gideon rolled off her. Kylie snatched a breath and reached up and turned off her lamp. They were in total darkness now, and she knew from the direction he'd moved that he would have to grope his way back to the side wall to fetch his lamp, presumably after he'd freed himself.

She rolled and crawled and flicked her lamp back on. Kylie turned her head and saw Gideon glaring at her, his hands still behind his back and his arms jiggling. He had managed to open the Leatherman and was cutting through his bonds. She looked to the side and saw his helmet. She scrambled towards it and heard him moving behind her.

'Bitch!'

Kylie grabbed Gideon's helmet, switched off her lamp and ran. He was armed, but blind without his lamp. She almost fell and her nose throbbed in agony. She had no idea where she was going, but she knew now she needed to get away from Gideon. Ahead she heard gunfire and another explosion.

Too late, Kylie heard a muffled sound and stumbled into something yielding that wriggled and grunted as she fell. It was a man. She switched on her lamp and saw a black man with bound hands and tape across his mouth. More of Cameron's handiwork. The man widened his eyes at the sight of her. She ran her hands over his smelly overalls, looking for a weapon. Nothing. She heaved against him and rolled him over. Protruding from his side pocket was a curved metal magazine full of bullets. She thought it looked like it came from an AK-47 – she had paid to fire one at a crazy backpackers' camp in Vietnam when she had travelled there in her early twenties. The man had nothing else. She heard footsteps echoing behind her and stumbled on in the darkness.

Kylie used her lamp sparingly, switching it on to show her the next section of tunnel in case of obvious obstacles, then turning it off so as not to give Gideon any advantage. She knew he would be moving slower than she was. The next time she switched on her lamp and shone it around she saw a rifle leaning against the side wall. A few paces from the weapon, as if tossed aside, was a banana-shaped magazine, which, when she picked it up, she saw was full of bullets.

12

Wellington marshalled his armed men. He had a security force of fifteen *zama zamas* armed with a variety of weapons, including shotguns, pistols, AK-47s and hand grenades. He called these men his lion cubs.

'Take the side tunnel and cut the white men off before they get to the main shaft. You must stop them or we are all finished.' The men nodded in the gloom.

Wellington had run from the fighting, but could still hear a man firing his AK-47 at McMurtrie. He had recognised the lone figure from his picture on the Global Resources website and wondered if there were more men behind him. Loubser was on the run with McMurtrie, and Wellington was not finished with him. 'Bring Loubser back alive.'

The men jogged away to encircle Cameron and Chris, as Wellington went off in the opposite direction. He ran back to the old refuge chamber that he'd appointed as comfortably as possible as his underground home. There was a deep freeze full of beer, a single bed, a bedside table and chair and a small electric cooktop. He moved the freezer and brushed away dirt from the rock floor. He lifted a metal lid on a cavity and took out a bag of gold. It was the latest takings from the mine. He put the bag in a backpack, put on a mining helmet and lamp, and changed from his normal underground working clothes of jeans and a T-shirt into a set of clean Global Resources overalls. He exited his quarters and ran deeper down the tunnel, away from the gunfire and explosions.

*

'Keep going, towards the shaft. I'll be right behind you,' Cameron whispered to Chris.

'No, come with me.'

'No, it's fine, Chris, just keep going. There's only one man behind us. I have to get him. Go.'

Chris paused for a moment, then turned, walked a few steps and looked back. 'Thank you. For coming for me.'

'Go.'

Cameron lay down next to the side wall, making his silhouette one with the rock. He laid down his shotgun and pulled out his nine-millimetre pistol. He heard the footsteps coming down the tunnel. The man approaching loosed off a burst of three rounds and the AK, true to its nature and the inexperience of the firer, kicked high and to the right. Cameron knew the man was trying to provoke a reply, so he forced himself to lie still. When the gunman came alongside him Cameron had already moved into a crouch and he launched himself at the man.

The gunman was young and lean, and quick. He thrust back with the butt of his AK and caught Cameron in the solar plexus. Cameron lost his grip. He sensed the man swinging the barrel around so he fired his Sig twice and heard the thud of bullets hitting flesh and the man's yell of pain. He switched on the infra-red beam and saw the man's lifeless body sprawled on the rock. One of the bullets had drilled him through the forehead.

'Cameron!'

He got up and started moving and as he rounded the next bend in the tunnel he saw Chris Loubser, trapped in the beam of a lamp with his hands up. A *zama zama* with an AK was pointing his rifle at him.

'Shit.'

*

The pirate miner with the AK stood over a filthy, dishevelled Chris Loubser and said to the man next to him: 'We take this one back alive. The other one, the boss from above, we kill.'

Kylie crouched further down the tunnel, hiding, but in earshot of the men. She realised there must be others coming. She had sat there for a minute or so watching as the *zama zamas* bailed up Chris, wondering what she should do. It looked like she would soon be outnumbered.

'Let him go, take me instead!' Cameron called from further up the tunnel.

The man shifted his aim from Chris and opened fire into the blackness. Chris put his hands over his ears, sank to his knees and screamed.

Kylie had fitted the magazine to the empty AK-47 she had found lying against the side wall – she presumed Cameron had taken it from the bound and gagged man and dumped it, perhaps planning on retrieving it on his way back to the shaft. Cocking the weapon had taken some fiddling, but she'd eventually remembered how she had pulled back the lever in Vietnam in order to load a round into the chamber.

'Oh, God, forgive me,' she whispered. She raised the rifle to her shoulder, braced herself for the recoil and pulled the trigger. Nothing happened.

Kylie's mouth was parched and her heart was pounding. Her hand was shaking as she briefly contemplated that madness of what she was trying to do – shoot a man. She took a breath and forced herself to think, and to try to remember what she'd been shown on the firing range. She ran her fingers over the left, then the right of the rifle and found the selector switch. She pushed it down, raised the rifle again, and pulled the trigger again. This time flashes exploded from the barrel and the rifle kicked back into her shoulder, knocking her backwards a little. The man who had been firing yelped in pain and was pitched forward. Kylie didn't have time to ponder the enormity or repercussions of what she'd just done; her body was firing on pure adrenaline. She ran towards Chris, who was cowering close to the ground. As she passed the entrance to the side tunnel bullets erupted and zinged off the rock beside her. She turned as she jogged and held the trigger and pointed into the tunnel where the flashes had come from. The rifle bucked in her hands and there were more calls of pain. She ran on, trying unsuccessfully to block out the screams she left in her wake.

The man she had shot was lying on the rock floor writhing in pain, blood frothing at his lips. Kylie felt nausea rising up inside her and swallowed it down. Part of her wanted to throw down the rifle and try to save the man she had hurt, but she instinctively knew that to do so could cost her her life, and the lives of others. She forced herself to turn from the man's torment. She went to Chris. 'Come on!' She grabbed his shoulder and tried to get him to stand.

There was movement in front of her and shouting from behind.

A figure loomed out of the darkness, into the cone of light cast by the wounded man's lamp. Kylie raised the rifle again, aware she was ready to kill if she had to, and pointed it at the man, her finger curled around the trigger. He held up a hand. It was Cameron, festooned with weapons and his angry face blackened.

He shook his head. 'You were mad to come down here.'

'*I* was mad? I just saved your friggin' life, mate.' Despite her tough talking, she could feel her whole body begin to shake. She lowered the rifle; it suddenly felt like it weighed a tonne. 'Cameron . . .' She felt the tears welling behind her eyes.

He strode to her and wrapped a free arm around her shoulders and squeezed her for a second before letting her go and looking into her eyes. 'You did what you had to. But it's not over yet.' A probing burst of bullets fired blindly from around a corner tore up the tunnel and the three of them dropped to the ground. 'Shit. How many more are there?' Cameron asked.

'I don't know.' Kylie's tears were gone. His touch had reinvigorated her. 'There was plenty of movement in the side tunnel. I think I hit a couple.'

He shook his head. 'This is not good.'

'*Senhor*,' a voice said. 'Come with me. This way.'

Kylie, Cameron and Chris crawled towards the voice.

'I know the way out, *senhor*,' the voice said. 'It is normally guarded, but Wellington has all his spare men out looking for you.'

'Why should we trust you?' Kylie asked the voice.

*

Luis thought it a good question. 'Because you have no choice. Because this is my chance to escape here, too.'

'This is Luis. He's a good *oke*, Cameron, you can trust him.' It was Loubser, his voice shaky. 'They call him the Professor.'

The moment the gunfire and explosions had begun Luis had abandoned his foolish thoughts of taking over the illegal operation from Wellington. All he wanted now was to see the sun again, to feel the Indian Ocean breeze on his face, to smell the salt in the sea air and to be with his wife and child once more.

'Come,' Luis said. 'You cannot make it to the main shaft. Wellington has many armed men. There is another way.'

Luis got up and edged along the side wall of the tunnel. If these whites were too stupid to not follow him, then that was their problem.

'Wait for us, we're coming,' the woman said in the darkness. Luis had no idea what she was doing down here, holding a rifle. She was crazy, or perhaps brave. He had heard the exchange between the man and the woman. Like lovers fighting, he thought.

'There is another side passage up ahead,' he said to them. 'Stay close to me. No lamps.'

'I thought you said all the armed men had gone looking for us,' the man, McMurtrie, said.

'They are the armed men. There are more than two hundred *zama zamas* down here. Men have scattered everywhere, but most of us carry a knife or weapon of some sort. You are among thieves, *Senhor* McMurtrie.'

'Two hundred? Jeez,' the woman said.

'Shush,' Luis hissed.

He led them through a maze of side tunnels and stopes. As Luis had run from the firing and noise, he'd caught sight of Wellington leaving his office, a daypack on his back. Their so-called fearless leader was abandoning his men. Like all bullies, he was a coward. Luis knew Wellington would be heading for the emergency exit from the disused mine whose old workings occasionally intersected Eureka's *madala* sides. The exit route, which Wellington used whenever he was smuggling gold out, was made up of nearly a kilometre of stairs, laid into the rock of a steeply inclined shaft. Luis was now aiming for the same way out; he just prayed Wellington would not be around one of the corners waiting for them. In truth, he didn't know for sure if the exit had been left unguarded, but the GR people had an AK, a shotgun and a pistol – they represented Luis's best chance of escape.

Luis heard voices behind them. 'Hurry. The others will guess where we are going.'

'Where is that, exactly?'

'This tunnel leads to an incline shaft in the disused mine next to Eureka. There was once a chairlift there to carry workers.'

'There may be a man still guarding the door to the shaft.'

'Shit,' McMurtrie said. He came to Luis and tugged his sleeve. 'Wait, take this.'

McMurtrie pressed a pistol into his hand. It was the first time since the end of the civil war in Mozambique that he had held a weapon. He tried to hand it back.

'No. Take it. You're going to be able to get closer to a guard than any of us.'

'And if I kill a man my crimes will be much worse when you hand me over to the police, above ground.' He suddenly resented these people and their kind, who had sacrificed his career and years of hard work for the sake of ethnic tokenism and union intimidation.

'You're helping us escape. It won't be forgotten,' McMurtrie said. 'I give you my word,' he added in Portuguese.

Luis sighed but hurried on, slipping the pistol into the imitation leather bumbag he wore around his waist and zipping it closed. He didn't have much choice.

*

Wellington was almost out of breath from running by the time he reached the emergency exit. He tried to slow his breathing for the ordeal that lay ahead, climbing the interminable flights of stairs that followed the track of the disused chairlift, up the inclined shaft. He made the tortuous journey once a month and each time it seemed more difficult.

Jonas, the sentry, lowered his AK-47 when he saw who it was. 'What's happening, boss?'

'Nothing. It was only one man. He came to rescue the *murungu*, Loubser. A fool. My cubs will have dealt with him by now, but some of the men will be alarmed. Shoot anyone who tries to escape, Jonas.'

The man smiled. Jonas, a fellow Shona, was wanted for murder above ground. He could never surface and Wellington kept him happy with *dagga* and the occasional whore. He had killed on Wellington's orders three times in the past to maintain discipline underground. 'Yes, boss. Are you coming back?'

Wellington clapped him on the arm. 'Of course, *shamwari*, and I will bring you a present. One with a nice round bottom.'

*

'Luis,' Cameron called softly to the panting Mozambican, 'where do you keep your explosives?'

'Just a little further on from here. There is another disused refuge chamber.'

'Cameron, the guys down here are crazy,' Chris said. 'They mine the safety pillars. If you let off a big bang you could cause a major rockfall. You heard what Luis said – there are more than two hundred people down here.'

Cameron was annoyed with Chris's whining tone. He seemed to forget the band of men following them was out to kill them, although they had been told to take Chris alive. Cameron had reverted to his military persona. Achieving their mission – in this case escaping alive – was all that mattered.

'Just keep moving, you two,' Kylie said from ahead.

He had to give it to her, she was gutsy, coming after him, even if she had screwed up by bringing Gideon with her. Cameron thought of Jessica and wished he had told her he loved her the last time he'd seen her. She would be home from school now, making herself tea.

Cameron still had his night-vision goggles on and he saw through the open door of the refuge room stacks of sticks of cartridged explosives, probably stolen from the stope faces of his mine when the *zama zamas* rushed in at the end of a shift and cut the igniter cords before they could reach the fuses.

'Carry on,' he said to Chris and Kylie. 'I won't be far behind.'

'Cameron . . .' Chris began.

'He knows what he's doing,' Kylie said. 'Stay close to me, Chris.'

She had, Cameron thought, an incredible knack of in turn pissing him off and pleasantly surprising him.

Cameron worked quickly. He didn't know how far behind them the *zama zama* gunmen were. Some or all of them would know the shortcut and would guess where they were heading. Despite Chris's concerns, a rockfall was exactly what Cameron wanted to create, between the exit and the men chasing them. With any luck he would not only stop the gunmen, but also block this rat run for good.

Cameron gathered half-a-dozen sticks, each about thirty centimetres long, and bound them together with some duct tape he found lying on the ground. From a roll of igniter cord he unwound about fifty centimetres, cut it and wired it to the fuse of one of the sticks.

In his mind he double-checked his rough calculation: igniter cord burned at two metres per minute, so fifty centimetres would give him about fifteen seconds before detonation.

When he was finished he switched his night-vision goggles to infra-red and ran along the tunnel, cradling the explosives, and caught up with the others. He came first to Chris and Kylie, crouching and pressed against the rock wall. He laid his hand gently on Kylie's shoulder and she jolted. He pressed his lips to her ear. 'What's happening?' He could smell her shampoo and her perspiration.

She moved her head so she could reply. 'Luis is ahead, talking to the guard.'

'Jonas, *please*, my friend. As I just said, Wellington asked me to bring this gold.' The figures were indistinct at this range, but Cameron could see that Luis, dwarfed by the muscled sentry, was holding up what looked like a bumbag, its belt hanging loose. 'I can show you.'

The guard took half a step back and raised the rifle. 'Wellington said to shoot anyone who tried to get out. He mentioned nothing about you or more gold.'

'He forgot, my friend. This is the last batch I produced. He told me before the shooting began to bring it to him as soon as I was done. Do you want to be the one who tells him, when he returns, that you stopped me from saving his gold? This raid will slow production for some time while the boss relocates us to other *madala* sides. Every gram of gold counts now.'

There was a moment of tense silence.

'Here, let me show you.'

'Toss it to me. Keep your hands in sight,' the guard barked.

A voice called from down the tunnel behind them. 'Jonas! It is us, the lion cubs. We are coming. The whites are heading your way.'

Luis began to pull the pistol out.

Cameron took a cigarette lighter out of his pocket and lit the ignition cord attached to the sticks of explosive, then tossed the bundle as far as he could down the tunnel in the direction from which they had just come.

Cameron grabbed the AK-47 from Kylie, raised it to his shoulder and took aim, but he was a fraction too late. Jonas fired and Luis was knocked backwards. 'Down everyone!' Cameron yelled.

The guard loosed a burst towards him but Cameron kept his cool and took his time. He fired twice and both bullets caught Jonas in the chest. The next instant Cameron was pitched face forward, skinning his hands and knees on the floor as the tunnel behind them erupted in a storm of fire, rock and dust from the explosion he had just triggered.

As he dragged himself to his feet, Cameron's ears were ringing, and when he wiped his face he saw blood was coming from his nose. He went to Kylie, knelt, switched on her headlamp and then helped her up. 'Are you OK?'

Her reply was barely audible but she coughed and gave him a thumbs-up. They made their way over to Chris as around them the rock protested, creaking and groaning. Cameron, still holding the AK at the ready, looked back to the site of the explosion as rugby ball-sized lumps of rock started dropping from the roof of the tunnel. 'Run,' he said to the others. 'It's about to go. Wellington's men are on the other side of a cave-in.'

'We just leave them to die?' Chris asked.

Cameron shook his head. 'We'll send mine rescue down later, once it's stabilised.'

Kylie was already ahead of them, kneeling beside Luis.

'Where's he hit?'

'Midriff. I think it's his side.' Her hand came away wet as Cameron joined her.

'Luis, can you hear me?'

The man blinked, then nodded. Cameron took his knife from its scabbard and cut away one of the sleeves from Luis's overall top. He balled the material and pressed it against the wound then placed Luis's hand over it. He hoped it had missed his stomach. 'Keep pressure on this. Do you understand?'

Luis nodded.

'What are we going to do with him?'

Cameron clenched his jaw.

'Cameron, he saved our lives. He took a bullet for us,' Kylie said.

Cameron knew the smartest thing would be to leave Luis here. The man was a criminal, but Kylie was right. Cameron was torn between the need to get Kylie and Chris above ground as quickly as possible, helping Luis, and trying to catch up with Wellington. But he had given the man his word.

'I'll carry him,' Chris said.

'I can help,' Kylie added.

'It's more than a thousand metres up. Climbing all the way,' Cameron said.

'I'm the youngest, and the fittest,' Chris said.

It was a statement, not a boast. Cameron gave the AK-47 back to Kylie. Chris was already on one knee in front of Luis, lifting him in a fireman's carry. The African groaned with pain.

'I'll go ahead,' Cameron said.

*

Wellington heard the gunshots below, then felt the thump of the shockwave and the rush of hot air and dust wash over him as the explosion sought an outlet. He forced his aching legs to carry on, one step after another.

He was wheezing and sweat drenched his clothes. It was never an easy climb, but he usually had the luxury of taking a few breaks on the way up at the regularly spaced landings where workers had once hopped on and off the old chairlift to access the different levels of the mine. He could hear voices, indistinct and unfamiliar, after the explosion had died down. Wellington pushed himself upwards, and tried to ignore the pain in his calves and his shortness of breath.

*

Cameron paused. He knew Kylie and Chris would be making slow progress below him. He wondered if Luis would survive the climb.

He cocked his head and listened again. There it was, the soft echoes of movement above.

Wellington.

He unslung his shotgun and held it at the ready. If he could cut the head off this leech that fed off Eureka's honest earnings he could leave the mine and the company in a better position. Perhaps Jan would even reconsider keeping him in charge of the mine to finish mopping up the *zama zamas*. Of course, Jan might still decide to fire him for going against his orders.

Cameron started climbing again, faster than before. He would catch this bastard. He forced his body towards the light he still couldn't see but knew was at the top of the climb.

At the next landing, Cameron savoured a few moments of the comparative bliss of walking on a level surface for about thirty metres before the shaft rose again.

He was breathing hard as he reached the end of the platform. He heard then saw a rock bouncing down the steps. Cameron raised the shotgun to his shoulder and fired up the shaft, into the darkness.

'Cameron?' he heard Kylie call from far below. 'Are you all right?'

'Wait where you are.'

Cameron leaned into the shaft and saw a figure moving. The man turned and fired two shots which glanced off the rock a metre from him. Not a bad shot, Cameron thought, given the man was shooting into blackness. He probably knew the shaft well and had guessed where Cameron had paused.

'Stop, Wellington. We knew about this shaft. The police are waiting for you at the top,' Cameron called in the darkness.

Wellington laughed at his bluff and Cameron heard his footsteps on the rock stairs.

'Cameron, let him go!' Kylie called from the depths. 'Luis is getting worse. We've got to keep moving.'

His quarry would have heard the woman. Cameron paused and listened to Wellington's exertions. The man knew he was almost home free. Cameron could smell the change in the air. The sweet smell of above ground was filtering down, no doubt fuelling Wellington's escape efforts.

Cameron heard Kylie and Chris start climbing again. From the sounds coming from below they weren't as far behind him as he'd thought. Chris had snapped out of the daze he'd been in when Cameron had first found him and was now putting his youth and strength to good use.

'Be a man, McMurtrie,' called a voice from above.

Cameron's hand closed tighter around the grip of his shotgun. The bastard was taunting him.

'I'll be back, you know.'

Cameron knew Wellington was probably correct. He had rescued Chris and killed a few *zama zamas*, but he hadn't had time to destroy any of Wellington's gear or processing plants, and there could still be more than a hundred illegals unaccounted for, scuttling away like rats into more disused workings. Cameron would move to his office job and Wellington would return to what he'd always been, the mine boss.

Cameron also knew he should stay put and wait for the others. Instead, he started to climb again.

*

Wellington paused at the next chairlift landing, shrugged off his daypack and unzipped it. He was one more flight of steps from the entrance to the disused mine. There was still a risk that McMurtrie and the others would emerge from the escape shaft in time to catch him fleeing across the open ground and old mine dumps. It was a long way to the fence and the gold in the pack was heavy.

McMurtrie probably had a cellphone or radio and would call security or the police to intercept Wellington before he could exit through his concealed cutting in the old mine's security fence. Wellington needed to ensure there would be no pursuit and the best way to do that was to kill McMurtrie.

But he couldn't risk getting into a gunfight with McMurtrie, as Loubser had let on that McMurtrie was an ex-recce commando.

Loubser had also told him, during one of their many conversations, that McMurtrie's wife had run off with another man, to America. 'I'll go see your wife for you if you like,' he called down below. Wellington smiled to himself when he heard the other man's grunted exertions.

Wellington lay on the edge of the parapet overlooking the steps below him and waited for McMurtrie to appear. He couldn't see him, but he would hear him. From the glimpse he'd had of McMurtrie earlier, it looked like he was wearing night-vision goggles. A handy device, Wellington thought, and he would have to invest in a pair for himself before returning to take over Eureka again.

He heard McMurtrie's breathing and his footsteps slowing as he prepared to move to the next level. Wellington picked up the hand grenade he had taken from his pack and pulled the pin. He let the lever fly off the side of the orb.

*

Cameron heard the metallic clang of something hitting the side wall of the escape tunnel and looked up. He caught a brief glimpse of Wellington's face, but was preoccupied by what he saw falling from the man's outstretched hand as he disappeared from view.

'Grenade!'

Cameron reached for it as it bounced from the floor of the shaft onto the concrete landing in front of him. He watched, momentarily transfixed in horror, as it rolled past him along the platform.

'Shit.'

'What is it?' Kylie called up from below.

She must not have heard him. 'Hand grenade! Get back!'

Kylie's head and torso came into view as the grenade slowed to a stop two metres from her. Chris's face appeared, contorted with the labour of carrying Luis. Cameron rushed along the landing and pushed Kylie in the chest with the palm of his hand, knocking her backwards into Chris, who cried out in surprise as they tumbled back down the last few stairs.

Cameron dived on top of the grenade.

PART TWO

13

The fisherman preened his feathers in the deep shade of the sycamore fig. He needed the darkness and he needed food for his two young chicks. The voices and the light that searched the trees for him and his family most nights had cost him a meal again the previous evening. He hated the light.

The sun, too, was his enemy. He nestled deeper into the shadows moving slowly and carefully along the branch as the moving rays began to pick him out. His young slept and his mate blinked her eyes from the nest.

She was the only one he had been with; they would be together for life. They had successfully raised just two offspring from six eggs in the past three years. Their habitat was being disturbed along the river, by flood, by predators and by man.

Their roost was far from ideal. The fig was a big tree, but the elephants drank and browsed here often. The massive pachyderms would rub themselves against the trunk, shaking the nest as though the earth itself was moving. In the summer, when the tree fruited, they would have to move because the resident troop of baboons would raid the tree, gorging themselves on its juicy bounty.

He swivelled his head slowly and checked his surroundings. One of his chicks squealed. When the fisherman looked upriver again his head froze as he caught the fast-moving sweep of a shadow on the surface of the river below their perch. A second later he heard the sound that was part of the daily symphony of the bush, yet one that always caused him concern. *Wee-aah, hyo-hyo-hyo*, cried Inkwazi, the African fish eagle, in his ringing, rising and descending tones as he called to his mate.

Like the fisherman, Inkwazi was a devoted partner to his female and together they were also struggling to raise a family. But whereas the fisherman relied almost solely on the river for his food, the fish eagle's name was something of a misnomer. He and his wife could, and would given half a chance, feast on lesser birds. The fisherman sat very still.

Along the branch, however, one of his young, denied his feed from the night before, cried out in hunger. The owl turned his head at the sound of beating wings.

Inkwazi had heard the noise or glimpsed the slightest of movements in the dappled shadows of the fig. He dived from his own perch, flying fast, aiming for the kill.

14

ONE WEEK LATER

T ertia Venter received the message by radio that her guests had entered the Sabi Sand Game Reserve via Shaw's Gate and were on their way to Lion Plains. She hoped a rogue elephant stopped them en route and trampled the mining executives to death.

The other operators and landowners in the reserve had all signed her petition condemning the mine, but none of them would be as directly affected as she by Global Resources' plans. She appreciated the other lodges' support and solidarity, but they didn't want to contribute to a legal case and Tertia couldn't afford a high court challenge by herself.

She knew her strategy of taking a high-profile stance against the mine in the media was a two-edged one. As well as several articles in the *Sunday Times*, the *Citizen*, and the Afrikaans newspapers *Beeld* and *Rapport*, and a feature story on the local television current affairs program *Carte Blanche*, Tertia had also attracted the interest of the South African correspondents of CNN and BBC World and the Australian ABC. While she felt she was gaining traction – two international environmental peak bodies had recently issued a media release condemning Global Resources, and the South African government for approving the company's application – she knew the publicity had also cost her business. She'd had feedback from her neighbours from clients who had been considering staying at Lion Plains but had mistakenly thought the mine was already operating. People could be stupid – they absorbed only the worst of the facts they saw on TV or read in a newspaper – but many other strangers had contacted her via Facebook to express their support for her and some had made a point of booking with her so they could person-ally vent their anger about the mine while staying at Lion Plains.

There were plenty of people out there with a passion for wildlife. Passion, she mused, was a funny word – and one that had been absent from her life for so many years, until the mine proposal came along.

Tertia had lost the deeds to the property in a land claim by the local community several years earlier, but thanks to what she believed were her close ties to them she had negotiated a contract to lease the rights to continue operating Lion Plains Lodge on the communal lands for a nominal annual fee. Tertia had received compensation from the government for the loss of ownership of the land and, although she knew the amount was the land's fair value, she had decided not to buy somewhere else or emigrate to Australia, but to plough most of the money back into Lion Plains. Many had thought she was crazy, but she had built another camp on the property, the community received a good profit from her game lodges and Tertia had been more or less happy with the outcome. Now, of course, the community knew it could make far more from the mining company, and her five-year initial contract had not been renewed. But she wasn't dead yet; she would show them all – the community, Global Resources, and the government, that they'd been wrong to cross her.

The Eureka *bakkie* pulled up in front of her lodge. She watched them get out. There was a woman, who would be Hamilton, with a sticky plaster over a swollen nose – served the bitch right, whatever happened to her – and the man she knew was Cameron McMurtrie. She had last seen his blackened, sweat-streaked face on the front page of the *Star*, after the mine rescue.

Chris Loubser, the project's environmental officer, had come to her seven months earlier to explain how his company was going to destroy her life and the land she loved.

He walked fast, to overtake the others. 'Tertia, *howzit?*'

She folded her arms. 'How do you think? Can you imagine what I've been going through?'

He smiled. '*Ja.* I've had an interesting time, too.'

'So I read.'

'Let me introduce you to Dr Kylie Hamilton, head of health, safety, environment and community at Global Resources.'

'Hmph, chief window-dresser by the sound of it.'

Tertia made no move to approach the other two, and they were smart enough not to extend a hand for her to pointedly ignore. Normally guests would have been greeted by a ranger and tracker, who would have loaded their luggage into a game-viewing vehicle for transport to their suites. Technically this lot were guests, as they were staying the night – Tertia had invited them as she wanted the senior people, particularly the foreigner, to see first hand what they were about to destroy – but she would not be going out of her way to make them feel at home.

'Tertia, please,' Chris appealed to her. 'And this is Cameron McMurtrie. He's taking over as Global Resources' head of new project developments.'

'Please excuse me if I don't hand you a welcome fruit cocktail,' Tertia said. 'If you load your luggage into the game viewer I'll send someone to park your *bakkie*. It's a short drive to the lodge where you're staying and we can have a game drive on the way.'

Kylie Hamilton walked to the open-topped Land Rover and hefted her bag onto the rearmost of the three tiers of seats. The men did the same and they all clambered up and into the vehicle.

Tertia got into the driver's seat and took another look at the newcomers, on the pretext of making sure they were all seated. In fact, she wouldn't have cared less if one had fallen out and been cleaned up by Stompie, the cranky old male lion with only half a tail, and brother to Big Boy.

The woman was trying to smile, but it looked like the action made her swollen nose hurt. McMurtrie had a plaster over a cut above his left eye. He was a good-looking man, but not nearly as handsome as Chris Loubser. Despite her shock and anger when he had first come to Lion Plains to deliver the bad news to her that the mining project had been approved, she still thought him one of the most attractive young men she had ever laid eyes on. He smiled at her and she scowled and turned the Land Rover's key.

Tertia attacked the track to the lodge, aiming for every rut and pothole she could see. Twice she had the satisfaction of hearing the woman gasp behind her.

'No point in grading the roads as we get so few guests these days,' Tertia said in the wind, not deigning to look back at her passengers.

'Stop!' the woman called from behind her.

Tertia instinctively pushed the brake and clutch and looked back. The dust cloud that had been trailing the Land Rover now enveloped them. 'What is it?'

'I just saw an elephant!'

Kylie, the senior member of the group, was as wide-eyed as a five year old on her first visit to the Kruger Park. Tertia had seen that look countless times, in people of all ages when they first encountered Africa's glory. Despite her hatred of the woman, of all of them and their filthy business, this was what she had hoped for. The woman was pointing.

'Back there.' Kylie looked at Cameron McMurtrie and Chris, who were both smiling.

'We saw it,' Cameron said.

'Please won't you reverse, Tertia?' Chris said. 'I'm sure Kylie would like to have a better look.'

'*Ag. Pleez,*' Tertia mimicked. They were coming here to raze this place and relocate or destroy everything that lived here.

'Sorry,' Kylie said, trying to be professional again. 'We've got a meeting to attend. It's OK.'

Tertia took her hand off the gear lever and waved it in the air. 'It doesn't matter. It's a foregone conclusion. I'll show you old Marula if you wish.' She dropped her hand and found reverse, not caring how bumpy the return journey was on them. Looking back over her shoulder she saw the woman frantically scrabbling in her daypack for her camera.

'There it is,' Kylie hissed. 'Oh. My. God.'

'An old bull,' Cameron said, leaning back in his seat as Kylie raised the camera to her eyes, then cursed, lowered it and quickly removed the lens cap.

'Sixty, sixty-five, I reckon,' Tertia said. 'Just think of how much history he's seen, and now –'

'Tertia, you know he's a lone bull who follows the breeding herds which move in and out of the national park,' Chris said.

'*Yes,* I know, but he *always* comes back to Lion Plains, as do the breeding herds, and Marula has lived most of his life in the Sabi Sand. It's his home.' She swallowed as her voice caught. 'Now there'll be even less of the greater Kruger Park for them to feed in, which will add to the pressure on the rest of the reserve.'

The Australian woman was lost to their conversation, snapping picture after picture with her expensive digital camera. Finally she lowered it and just gazed at Marula. 'He's beautiful.'

Tertia saw the look again. It had changed, as it did for most people, from surprise to awe to rapture. She had seen people cry at their first elephant sighting. Kylie put her hand on her heart. It was an instinctive gesture, not meant to be seen. Tertia loved seeing this type of reaction in first-time visitors. She wanted not to hate the woman at this moment, but business was business.

'His name is Marula,' she said softly.

'Like the drink they were offering on the South African Airways flight?' Still not taking her eyes off him.

Marula snatched a tuft of grass with the finger-like tips of his trunk, brushed it against his leg to remove the loose soil, and popped the brittle blades into his mouth. 'That's Amarula, but it's made from the same thing, the marula fruit. All elephants love the fruit, when they ripen, but Marula's always been particularly berserk for them. We tried putting up a boma many years ago – that's a fenced enclosure – to keep some rhino we were relocating to the reserve from the Kruger Park before the fences came down between us and them. The idea was the rhino would get used to their surroundings. Unfortunately one of Marula's favourite trees was in the boma and he destroyed the fence faster than we could erect it. We had to relocate the boma eventually.'

'Look at his eyelashes,' Kylie said.

Tertia saw how the majesty of the animal was working its magic. This woman had made it to the top of a man's game by not taking shit from anyone, and now she was totally disarmed, rendered child-like by an old elephant. Tertia hoped she could make this work to her advantage. 'He comes here every year, following the ancient game trails that are programmed into his memory like some mammalian GPS. This is where he feels comfortable, Kylie, where he feels at home.'

The woman blinked, as though coming out of a trance, and Tertia wondered if she had overdone it a bit by suddenly using her first name. 'Ancient?'

'His ancestors would have followed the same routes,' Tertia said.

'Hang on,' Kylie said, looking away from the elephant. The glow had faded and her emerald eyes locked onto Tertia's. 'You just said "before the fences came down between them and us", didn't you?'

Tertia shrugged. She turned the key in the ignition.

'Lion Plains didn't become part of the greater Kruger National Park until 1993. Before that you were simply part of the Sabi Sand Game Reserve, fenced off from the national park. That elephant's only been roaming the greater Kruger for the past twenty years, not for generations.'

Tertia waved her hand in the air again, then engaged gear.

'In fact,' the Australian droned behind her, 'from what I've read, it's likely his ancestors would have been born in Mozambique as so many elephants had been killed in this part of South Africa that by the time he was born they were almost eradicated. His parents prob-ably moved from Mozambique into the lowveld and then eventually onto your farm about the time your family was switching it from cattle to game.'

Tertia looked back over her shoulder as she drove. 'What's your point?'

'His family has relocated a couple of times. He can do it again.'

Tertia sighed. She had underestimated the woman, but she wasn't ready to give up yet, no matter how hopeless the odds. 'Maybe. But he'll be going backwards next time, not forwards.'

*

Chris had seen how Tertia had continued to seethe on the rest of the short drive to Lion Plains. She'd thought she had the measure of Kylie, but the Australian had pulled back from her moment of weakness – her first sighting of an elephant in the wild – and set Tertia back on her butt.

He was pleased they were staying the night, even though Kylie had questioned the need for it at first. It was three in the afternoon when they arrived at the lodge, allowing them just half an hour before high tea, followed by the regular afternoon game drive at four.

Tertia stopped the Land Rover and, after curtly telling them the schedule, walked off to her office.

'We can skip the game drive if you want,' Cameron said to Kylie.

Chris didn't appear to be part of the decision-making process, but he was fine with that.

'Oh well, we're here now, and I don't know if I want to spend any longer with that woman than I have to,' Kylie said with a laugh, which Chris thought was forced.

The truth was Kylie now actually *did* want to get back into an open Land Rover and go for another drive. Certainly she was right – it would be a more pleasant experience than spending an hour or two more than necessary across a table from Tertia – but he had seen the same thing that Tertia had. Kylie had just sampled her first real taste of Africa and she was ready for more.

Two guides arrived and took Cameron and Kylie's bags and led them off to their rooms. 'See you at three-thirty?' Kylie said to him.

'*Ja*, I'd never miss a game drive,' Chris said. He loved the bush. She gave him a wave and walked off behind the guide.

Chris wondered what Cameron thought of the exchange between the women. Cameron had been quiet on the trip up from Barberton – quiet since the rescue.

Chris had thought they were all going to die – Cameron for sure – when he had leapt on the grenade. Cameron had been annoyed at him, he knew, for telling the reporter from *Beeld* about the incident with the grenade. When he thought about it now it seemed like something out of a movie, but at the time his terror had been all too real. And Cameron, why had he done that? Chris liked to think he would have sacrificed himself for the others, but he doubted it.

Kylie's reaction had been interesting, too. She had run towards Cameron, not from him. Chris couldn't have done much of anything. He had Luis on his back so he couldn't have jumped. He had fallen onto the rock-cut steps and waited for the explosion that should have shredded Cameron's body.

But it hadn't happened. The grenade was a dud.

Cameron, shaken but still in control, had eventually got to his feet and ushered first Kylie and then Chris and Luis to the next landing. He then kicked the grenade down the shaft to the next level. Explosive Ordnance Disposal technicians from the army had later been called in to get rid of the explosive and to search the *zama zamas'* workings for more explosives and weapons.

Nine of the illegal miners had been killed in the rockfalls and thirty had been rounded up, some of them injured, by the police who had been forced, belatedly, to go underground after Cameron's one-man commando raid had rescued Chris and disrupted Wellington's operation.

Wellington himself had got away. While Chris knew the other *zama zamas* would have escaped through the labyrinth of old tunnels and some might have stayed to regroup and start work again, Wellington's operation had been dealt a blow that might end it forever in Eureka. Much of his equipment had been destroyed or confiscated, and his workforce slashed.

Chris checked his watch. It was 15:10. He had less than twenty minutes. He knew he should probably go to his room and check emails. Instead he walked into the old farmhouse that had been converted to the lodge's dining and bar area.

He went through the entrance foyer and turned right down a corridor that led to a new extension that housed the lodge's administrative offices. The administrative assistant's office was empty. Tertia's was next door.

Chris felt his pulse start to throb in his carotid artery and he was suddenly short of breath as he put his hand on the door handle. He turned the knob.

Tertia looked up from her laptop, unsmiling.

Chris kept his eyes on her and closed the door behind him.

She glanced down, looking at her watch. 'You have to be on a game drive in eighteen minutes.'

'I know.'

'Do you want to talk about what happened to you?'

He gave a brief shake of his head and took a step towards her desk.

She swallowed, then just sat there, lips slightly parted.

He walked to her, around the desk, and she looked up at him as he stood, so close that his leg was touching her thigh.

Tertia looked up at him. 'There isn't time.' But she was already wetting her lips with the tip of her tongue. He could see the rise and fall of her chest.

Chris didn't bother trying to convince her with words. He reached for his jeans and unzipped his fly. She swivelled in her office chair and spread her knees so her khaki skirt was hiked up and her legs were either side of him. Still sitting, she leaned forward and pulled his penis from his pants. She glanced up, catching his eye, and he saw her sly smile.

He wrapped his hand in her hair and guided her face onto him, just as she opened her mouth to take him. She wanted him as much as he wanted her, but it made him feel good to gently push her head down. She moaned, deep in the back of her throat, as he felt her lips brushing against his groin.

Chris relaxed his grip but kept his hands in her hair until he was close. When he was nearly ready he pulled away, revelling in the cheated look on her face, her wanton smile. He was breathing deep now, hungry for release. He swiped the accounts and letters and pens and paperclips from her desktop with the back of his hand, and when he saw her flash of annoyance he grabbed her by the elbow and lifted her from the chair so that her bum was against the edge of her desk.

He lifted her legs and pushed her skirt higher up her thigh. Her lacy pants came away in his hand with one forceful tug. She opened herself for him and wrapped herself around him as he drove into her in one long, hard thrust. She grunted, animal-like, as he fucked her.

Chris felt her fingernails on his back, clawing at him under the blue cotton of his Global Resources shirt.

'Yes,' she hissed.

He held her down, his hand on her chest, preventing her from hugging him, as he exploded inside her and felt the spasms of her body gripping his at the same time.

Chris pulled out of her, wiped himself with his hand and rubbed it up the inside of her thigh. Her eyes stayed on his. 'I'm glad you're back safe,' she whispered.

He put her torn pants in the pocket of his jeans and walked out of her office, closing the door quietly behind him so no one would hear.

15

Kylie sat next to Cameron on the first tier of seating in the open-top Land Rover, just behind where the guide would be sitting, and checked her watch.

'Shall we wait a while longer?' asked the guide, Tumi Mabunda, who looked no older than twenty-four. She had intricately braided hair, and a tailored uniform, and copper and elephant-hair bracelets encircled her wrists.

'Chris definitely said he was coming,' Kylie said. She was a punctual person who expected the same of others. This wasn't a business meeting, but she found herself itching to get on the road. She thought of the elephant, how content it seemed and how relaxed it had been around them.

Cameron nodded but didn't seem to be worried by Chris's tardiness. He looked out over a tributary of the Sabie River, which snaked its way through a valley flanked by thick riverine forest, at the base of the rise on which Tertia's lodge was set.

She wondered what was going through his mind. He'd been very quiet on the drive up from Barberton. 'You know,' she said, 'the company will pay for a counsellor, if that's what you want.'

He smiled a little and snorted. 'No, no. I'm fine on that front.

I don't want to sound like a Rambo, but I saw much worse during my time in the army. My thoughts are elsewhere, that's all. I'll be ready for the meeting with Tertia later, though, don't worry.'

'You're thinking about your daughter. Jessica?'

He looked at her. 'How did you guess?'

'What you did, for us, was incredibly brave, but it probably hurt her.'

He nodded. 'You're right. I think she thinks I have some kind of death wish, and that it's somehow a reflection on her. I thought she'd be proud of me, but she was just angry.'

'It's none of my business, but with your wife . . .'

'Sorry, Kylie, but you're right. It's my business, no one else's.'

He was a prickly man, she thought. She had only been trying to reach out to him. She realised she hadn't actually thanked him for what he had done for her, for all of them. If the grenade *had* gone off he would have been killed for sure, and she would have at least been wounded. Cameron looked at her, and she wondered if he was still thinking about the business with the grenade and the men he had killed, despite his bravado and his problems with his daughter.

'Sorry!' Chris strode up the pathway from his suite, tucking in a shirt as he walked.

Kylie saw he had changed and when he climbed on the Land Rover she saw his hair was damp. He smelled of soap.

'*Ag*, I dozed for what I thought was ten minutes and it turned out to be twenty. Sorry, but I needed a shower to wake up again.'

'That's fine,' she said. Cameron was gazing out over the river.

'Right, shall we be off?' Tumi asked. She started the engine and the Land Rover belched a cloud of black diesel. 'This one we call Old Smokey. Should have been replaced a couple of years ago, but with things as they are . . .'

Kylie wondered if they were going to be preached at the whole time.

'Sorry,' Tumi said. 'I didn't mean to talk politics.'

'It's fine,' Kylie said. 'I understand how hard it must be for all of you who work here, knowing the lodge is going to close.'

Tumi shrugged. 'Most of the guides and the other staff who work here – the cooks, the cleaners, the maids – are from the local community. Some of them will get jobs at the mine, and those who don't will probably be absorbed onto the neighbouring game farms. The ones looking at jobs at the mine are expecting pay increases. Business hasn't been good here and no one's had a rise for a long time. The guides mostly work for tips, in any case.'

'So some of you will be better off,' Kylie said.

Tumi looked back at her. 'I have got a degree in business, but I decided to come work in the bush for peanuts. My parents wanted to disown me, but there's nowhere in the world I'd rather be.'

Kylie sat back in her seat.

'Tumi,' Chris asked from the back, 'can you take us to the Sunset Dam?'

'*Yebo*,' said the guide.

'That's the location where we're planning to mine first. The gravel road we're on now will be the main access road,' Chris said for Cameron and Kylie's benefit.

Kylie had studied a map of the proposed development, overlaid on an aerial photograph. The countryside hadn't looked like anything special when she'd looked at it in one dimension. She'd thought it would be just flat land and scrub, but it was crisscrossed with stream beds, mostly dry, that were shaded with tall mature trees and thick vegetation. Here and there were granite boulders and other rock formations.

The movement of the Land Rover produced a warm breeze and the lowering sun was casting a mellow golden wash over the bush so that the bark of a tree they were passing glowed almost pink. Birds called and Tumi stopped the Land Rover and turned off the engine.

'That's a lilac-breasted roller,' she said.

After a couple of seconds of searching, Kylie saw the bird. Apart from its eponymous breast, it had a white crowned head. When it turned its face to the breeze and took off, before she could even switch on her camera, its wings shone a brilliant, electric blue. It was, she thought, the most beautiful bird she had seen in her life.

161

'Lovely,' Tumi said, and Kylie could tell she meant it.

Tumi started the engine but drove only three hundred metres before switching off again. 'What is it?' Kylie whispered.

Cameron lifted a finger and pointed into the bush, off to the right. 'Don't you see it?'

She shook her head.

He put a hand on her shoulder and gently turned her until she was looking at a tree.

He left his hand on her and it unsettled her slightly. It wasn't until she heard, then saw a swish of long black hairs, on a tail, that she saw the giraffe. It was no more than five metres from the edge of the road. 'I can't believe I didn't see it.' Instinctively she placed her hand on his, by way of thanks.

Cameron gently slid his hand from under hers. 'Your eyes take a bit of time to adjust from the city to the bush. Things can be staring you in the face, yet you can't see them because your eyes are still in city mode.'

Kylie found herself mesmerised by the statuesque, beautiful female. She could tell, thanks to Tumi, the sex of the giraffe by noting the tufts of hair on the tips of its horns; the males' horns were bald. 'She walks like a supermodel.'

Chris laughed and when Kylie turned from the giraffe, slightly embarrassed, she saw Cameron was smiling, for the first time since she'd met him.

Tumi lingered at the sighting for a couple more minutes before starting the Land Rover's engine. As they drove away Kylie looked back at the giraffe, contentedly munching on leaves. She'd never imagined she would be so moved by the simple sight of an animal in the wild. She had seen giraffes in the zoo as a child in Australia and didn't remember feeling nearly so engaged. Perhaps it was the setting.

Kylie knew she would have to refocus her mind soon to get ready for the meeting with the feisty Tertia Venter. Chris had been on leave in the days following his rescue and had slept in the back of

Cameron's car on the drive up from Barberton, so they'd had little time to talk through the details of the new strategy. She couldn't do so in front of Tumi, so they would be winging it for the meeting.

Jan had stated the obvious, that Global Resources was starting to feel the impact of Tertia's vitriolic PR campaign. The company already had in-principle approval to start mining, pending final sign-off on their environmental impact statement, which their government sources and local advisers were telling them was a fait accompli. Still, Tertia's alarmist claim that animals in neighbouring concessions would be poisoned by contaminants from the mine entering local watercourses was causing some angst among shareholders in Australia. Kylie had been assured Tertia's claim was nonsense, designed purely to grab headlines – but that's precisely what she had done. Jan's PR people, including Musa Mabunda, Tumi's brother, were continually on the back foot, trying to put out the fires that Tertia kept lighting.

Chris had come up with a scheme that would hopefully silence her. Kylie wasn't convinced it would work, but Chris said he had built up a measure of rapport with the woman and thought his idea would appeal to her. They would soon see.

Tumi's radio beeped to life. '*Tumi, Tumi, Quentin, copy?*'

Tumi keyed the handset. 'Go Quentin.'

'*Tumi, I've got the* mafazi ngala *with* mapimpans. *She's* lalapanzi, *eastern side of Sunset, copy?*'

'Roger, thanks Quentin, I'm coming to you just now. We were heading there in any case.'

'What did all that mean?' Kylie asked.

Tumi shifted down a gear and accelerated. 'Hang on, everyone.'

'You'll see,' Cameron said. He looked back at Chris and winked.

Kylie turned to Chris, who grinned and said: 'Don't look at me, my Shangaan is rubbish, man.'

Kylie shook her head, aware that everyone on the vehicle knew what was going on except her. She grabbed the metal railing in front of her as Tumi bounced through a dip into a dry creek bed and up out the other side. She was content just to hang on and enjoy the ride and found she couldn't suppress her smile.

'This is Sunset Dam,' Chris said in a low voice five minutes later as Tumi slowed the Land Rover to a stop and pulled her binoculars out of the daypack on the seat next to her.

It was an aptly named spot, Kylie thought. The red sun was reflected in the waters of the dam, which rippled gently in the light breeze.

'There,' said Tumi, pointing into the setting sun.

'Well, whatever it is, it's not on the eastern side of the dam, like that guy said on the radio,' Kylie said.

'No, look,' Cameron interjected, pointing now as Tumi engaged gear again and started driving close to and then around the edge of the dam's lava-coloured waters. 'She's moving them.'

'Who's moving who?' Kylie was getting exasperated now.

Cameron laid a hand on her arm again, and his touch served to soothe her, as much as it surprised her again. She wouldn't have thought him the touchy-feely type. Again he showed her where to look.

'Oh my,' she said, finally spotting what all the fuss was about.

Tumi put the Land Rover in neutral and coasted slowly, silently, a little closer, until they were about fifteen metres from the cat.

The lioness turned her golden eyes to look at them. The fur of her belly, her ears and that of the tiny squawking bundle she carried in her mouth were all suffused with a halo of golden light by the sun behind them. She walked in front of them, not two metres from the Land Rover's bull bar, not seeming to mind it or the humans on board, and deposited her tiny baby cub with the utmost delicacy under a bush at the base of a tall tree.

Tumi swivelled in her seat, grinning like a child. 'She only had these cubs five days ago. Look how gentle she is with them.' The lioness lay down on her side, keeping a watchful eye on the humans.

Kylie thought her heart would melt as she accepted Tumi's proffered binoculars and watched the cubs clambering over each other to get to their mother's teats. They squeaked and snarled in imitation of the fearsome adults they might one day become, fighting for the right to feed first.

'They're *adorable*,' Kylie said.

'Yes,' Tumi agreed.

'So, anyway, this is where the first open-cut mine will be established,' Chris said softly behind her.

Kylie looked from the lioness and her cubs across the sun-bathed waterhole and at the surrounding wilderness. She sighed. Then, simultaneously, all three of their cellphones beeped.

*

Cameron had tried to make five calls from the bouncing back of the game-viewing vehicle before they made it to the lodge, but everyone seemed to be on the phone or busy elsewhere. Kylie, meanwhile, had spent most of the trip talking to Jan, in Australia, even though it was around two am in Sydney.

Cameron sat on the bed in his suite scrolling through emails on his laptop, searching for news. There was a knock on the door and when he opened it Kylie walked in, holding her phone to her ear. 'Tell me, Musa, how come we're being called so late in the day for comment?' she said.

Kylie stood still, waiting for an answer, and Cameron moved his computer bag off the chair so she could sit down. She waved away his offer, so he sat down and resumed checking.

'Hello?' Chris said softly from the open door. Cameron beckoned him in.

'Well, it's just not acceptable,' Kylie said. She listened for a few seconds more. 'All right, Musa, call me as soon as you hear anything else.'

'What did he say?' Cameron asked.

Kylie exhaled and sat down on the end of his bed. She ran a hand through her hair. 'I was probably a bit hard on Musa. He's just the messenger. Just as he said in his text message to us, the *Mail and*

Guardian is running a story in tomorrow morning's edition that says miners at Eureka are being exposed to grossly unsafe levels of silica and other pollutants.'

'Yes, but that's ridiculous,' Cameron said.

'Well, there's more. It turns out that the claim isn't *ridiculous*. Musa's been in touch with your air pollution monitoring consultancy . . .'

'APMS – Air Pollution Monitoring Systems,' Cameron said.

'Yes, well, whoever they are, they told Musa that what the paper is going to report *is* correct. The head guy, Johan something, was in the process of preparing a confidential report for you, but it appears one of his staff has leaked it to the press.'

'*Jissus*.' Cameron shook his head. 'I was just trying to call him but his number was engaged. It must have been Musa talking to him.'

She looked across the room at him and he saw the cold fury in her eyes. 'It shouldn't be up to the company PR man to be finding this stuff out, Cameron.'

'It's my fault, too,' Chris said. 'I usually check in with APMS once a week, but after, well, after what happened to us underground I neglected to call Johan this week. He might have given me a verbal heads-up. I'm sorry.'

Kylie waved off his apology 'It's not your fault, Chris.'

Cameron bridled at her tone, and her stare. He couldn't believe this was happening. There had to have been a mistake made somewhere. 'Chris, you of all people know how stringent our dust control measures are. What do you think happened?'

Chris shrugged. 'You didn't have any breakdowns of the ventilation system while I was underground? It could be the samples just came from one day where there was a problem.'

Cameron shook his head. 'No ways. I was keeping an eye on your stuff the whole time you were missing. I would have known if there'd been a breakdown.'

Kylie stood and started pacing. 'Look, there'll be time to find out what went wrong soon enough, but the key thing we have to do now is find a way to turn this around in the media.'

'No,' Cameron said. 'The key thing here is the safety of my workers.'

She stopped and put her hands on her hips. 'They're not *your* workers, Cameron. I was just on the phone to Jan. Your transfer to acting head of special projects is now taking effect immediately. We're putting Coetzee in charge of the mine as of tonight.'

He jumped to his feet. 'What? You can't do this to me.'

She squared up to him, even though he was a head taller than she. 'I can and I just have, with Jan's blessing.'

'You're making a mistake. I need to get back to Barberton and find out how and where this happened.'

'No, Cameron. Coetzee is overseeing the investigation, which is going to be carried out by a team from APMS. Musa's drafting a media release now saying that work is to be suspended at Eureka pending an urgent review of ventilation systems and intensive site monitoring. The government and union are being invited to send a representative to observe the investigation. Don't try and accuse me of not putting the safety of our workers first – I've already ordered the mine shut down. It's you who dropped the ball here, Cameron.'

He clenched his fists in futile rage. Who did she think she was? He knew his mine and he knew his record, and Chris's, on safety. He looked at Chris and the other man just shrugged. 'Maybe they mixed up the samples.'

'Musa asked Johan if that was possible,' Kylie said. 'He said that Eureka's samples were the only ones they were working on this past week. He personally did a second and third analysis of the samples to make sure the findings were correct. He said he only found out yesterday. He was just about to put in his report when the leak happened.'

Cameron sat down again, defeated. Kylie's phone rang and she jabbed the answer button.

'Kylie Hamilton.' She listened. 'Shit, Musa, this is going from bad to worse. OK, call me after you've watched it.' She hung up. 'Fuck.'

'What is it?' Cameron asked.

'The union's just declined our invitation to take part in the review and they're saying that they're calling for an indefinite strike at the mine, pending the outcome of the review. On top of that, the *Mail and Guardian* is worried other media outlets will jump on the story so they're going proactive with it and offering a preview of the article to SABC 1. It's going to be on television tonight – claims that we're exposing workers to "lethal" levels of contaminants.'

'Is Musa going to go on TV?' Chris asked.

Kylie shook her head. 'No. The timing of all this couldn't be worse. We're stuck out here in the bloody bush, Musa is in Botswana visiting a diamond mine and Jan's in Sydney. And now we've got to go and face that witch, Tertia Venter.'

Cameron held his tongue. He simply couldn't believe he wasn't being allowed to manage what was going on in the mine – *his* mine. But Kylie was right. Their meeting with Tertia was in minutes, yet they hadn't had any free time to discuss their strategy, or Chris's bold offer on behalf of Global Resources – the purpose of their visit to Lion Plains. They would have to wing it.

Cameron's phone rang and he looked at the screen. It was Jessica. For a moment he considered not answering it. Kylie looked at him. Screw her, he thought. 'Hello my girl.'

'Dad, when are you coming home?'

'I told you, Jess, tomorrow, remember?' She had never minded him going away before, not even since Tania had left home. He wondered if she was still angry at him over what had happened down the mine. 'Are you all right?'

'I suppose so. The alarm went off before.'

'What?' He felt his heart rate increase.

'Petty's here. We checked. She said she thought it was maybe a genet tripping the beam again, like last time.'

Kylie tapped her watch, so he could see. It was time for their meeting with Tertia. 'OK. Look, call me if it goes off again. I have to go now, my girl. Tell Petty, too, that I said to call me, all right?'

'Yes, Dad.'

'Love you.'

'*Ja*, me too.' She hung up.

Cameron stood up. 'Okay, let's do this.'

Chris, who was the only one who had visited Lion Plains before, led the way across the grass through the darkness to the main lodge. There was one other party staying, a group of noisy Americans who were in the lounge area drinking. Chris led them down the corridor and knocked on a door.

'Good, come in,' Tertia said, ushering them inside and hurrying back to her desk. 'You're just in time. Have a look at this.'

Tertia swung a computer monitor around so they could all see it. The SABC 1 news in English had just started.

Cameron recognised file footage of the outside of Eureka, including the Global Resources sign, and the pictures then switched to men drilling underground as the reporter continued her monologue.

'*The mine workers' union today called for strikes at all Global Resources mines, saying it was intolerable that management and their paid consultants were dealing in so-called "confidential reports" about dangerous pollutants while workers were being put at risk. A spokesman for Global Resources said the company was waiting on delivery of the APMS report, but that a review of ventilation systems and an intensive program of air quality testing would commence tomorrow. A spokesman denied the company had been forced to act by the* Mail and Guardian's *story. Global Resources is currently awaiting approval for a controversial project to mine coal in the Greater Kruger National Park.*'

Cameron saw that Kylie was quietly seething at the inaccuracies in the story. Tertia, on the other hand, couldn't hold back her smile. She placed her hands palm-down on her desk, which Cameron noticed that, unlike his, was spotlessly clean with everything laid out in a precise order.

'Now, what can I do for you, other than hand over my life's work for you to bulldoze?'

Kylie's jaw was clenched. Cameron studied her face, but she was inscrutable. He suddenly understood why she had cut him out of the review process at the mine. She was setting him up as a scapegoat.

He'd been a fool to think she might actually be a decent person. She was an attractive woman, even more so out of her mine overalls or corporate armour. The soft lighting of the suite caught a pale high-light in her auburn hair, reminding him of a vein of free gold that was occasionally visible in a piece of ore, but those emerald eyes that he'd thought so nice when he first saw her, drilled back at him now. His mind flashed back to the moment when he'd found her underground, the rifle held in shaking hands and how his heart had almost turned molten when he saw her lip trembling. It had felt good to hold her, if only for a second. But he had let the fact that she was a woman cloud his judgement. She had looked relaxed and happy in her shorts and T-shirt and sandals on the open vehicle and her face had reflected the innocent wonder of someone encountering the true beauty of Africa for the first time. But at the end of the day she was a single-minded businesswoman, ambitious and unafraid to hang people out to dry to attain her goals – GR's goals. And that included him. He felt deeply embarrassed now that he had put his hand on her arm as he pointed the animals out to her. She must think him an idiot. And then she had turned on him. His wife had left him, his daughter no longer trusted him, and his boss had just put him into occupational limbo.

Chris cleared his throat. Although he was the most junior of the three, it seemed to Cameron he was the only one not knocked over by the events of this afternoon, even though air quality monitoring and assurance was his responsibility. 'Tertia, thanks very much for agreeing to meet us this evening.'

'I appreciate you're all busy,' Tertia continued, nodding at the screen, which had now changed to a story about political corruption, 'and about to get busier. Did you enjoy your game drive, Kylie?'

The question seemed to stop Kylie in her tracks. 'Well, yes, I did, actually. We saw a lioness with the tiniest cubs.'

'Such a shame your mine will destroy her home.'

'Tertia, please,' Chris said.

'Sorry, I can't help speaking the truth.'

Chris looked at Kylie.

'Go on, Chris. Credit where credit's due, this was your idea,' Kylie said.

He nodded, then drew a breath. After a pause he said, 'Tertia we, that is, Global Resources, want you to stay on here, after the mine is open.'

She pushed back her chair and crossed her legs. 'And why would I want to do that?'

'The mine, as you know, is not going to consume the whole of Lion Plains. There's going to be a buffer zone all around it so that it doesn't impact on the neighbouring reserves.'

'Hah! I've seen your thin green line on the maps. It's nothing but a PR stunt. All that talk about game corridors is rubbish. You'll force wildlife from tens of kilometres around the mine to move out of the Sabi Sand back to the Kruger Park. The elephants will add to the problem of overpopulation and the wild dogs that usually roam through here will be cleaned up by the park's lions.'

'Please, hear me out, Tertia.'

She folded her arms tightly across her chest. 'Go on then.'

'We know the mine will have an impact on wildlife in the local area, but Global Resources wants to do its bit to help conserve endangered species. What we'd like to propose is the establishment of a research camp, set in the bushland corridor around the mine, near the border with the property to the north. There are a number of research projects underway in the Greater Kruger at the moment, as you know, but they tend to be stand-alone projects with little coordination. Also, the researchers are either self-funded or supported by the lodge where they happen to be based. Their resources vary greatly.'

'I know all this.'

'I know you do. So what Global Resources wants to do is fund a base camp for researchers in the reserve; a place where they can come together, stay, and compile their data. It'd be a commercial operation as well, with a limited number of tourists paying to work as volunteer assistants to the various researchers.'

'What's it got to do with me?' Tertia asked.

Crunch time, Cameron thought.

'We'd like you to run the camp and to oversee the volunteer program. I've already sounded out the local community and they're supportive of the idea, in principle. You'd get to stay in the reserve, Tertia.'

'As a paid employee of Global Resources?'

Kylie stepped in. 'The research camp would be set up as a separate trust, overseen by a board with representatives from the local community, peak wildlife bodies and the company. But, yes, the majority of the funding will come from Global Resources, supplemented by whatever income you generate from hosting the paying volunteers.'

'Yes, then I'd be a paid employee of Global Resources.'

Kylie shrugged.

'You think this is about money for me, or that I just want to protect my home in the bush?'

Cameron could see the seething hatred in Tertia's eyes. She was about to erupt.

'No, not at all. We know you care about the environment,' he said.

'No! You think I'm some spoiled white woman who thinks she has a God-given right to live here, and that I don't really care about the bush or the wildlife or the local people and their traditional claim on the land.'

'Absolutely not, but –' Kylie tried.

'Well, you're wrong. What this is about is mining in a protected area, in a wildlife paradise. You cannot develop a mine in the greater Kruger Park, no matter what any bloody government or any bloody *traditional owner* says. You cannot have a mine belching noise and light pollution and dust and machinery exhaust fumes within view of a national park. It's an abomination.'

Kylie balled her hands into fists and took a breath. 'There are precedents.'

'Pah!'

Cameron wondered why they were here, why Chris had bothered coming up with the compromise, and why Kylie would want to put herself within reach of Tertia. The government had given the land to the local people and they wanted a mine, simple as that. The problem with his Australian superiors, and he now lumped Jan into that category, was that they cared more about perceptions than realities, more about public image than real people. They could have been rid of the *zama zamas* by now if he had been given free rein to do his job and, whatever Cameron's and Chris's personal views about mining in a wildlife area, they should just get on with this job instead of trying to pacify a woman who would hate them until the day they died. Perhaps hard-as-nails Kylie had met her match with this female wildcat.

'Tertia, please,' Chris said. 'We're only trying to help you. Can't you maybe think about this for a while, maybe meet us halfway somehow?'

Tertia uncrossed her legs, pushed back her chair on its castors and stood. She glared down at Chris and then at Cameron, pointedly ignoring Kylie. 'I'm not going to be your trained monkey who tells the world how much Global Resources cares for the environment. I'm not going to be silenced by the offer of thirteen pieces of silver. I'd rather die than see your filthy mine ravage this paradise.'

Cameron looked at Chris and saw he was crestfallen. The boy had told him he was sure she would go for it, that he had built up a rapport with her over the months and could get her on board.

Tertia finally turned her glare on Kylie. 'You may have convinced yourself that what you are doing here is somehow justified, or beneficial for the local community, but you've been out in the bush now. You've seen what this place is like. I can't believe you can still be so cold-hearted, so intent on destroying all of this, in the name of your corporate greed. This is not just a question of what can or can't be seen or heard from within a nature reserve, this is about saying enough is enough, we will not squander our natural heritage. Global Resources is wrong, the local community is wrong, and our greedy corrupt government is wrong. I *will* stop this mine and I *will* *not* take your blood money.'

Kylie looked up at her and seemed, to Cameron, to be lost for words.

Tertia brushed a strand of red hair from her face and composed herself. 'You're welcome to stay to dinner – in fact you must, as you're not permitted to drive through the reserve now that it's dark. But you'll forgive me if I don't join you.'

16

A small herd of six elephants, visible in the light of the near-full moon, emerged from the pool in the mostly dry river. The lead one, which Kylie guessed was the matriarch, raised her trunk into the air and sniffed, checking the way was clear. She knew where she was going, and how to protect those who depended on her.

In contrast, Kylie felt helpless.

She sat on the timber verandah of her suite and wondered what she should do next. She had just finished a Skype call to Jan. Lion Plains had a strong wireless signal and she had been able to use the webcam. She wondered if his ruddy complexion was due to his morning workout or his anger. A bit of both, she suspected. She checked the notes she had made on her laptop, as the elephants sloshed through the puddles, and played back the conversation in her mind.

'Chris was sure Tertia would go for the research camp proposal, and so was I,' Kylie had said to him.

Jan had shaken his head. 'It was doomed from the start, Kylie. I should never have allowed you to go to Lion Plains.'

She had bridled. It hadn't been a matter of Jan 'allowing' her to go to Lion Plains. She had made the call herself. She wanted to get

Tertia out of the media spotlight, if not completely onside, and she and Chris had made the fundamental error of thinking that Tertia was motivated by greed and self-interest. It appeared she really did care more about the animals and the land at Lion Plains than herself. Kylie found herself grudgingly respecting the formidable redhead.

'I want you and Musa to get on top of the local media tomorrow, your time,' Jan had said to her. She had been about to suggest the same thing, that they go proactive with the press, inviting them to Eureka to explain how they were going to conduct their full review. Jan was second-guessing her every decision and treating her like an idiot. She had felt chastised and angry at the end of the call.

Kylie had walked out onto the verandah to get some air and try to wind down. It was only ten o'clock and she had held off having wine with dinner as she knew she would be talking to the boss.

Her eyes were drawn back to the giants gliding silently along the sandy riverbed. The elephants were black on their lower parts, where they'd been in the water, while their backs shone grey in the light of the moon. Owls called to each other from nearby trees.

She had been in the African bush less than a day but she was already starting to understand Tertia's love for this place. It was heartbreakingly beautiful here.

Kylie got up, poured herself a glass of wine from her suite's fridge, kicked off her shoes and returned to the swinging chair on her verandah. As she sipped, her anger mellowed into moroseness. It all felt so hard, and she felt completely alone. She had left Chris and Cameron at the dinner table to make her call and she wondered if they were still in the dining room, or the bar. She had to have a clear head for the next day, but she was too wired to sleep just yet.

She downed the wine, went back into her suite and called reception. 'Are Mr McMurtrie and Mr Loubser still in the restaurant?'

'I'll check for you now,' the woman said. A few moments later she returned to the phone. 'They are in the bar, madam.'

That clinched it. Kylie asked the receptionist to send a security guard to fetch her and the man knocked on her door five minutes later. He led her back to the main building, shining a high-powered torch ahead as they walked.

An eerie *woo-oop* noise called from up the river. 'What was that?'

'Hyena, madam. Close-close,' the guard said, grinning.

Kylie closed the gap between her and the man. There were no fences around the camp. It was a little scary, but exciting at the same time, just like her close encounters with the lions and elephants on the game-viewing drive.

When they got to the lodge she thanked the security guard and walked into the lounge. Cameron was alone, sitting on a lounge chair, a tumbler of Scotch and ice on the coffee table in front of him.

'Are you the last man sitting?' she asked.

'Chris is in the bathroom.'

'Mind if I join you?'

'It's a free country, more or less.'

She took the chair opposite him and the barman came over to take her order. 'Gin and tonic, please.'

'Double or single, madam?'

'Double.'

'Same again,' Cameron said to the barman and raised his glass. 'One of those nights?'

'I'll drink to that,' she said.

'How was your call to Jan?'

She shrugged. 'How do you think? He's justifiably pissed off.'

'Well, there's nothing you could have done to change the news.'

'Or you.'

He raised his eyebrows at the olive branch she'd just offered. 'I still can't work out how those samples could have come back so high.'

'We'll get to the bottom of it,' she said. The barman brought her drink and she thanked him and took a long sip. 'I'm sorry about earlier this evening. The truth is that we do need you in this position, overseeing our new projects. You shouldn't see it as a move sideways, Cameron.'

He didn't look convinced. 'Everyone in the industry will look at the story tomorrow and read that Coetzee's running the investigation.

It'll look as though I've been moved out as a sacrificial lamb.' He stared down into his fresh drink.

'I didn't think you were the sort of man who cared about what others thought of you.'

'I think the only thing that matters to me now is what my daughter thinks of me.'

She sat back in her chair and regarded him. He was a big guy, broad across the chest, with muscled arms, but tonight he looked small, as if part of him was missing. He was a different man to the one she had seen underground, face blackened, with the shotgun in his hand, leading them through the darkness to the escape tunnel. It was as if the mine, and life underground, defined him and, like a fish out of water, he struggled to function above ground. Other men might have revelled in the position he had been put into, travelling throughout southern Africa assessing and monitoring the company's myriad new projects. But Cameron McMurtrie just wanted to be back in Barberton, running his mine. She had cried in the privacy of her office the day she had to leave the coalmine she had managed, but she knew there was more to her life and career than the mine.

'Maybe we can reassess things when the Lion Plains project is up and running,' she said.

'Maybe I'll be in Mozambique running fishing boat charters by then.'

'I don't respond well to threats, Cameron.'

'It wasn't meant as one. All I want now is a bit of stability for Jess. If I can't be in Barberton with her, then maybe it's time for me to move us somewhere else, start afresh.'

She sipped her gin and tonic. 'That's your right, Cameron, but I need you here now.' She looked into her glass.

'What is it? Something else on your mind?' he asked.

'I've been thinking about what you did underground, with the hand grenade. I can't stop thinking about it, in fact.'

'It was nothing.'

'No, it wasn't. You were prepared to sacrifice your life to save us.'

She lifted her face and he looked her in the eyes. 'And you came towards me, not back down the stairs. You grabbed me and tried to roll me off the grenade. If it had been live you could have been killed. Why did you do that?'

She didn't know the answer to that, although she'd given it quite a bit of thought. Kylie didn't think she would have risked her own safety to try and save a complete stranger, and it wasn't just because Cameron was a work colleague. In that brief moment in which she'd made the decision to go to him, instead of back down the stairs to safety, she had been worried for him and his daughter. Even in his self-pitying moments, like now, there was something strangely appealing about Cameron. Perhaps it was because of this, not in spite of it, that he'd grown on her. He had been dealt the dual blows of losing his wife and the job he loved, and Kylie felt partly responsible for his current state of mind. And it was the very fact that he had been prepared to give his life to save theirs that made him much more than the broken man slumped in the armchair opposite her. You didn't come across many bona fide heroes in life, Kylie thought, but she thought she was looking at one now.

'I don't know,' she said.

'*Howzit*,' said Chris as he walked back into the lounge bar. 'Windhoek please,' he added to the barman.

'Shithouse,' said Kylie, raising her drink to him. 'And you?'

He smiled. 'Well, since my grand scheme to win Tertia over failed, and the drinks are included in the rate the company is paying for us to stay here, I think we owe it to ourselves to waste as much of her liquor as possible.'

'I'll drink to that,' Cameron said.

'Me too.' Kylie lifted her glass again, smiling for the first time in hours. The barman brought Chris his green bottle of beer and they clinked. 'Same again.'

They were into their fourth round and it was after eleven when Cameron's cellphone rang. He stood, a little unsteadily, and walked out on to the verandah. Kylie was at the point where she knew beyond a doubt that the sensible thing for her to do would be to finish this drink and go to bed, but in the same instant she called the barman over and ordered the same again for all of them. Chris gave her a wicked grin. He was handsome, she thought, though too young for her.

'That dress really suits you,' he said, his blue eyes glittering with the booze and the candlelight.

'I bet you say that to all the girls.'

He shook his head slowly. 'No, only the pretty ones.'

She laughed. He seemed to have recovered from his time underground. He was the antithesis of Cameron. Chris appeared to enjoy being away from the mine, above ground and on the road. Also, unlike Cameron, he seemed to have taken Tertia's rejection of their offer in his stride.

'Are you married?' he asked her.

She sat back in her chair, accepted the new drink from the tray carried by the barman and regarded him through narrowed eyes. 'No.'

He stared at her, ignoring his drink.

His stare unnerved her and excited her at the same time. He was like a young lion, she thought, with his piercing eyes and his mop of fair hair. She knew from studying his personnel file while he was missing that he was six years younger than her and single. Kylie had made it a rule since starting work not to get involved with anyone in the office – or in a mine. She had so far kept her personal and work lives separate – not that she had much of a personal life.

Chris, from the little she knew of him, from his smile and the time they'd spent together since his rescue, struck her as trouble. He was handsome, yet appeared vulnerable as well. He had told her he had been terrified during his time as a hostage underground. She had seen him cowering, waiting for Cameron to pick him up by the scruff of the neck, literally, and rescue him, yet here he was coming on to her like a professional. She imagined he'd had plenty of experience with women.

Cameron walked back into the lounge. 'You won't believe who I've just been talking to and what he wants me to do.'

*

When they arrived back at the mine the next morning, all a little fuzzy around the edges from hangovers, they went straight into meetings. Predictably, once he had heard the strategy they had developed over too many drinks at Lion Plains, Hein Coetzee tried to overrule Cameron, but Kylie put him in his place, telling him that what Cameron was proposing had her approval.

Cameron nodded his thanks to her as Hein retreated to his old office – the deputy manager's. For today. Perhaps for the last time, Cameron was back in his chair behind the door that said *Mine Manager*. There was serious work to do and Kylie had told him, and Coetzee, that they would both be involved in planning for the media conference that was to be held in the mine at two o'clock that afternoon. But first, there was another meeting to attend.

His phone buzzed. 'Hello, Hannelie.'

'Mrs Correia is here to see *Mr* Correia,' she said softly. 'You wanted me to let you know when she arrived.'

'*Dankie*, Hann,' he said.

Cameron stood and picked up a document. It was a report on water recycling at the mine, of no importance to the meeting, but it would serve as a prop. He walked out to reception, headed towards Hannelie and made as if to pass her the document, when he saw the African woman sitting in reception in a threadbare but ironed sundress. He looked at her, then at Hannelie and then back at the woman.

'Morning, how are you?' he said to the woman.

She looked nervous. She swallowed, then said, in English with a Portuguese accent, 'I am fine, thank you. And you?'

'Fine. It's Mrs Correia, isn't it?'

Now she was startled. She rose to her feet nervously as he approached her. 'Yes, that is me. But I am sorry . . .'

He held out his hand. 'No apologies necessary. I'm Cameron McMurtrie, the mine manager. I recognised you from the photo on Luis's desk. He talks about you so often, and young Jose, that we all feel like we know you both already. He mentioned you were coming from Mozambique to see him and would be stopping by the mine.'

She shook his hand and smiled. 'I am sorry for the inconvenience of visiting. But I haven't seen him for so long and I read about the troubles you had here recently. Is he here?'

'Miriam, there's a reason I asked Hannelie over there to let me know when you arrived.'

'There is? Can I see my husband?'

'Yes, of course, but I know what a modest man Luis is, as well as being my hardest working member of staff. I'm not sure if he told you, but he was injured in the business that went on last week, when another of our men was rescued.'

Her eyes widened. 'Injured? I haven't heard from him. I have no telephone.'

Cameron placed a hand gently on her arm. 'He's fine, Mrs Correia. But he was involved in the rescue of his colleague, Chris Loubser, and he was wounded by a gunshot when he put himself between Chris and myself and an armed criminal miner. He saved our lives.'

'Is he here? Is he in hospital?'

'He was released from hospital last night and told to go to his lodgings, but instead he insisted on coming to work. He is in his office, but I wanted to meet you first, to prepare you, and to let you know how grateful I am – how grateful we all are for Luis's years of hard work underground, and for saving the lives of his friends and colleagues.'

She looked overwhelmed by the news. 'I don't know what to say. But I must see him, please, Mr McMurtrie.'

'It's Cameron. And I'll take you to him personally, right now.'

'*Obrigado*. Thank you, Mr Cameron. Please call me Miriam.'

Cameron led her down the corridor to a door that said, *L. Domingues Correia – Chief Metallurgist*. Hannelie had made it on her computer an hour earlier. Miriam put her hand to her mouth. Cameron knocked on the door.

'Come in. Morning, Cameron,' Luis said, looking up from a sheaf of papers, over the top of reading glasses perched on the end of his nose. He wore a crisply ironed blue chambray shirt with the Global Resources logo embroidered above the breast pocket.

'Morning Luis, I've got a visitor here to see you.'

Cameron stepped to one side and Miriam moved past him. Luis stood, and flinched at the pain the action caused and put a hand to his side. Miriam gasped and moved to him, clearly torn between a desire to fling her arms around him and the need to show some decorum in front of her husband's boss. 'I'll leave you two alone for a little while, but I need to see you in the boardroom in fifteen minutes, Luis. It's very important.'

Miriam cast a glance over her shoulder.

'Miriam, you can come to the boardroom as well. I have to make an announcement to my senior management team and it concerns Luis.'

'Yes, *senhor*. Thank you.'

Cameron nodded. 'Fifteen minutes,' he said again as he closed the door on them.

Cameron walked down the corridor, smiling to himself. Kylie emerged from the boardroom. 'How did the reunion go?'

'I thought she was going to cry when she saw him. I've given them fifteen minutes,' Cameron said.

Kylie checked her watch. 'OK. Then we need to get them out of the boardroom half an hour after that, no later. I need to prepare for the media conference. I don't want to seem like a hard arse, but we do have some real work to do here as well, you know.'

'You're anything but a hard arse. I half thought you'd go back on agreeing to help Luis after he called me last night.'

'I almost did when I woke up. I hope you feel as ill as I do this morning. I know I was pissed but I still don't know how I let you talk me into going along with this little charade. Coetzee's got the hump and I wouldn't be surprised if he dobs us all in to Jan.'

'Luis saved our lives, Kylie. I visited him in hospital and he told me his story. He's had a rough time in South Africa and all he ever wanted was a proper job. He's got more qualifications than most other men I've worked with.'

'I know, so you said last night when you were drunk and working your magic on me. You *know* we still can't offer him a real job, though, Cameron. He's an illegal immigrant and was a party to defrauding us of millions of rand worth of gold.'

He nodded. It was part of the deal they'd struck over two more rounds of drinks at Lion Plains.

Cameron had unknowingly set the whole thing in motion when they had emerged from the mine. Cameron and Chris had carried Luis to a waiting ambulance, before the police had time to speak to him. 'When you get to the hospital, tell them you work for us,' Cameron had whispered to the barely conscious Mozambican.

Cameron had called into the Mediclinic at Nelspruit the next day, once he had finished giving a detailed statement to the police. Luis had undergone surgery, but the bullet had passed through the flesh above his left hip, missing his vital organs, and the doctor predicted he would be released within a week.

Luis had been in a panic after the operation, and pleaded with Cameron for a legitimate job with Global Resources, not at Eureka but at any other mine. Cameron had told him that while he was happy to continue the charade with the hospital so that Luis's medical expenses were covered, he was realistic too: there was no way he could give Luis a real job.

Cameron had thought that was the last of it, until he'd taken Luis's call at the lodge the night before. Luis had talked quickly and urgently: there had been two alarming developments. First, Wellington Shumba had found out where Luis was and was threatening to kill him, and second, which seemed of even more concern for Luis, his wife was on her way from Mozambique to visit him.

Luis's cover had been blown when he'd been spotted shuffling down the Mediclinic corridor by one of the four badly injured *zama zamas* who the police had pulled from the rubble of the collapsed tunnel in Eureka. Although there was a police guard on their ward, the men must have had a way of communicating with Wellington, as a nurse had delivered a telephone message to Luis's bedside that read: *I will see you back at work as soon as you are released. W.* Luis had explained the unwritten threat in the note. He knew too much about Wellington and his illegal pipelines in and out of the mine. The Zimbabwean could not afford to have Luis at large, or in police custody. Luis promised that if Cameron offered him a job, somewhere far from Barberton, he would tell him and the police all he could about Wellington's operations.

Luis's contact with his wife had been via letters sent to a post box at Barberton, which was cleared by a legitimate miner above ground, who then added Luis's mail – mostly letters from his wife and son – to the regular shipments of contraband carried underground to the *zama zamas*. The miner, who had become something of a friend to Luis, visited him in hospital to bring him his latest mail. To Luis's horror, the last letter from his wife revealed she was travelling by *chapa* from their home far in the north to the border post at Ressano Garcia, where she expected to leave the Mozambican minibus taxi and transfer to a similar vehicle on the South African side at Komatipoort and make it to Barberton by the next day.

Cameron had heard Luis out, and then promised him that he would discuss his requests with his superior – Kylie – and call him back that night.

'I'm not giving in to blackmail,' Kylie had said, over yet another drink. 'We can't offer him a job at any of our mines – word would get back to the union too soon about his background. He's admitted he has had direct contact with your people at Eureka.'

Cameron had liked how she had said 'your people'. He did still think of himself as manager of the mine, whatever the politics and whatever she and Jan wanted to call him. 'You're right. He can't expect us to help him, and only tell us what he knows about Wellington if we give him a job. We could turn him over to the police.'

'We probably should,' Kylie had said.

'But he did save our lives by taking a bullet from that sentry,' Cameron said. Suddenly, through his drunken haze, the answer came to him. 'The reward!'

'What reward?' Kylie asked.

Chris had sunk into one of the lodge's deep armchairs and his head was lolled back and his eyes closed.

Cameron snapped his fingers. 'Six months ago I posted a reward of a hundred thousand rand for information that led to the breaking up of the *zama zama* gang at Eureka. None of my guys came through with any information; they were all obviously too scared of Wellington to give him up, or worried the legitimate miners supplying the *zama zamas* would get them if they gave information that ended the smuggling.'

'So?' Kylie asked. The alcohol was slowing her uptake.

'So, I didn't specify that it had to be a Global Resources employee to claim the reward. If Luis gives us the dirt on Wellington, then he's entitled to the money. It's not a fortune, but it might be enough for him to get back to Mozambique and set himself up in some sort of business.'

Kylie looked dubious. 'He's a criminal, Cameron.'

Cameron had shrugged. 'So what? Plenty of criminals collect rewards for spilling the beans on each other, and plenty do deals with the police and prosecutors to avoid being convicted. We'd be offering Luis the same thing.'

And Luis had gone for it.

To Cameron's surprise it had been Kylie who had come up with the idea of staging a meeting for Luis and his wife at the Eureka offices. Cameron had laughed at the prospect and now that it was happening it still put a smile on his face. Kylie had a heart after all. She winked at him as Luis walked, still a little painfully, arm in arm with Miriam to the boardroom.

Chris was there, as were Hannelie, Coetzee, Casper and Roelf, all of whom Cameron had confided in.

'Thanks everyone for coming, and for those of you who don't know her from her picture, allow me to introduce Miriam Correia to all of you.'

Miriam looked embarrassed by the attention paid to her, but smiled and nodded greetings to the rest of the team.

'I'd like now to hand over to Global Resources' head of health, safety, environment and community, Dr Kylie Hamilton.'

Cameron sat and Kylie stood. In front of her was a picture frame glass-side down.

'Thanks Cameron, and thanks everyone for making time to join us here for what is a very sad, but also happy moment for Eureka. Sadly, Luis met with Cameron yesterday and, quite unexpectedly, tendered his letter of resignation from the company as chief metallurgist at Eureka.'

Cameron saw Miriam's eyes widen as she turned to her husband. Luis put a hand on her arm to quieten her for the time being.

'While this was a sad moment for us, Luis's reason for leaving touched our hearts. I hope I'm not embarrassing you, Luis, when I explain to the rest of the team that your prime reason for leaving was your love for your wife and son. Many miners spend long periods away from their families and sometimes those relationships suffer. No one will begrudge you wanting to go back to Mozambique and I am sure you'll be very happy being back home on the coast at Inhambane.'

Miriam was grinning. Cameron had wondered if she would be angry to see her husband lose his supposedly well-paid job at Eureka. Cameron had no idea how much Luis had made from Wellington's illegal underground mine, but he guessed it had not been a fortune.

'As you're all aware,' Kylie continued, 'Luis was injured by a gunshot during the rescue of our colleague Chris, just a week ago. He put his life on the line to protect others who were taking part in the rescue operation. As Luis hasn't been with us long enough to claim any retirement benefits, and is leaving us of his own volition, he isn't strictly entitled to much more than some accrued holiday leave, but in recognition of his bravery and the injury he's suffered, I'd like to, on behalf of the company, offer him a small token of Global Resources' esteem and a certificate of appreciation for his bravery underground. Please step forward, Luis.'

Luis winced as he stood, clasped his wife's hand, then let go of it. Kylie shook his hand as she handed over the framed certificate and then an envelope.

Cameron saw Luis was too embarrassed to say anything. He opened the envelope when he sat down, and passed it to Miriam. His wife put her hand over her mouth to stifle a gasp when she read the amount on the cash cheque. Cameron looked at Kylie and winked at her. She smiled at him.

17

'Wellington's buyer is an Arab named Mohammed,' Luis said.

Kylie sat back in the boardroom chair and folded her arms. Miriam was in Luis's 'office' reading a magazine and drinking a cup of tea. It was time for her husband to live up to his end of the bargain. 'Come *on*, Luis. You've got to be kidding. You have to give us more than that. An Arab named Mohammed?'

He nodded. 'I am sorry. I know they meet sometimes in Malelane.'

'Where?' Kylie asked.

Cameron explained: 'It's a small town north of here, on the N4, not far from the Mozambican border. It's based around cane farming and it's a shopping stopover for people coming from Mozambique to South Africa or vice versa. But Kylie's right, Luis, we need more than that.'

Luis nodded and sipped from a glass of water. 'I think this Mohammed comes from Mozambique, or takes the gold there. Wellington has also sometimes been there to meet him; I've heard Wellington bragging about . . . well, bragging about being with people and having fun in Maputo.'

Kylie was touched by his modesty. If Luis had been present at some of the conversations she'd had with miners in Australia – mostly started with the aim of embarrassing her as the only woman present – his toes would curl. 'What sort of people does he like to "be" with?'

Luis shifted in his chair and looked to Cameron, who gave a slight nod of his head. Luis took a deep breath, then finally looked at her. 'He rules by fear and he enforces this fear by taking what he wants, who he wants. He will "be" with whomever he wants at that moment – the women the miners would sometimes smuggle down, even young ones, even men if he wishes. I heard things, terrible things down there.' He closed his eyes.

'I'm sorry, Luis,' Kylie said.

He opened his eyes and looked into hers. 'Please tell me, Dr Hamilton, that you are not thinking of going after him.'

Kylie chewed her lower lip. Her gut instinct was that Luis was a decent man who was genuinely trying to repent for his life of crime, but there was no way she was going to tell him what she intended to do, partly because she didn't know. She was beginning to understand what had made Cameron defy her orders and Jan's and set off on his one-man vigilante mission. The police here were useless, his own bosses were sitting on their hands, and this bastard Wellington had killed one of his men, kidnapped another and was laughing at him. 'That would be a matter for the relevant authorities,' she said.

Luis interlaced the fingers of his hands and studied them for a few moments. He seemed to be deciding, Kylie thought, whether to continue telling them what he knew. She thought it would be best to say nothing, and let him fill the void. She glanced at Cameron whose rough-hewn face was immobile. He was quite a good-looking man, in a craggy sort of way. Luis exhaled. 'You were right about how he transports the gold. There are crossing points between Swaziland and Mozambique where the gold is moved by one vehicle, then carried through or under the fence, and then loaded onto another.'

'How does he get it across the border from South Africa to Swaziland?' Kylie asked.

'Underground?' Cameron ventured. Luis nodded his assent, so Cameron continued, for her benefit. 'There are old tunnels that date back decades, perhaps a hundred years even, linking mines in South Africa and Swaziland.'

'Yes,' Luis confirmed. 'But do not ask me where they are, because I was never shown. Wellington compartmentalised the operation and only he and Ncube knew how all the pieces fitted together. Originally the Lion would use men to carry the gold part of the way to Swaziland, then others would meet them there. The ones on the South African side would never be able to find the escape holes on the Swazi side, and those on the Swazi side would likewise not be able to find their way into the heart of the operation at Eureka without Ncube or one of the porters. Lately, though, he has been carrying the gold himself.'

'What are you going to do now?' Cameron asked Luis.

He shrugged. 'I cannot stay here, I must leave as soon as I can.'

'Will you go back to Mozambique?' Kylie asked.

Luis put his glasses back on. 'I think that is best. Your gift – please do not think I am ungrateful – will only go so far here in South Africa. In Mozambique my family has land. It is not much, but perhaps I can buy some seed and some tools and go back to doing what my ancestors did, living off the land, or fishing.'

He wasn't playing them, Kylie thought, just telling it as it was. He had broken the law and was in South Africa as an illegal immigrant. In her country he would be scooped up and put in a detention centre before being deported. At least this way he was going home with something in his pocket. Still, she thought, it was a shame that they couldn't use his knowledge and experience. If it leaked out that Global Resources was employing ex-*zama zamas* with no work papers they would be in even hotter water with the unions and the government than they were over the air quality results. 'Is there anything else you can tell us about Wellington?'

'Yes, Dr Hamilton. I will tell you to be careful.'

*

Two doors down from the boardroom, Chris checked his computer clock for the tenth time in three minutes. There was a sound like a bubble popping up on the surface of water and he felt a corresponding surge of adrenaline.

Safarigirl43 is online, said the small pop-up on the screen. He maximised the chat window and saw she had written *Hi* and nothing else.

Just got here myself, he lied to her. He didn't want her to think he had been sitting here, like Pavlov's dog, waiting for her permission to drool.

Ja, right, lol, she typed. *You've been waiting for me, haven't you?*

She had his measure, and more. He was sure she was as addicted to him, and to all this running around, as he was to her. He just didn't want to show it. He couldn't let it become so encompassing that he would make a mistake.

Are you hard for me, lover?

He was. *Just thinking about how hard I fucked you on your desk.*

Lol. It was the way they were. She liked him to be forceful with her when they met in the flesh, but she pulled the strings the rest of the time. *Did you get a* snotklap *from your lady boss, my poor baby, when I rejected your offer?*

She was OK about it with me, but I'm sure she was pissed off.

Where's the info you were going to send to me, about your past air quality monitoring results?

I haven't got it all together yet. It was the type of information any shareholder or analyst could ask for. They were required to submit regular reports on air quality monitoring to the government's Department of Mineral Resources, so technically he wasn't leaking information to Tertia, just facilitating her getting it.

Get it for me, baby. I need it.

OK. The deception went against his grain, yet excited him at the same time. It was like his relationship with her. She was eight years older than he, and though she was an attractive woman he could have had his pick of the twenty year olds in town. She was experienced, and they had done things that most of the girls closer to his age would have blushed at. She was the enemy of Global Resources, but he was desperately, completely in love with her.

When is her press conference?

Half an hour, he typed. It was public knowledge, the details available on the Global Resources media alert that had been emailed that morning and posted on half-a-dozen news and mining websites, and the company's.

He clicked on the folder that contained the air pollution monitoring reports and returns to the government. It was all there, the mine's history of compliance over the past ten years. It would make for dry reading. He went back to the chat window and hovered his cursor over the file-sharing icon.

Unzip your trousers for me. In your office, she typed.

She had never told him to do that. Not at work, at least. When he had tried it with her once she had said no, flat out. She would not risk one of her staff catching her. Yet she'd been quite happy for him to fuck her on her desk. The limits of this thing were being pushed all the time. He ran a hand through his hair. He thought of her grunting as he thrust in and out of her.

'No,' he whispered. He put his hands on the edge of his desk and pushed his office chair back.

Are you there, baby?

She knew he was. She knew the turmoil in him; the guilt; what he was going through for her. She was using him. And he loved it. He tried to be strong, and to hold off replying. He wanted to close down his computer now, to be done with her forever. *I'm sending you the file you want now*.

She ignored his message. *Do it. For me.*

He reached for his zipper.

*

Cameron knocked once on Chris's door then opened it. Loubser looked up, startled, and rolled his chair closer under his desk.

'Surfing porn at work? That's in contravention of the Global Resources internet protocols and a punishable offence.'

'No, boss. I . . . *sheesh*, you just gave me a fright is all, man.'

Cameron scoffed. 'No problem either way.'

Chris's face flushed even redder. Cameron wondered if he'd cut too close to the bone. In any case it didn't matter; there was work to be done. 'Kylie's going to front the press in twenty minutes. She says you're going to as well.'

'But boss, hell, I don't want to face those vultures. I thought head office said it was going to be Kylie and Hein talking about the review.'

Cameron knew he had to be patient, despite Chris's whining. 'They did, but I suggested to her it would be good to have our expert in air quality monitoring there to back her up and to answer any technical questions the jackals might have. She's ignoring head office and I agree with her. Hein's relieved. Besides, this is your area of the business that we're being slandered over, so it's only fair that you get up there and tell them what we do in terms of monitoring, and how good our results have been so far.'

Chris scratched his head, and used his mouse to click something closed on his computer. 'All the same, I'd rather be underground again with those bastard *zama zamas* than facing that lot.'

There were parts of Cameron's job that he didn't like – most particularly dismissing people. However, he took responsibility for his decisions and stood by them. Chris was the man in the firing line over air quality monitoring. It might not have been his fault that something had gone wrong somewhere, leading to an off-the-scale reading, but he was the best man to explain to the media how seriously they took pollution control and monitoring at Eureka, and how best they could prove that this had all been a mistake. Or, if it wasn't a mistake, how they would find the problem, fix it and ensure it didn't happen again. 'I understand, but we need you now, Chris.'

Reluctantly, Chris rolled back his chair and stood.

They went to the boardroom and Cameron opened the door. Kylie was leaning forward on the table, talking into a hands-free unit used for teleconferences. She nodded to them. 'Musa, Chris and Cameron are here now.'

'Hi guys,' Musa Mabunda said from the tinny speaker as they took their chairs. They greeted him back.

'Musa, it's Chris here. Can you please tell me how I explain what went wrong when we don't know?'

'That's why we're having the investigation,' Kylie interjected. 'Basically what we're going to do is a complete environmental audit which will prove that these results couldn't have come from Eureka. Unless, of course, there's something going on I don't know about.' She looked at Cameron, Chris and Hein Coetzee in turn. None of them said a thing.

'Kylie's right,' said Musa. 'Stick to the facts and explain how we test, what we test for, and state that we'll fix any problem the audit finds.'

Kylie ran them through the order of the media conference; she would give a prepared statement and then take questions. She then asked Cameron, Hein and Musa to play the parts of hostile journalists and bombard her and Chris with questions.

At the end of the rehearsal she said, 'Right, is everybody ready?'

'No,' said Chris.

*

Wellington lay on the bed and used the remote to switch on the television in his room in the Cardoso Hotel in Maputo. The hotel overlooked the harbour. It was new enough to be comfortably modern, and old enough not to be out of place in Maputo's European-feeling architecture.

The girl was in the shower.

He flicked through the channels to the SABC live news channel. The woman he had seen underground appeared on the screen, behind a cluster of microphones bearing the logos of South African radio and television stations. He had only caught glimpses of her underground, and she had been wearing sexless overalls and a helmet. She was in something corporate for the media conference, a white blouse with the top two buttons undone, and a blue jacket. He couldn't see her from the waist down, except in his mind's eye. He knew from his sources that she was a senior executive with Global Resources, from Australia.

The whore emerged from the bathroom, the snowy white towel knotted just above her breasts, setting off her milk-coffee coloured skin nicely. She was almost white, this one. He'd specified her to feed one of his many fantasies, but now she was blocking his view.

'Get out of the way, bitch.'

She pouted, paused, then stepped to one side and looked at the television.

'Come here, baby,' he said, his voice silky, as though he hadn't just abused her. He moved to the end of the bed so he was sitting on the edge, his feet on the floor. He had his shirt off. 'Kneel down.'

She did as he told her and she undid the knot of the towel, letting it fall around her. He returned his gaze to the television.

The woman on the television was wrapping up her prepared statement. 'Are there any questions?'

Wellington unzipped his jeans. The girl took her cue and freed his shaft. She ran her hand up and down it. He leaned back and placed his hands on the bed behind him.

A male reporter asked the woman what comment Global Resources had about the mining union calling a strike at Eureka and boycotting involvement in the monitoring review.

'You'd have to ask the union that. The fact is that we have suspended operations at the mine pending the outcome of our investigation and review. We don't want our workers going underground until we can get to the bottom of this, so the strike is irrelevant.'

Wellington smiled as he grew hard under the woman's ministrations. She rolled a condom over him and lowered her mouth to him. There would be no rubber between him and Kylie Hamilton if he ever got hold of her. He let the fantasy flit at the corner of his mind as he forced himself to concentrate on the screen and not the woman between his legs.

A woman from the press pack spoke up. 'Annelien Oberholzer from *Beeld*, Dr Hamilton. How often in the past have air pollution monitoring results exceeded the mandated maximum?'

Kylie nodded, as if she had been expecting the question. 'Global Resources has never been prosecuted for exceeding the maximum allowable levels in dust samples.'

'That's not what I asked. My question was, how many times have results exceeded the mandated maximum levels?'

The Australian woman's confidence started to crack. She looked to her left and the camera panned to the handsome face of the white man, Chris Loubser. Wellington's pulse quickened. He reached for the prostitute and wound his hand in her braided hair. She moaned on him.

'Chris? Perhaps you could confirm this,' Kylie Hamilton said.

He blinked a few times, then licked his lips. His face was bathed in the harsh light of the television cameras. 'Umm, well, off the top of my head, about a hundred and twenty-two times.'

There was an audible murmur in the ranks of assembled journalists.

'So this is far from an isolated case of Global Resources breaking the law,' said another reporter.

'What was that number again, and over what time period?' Oberholzer asked.

Wellington laughed out loud and slapped his thigh. The girl started and glanced up at him, wide eyed. 'Nothing,' he said to her, 'keep going.' They were making Loubser say it again so there was no doubt the number was on the record.

'A hundred and twenty-two times in the past ten years,' Chris said.

'Dr Hamilton, did you know that Global Resources has broken the law, and endangered the lives of its workers, on average, once a month over the past decade?' the reporter from *Beeld* asked.

The camera panned back to Hamilton. She glanced at Loubser then back down the barrel of the lens. She looked flustered. Wellington wanted to laugh again, but also didn't want to break the girl's rhythm as she worked him close to the edge.

'I'm sure this can be put into perspective,' Kylie said.

Before she or Loubser could explain, a journalist said: 'Dr Hamilton, you said in your earlier statement that the matter reported in the press was, quote, "an isolated incident". Clearly it wasn't, so were you lying or were you just not aware of what was going on at this mine?'

'Neither, I just –'

'Dr Hamilton,' Oberholzer interrupted, 'the ANC Youth League's spokesman said today that your criminal negligence of health and safety at Eureka means the government should reject your plans to mine in the Kruger Park. How confident are you that the environmental impact assessment for the Lion Plains mine will be approved now that your record on pollution monitoring has been made public?'

'I . . .'

The television screen returned to the studio, where the pretty anchor woman said to her co-host, 'Well, Vusi, that looks like a very rattled Dr Kylie Hamilton from the mining company Global Resources. We'll be watching this story with interest, and also the company's plans to mine in the greater Kruger Park, which must be looking a little shaky now.'

Wellington closed his eyes and pictured himself back underground, with the Australian mining executive on her knees, in the dirt. He bunched the whore's hair tighter in his fingers and she moaned compliantly for him.

Yes, Dr Hamilton would like it, though she might protest at first. He might not have to force her at all, once she realised there was no escape.

There were loose ends to be tied up. The traitor, Correia, would have to be eliminated before he could slip across the border into Mozambique. McMurtrie and the woman had seen him, so as long as they were alive he was at risk if he ventured back to Barberton. A car-jacking might be the best way to get rid of them, however Wellington wanted to feel her mouth on him before he killed her.

The smart thing would be for him to melt away and find another mine or another line of work. But he knew Eureka like it was his own. He wanted it all. The mine, the woman, the gold.

He would have it all. He closed his eyes and felt the surge of power from his loins.

*

'My office, now,' Cameron said to Chris as they left the boardroom.

Coetzee was escorting the last of the journalists and camera people out of the administration building, a task he seemed to relish. One of the photographers told him to take his hand off his arm.

Kylie followed them into the office which, Cameron realised yet again, was actually not his any more. He struggled to keep his fury in check. 'Sit down. What the hell were you thinking, Chris?'

Chris held out his hands. 'Musa said not to lie. *Jissus*, Cameron, what was I supposed to say?'

'How about putting it in context?'

'OK, let's everyone cool it,' Kylie said. 'Cameron, to be fair to Chris, you don't know how strenuous it is facing the media until you've had to do it.'

He shook his head. 'I have had to do it. But the way that just went makes it looks like we've got a serial problem with air quality.'

'*Have* you?' she asked.

God, she could be infuriating, he thought. 'No. Whenever we do get an elevated reading we report it and fix whatever's caused it. What you should have said,' Cameron fixed Chris with his gaze, 'was that three weeks of those readings came from when the ventilation system in number two shaft was down. We stopped mining and sent workers down in breathing apparatus to fix it, but the whole time we continued to do air quality monitoring and report the findings to the DMR. No one was breaking any laws and no one was at risk. Why on earth didn't you say that?'

Chris looked sheepish. 'They didn't give me time. I was nervous. I felt like an impala in a spotlight.'

'I'll get Musa to issue a statement of clarification,' Kylie said. 'Chris, I want you to talk to him and give him all the facts and put it all in context.'

'*Ja*, all right.'

'Hell, it won't do any good. The vultures have got their headline already. *120 BREACHES AT KILLER MINE*, or something like that,' Cameron said. 'At this rate we'll be out of business before the end of the year.'

There was a knock at the door. Coetzee opened it and walked in. 'The criminal miner is asking if he and his wife can leave now.'

Cameron stood and said to Chris, 'Get on the phone to Musa now. I'll see Luis off.'

He walked out into the corridor where Luis and Miriam were waiting. Luis had changed out of his Global Resources shirt and into a plain one. It was another of Cameron's that he had brought from home. He held out his hand and Luis took it, touching his own right forearm with his left in a gesture that said thank you very much.

'I'm sorry you have to leave us, Luis.'

He nodded, and Cameron saw the sadness in his eyes. 'I am sorry, too, but I have been away from my family for too long. I think it is time that I went home.'

He knew how Luis felt. He had left Jessica in the care of his neighbours for too long. He clapped Luis on the arm. 'Thank you.'

'*Obrigado*. If you come to Inhambane, please look for me. Here is my Mozambican cellphone number.' He handed Cameron a piece of paper.

'We'll be sorry to lose your husband,' Cameron said to Miriam. She didn't seem sad at all that he was leaving South Africa. 'I'll get one of our drivers, Sipho, to take you to Nelspruit. You should be able to get a bus or taxi from there to the border.'

'*Obrigado*.' Miriam took his hand in both of hers.

Chris and Kylie came out of Cameron's old office as he was telling Hannelie to organise Sipho. They all said their goodbyes.

'Stay safe,' Cameron said to Luis.

'You too.'

18

Vusi Khumalo and Danger Maseka were playing pool in a shebeen in Emjindini when the call came through.

'Sharp, my brother,' said Danger when Vusi put his hand over the mouthpiece and whispered that it was the boss on the line. 'We are back in business,' he added when Vusi finished the call.

They drained their Black Labels and went straight to the black Golf GT. Vusi had stolen it a week earlier and it now sported a new colour scheme and plates and dark tinted windows. Vusi felt the adrenaline kick in, out to his fingers and toes as he revved the engine and sent up a fantail of red dirt as they skidded to the tar road. A mangy dog barked and jumped out of their way just in time to save itself. The young men laughed.

Danger lit a spliff and dragged deep before passing it over. Vusi inhaled the marijuana smoke and held it in his lungs, feeling it even out the rush. As he drove, the needle sitting on one-twenty, he reached down between his legs and under the seat for the Colt .45. It was a cannon, and it had been too long since he'd used it.

'I was wondering,' said Danger as he took the spliff back, 'if we would hear from Wellington ever again.'

Vusi laughed half-heartedly. 'Don't ever let him hear you say that, my brother. Just be thankful we *are* back in business and he has called on us.'

'Amen.' Danger tuned in the car radio to some hip-hop, but Vusi reached over and turned it down.

He explained the details of the job to Danger, who lifted his T-shirt and slid out his Glock. Danger thumbed the magazine release, checked his load, then rammed it back home again. He pulled back the slide and released it, chambering a round.

They passed through Barberton and out onto the R38. Both men scanned the road.

'There he is,' Vusi said, spying the mine *bakkie* ahead of them, flying the orange day-glo safety flag from its rear bumper. 'I knew we would catch them. That Sipho drives like a woman.'

Vusi eased off the accelerator, not wanting to get too close to the truck until it was time. There was too much development on the roadsides around here. He would wait until they were on one of the stretches where the bush grew close to the road.

It would not be an easy hit, but Vusi liked a challenge. And an even bigger challenge would be keeping his boy Danger focused. 'We go for the rear tyres. Shoot them out, then close in on them when they go off the edge.'

'No. Just overtake them and cap Sipho.'

Vusi shook his head. 'Too dangerous. He might roll the *bakkie* and kill them all. We have our orders. We must do this job correctly, but we must also be fast.'

'Go past them,' Danger suggested, 'and we lay some rubber and stop close to a tree. Make it look like we have crashed. I will flag them down and when Sipho stops and comes to help us, we kill him.'

Vusi knew this was why the boss had called him and not Danger. He took the time to think things through and the *dagga* made him think clearly, unlike Danger who was turned into even more of a madman by the weed. 'My brother, if you were Sipho, would you stop for you?'

Danger had to smile at that one. 'All right. We do it your way.'

*

Luis saw the eyes of Sipho, the cautious driver, flick up once more to the rear-view mirror. Luis, sitting in the back seat of the Hilux next to Miriam, looked over his shoulder. A zippy black Golf with tinted windows was accelerating fast behind them. It came up close to the tailgate.

'Boys.' Sipho clicked his tongue on the roof of his mouth and shook his head.

Luis took his wife's hand and squeezed it. 'It is good to be going home.'

'I can't say I am unhappy,' Miriam said.

'Of course, I don't have a job any more.'

'We will manage,' Miriam said.

As Luis turned his eyes back to the road in front, there was a series of bangs. Luis, who had served during the war, could not mistake the sound for anything else. Sipho, however, was caught unaware and seemed confused. The steering wheel bucked in his hands as the rear of the Hilux slid from side to side.

'Get down!' Luis pushed Miriam down with a hand on her shoulder.

Sipho was panicking, overcorrecting. 'They shot out a tyre, maybe two!' He eased his foot off the accelerator.

'Go faster – forget the tyres,' Luis said.

The Golf sped up beside them and Luis saw the squat black pistol in the passenger's hand through the wound-down window as the gunman waved at Sipho to pull into the kerb. Sipho eased off the accelerator again.

'No, don't stop! Ram him,' Luis ordered Sipho.

Sipho glanced at him, then at the road. 'No! These men just want the *bakkie*. They can have it.'

'Sipho, listen to me. Those men, they don't want the *bakkie*, they want me.'

The driver of the Golf was blowing his horn and his passenger was waving his pistol at them, furiously gesticulating for them to pull over.

'*Eish*, they can have you!' Sipho said, not looking back. The Golf kept pace with them.

'They won't leave witnesses. If they kill me they will have to kill you too.'

Miriam looked up at him and grabbed his arm. 'Luis, what do you mean? Who are these men? You have done nothing wrong.'

Luis swallowed back a rising tide of nausea. His sins were being visited on him, along with his wife and the innocent driver. At least one tyre slapped noisily on the road as the truck continued to slow. Luis lowered his head below the sill of the window and said to Miriam: 'Listen to me, get ready to jump.'

'No! I can't.'

'You must. It's our only chance.'

He opened his door just a fraction and got ready to remove his seatbelt. 'On three, my love.' He undid her belt and grabbed her forearm.

She looked into his eyes. 'I am scared.'

'What are you doing back there?' Sipho asked, his eyes still alternating wildly between the road ahead and the car beside them.

Luis ignored the driver and clasped his wife's hand. 'We will die unless you jump, my love.'

'All right, I am ready.' She straightened her torso, readying herself to follow him out of the vehicle.

Luis glanced to the right and saw the mean young face over the top of the pistol. The boy smiled at him, then pulled the trigger. The pistol bucked in his hand twice. Luis flinched and ducked and heard the right rear passenger window shatter. 'Miriam!'

Sipho winced as broken glass spattered the back of his head. He risked a glance back. 'No!'

Too late, Sipho accelerated and swung wildly to the left, then back to the right, and the Toyota sideswiped the Golf.

Luis clutched Miriam to him and looked into her wide eyes. She was dead already. Blood oozed from the entry wound on her right temple. The left side of her face was a mass of shattered bone and spilled brains that soaked his shirt. She stared at him accusingly and he knew she would watch him, like that, forever. If it wasn't for their son he would leap through the broken rear window now and throw himself at the Golf, like a lion on a buffalo.

Reluctantly, Luis laid his wife's body against the seat, unclipped his seatbelt and opened the door.

Two more gunshots sounded and bullets slammed into the truck's engine bay. A cloud of steam erupted from the bonnet and washed over the windscreen as Sipho hit the brakes. 'Where are you going?' Sipho screamed.

Luis ignored him and leapt out of the slowing *bakkie*. He hit the gravel verge of the road hard, and rolled, trying to keep his arms and legs tucked in tight as he tumbled. He felt something tear in his side, where the gunshot wound had been stitched. The wound was not as serious as it looked, but he felt blood wetting his shirt as he bounced to a halt by a tree. He got up, drew a ragged breath, and ran into the bush. Tears welled in his eyes as he stumbled on.

*

'What was that?' Vusi yelled.

'What?' Danger's eyes were wide and bloodshot with the lust of battle and the residual effects of the marijuana. He had ejected the magazine from his pistol; he was either out of ammunition or had a stoppage.

'He's gone,' Vusi said. 'And hurry up and reload.'

'No, he ducked down.'

'Look, you fool, the passenger door is swinging open.' Sipho was coasting to a halt. Vusi drew his own pistol for the first time and leaned across Danger, took aim and fired. The first shot missed so he fired again. Danger yelped like a dog at the thunder and flash in the car from the .45's barrel. The second shot took the top off Sipho's head. He slumped to the side and the Toyota veered lazily off the road and smacked into a tree.

Vusi pulled over, leapt from the Golf and ran to the *bakkie*. Steam hissed from the punctured radiator and twisted metal pinged as it cooled. He smelled the blood from inside. He stuck his head in and confirmed what he had seen. 'Shit, man. He jumped. You should have been paying more attention. And you shouldn't have shot the woman so soon.'

'But the boss said –'

'Shut up, Bright. We have to find the Professor. The boss will kill us if we lose him.'

'Don't call me that.' He tapped his chest with the barrel of his Glock. 'I am Danger. Come, my brother, let's see what they have in their pockets.'

Vusi shook his head. A poor Mozambican woman dressed in near rags and a mine driver. There would be nothing. He saw the sticker for the satellite tracking service on the remnants of Sipho's window. They were Wellington's enforcers, but only part-time car thieves. Vusi had no idea how to find a tracking device. There was the risk Sipho had set off some sort of panic button while they were shooting his tyres out. 'We can't stay here.'

Danger was tugging at a ring on the dead woman's finger. 'Wait.' He reached into the back pocket of his jeans and pulled out a flick knife, releasing the blade.

'*Eish*. Come, man.' Vusi shook his head as Danger began sawing at the dead woman's finger. 'The boss . . .'

Danger glared up at him, his hands slick with blood. 'Fuck the boss. The Professor is long gone.' He went back to his cutting.

Vusi ran back down the road to where he thought the Mozambican had jumped from the car. Someone had to follow the boss's orders.

He turned his mind to the ground, where the answer always lay, as his father had often told him. His father had been a poacher, before he'd died of the wasting disease, and he had taught Vusi much about following spoor. Fleetingly, Vusi had thought about a career as a game ranger, but then he had found work on the mines and from there drifted across to the *zama zamas* where he could make more money. Wellington had spotted his dedication and ruthlessness – he'd once beaten a fellow worker to death when Wellington ordered the punishment, and had since used his .45 to cap a rival gangster from Johannesburg who had tried to rip Wellington off during an arms deal.

Vusi found the scuffed dirt where the man had rolled from the car and hit the ground. From there it was easy to see the path he had trodden through the bush. He held his Colt at the ready and was about to set off when his cellphone vibrated in his pocket. He stopped and looked at the screen and saw the number of the Mozambican pre-paid sim card.

'*Yebo* boss?'

'Is it done?'

'Ah . . .'

'Idiots. Tell me what went wrong.'

Vusi swallowed. 'I'm following the Professor now. He got away on foot, boss. I will get him.'

'I didn't ask you what you were doing, I asked you what went wrong.'

It was the way of the man. Enforcement of his will, and retribution, were more important to him than getting a job done. Wellington could accept that sometimes people would fail, as they were only human, and seemed almost to enjoy receiving bad news as it gave him a chance to demonstrate his power. 'We shot the tyres of the *bakkie* out and then Danger shot the woman.'

There was a pause. 'So instead of thinking it was a common hijacking they knew you were going after the Professor and his wife.'

Wellington was as clever as he was evil, Vusi thought. 'Yes boss.'

'The mining vehicles all have satellite trackers. There will be a response team on their way now.'

Vusi cocked his head. As if on cue he heard the mosquito buzz of a helicopter, far off but getting closer. 'I think they are on their way, boss.'

'Go back to the *bakkie*.'

Vusi almost objected, but held his tongue, turned back to the road and ran towards the crashed Toyota. A BMW X5 slowed to look at the Hilux but didn't stop. This was South Africa. 'I am almost there, boss.'

'Is Danger still there?'

Vusi could see Danger's knock-off Levis, low on his hips so his similarly authentic Calvin Kleins were showing. He was leaning in, still hacking at the body of the dead woman. 'Yes boss.'

'Call him. Tell him I want to talk to him.'

Vusi could see the speck of the helicopter now. His heart was racing. He wanted to run into the bush. 'But the Professor, boss . . .'

'Shut up, you idiot. Do as I tell you, boy.'

'Danger! Danger, the boss is on the phone.'

Danger straightened and looked back at Vusi. He held up the small band of thin, cheap gold, a broad smile on his face as he wiped the blade of his knife on his jeans and folded it closed against his thigh. 'Tell him I'm coming.'

'He's coming, boss.'

Danger walked towards him.

'Kill him,' said Wellington. 'Then go find the Professor. I want him alive, remember.'

Vusi licked his lips as his friend approached him. He could ignore the order and they could both try to run, but Wellington had contacts throughout South Africa and into neighbouring Mozambique and Zimbabwe. Wellington was in Mozambique now, judging by the number he was using, but he could be less than ninety kilometres as the crow flew. The helicopter was plainly visible now. The pilot had lost altitude and was racing towards the *bakkie*. Danger looked up over his shoulder. 'We must run, brother.'

'Kill him.'

It would be better this way than if Wellington killed him slowly himself. Vusi raised the .45 and shot Danger in the face. The bullet entered his friend's open mouth and smashed through his neck bones on the way out. Danger fell backwards, paralysed but not dead. Blood gurgled from his mouth and his wide eyes begged an answer. Vusi kept the phone to his ear as he aimed at Danger's forehead and fired again. They had known each other since their first day at school, but Vusi's fear of his employer was far greater than his loyalty to his friend.

'Good boy. Don't lose the Professor or I will find you myself,' Wellington said. 'I want him alive, understood?'

'Yes, boss, I understand. I must bring the Mozambican to you alive.'

Vusi ran into the bush, the hot bile rising up the back of his throat, burning him from the inside.

*

The police had cordoned off the crashed *bakkie* and undertakers were loading the three body bags into a white minivan when Kylie and Cameron arrived at the crime scene.

'Do you want to stay in the truck?' Cameron asked as he switched off the Hilux's engine.

'No. I can handle it.'

He nodded. He knew she could. He had thought she would be a cowardly corporate type, too worried about her manicured nails and power suit to go underground, but she had followed him down there and she had seen first hand what the *zama zamas* would do for gold. She had guts. She could still annoy him with her supercilious attitude, but she was growing on him. He had been wrong to underestimate her. She had made it to one rung from the top in the company and he knew Jan's reputation well enough that Kylie's rise was about her, not some gender window-dressing.

A police captain in a blue SAPS uniform waddled over. Cameron recognised him. He had spoken to him in the past about the *zama zamas* and various crimes and the man had always promised to follow up and get back to him, though he never did. They greeted each other and shook hands.

'I'm sorry about the loss of your worker,' the captain said.

'So am I.' Sipho had a wife and three children. This was happening too often.

The captain checked his notebook. 'The woman carried a Mozambican temporary travel document. She was Miriam Correia. Did you know her?'

Cameron shrugged. 'She came to the mine looking for her husband.' It was the truth, but he didn't want to give out any more.

The policeman gestured to the white van. 'There is another body in there. It's a local boy, named Bright Maseka. He's got a record as long as my arm. I take it he wasn't the woman's husband.'

'No,' Cameron said, surprised. The satellite tracking company employees, who were first on the scene, had told him there were three people dead at the truck wreck, a woman and two men. He had assumed one of them would be Luis.

'What was his name?'

'Mr Correia.'

The policeman pursed his full lips. 'If there was someone else in the vehicle with the dead woman and your worker, then he – or she – may be an important witness. Someone killed Bright Maseka, and even if it was in self-defence we need to talk to them. How many people were in the truck when it left the mine?'

Kylie took a step closer to them. 'I'm Dr Kylie Hamilton, from Global Resources. Cameron and I were in a meeting when Sipho left with Mrs Correia. We didn't see him leave the mine so we don't know for sure if there was anyone else in the truck. There could have been.'

Cameron was impressed by her again. She had picked up his vibe about the police officer. 'Is that the hijackers' car?' He pointed to the black Golf.

'We think so. There are some spent bullet casings in it.' A pair of crime scene investigators in disposable overalls was searching the hatchback.

'Do you have a Mr Correia working for you?' the policeman asked.

'No.' Cameron felt a moment of relief. Again, he wasn't lying to the police. He needed to keep steering the conversation away from Luis, and the fact he and Kylie had been harbouring a *zama zama*. 'What do you think was the motive for this – whatever happened here?'

'Simple carjacking and robbery,' the captain said too quickly. 'The Golf was taken from outside a pub a few days ago. The dead man, Maseka, was known to us as a local thug. It was only a matter of time until he tried his hand at carjacking. You may not have seen anyone leave the mine with Mrs Correia, but my sources tell me that a Mozambican illegal immigrant, Luis Correia, was in this car.'

'No one by that name has ever worked at Eureka.'

The cop nodded, both of his chins wobbling, 'Be that as it may, we have now started a search for this man Correia as we need to question him over the shooting of Maseka. My theory is that he shot the car thief, perhaps in self-defence, and is now worried that if we catch him we will lock him up.'

'And will you?'

'Yes. At least until we work out what to do with him, and confirm the circumstances of the shooting. If we don't charge him over the death of Maseka and he is an illegal, we will deport him to Mozambique, but if he's carrying an unregistered firearm he may face charges over that.'

A white *bakkie* approached them from the direction of Nelspruit, the next nearest major city. The driver indicated and pulled up alongside them. A sign on the truck said, *Mpumalanga Dog Squad*. A burly man with a sun-reddened face and arms got out.

'Our priority now is to find this Correia. Is there anything else you want to tell me, Mr McMurtrie?'

'Our first priority, Captain,' Kylie interrupted, 'is to contact the family of our murdered employee.'

'Of course,' said the captain. 'But I will be in touch.'

Cameron and Kylie walked back to his Toyota.

'How can he have known about Luis?' Kylie said as she opened the door and got in.

'Wellington's got eyes and ears everywhere, especially at the mine where half my staff were supplying the *zama zamas*. I wouldn't be surprised if the captain's in his pocket, because I'm pretty sure his boss, Colonel Sindisiwe Radebe, is. That's why the local cops have been so reluctant to do anything about the illegal mining for so long. What worries me now is that if they find Luis he'll be in for much worse than deportation or a slap on the wrist over an illegal firearms charge.'

'Do you think he managed to get hold of a gun somehow between getting out of hospital and to the mine?' she asked.

'No, I didn't,' said a voice behind them.

Cameron and Kylie both looked around, into the rear of the double cab. There, lying on the floor at the bottom of the passenger bench seat, was Luis.

19

Luis Domingues Correia had known tragedy and disappointment all his life, but the death of his wife was threatening to unravel him.

His body shook as he lay curled in the foetal position under a tarpaulin in the back of Cameron McMurtrie's truck. Above the tarpaulin was the black vinyl cover of the Toyota's load area, stretched tight to its tie-down points on the sides. Sweat ran from every pore and he blinked away salty drops that may have been perspiration, or perhaps tears. He doubted, however, that he had any of the latter left in his body.

His father had been an early recruit to Frelimo, the *Frente de Libertacao de Mocambique*, the Front for the Liberation of Mozambique, and had been killed in 1970 during the colonial government's military offensive against the guerilla movement, known as Operation Gordian Knot. Luis had been just six years old at the time and his mother had only just begun to inculcate a true hatred of the colonialists when they disappeared. In 1974, following a revolution in their own country, the Portuguese gave up their colonies, including Mozambique, and Frelimo was handed victory and a country to govern.

But Luis was not to be cheated out of a war. Others outside of Mozambique had an interest in destabilising President Samora Machel's fledgling socialist independent state. White Rhodesia, nearing its death throes, ploughed guns and ammunition and landmines into the Mozambican right-wing opposition, Renamo, fuelling a civil war designed to disrupt Mozambique's ability to provide a safe haven for Robert Mugabe's Zimbabwe African National Union and its national liberation army guerrillas who used Mozambique as a base to launch raids back into their homeland, Rhodesia.

As the son of a revolutionary martyr, Luis was offered the chance to study abroad, in East Germany. The Soviet bloc supported Machel – until he tired of their rapacious demands on his resource-rich country and booted them out in the early 1980s. By then, however, Luis had already earned his Bachelor of Science with majors in Metallurgy and Engineering.

The consensus among those who sent Luis away was that he would return to play a senior role in kickstarting Mozambique's mineral economy. But the war between Frelimo and Renamo continued even after Zimbabwe gained independence in 1980, and Luis found himself not supervising new mining projects but rather carrying an AK-47, hunting Renamo soldiers in the bush of Gorongosa National Park, once the country's flagship game reserve and now an open-air slaughterhouse for man and animal alike.

He had a brother who had been killed in the Rhodesian raid on Mapai and a sister who had lost both her legs beneath the knee to a landmine. She'd lived for six months before dying of infection. His mother had miraculously survived the war.

His son and mother in Inhambane were all that was left of Luis's family. The war had touched everyone, and the darkest days of his time in uniform were coming back to him, here, now. He heard the screams and the bullets again. Perhaps it was seeing Miriam's mutilated body that took him back to that hell again, to the day in 1987 when he had nearly died.

*

The rocket-propelled grenade whooshed over his head, trailing a stream of dirty smoke across the battlefield, and exploded against the wall behind Luis. He screamed as he felt shards of shrapnel and dislodged masonry pepper his back. The jagged metal burned.

The Renamo rebels were advancing. Luis gritted his teeth against the pain and squeezed off the final three rounds from the last magazine he had for his AK-47. One of the enemy fighters fell, but Luis couldn't tell if he had hit the man or if he had dived for cover. He reached under the scorching hot barrel of his rifle, flicked out the folding bayonet and fixed it in place. He had heard of the atrocities committed by the Renamo rebels when they took prisoners. Luis would fight to the death.

He ducked back through the doorway in the wall that had just been hit by the grenade. The building was an old store, built by the Portuguese. It was in ruins now. He stepped over fallen shelves, empty tins of fish, shattered bottles of Dois M beer and a tangle of torn women's clothing. Anything that could be eaten in Mozambique was consumed on the spot or looted.

Luis went to the rear of the store and saw young Joao lying on his back, a bullet hole drilled through his forehead and blood and brains pooled on the tiled floor. Luis crossed himself. He had assumed the worst when he had no longer heard Joao's AK-47 firing, and when his call for more ammunition had gone unanswered. Luis moved to the rear door and, keeping his back pressed to the wall, peeked out. He saw a Renamo man in camouflage darting through the bush.

Luis could surrender and, if he was lucky, be executed on the spot. If God had abandoned him, along with his country, then he might be tortured for information, or for fun. He heard the Renamo men calling to each other. They were readying for an assault on the store. Luis said a quick prayer – although it was against regulations – and charged out the door.

Men shouted as they saw the lone fighter running towards their cordon, his AK out-thrust with its bayonet fixed. Luis yelled a berserker's war cry as gunfire crackled around him. The Renamo men had to turn to draw a bead on him and ran the risk of shooting each other as Luis crashed through the thornbush and vaulted an empty petrol drum. He felt a bullet tug at his sleeve and burn his arm, but he had taken them by surprise.

His lungs were burning as he took fallen palm trees in his stride. He heard the confusion and began to think he might make it to safety.

'Stop!'

A man stepped out from behind a tree and brought his AK to his shoulder, taking aim at Luis. He must have been less keen than his comrades, Luis thought, lagging behind the advance on the store. If he had been a hardened Renamo cadre he would have stayed in cover and shot Luis. His suspicions were confirmed by the way the barrel of the rifle wavered.

Luis screamed again and ran straight for the man. If he shot him, then so be it. It would be better than enduring the torturer's knives. Luis's senses were recording, in detail, every moment of his last seconds on earth. He saw the fear in the man's eyes, watched his finger curl and squeeze. But there was no sound. The man lowered his rifle and worked the cocking handle. It had jammed or misfired. Whatever the case, Luis had been saved. All he needed to do was dispatch this inept fool and carry on his way.

The man fumbled with his rifle and raised it to try to ward off Luis's charge. Luis turned his own AK in his hands and smashed the other man's weapon out of the way with a butt stroke. The younger, smaller man teetered under the force of the blow and Luis pressed home his advantage, bringing the butt of his rifle up into the man's cheek and slamming him backwards. The man sprawled on the ground on his back, arms outflung.

Luis stood over him and twisted his rifle again so that the sharpened point of the bayonet was pointing down at the man's belly. He raised his arms to deliver the killing thrust. The top few buttons of the Renamo man's Rhodesian-supplied camouflage shirt were open and something glittered on his chest. Luis saw the silver crucifix and paused, just before the tip of the blade touched the man's skin.

The man reached up for him with open hands, his rifle lying useless on the ground beside him. 'Mercy,' he said in Portuguese.

Luis blinked. His chest rose and fell and he felt the mist clear from his mind. What had become of his country? What had become of him?

He heard voices behind him. He knew he should kill this man, now, and take his ammunition. But he couldn't do it. He felt tears pricking the backs of his eyes. He stepped away from the prone form and started to run again.

The men tracking him were calling to each other in a mix of Portuguese and Xitswa. They were getting close. There wasn't even time for him to check the terrified soldier's pouches for more magazines. Besides, there were too many of them for him to take a stand against.

He started to run, but had covered no more than twenty metres when he heard another voice yell a command in a different language. Behind him, he heard the metallic snicker of a rifle being cocked, and then a single gunshot. Then his world went black.

*

Luis forced himself back to the present, to try to evaluate what he would do next, where he would go. There were horrors aplenty to confront in the present without the demons of his past resurfacing. He had a clear and present enemy today – Wellington Shumba, the Lion. Wellington had seemed something of a saviour at first, but Luis had soon learned he was an angel of death. And there was no escaping him or his reach.

After running into the bush he had circled back to the crashed *bakkie*. He needed to know what had happened and who had killed his wife and the driver, Sipho. He had hidden in the long grass at the verge of the road and watched as one of the gunmen had spoken on his phone and then used his pistol to shoot his comrade in the head while still talking.

'I understand, boss. I must bring the Mozambican to you alive,' the young *tsotsi* – criminal – had said into his cellphone.

When the killer had headed back up the road, scanning the ground, Luis had known he had limited time to get away. He couldn't run, however, before saying goodbye to Miriam. He had crept to the wreck and found her there. Luis had pressed a knuckle to his mouth and groaned like a dying animal when he saw the blood on her hand where the bastard had cut off her finger. Luis had become desensitised to death and gore decades ago, but the sight of his wife's severed finger lying on the blood-soaked upholstery of the mine truck had been too much for him. He had sunk to his knees, and might have stayed there if it hadn't been for the buzz of the helicopter.

He had pushed himself deep into cover, shivering and shaking with rage and fear despite the heat of the day. The noise of the chopper blades took him back to the war years.

By the time the tremors had subsided the police were at the crash site, responding to the radio call of the privately operated tracking-company helicopter that hovered above the stricken Toyota and its grisly cargo of death.

When he saw the fat policeman and his underlings peering into the truck, Luis decided to give himself up. He could not run any more. He would surrender and tell them everything he knew about Wellington. With luck they would cart him in the back of a police *bakkie* with a dozen or more other illegal immigrants who had chanced their luck in this land of blood and gold and drive him back to the border crossing at Komatipoort. From Ressano Garcia, as the other side of the border was known, he would, perhaps after a beating from the police or army, make his way home to his son.

He had placed his palms on the ground and begun to raise himself up when the young man emerged from the bush and waved to the policeman.

'Don't shoot, *baba*,' the thug called to the policeman, whose hand nonetheless went instinctively to the black Z88 automatic on his belt.

The police captain walked away from the others, grabbing the youth by the collar and taking him into the tree line. They stopped, not five metres from where Luis had lowered himself back into the grass.

The policeman backhanded him in the face, almost knocking him off his feet. 'I just got the call from Wellington. You fucked up.'

The angry young man clenched his fists, though kept them by his side, and spat blood. 'Danger fucked up.'

'Your handiwork?' The captain tossed his head back towards Luis's dead wife and the other two bodies.

'I didn't kill the woman or the driver, *baba*. Like I said, it was Danger who screwed it for us.'

'We need to find the Mozambican,' the policeman said. 'He'll take the blame for killing Danger. We might even frame it as him setting up a hit on his wife.'

The youth nodded, smiling at the policeman's guile, his hands relaxing by his side. '*Yebo*. That's cool. But doesn't the boss want the Mozambican alive? That's what he told me, *baba*.'

The cop chuckled. 'Yes, he does, and we're going to deliver him that way. If the man's wanted for the murder of his wife he won't last long above ground. Wellington will keep him locked up underground like a caged pet forever.'

Luis had started shivering again as he lay in the grass, ants crawling over him. Wellington had the police captain in his pocket and was determined to destroy Luis's life. If it wasn't for his son, the man would have succeeded – Luis would have given up. But the dreadful thought of Wellington coming after Jose washed through his body and turned his insides to water. He clutched at the tufts of grass in front of him to steady himself. He was a fool. He should have accepted his lot in life and stayed underground, and not done anything to assist McMurtrie and Hamilton. He was making reasonable money as a *zama zama* and at least some of it had been getting back to Miriam and Jose. And now she was gone. He could not go on.

No.

He dragged a breath into his lungs. He had seen death, in the war, and he had survived. He would mourn for his wife when he could, but his priority now was Jose. He must be strong for him.

'Go look for the Mozambican, boy,' the captain said, belittling the carjacker. 'And pray you find him before my dog squad arrives and catches him. You might be able to save your skin with the boss if you can deliver the Professor to him. Alive, remember?'

'*Yebo, baba.*'

Luis had lain in the grass while the youth went in search of him. He'd watched the police search the *bakkie*, and the coroner's men lift out the blood-soaked bodies of his wife and the driver, Sipho, and zip them into body bags.

He didn't cry for his dead wife. Instead he let his anger and grief and his hatred of Wellington fuel him. In his mind, he was back in the bush again, during the civil war. He had killed for stupid, outdated ideologies that had delivered his country nothing but poverty, even in victory. But he had killed.

Luis felt the fear and the adrenaline surge that followed it. He looked around him for a weapon. There was none, but that did not matter. The *tsotsi* had taken his orders over the phone, from Wellington. That phone was a link to the man who all but destroyed his life.

Luis edged backwards, away from the police, and went in search of the criminal. The young one had moved quietly and Luis glimpsed the back of his white T-shirt before he heard him. Luis, too, could move as quietly as a leopard through the bush, though it had been many years since he had needed such a skill. He placed each step carefully.

Slowly, he closed in on his prey.

With a knife or a gun he might have simply held him up and taken his phone or scared him into revealing what little he might know about Wellington's whereabouts. But that was not an option. He vaguely recalled this young enforcer delivering a beating on Wellington's orders a year or so ago. A *zama zama* had been caught sleeping during his shift. The man's head had hit a rock when the youth had knocked him to the ground the first time. He had died quickly. It might have been forgivable, as an accident, except Luis had seen how the unfeeling young man had pounded the dead man's skull to a pulp under his work boot, in the hope of winning a smile from Wellington. Luis didn't know if psychopaths were drawn to each other, or if they were nurtured by men such as Wellington.

Luis closed the distance between himself and the *tsotsi* and reached out and wrapped one arm around his neck, squeezing the cry of pain and alarm before it could form. He placed his other hand behind his quarry's neck and pushed his arms against each other. He heard the snap of the enforcer's neck and felt the body go heavy in his grip. He let the dead boy slide to the ground. Luis stood over him for a second, his breath blowing hard through his nose as he fought to keep the rising tide of red rage under control. He dropped to one knee and quickly, efficiently searched the body as if it was just another dead Renamo man. He found the .45 stuffed down the boy's jeans, under his T-shirt, and transferred it to his own belt. In his back pocket was the telephone. Luis pushed a button and the screen lit up. He found the menu and then selected recent calls. The last incoming call was from a cellphone number beginning with +258, the country code for Mozambique.

Luis pocketed the phone and headed back to the road, leaving the boy's body for the police or some wild animals to find.

When Cameron had pulled up in his mine company Toyota the police had been distracted by his arrival. Luis had leopard-crawled through the grass and under Cameron's Hilux. Emerging on the far side, out of sight of the assembled police, he had been able to quietly open the rear door of the double cab and slide inside.

The hum of the highway was softening now, the vehicle slowing. Luis crossed himself, in the baking darkness in the back of the pickup truck, and prayed that the white people who were helping him would hold their nerve.

*

Kylie wasn't used to breaking the law and she was feeling slightly nauseous as Cameron drove through one side of Barberton and out the other, then turned left to climb the narrow dirt road to his home high in the hills. They had already stopped at the Diggers' Retreat on the way back from the crime scene for Kylie to quickly pack up and load her luggage.

He glanced over at her. 'You look a little pale.'

'I'm fine. No, actually, I'm not fine.'

Cameron turned his attention back to the road. 'So do you have a better plan? We know from Luis the local cops are crooked – I could have told him that, but now it looks like they were in on the plan to kill his wife and capture him. He's also our best lead to Wellington. We need to get him in front of someone at the National Prosecuting Authority.'

Kylie exhaled. She didn't know how to function in this country. She was out of her depth, but bubbling underneath her uncertainty was the bitter bile of anger. She, too, wanted this Wellington out of business – permanently – and she knew, deep down, she was willing to do whatever it took. 'You said we were going to take Luis somewhere safe. Not to your home?'

'No. I just need to pick up Jess and some stuff. My wife's parents own a holiday home near the Kruger Park. We can go there. I doubt Wellington or his people would know of my connection to the place; we've only stayed there a couple of times.'

They turned into his driveway and Jessica opened the door and came out to greet them at the sound of the engine.

'Dad, I heard about Sipho.' She wrapped her arms around her father and looked past him at Kylie.

Cameron kissed his daughter on the top of the head. 'Jess, this is Dr Kylie Hamilton, my boss, from Australia.'

'Hi.' Kylie took Jess's hand and was surprised by her firm, confident handshake.

'Nice to meet you, Dr Hamilton.'

'Call me Kylie, please.' The teenagers she knew in Australia, including her nieces and nephews, were uniformly surly, noncommunicative and spoilt.

'Would you like a cup of tea?' Jess asked her.

'Jess,' Cameron interjected, 'we can't stay for tea. I want you to get some clothes and stuff for a couple of nights in the bush. Kylie and I are going to stay at Ouma and Oupa's place at Hippo Rock, and I want you to come with us.' Jess had always referred to Tania's parents, who were Afrikaners, as grandma and grandpa in their mother tongue.

Jessica raised her eyebrows. 'What about school?'

'You can use a couple of days off, after all the drama we've had going on in our lives. Come. It'll be fun. Kylie, if you don't mind, there's a camping mattress rolled up in the garage – you might like to put it in the back of the *bakkie*.'

'What do we need to take the camping gear for, Dad? That house is fully furnished,' Jessica said.

'Never mind, I'll explain later.' He looked back at Kylie, who nodded to him, signalling she understood what he wanted. Cameron bustled Jessica inside.

Kylie opened the tilt door of the garage and saw shelves on the far wall neatly stacked with camping and fishing equipment. She saw three mattresses and took one outside to the *bakkie*. She unhooked the vinyl covering down one side of the truck and peeled it open. Luis blinked up at her. His eyes were red. 'I'm sorry, Luis. I'm not at all sure where we're taking you, but Cameron has a plan. Here, this will make the ride a bit more comfortable.'

She undid the strap around the canvas-covered foam mattress and with Luis's help unrolled it. He shifted and then lay on it, nodding his thanks. He said nothing, just stared up at the sky. Kylie heard Cameron and Jessica talking and partially closed the cover again. Luis made no complaint. Kylie walked across the lawn and met Jessica halfway. Cameron's daughter had a carry bag and Cameron, she saw, had his gun bag again. 'Let me help you with those,' she said to the girl.

'I can manage.'

Kylie heard the defensive note in the reply, but smiled. 'I know you can, but I'm sure you need to lock up the house, right?'

'Oh, OK, sure.' Jessica handed Kylie her bag and she and Cameron went to the truck.

'Couple of hours,' Cameron said to Luis. The Mozambican just nodded again. Cameron unzipped the gun bag so Luis could see the shotgun inside. 'It's loaded.' He laid the bag next to Luis, along with the rest of the luggage. Cameron was securing the last of the stays on the cover when Jess pulled the back door to the house closed and jogged across to them.

They got into the vehicle, with Jessica in the back seat. She took out her cellphone from the pocket of her jeans. 'I'm warming to the idea of a couple of days off school. Wait till I SMS Mandy, she'll be so jealous.'

'Keep her guessing, Jess. I'd rather you didn't tell anyone where we're going. I'll call your school and tell them you're sick.'

'Why all the secrecy, Dad?'

'I'll tell you the full story once we're there, Jess. Now I need to focus on the road.'

They drove down the hill to the main road, back to Barberton and turned left towards Nelspruit. Kylie asked Jessica questions about her school and her life in Barberton, partly to deflect her curiosity about their trip, and partly because she was genuinely interested in the replies. Unlike her taciturn father, Jess seemed bubbly, outgoing and personable. Like her father, she was also smart.

'I'd like to go into mining when I finish university,' Jess said, 'even though Dad doesn't want me to.'

'My father was against it as well, but there are plenty of opportunities for women in mining,' Kylie said.

'I'd really like to hear about how you got to such a senior position. Is your doctorate in engineering? People say it's a man's business, but I'm fascinated by building stuff and how things work.'

Kylie talked about some of the difficulties she'd encountered in the still predominantly male workforce, but told Jess she should follow her dreams regardless of what other people told her, and without worrying about preconceptions. It was nice to talk to another female. Cameron, she noted, was content to stay quiet and concentrate on the road. As well as they were getting on, Jess was going to be in for a shock when they eventually let on who was in the back of the *bakkie* and why.

The drive took them across the N4 at Nelspruit and Kylie recognised the countryside they had passed through on their way to Lion Plains, through the pine and gum plantation-covered hills around White River. 'Is this place we're going to near the Sabi Sand Game Reserve?'

'It's only a few kilometres from it,' Jess answered for her father. 'My grandparents own the house and it's *lekker*. I just wish we'd been to Hippo Rock more often. I guess this'll be the last time, hey Dad?'

Cameron shrugged. 'Your gran might still be happy for you to use it. She hasn't asked for the spare keys back.'

Kylie had heard the sadness dulling the girl's bright mood. She wondered if Cameron's mother-in-law was angry at her daughter for leaving him and Jess. 'What is this place we're going to, anyway?' Kylie asked.

'It's a wildlife estate, on a private nature reserve,' Cameron answered. 'It's an old game farm that was given to the local community during the land redistribution program. Some developers hooked up with the local people and they built holiday homes on it for rich people from Jozi and Cape Town. It's pretty cool – there are zebras and wildebeest and giraffe and stuff on the estate and it borders the Sabie River, so it's technically part of the greater Kruger Park.'

'But there are no dangerous animals around the houses, I'm assuming?' Kylie said.

'No, not really. Just a couple of leopard,' Jess said nonchalantly. 'But there are no fences around the houses, so don't go walking about at night.'

'*Just* a couple of leopard?' The concept sounded weird, yet quite exciting. Kylie couldn't imagine a housing estate in Australia where dangerous animals patrolled the neighbourhood.

They wound their way through hills covered with pine and banana plantations and Cameron stopped at the bustling town of Hazyview to pick up some meat and groceries at the Checkers supermarket. Kylie tagged along behind Jess and her father, who seemed to know where everything was and what was needed for their stay. She left them and wandered outside and leaned against the *bakkie*, ready to load the food in before Jess could look inside. She would learn the truth of what they were doing soon enough. It was insane; they were hiding a fugitive from the law in order to protect him, and themselves possibly, against a crazed killer.

With the supplies packed and Jess none the wiser, they drove another thirty-five kilometres, passing through the town of Mkhulu, which Cameron said had grown in leaps and bounds in the past seventeen years. He slowed and Kylie saw a sign to Hippo Rock Private Nature Reserve on the right.

'A few of these places have sprung up over the past thirty or so years – Marloth Park, Mjejane, Elephant Point, Sabiepark. They're residential or holiday home estates where people come to try and get away from real life for a while.'

Kylie checked the wing mirror again – she'd noticed Cameron doing the same throughout the drive. She was sure no one had followed them. Cameron slowed and turned right.

A security guard in green uniform and canvas and rubber combat boots stepped out of a brick and thatch gatehouse and saluted. Cameron greeted the man and took out a plastic laminated identity card. The guard gave him a clipboard with a registration form on it and Cameron filled it out.

'The security is really tight here,' Jess told Kylie. 'We get an ID card because of my mom.'

From the car, Kylie saw half-a-dozen warthogs down on their knees, rooting around in a green lawn watered by a sprinkler. The bush beyond, however, was dry and brown.

Cameron handed the clipboard back to the guard and they set off again. He took it slow on the narrow dirt road and they passed a series of houses, constructed in the same brick and thatch as the gatehouse, nestled away in the bush.

'Zebra!' Kylie couldn't help but cry out when she glimpsed the black and white through the dull green bushes.

Jessica laughed at her childish excitement. Kylie wished she had her camera, but then remembered Luis lying sweltering in the back of the truck; the man had just lost his wife. She felt guilty that she could be distracted so easily when Luis was suffering so much.

Cameron turned into an even narrower road that twisted down a hill and led to a house that looked as unassuming as the others they'd passed. Cameron let them in via the back door and when he threw open the musty curtains on the far side of the lounge room Kylie was taken aback by the majesty of the view. 'The Sabie River,' he said. 'It means fear.'

Dark waters rushed around smooth granite boulders that shone pink in the afternoon sun. A small chocolate-coloured antelope with white spots and stripes – 'Bushbuck,' Jess informed her – leapt away into a thicket as Jess slid open the doors. Kylie shielded her eyes and saw an elephant ambling down to the river on the other side, which Jess told her was the Kruger National Park. It was paradise, but it was time for them to explain to Jess what they were really doing here.

'Jess, come outside with me, to the *bakkie* again,' Cameron said.

Kylie followed them out, and Cameron gestured to a wooden bench. 'Sit down for a minute, Jess.' His daughter did as he asked and Kylie, on impulse, sat next to her and placed her hand over Jessica's protectively.

'What is it?' the girl asked, looking up at him, though she didn't move her hand.

Cameron moved to the rear of the *bakkie* and started undoing the stays on the cover. 'Jess, there is a man in here, hiding.'

Jess put her free hand over her mouth. Luis sat up.

'Oh my god.'

'It's all right, Jessica,' Kylie said.

Cameron quickly explained who Luis was and how he had just lost his wife in a shooting.

'The one where Sipho was killed?'

'Yes,' Cameron said. 'Jess, I don't want to alarm you, but Luis is important to our investigation into the deaths of Paulo Barrica and Themba Tshabalala. He's crucial to bringing down the criminal miners. I needed to get him away from Barberton, and I didn't want to leave you on your own.'

She nodded. Luis climbed down out of the truck and walked to her. 'How do you do?'

'I'm very well, thank you.' Jess left Kylie and took his hand. 'I am sorry for your loss.'

'Thank you.'

Kylie was amazed that Jess seemed to take all this in her stride, but then she guessed growing up in Africa was different to growing up in Australia. In her country people didn't get shot underground, or murdered for their cars. Nor did they live in housing estates with resident leopards.

They went inside and Cameron showed Luis and Kylie to their rooms. Kylie protested that he didn't need to give her the master bedroom, but when Jess walked down the corridor, past the smaller of two spare bedrooms that had been assigned to Luis, he said, 'I'll sleep in the room with the two singles, with Jess. I want to keep an eye on her until this thing is sorted.'

'I understand,' Kylie said.

Each of the bedrooms and the living room looked out over the river. Kylie slid open a glass door to get some fresh air into the musty master bedroom. When she stepped out onto the timber deck she heard a deep honking. Leaning out over the railing, she traced the sound and saw a pair of pink and grey ears wiggling and an exhalation of air and droplets before the massive head disappeared. A hippopotamus. She turned at the sound of footsteps on the stone floor behind her.

'He's just checking us out.' Cameron walked out onto the verandah, which ran along the whole front of the house, and stood beside her.

'It's lovely here,' she said. 'It's just so sad we have to be here in such terrible circumstances.'

'I know. And we've still got work to do.'

'We can go over the review of operations in Zambia here, this afternoon. Maybe we don't need to fly up there.'

Cameron shook his head. 'No, you have to go to Zambia. The new mine up there is a crucial part of the company's growth strategy and, well, don't take this the wrong way, but . . .'

'Go on.'

'You need to assess the situation up there in person. You've seen for yourself that conditions here on the ground in South Africa are different to how you imagined them in Australia, yes?'

She didn't like being admonished but she had to admit he had a point.

'And you can't let this bastard Wellington bring the company to a halt. He's shut down Eureka but he can't stop the whole show.'

'You're right,' she said.

'Tomorrow I'll try and find someone in Pretoria we can hand Luis over to, but we have to give the guy at least a little time to grieve for his wife. Also, I have to sort out the transfer of her remains back to Mozambique and go and see Sipho's family.'

It seemed to her as if saying the words made the weight of his commitments finally register. Cameron put his hands on the balcony railing and she saw his body sag. He looked out over the river. 'I can't let him win.'

She put a hand on his shoulder. 'I know. He won't.'

He looked at her and she saw the hardness in those sad eyes. She moved her hand, but he kept staring at her. Kylie swallowed. Her heart was beating faster. Despite the absurdity of all that had gone on since she'd arrived in South Africa, and before that with the deaths of Tshabalala and Barrica, she wouldn't have wanted to be anywhere else than right here, right now, on the banks of a river called fear. In Australia her idea of confrontation was boardroom jousting by video conference. Here it was like being in a war zone: terrifying, electrifying, seat-of-the-pants stuff, with all its attendant tragedy. Cameron had tried to make decisions on mine security like a commander on a battlefield, while she and Jan had been over-laying first-world health, safety and environment rules or, at best, acting like armchair generals totally distanced from the frontline.

'Let's go for a walk,' he said at last.

'OK,' she breathed.

Jess was in the lounge room reading a book, legs and feet curled under her in an overstuffed beige two-seater lounge whose dust cover was lying on the floor. 'Come, my girl, we're going for a walk.'

She looked up from the book. 'Dad, you know exams are on soon. I *have* to study.' She glanced at Kylie, then looked away.

Cameron looked as though he was debating overruling her, and was probably torn between his desire to cosset Jess and his relief that he had a seventeen-year-old who actually wanted to study. Also, Kylie guessed he didn't want to frighten her. 'All right. Luis is in his room, lying down. Call me if anyone – and I mean anyone – comes near the house. Don't open the door to anyone.'

'OK, Dad. Enjoy the walk. Kylie, mind the buffalo.'

'Haha.'

'She's serious, but let's go.'

Cameron took a carved wooden walking stick from an earthen-ware pot by the back door and Kylie followed suit. 'Will these protect me from the buffalo?'

Cameron laughed. 'No. Snakes, maybe, but if we come across an angry buffalo just climb the nearest tree.'

'You're joking, right?'

'I never joke about buffalos.'

'I might stay and study, too.'

'Come.'

She followed him out the door, sticking close. The African bush wasn't too different to some of the vegetation she had seen in northern Australia, but as Cameron led her onto the narrow path that followed the riverbank, she was acutely aware that there were many things out here that could kill her.

Cameron stopped and as he knelt down his shirt rode up a little and she could see the pistol tucked in the waistband of his jeans. It was a reminder that not all the danger around them moved on four legs. 'Leopard. See the pug marks?'

She bent forward and saw the faint indentation on the ground. 'Do they get lion here in Hippo Rock?'

'Not often, but they've been known to cross from the Kruger Park on the other side of the river. There's a low electric fence meant to deter the buffalo, hippo and elephant, but anything that can jump can get in here. We've also got a communal picnic site on the other side of the fence, on the banks of the river. That's the place to watch out for the buffalo and any other nasties that might have crossed.'

'It's all so deadly, but beautiful at the same time.'

'I know plenty of *okes* who have moved to Australia, but I could never leave all this – the bush.'

'I'm beginning to understand how you feel,' Kylie said.

As they walked, Cameron pointed out trees and their uses in traditional life and medicine, such as a giant leadwood whose ash could be used as a tooth-cleaning powder, and the gwarrie bush, whose chewed twig ends made a bush toothbrush. He showed her a paradise flycatcher, a beautiful bird with a blue head and orange body, and she learned the mournful cry that echoed along the river was that of the African fish eagle. One of the snowy-hooded eagles showed itself, diving out of a tree in front of them to swoop down and pluck a squirming barbel, a catfish, from a pool isolated from the main river in the course of the dry winter.

'As the river drops, more stuff will begin crossing over here. Hippo Rock's vegetation isn't as overgrazed as in the park, and it's too tempting for elephants to refuse in the dry season.'

She wondered what it might be like to live in a place where elephant, lion and leopard were your neighbours. The demarcated walking trail they were following took them away from the river for a while, around the outer edge of the estate. A herd of semi-tame zebra were grazing around another Hippo Rock house, two of the gorgeous animals escaping the afternoon sun under the home's carport. For the first time in her working life she felt guilty that her company, Global Resources, was going to destroy a small part of the natural environment. Jan was from this area; why had he made the decision to mine in a piece of pristine African bush? She knew it was all about economics and supply and demand, but did he feel nothing for this place?

'You look concerned,' Cameron said.

'It's nothing.'

'You're going all the way to the top, Kylie. Everyone in the company knows it. You'll have to make plenty of tough decisions, unpopular decisions, in the name of business.'

She sighed. She had never questioned herself or Global Resources before. This continent had shaken her. 'I want the best for the company, and for the local community that will benefit from the mine, but . . .' She trailed off.

'Maybe this land shouldn't belong to anyone,' said Cameron. 'Not the whites who took it or the blacks who now want a turn at making money out of it. But that's not for us to say. You'll see when we get to Zambia; the government there is allowing exploration *inside* national parks because they need the money and they need the jobs. You understand our business – we dig stuff out of the ground. It's messy but it's essential.'

'I know.'

When they got back to the house Cameron started a fire in the *boma*, which he said was a term for the fire pit encircled most of the way around by a waist-high brick wall. They sat on benches made from old railway sleepers, the four of them all lost in their own thoughts as Cameron *braaied* lamb chops and *boerewors*, the thick 'farmer's sausage'.

Luis was keeping to himself and Kylie knew Cameron was deliberately not pushing him. After eating dinner inside, the adults returned to the fire while Jess showered. 'I will stay awake tonight,' Luis said at last.

'No,' Cameron said. 'You've had a harrowing day. I'll take first shift and you will sleep. I'll wake you when I get tired.'

Luis nodded, excused himself and went to his bedroom. 'You're making me nervous again,' Kylie said, looking around her into the darkness beyond the ring of flickering firelight.

'We're fine. It's just a precaution. We're safe here.'

*

'Kylie, I have to go. Please keep an eye on Jess while I'm gone.'

Kylie had stayed up with him the night before, until past midnight, and they had talked about their families and their lives, though not about Cameron's wife. She had tried to raise the subject, asking him if he had heard from her, but he'd told her that he didn't want to talk about it. She had backed off – it really was none of her business – but it had been nice to talk to him in a non-adversarial way for a change, and not about business.

She didn't want him to leave them. It wasn't that she was scared. It was more than that. 'I know you have to go out, but yesterday you told me you didn't want to let Jess out of your sight.'

'I have to drive back to Barberton to visit Sipho's family, and there are arrangements to make for Miriam's body to be sent back to Mozambique,' he reiterated.

Kylie almost said, 'Coetzee can look after all that', but she bit back the words. Cameron was no longer the mine manager, but she knew, as he did, that right now his promotion was in name only. The workers at the mine would expect him to be there, and from the little she had seen of Coetzee in action she now knew that Cameron would do a better job of this terrible business. Looking into his sad eyes she felt guilty that she had so quickly agreed with Jan that Cameron should be moved. She couldn't tell Cameron but she knew Jan's decision *was* in part because his wife had left him for another man. Jan had said Cameron's staff – the males in particular – would not respect a cuckold, but Kylie had thought that was bullshit. Jan had also been critical of the spread

233

of illegal mining underground but Kylie now knew, first hand, that sometimes the only way to fight the *zama zamas* was on their own terms, with guns and explosives.

She had been wrong. About Cameron. About a lot of things.

What disturbed her, however, was that Cameron was choosing to do his moral duty at the mine rather than staying to protect his daughter. No, she corrected herself. What disturbed her, she realised, was that she would have done the exact same thing. He put a hand on her shoulder and she didn't flinch.

'If I move now I can be back by nightfall. I've given Luis the shotgun, and my pistol is in my bag. The house has an alarm that's linked to the estate gate and security office; there's a panic button on the alarm fob on the key ring. But believe me, you'll all be safe. No one knows we're here. It's just a precaution.'

Kylie nodded. She and Jessica walked outside into the morning light and waved goodbye to Cameron. It was weird being alone with Jess, and Luis who said very little. They washed up after breakfast and Luis retreated to his room. Kylie made herself a coffee and a tea for Jess and they went out onto the deck. The Sabie River sparkled in front of them and Jess pointed out an elephant grazing in reeds on the far side.

'What do you think about your father moving to a new job in Johannesburg?' Kylie asked.

Jess shrugged her shoulders. 'He wants to stay in Barberton. The mine means everything to him.'

Kylie sipped her coffee. 'Is that a problem?'

Jess looked into her cup for a couple of seconds. 'My mom hated it there. I still don't know why she left, but maybe if we'd been in Joburg she would have been happier. But maybe not. I want what's best for Dad, so if this promotion takes him away from Barberton, then maybe he can start over.'

'What about you?'

She looked out at the elephant and then at Kylie. 'I hate Johannesburg. All my friends are in Barberton and I love coming to this place. But now my mom . . . I'd rather not talk about it.'

Jess got up and walked inside, leaving Kylie feeling like she'd overstepped an invisible line.

*

Cameron called at five. 'Kylie, I'm sorry, but it's been hectic here. Sipho's wife was distraught; I spent two hours with her, and the NUM – the National Union of Miners – rep wanted a meeting. I'm at Nelspruit now at the Mozambican consulate trying to sort out the paperwork for the repatriation of Miriam's body.'

The upshot was that Cameron would not make it back to Hippo Rock until eight o'clock at the earliest. Although the days in the lowveld were sunny and warm, the temperature dropped quickly with the passage of the sun, which set at half past five.

Inside, Jess took charge of the household and Kylie felt a bit redundant as the teenager asked Luis to light a fire in the fireplace and then started preparing a chicken curry. 'There'll be enough to reheat for Dad when he comes home.'

Kylie felt like a drink, but knew she should keep her wits about her. They were safe, she told herself, and no one in South Africa knew where they were. Luis went about the business of laying the fire in silence. He stayed kneeling by the fireplace, staring into the flames as the wood caught. Kylie felt terrible about what had happened to him, especially after he had saved their lives. She moved across the stone floor and placed a hand on his shoulder.

When he finally turned his face to her she saw the red-rimmed eyes. He stood and excused himself. He walked down the corridor to his room and Kylie heard the metallic snicker of the shotgun. While Jess's curry was adding warmth to the house and clearing some of the mustiness, Kylie went to the open door of Luis's room. He had removed all of the shotgun shells and was now in the process of replacing them, checking and familiarising himself with the weapon's workings. He seemed to take some measure of solace in the methodical work, so she left him.

In Cameron and Jess's room she saw Cameron's bag. He had quickly changed shirts before leaving and his dirty one was lying on his bed. On impulse she picked it up.

'What are you doing?'

Startled, Kylie turned to see Jess standing in the doorway, wooden spoon in hand. 'Um, your dad asked me to get something from his bag. I just had to fight my way through his dirty laundry.'

The girl strode across the room and took the shirt from her, folding it and laying it on a chest of drawers. 'I can take care of him, you know.'

'I'm sure you can.'

Jess's lower lip trembled. 'I don't hate you, you know.'

'I'm pleased,' Kylie said, although she tried to tell herself it didn't matter what the girl thought of her.

'It's not like I don't want him to see other women. I wish he would. And if we have to move to Jozi, then we'll make the best of it. It's just that . . . I . . . I hate her.'

Kylie opened her arms and the girl fell against her, sobbing into her breast. At first she didn't know whether to hug her or not, but she enclosed Jess in an embrace and it felt OK. She did not consider herself an emotional person, and had never had an interest in having children of her own, but somehow this felt right, and she wanted to absorb some of Cameron's daughter's pain.

There was a cough behind them. Kylie looked over her shoulder and saw Luis, with the shotgun.

'I will stay outside, until Mr McMurtrie comes back.'

'No, it's too cold, stay inside and have dinner with us,' Kylie said.

'Thank you, but no. Perhaps when he returns.'

Jess eased herself away from Kylie and wiped her nose and eyes with the back of her hand. 'Here.' She unzipped Cameron's bag and pulled out a nylon rain jacket with a fleecy lining. 'This will help keep you warm.'

Luis took the jacket, nodded his thanks and left them.

*

Luis could not explain to the woman and the girl why he felt uneasy. It had not been like this last night. McMurtrie was correct: he had been through hell yesterday and he was exhausted to the point of passing out. It was the mix of adrenaline, anguish, sorrow and hatred. It had left him feeling limp, and if it hadn't been for Jose he would have taken McMurtrie's gun and joined his beloved Miriam.

He had slept and been annoyed to wake the next morning and find that Cameron had not roused him for his shift. But then he had not felt like this last night.

Perhaps it was being back in the bush that had resurrected the dormant instincts that years of warfare in his homeland had honed. He could not shake the feeling he'd had all afternoon, that there was danger out there, far more deadly than any reptile or animal.

Luis patrolled the bush around the house silently. The moon was full, so he had no need of a torch. The gurgling waters of the Sabie glittered with the reflected white light. It was a poacher's moon, a killer's moon. The lights in the house went out, one by one. Luis checked his digital watch; it was just after eleven.

Although he knew that McMurtrie was probably right in thinking that Wellington could not know where they were, he also knew it was foolish to underestimate the Lion's connections and persistence. Besides, he wanted the man to come to them. He wanted to see the bald-headed Zimbabwean kneeling before him, praying for mercy, and to stare into the killer's eyes as he pulled the trigger on the shotgun. He had never taken joy in killing during the war, but he wanted that force of evil obliterated from the face and the bowels of the earth.

*

Wellington had driven through the afternoon from Maputo, crossing into South Africa at Komatipoort. From the Nelspruit bypass he turned north onto the R40 and headed through White River and Hazyview.

He didn't know the area well as this was a road for tourists bound for the Kruger National Park. Once through Mkhulu he could see from his GPS that the turn-off to Hippo Rock Private Nature Reserve would be in ten kilometres. He checked his speed and stayed a few kilometres below the limit. He didn't want to be pulled over by some bribe-seeking traffic policeman.

As he closed on the estate he noticed the high electrified fence. He knew from his research online that this was a veterinary control fence – not impregnable, but definitely live and possibly alarmed. The estate's outer perimeter was that of the national park, he had read, and the estate itself was separated from the Kruger Park by only a low fence. He cruised past the entrance gate and saw the lights were on inside and the boom gates were down. A security man in a green uniform stood by the boom. Wellington carried on down the road and passed another stretch of bushland that had been earmarked, according to the realtor's billboards out front, for yet another wildlife housing estate. He had spent time among lion, buffalo and elephant when he had crossed from his training base in Mozambique into Zimbabwe during the liberation war and could not imagine what type of madness would possess people with money to want to live among such creatures when they didn't have to.

On Google Earth he had seen the place that was now on his right, the former Lisbon Estate citrus farm. This sprawling farm, he had read, had been handed over to the local community as part of a land claim several years earlier, but the once profitable farm had been allowed to fall into ruin. He passed rows of dead fruit trees, the lines between them choked with long dry grass. The fence, which once would have been electrified to keep out baboons, monkeys and human intruders, was now just a tangle of rusting strands of wire. There was a caravan parked in the entrance road and the farm buildings he could see looked to have been burned and destroyed. It reminded him of his own country, Zimbabwe, where so much had been given away to so few, mostly to be pillaged and squandered. The abandoned farm was perfect for his needs.

There was plenty of traffic coming his way and as the sun had just set he guessed this was tourists and staff leaving the Kruger Park for the day. He carried on past the farm and a turn-off to the Sabi Sand Game Reserve on his left. When he saw the bridge across the Sabie River leading to the national park, he made a U-turn and retraced his route.

Opposite the sprawling, defunct citrus farm he saw a track leading through some sparse bushland towards what looked like a small holding. He pulled in there, and drove his Audi off the dirt road and into a stand of long grass. Satisfied the car was not visible from the main road, Wellington got out and opened the boot. He lifted the rubber mat and then hefted the spare wheel from out of its well. Below it was a canvas bag and inside that was a pair of binoculars and a disassembled AK-47. With practised ease he fitted the weapon's parts together. When he was done he attached a magazine, cocked the rifle and, after checking for traffic, crossed the road. The tangled, rusted remains of the fence were no barrier to him at all, and he stepped easily through the twisted wire strands.

Dressed in black jeans and a tight-fitting matching skivvy he was invisible as he moved down the rows of dead fruit trees, following the lines downhill towards the Sabie River. Something slithered away from his advance, but he paid it no mind. Every ten or twenty metres he stopped briefly and listened, but despite the possible presence of leopard he knew he had nothing to really worry about until he crossed into the national park.

McMurtrie's wife's family's house, he knew, was on the Sabie River and this was the estate's weakest security front. The fence around the rest of Hippo Rock was well maintained, but the fence in front of the houses along the river was by design low enough for animals, notably predators, to come and go. He smiled to himself. He had been wrong to send his young lions to bring back Luis. It was a job for an apex predator, and he was the top of his subterranean food chain. But by now the Mozambican would have talked too much and McMurtrie no doubt planned on using him to bring down the *zama zama* network once and for all. Wellington was not going to let that happen. He would make sure Luis was dead before anyone from the Hawks, the elite police unit, got to him.

Wellington heard the flowing waters of the river and moved cautiously to the lower end of the abandoned farm. There, at the high watermark of the Sabie, was the Kruger National Park boundary fence. This farm, he reasoned, would be a popular access point for poachers, so he began walking the electrified barrier. Just when he was about to start thinking of an alternate plan he found what he was looking for. A natural drainage line running between rows of trees passed under the fence. Rocks had been piled under the strands to try to plug the gap the fast-flowing water must have created during the last rainy season. Fresh dirt scrapings told him something, perhaps a warthog or hyena, or even a poacher, had been digging away under here to enlarge the crawl space. Wellington climbed down into the creek line, pushed his AK-47 and binoculars through the gap, then got down on his belly and wriggled under the fence, being careful not to touch the live strand of wire just above his back. When he was through he retrieved his equipment and started moving westwards, along the rest of the edge of Lisbon farm, towards Hippo Rock estate, further upstream on the river.

The previous two summer floods had thinned out the bush and Wellington was able to make good progress. The river was flowing, but had obviously dropped considerably with the passage of the dry winter. He walked cautiously through a thicket of reeds, always mindful of the buffalo that he knew would like to lurk here. The river on his left narrowed considerably where it passed through a natural weir made by a line of granite boulders. He decided to cross and to approach the estate from the far side of the Sabie. He would be deeper into the national park, and while this would increase his risk of an encounter with a dangerous animal, it would lessen the chance of his being spotted from one of the riverfront houses.

When he crossed he found himself not on the far bank, but on a long island. He decided to stay on this and soon came abreast of houses lit by lamplight and electricity. This was the place where rich South Africans and foreigners came to rough it, in luxury that would have been unknown to him if he had never thrown his lot in with the pirates. Wellington had seen a picture of the house McMurtrie was in. The reeds and almost luminous lime green fever trees on the river island afforded him plenty of cover despite the moon's brightness, and he was able to take his time, moving abreast of the bush mansions and studying them through his binoculars. Ten houses along he was sure he had found it. He focused his glasses on a rectangle of light and made out a woman. It was Dr Kylie Hamilton. His pulse rate increased and he surrendered to the thrill. The images of her he had fantasised about as the Mozambican prostitute had done her work came back to him.

The Australian woman left her room and he scanned further along the house until he settled on the lounge. There was another female there, younger, and the pair of them came out onto the front deck, overlooking the river, where their white skin was illuminated with the golden glow of a paraffin lamp. Wellington licked his lips. It was McMurtrie's daughter.

He forced his mind back to business. His priority target was Luis, who had to be killed. There would be security on the estate and it might not be possible to take out the Mozambican quietly. Still, he toyed with the possibilities the women presented him, but it was time to focus on business, not pleasure. McMurtrie was gone from the mine and his company was spiralling into a crisis from which it might never recover. The mine was closed to legal workers and its future was uncertain. Wellington had, to all intents and purposes, won. He could afford to be magnanimous to his vanquished foe. He would, he decided, spare the women, as long as they weren't witnesses to his killing of Correia, of course. All he needed was to ensure that Luis Domingues Correia did not rat him out to the National Prosecuting Authority or the Hawks.

Wellington watched the house for another twenty minutes, until all the lights went off. Correia, he decided, was either already sleeping in the darkened bedroom he had identified or, more likely, he was out on patrol or in a covert observation post. He slung his binoculars around his arm and over his back to keep them out of his way, checked the safety catch on his AK was set to semiautomatic, and moved down the sandy bank to the edge of the river.

*

Luis tightened his hand on the shotgun's stock and curled his finger around the trigger. He watched the figure in black wading through the glittering, swirling waters. The river was narrow and fast flowing, minimising the chance of a crocodile taking him, but Luis was amazed nonetheless by the lengths Wellington was going to in order to kill him.

His heart pounded with a mix of fear and excitement as he manoeuvred himself behind a stout leadwood; not even the AK's rounds would penetrate this tree. He laid his ambush, overlooking the hippo trail through the reeds that Wellington was heading for. If McMurtrie had left him a rifle instead of a shotgun, he would have killed the Zimbabwean already, but the range was too great to ensure a kill with the shotgun. No matter, close up would be fine. Better.

Wellington had dropped into a dip in the riverbed, out of sight, and Luis switched his eyes from the game trail, where he was sure his quarry would soon appear, to the reeds either side, alert for the swaying tops that would give away Wellington's progress as he moved through them.

He licked his lips. He could see nothing. Behind him he heard a vehicle engine, racing and straining through the gears. There were voices coming from within the estate. He looked over his shoulder and saw lights flickering through the trees.

'Luis, Luis! Are you there?' a woman's voice hissed.

Curse it, Luis thought. It was Kylie and he could make out her silhouette on the deck up the bank and behind him.

'Luis, Wellington's coming. I saw him cross the river.'

He wanted to tell her to get inside, but to speak would be to give away his position. Wellington had not come the way he expected. He realised, too late, that he had underestimated the Lion, who had also fought and lived through a war of liberation. He had expected Wellington to take the obvious path.

Headlights played across the river briefly from behind him and Luis heard voices calling. Kylie stepped back into the house and rushed to meet the men. Luis said a quick, silent prayer and stepped out from behind the leadwood. He raised the shotgun to his shoulder and rushed forward, into the reeds.

*

Wellington had backtracked, knowing it would only be a matter of time before Luis broke cover and exposed himself. What he hadn't counted on, though, was the estate's security vehicle charging through the night to the house and armed men jumping from the back of the *bakkie*.

He would have only one chance. He had circled the reed bed until he was hiding right below where the woman was hissing her warning to Luis. He brought the AK-47 to bear. Luis passed behind a tree, but Wellington trained his rifle on the spot where he would emerge at any second.

'Stop!' a voice called.

Luis froze.

'Shit,' Wellington whispered.

'Drop your weapon.'

A torch beam played on the Mozambican as he took a step further. He scanned the darkened bush around him, reluctant to give in.

'I'm with the women in the house. I am not the man you are looking for.'

Luis was almost in view. Wellington could get a bead on him if he moved just a little. He stepped out from beneath the overhanging wooden deck. Yes. He had Luis in his sights. As he took up the pressure on the trigger the night exploded with a gunshot and Luis fell to the ground, but it wasn't Wellington who had fired. Instead, the Lion ran into the reeds. There was furious shouting and bullets zinged around him, scything the reeds. He ducked behind a granite boulder, flattening himself against it to catch his breath, then switched his assault rifle to automatic, peeked around the rock, and sprayed the deck with a long burst of ten rounds.

*

Kylie ran back through the house and out onto the drive and met the uniformed estate security men as two of them were dragging a protesting Luis, his head a mess of blood, to their truck. 'No, no! He's with us. He's telling the truth; the real killer is out there, in the reeds.'

The last twenty minutes had felt like a bad dream. Unable to sleep, Kylie had eventually sat up in bed, hugging her drawn-up knees and looking out of her darkened room across the Sabie River. In the moonlight, she'd seen a shadow in the river, so she'd moved to the glass window and, to her horror, seen a man with a rifle wading through the water. Wellington. She'd immediately pressed the panic button on the key ring Cameron had left, and had woken Jess and spirited her out the back of the house and told her to wait in the walled enclosure where the washing was hung to dry. She'd crept back to the deck, taking Cameron's pistol with her, and tried to warn Luis, but he had not answered her.

Getting no response from Luis, and wanting to stay out of sight of Wellington, she had flattened herself onto the deck, in a dark corner, and had kept one eye trained on the river to track his approach. She'd lost him though; he must have moved into the shadows.

As she lay there, trying to keep her breathing quiet, she had become aware of soft movements below her. Peering through the gaps in the planks she was sure she would see a hyena or some other creature snooping about. It wasn't until he stepped into the open that she realised it was Wellington, who had somehow left the reeds and made his way up underneath the house.

He hadn't seen her yet, he was looking into the bushes. Without breathing, she silently stood up and hid herself in the corner against a wall. She quickly weighed up her options and was about to yell a warning to Luis, who was somewhere out there in the bush in the dark, when the security men shone a light onto Luis, illuminating his hiding place, and moved in to arrest him.

She glanced around to see Wellington starting to slip away into the darkness. It was down to her now. She couldn't let him get away. She pointed the gun down at Wellington and pulled the trigger. Her shot missed and he moved further into the bushland. Kylie had fired four or five more shots at the fleeing intruder, but he had gone. Lights had started coming on in other houses.

Chaos had followed – the security men had begun yelling at each other, and into their radios as they'd got a hold of Luis and moved him out of the bush and around the deck towards the front of the house. She'd intercepted them after taking the short route through the lounge room and then rushed towards them to tell them of their mistake.

Once they'd heard her explanation, they mobilised themselves and detailed one of the men to drive her, Jess and Luis to the estate's main gate. While Kylie went to get Jess, Luis's head was being wrapped in a makeshift bandage using a sweater. Two security men headed back to the deck to continue the search for Wellington.

On the way to the gate, in the back seat of the security double-cab *bakkie*, Kylie dialled Cameron's number. Jess was shivering beside her in her pyjamas. Kylie wrapped her arms around the girl and held her tight. 'Hi. It's me. Wellington found us. The security guys have chased him off, but he's still alive.'

'Is Jess all right? Are you OK? Luis?'

'We're all fine. The security guys roughed up Luis at bit; they didn't know he was with us.'

'Shit. How did Wellington find out you were there?' Cameron asked. By the sound of the background noise he was driving.

'I don't know. Where are you?'

'I'm on my way. I just left Nelspruit. I'll be an hour and a half. Stay with Frankie, the head ranger at the estate. He's a good *oke*.'

'Cameron, be careful.'

'Just look after yourself and Jess. I'm coming.'

She hugged Jess to her. On her other side Luis held a blood-covered hand to his scalp and stared out the window into the night.

At the gate they were met by a young man with fair hair who introduced himself as Frankie le Roux. 'I've just had a call from Cameron. I'll take care of you,' Frankie said. 'You can wait in my house for him. My wife, Sunelle, will get you some tea or a cool drink if you like. I'm busy right now talking to national parks on the radio. As this man who came to your place is armed and inside the Kruger Park, they are sending up their helicopter to look for him. There is also an army patrol nearby in the park, on anti-rhino poaching duty, so they're going to get him, I'm sure.'

'Thank you, I hope so. I really hope so.'

20

Wellington splashed through the waters of the Sabie River, too charged with adrenaline to even care about crocodiles and hippos. He had watched, enraged, as Luis had been clubbed down by a stupid security man and then dragged away. A split second later and he would have been able to kill him and then make good his escape.

He had looked up, as he ran, and seen the woman, Kylie Hamilton, firing at him. She had clearly seen him. If he made it out of this predicament she would die. Spotlights swept the river but he was already in the tree line on the national park's side. He was running, thornbushes and vines snatching at him.

Wellington paused to catch his breath and thought about where he was going. The quickest way back to his car was through the fence of the abandoned citrus farm, the way he had come, but the ease with which he had been able to use this ingress point told him that it would be known to the authorities as a route used by poachers.

He could move further into the park, hopefully confusing the people who would be mobilising to find him, or he could try to shoot his way out through the farm and the cordon that would soon be put in place.

A far-off noise made him look up. The buzzing was getting louder. He saw the light switch on from above and the looming presence of the helicopter forced his hand. He took out his cellphone and dialled the number he had memorised.

*

Two police cars raced past Cameron, blue lights flashing. At first he feared they were coming after him, as he was clearly speeding.

He had been pushing a hundred and forty through the hilly, sweeping bends between White River and Hazyview, so the cops must have been doing another twenty on top of that, easy. Hopefully they were heading for the same place as him. He pushed down his accelerator and did his best to keep pace with the patrol cars.

As they tore through Mkhulu township, lights on bright and Cameron hoping a stray cow didn't amble out in front of their high-speed convoy, an unmarked BMW, also sporting a blue light on the dashboard, loomed behind him, flashed him, then overtook him.

The police cars sped past the entrance to Hippo Rock estate and as much as Cameron wanted to be in the thick of the hunt for Wellington Shumba, he pulled into the entrance: his daughter was his number one priority. He showed his ID card at the gate and was ushered through to Frankie le Roux's house. The ranger and Kylie emerged from the house, and Jess ran around them to hug her father.

Frankie's radio hissed and he walked a few paces away, speaking in Afrikaans into the walkie-talkie.

'They've got him?' Cameron asked, still holding Jess.

Frankie nodded. '*Ja,* almost. He's on the run through the Lisbon estate. The park's helicopter's tracking him. He's running straight into our cordon and the cops have just arrived. Perfect timing.'

'So it seems.'

'Cameron, can I have a word?'

Cameron eased himself from Jess's embrace and she went to Kylie, who, Cameron noted, put an arm around her. The two men walked a short distance from the house to where Frankie's *bakkie* was parked. 'Who was the man staying with Dr Hamilton and Jess in your mother-in-law's house?'

'Just a labourer I picked up to do some work around the house,' Cameron said.

'You know we have people on the estate who can do that sort of work.'

'*Ja*, and your rates are too bloody expensive.'

Frankie didn't laugh at the attempted levity in Cameron's words. 'You know that's not true. Why did the gate entrance register show only yourself and the two women?'

'He was asleep in the back of my *bakkie*.'

Frankie shook his head. 'I'm not buying it, Cameron. We don't need this kind of *kak* on the estate. We pride ourselves on our safety and security record and you've got a "labourer" armed with a shotgun out in the bush taking on another *tsotsi* with an AK. Are you going to be straight with me?'

Cameron could see the bind he had placed Frankie in. 'Look, all I can say is that it's important we protect the man I brought into the estate. I thought we'd be safe here. He's going to be the star witness in a case that will put that man your guys are hopefully about to catch behind bars for the rest of his life. He's stolen and killed for years.'

'Well, you can hand him over to the police now. I'm going to see them. Are you coming with?'

Cameron looked at Kylie and Jess. 'I'll take care of Jess if you want to go,' Kylie said. She had probably overheard all they had said. 'We'll all sleep better if we know Wellington's in custody.'

The two men got into the *bakkie* with the Hippo Rock logo on the side. Frankie had a shotgun with extra shells in loops on the green canvas sling. Cameron was unarmed, which was probably a good thing because if he came within range of Wellington he would be seriously tempted to put a bullet in his head.

A few kilometres along the main road, the R536, Frankie turned right between the crumbling white stone gates of Lisbon estate.

Frankie's head of security flagged them down and they got out of the vehicle. Overhead a helicopter was circling, its spotlight playing down. They walked until they could see between two rows of dead trees and saw Wellington Shumba, the lion of the underground, walking, arms out, his rifle dangling by its sling. This time Wellington was the prey, not the hunter. Blue lights strobed and two police officers, guns drawn, ran to the Zimbabwean, grabbed his rifle and put him on the ground, face down.

'There's your man,' Frankie said over the whine of the helicopter's engine. Its work done, the aircraft's pilot doused his light and turned back to Skukuza. In the relative quiet that descended Frankie and Cameron moved forward.

More policemen covered Wellington, who was hauled to his feet, his hands manacled behind him now. They led him to a patrol car. Cameron saw the black BMW that had raced past him. Its driver's side door opened and a figure emerged.

'The guys who just cuffed him are local, but I don't recognise her,' Frankie said, noticing the woman getting out of the car.

'Colonel Sindisiwe Radebe, Barberton's police commander. Shit.'

'What's wrong with her? Crooked?'

'You remember the police commissioner who was put in prison for corruption?' Cameron asked, watching the colonel walk to where the other officers were holding Wellington.

'Who doesn't?'

'Sindisiwe used to be his aide. She learned from the best. The Hawks investigated her, but she squeaked through. She's not honest, but she is smarter than her old boss.'

'I'm taking custody of this man,' Colonel Radebe said to the officers who had put the cuffs on Wellington. 'I have a warrant for his arrest.'

The arresting officers were clearly outranked and after a brief discussion handed Wellington over to Sindisiwe and the four officers who had been in the cars that had passed Cameron earlier.

Cameron and Frankie moved closer and Wellington turned and

looked at Cameron. For a few brief seconds their eyes locked. A police officer put a hand on his bald head to protect it as he folded the criminal into the back of the patrol car. Sindisiwe Radebe walked over to Cameron and Frankie.

'Cameron, how are you?'

'Fine, and you, Colonel?' Cameron said. He knew he had been right not to bring his gun. He tried to bring his rage under control, but it was hard knowing this corrupt policewoman now had charge of Shumba.

'Fine, thank you. So, we have our man,' she said.

Cameron clenched his fists by his side. 'I called the National Prosecuting Authority. The Hawks will want to question Wellington.'

Sindisiwe shook her head. 'I'm afraid that's not possible, Cameron, and while you *were* the manager of the mine, you are not a law enforcement officer or a prosecutor, so it is not up to you who handles a criminal case. Do you doubt that I will handle this matter according to the letter of the law?'

Cameron bit back his reply.

She continued: 'I am looking for a Mozambican man named Luis Domingues Correia, the husband of the woman who was killed yesterday. I am going to ask you if you know where this man is.'

Out of the corner of his eye Cameron noticed Frankie moving back to his *bakkie*. He called his security men together. Cameron looked into the colonel's eyes. 'No.'

'You are sure? If you do not provide the police all of the information you have then you know you are committing a criminal offence, Mr McMurtrie.' Her false bonhomie had slithered into the night.

'I understand.'

'Very well. I have to take my prisoner back to Barberton; it's just fortunate that I happened to be in this area tonight when I heard the call of trouble on the estate. Who would have thought that Wellington Shumba would have been breaking into this place?'

'Who indeed.'

She lowered her voice. 'If you do happen to stumble on this man, Correia, remember he is a dangerous criminal. He may or may not have been part of the hijacking of your vehicle, even though you told my man at the crime scene Correia was never in the car. Things may be easier for you if this man was in custody, or somewhere where no one can find him. Think about it.'

The colonel got into her car and as it pulled away, blue lights strobing the trees on either side of the road, Cameron clearly saw Wellington's face as the Lion turned to him and smiled.

PART THREE

21

It was just the three of them now, the fisherman, his mate and their one surviving chick.

Inkwazi had struck the nest with the speed and devastating ferocity of a bolt of lightning, and the fisherman had barely registered the blur of russet and white feathers before one of his offspring had been grabbed then carried off, screaming, in the fish eagle's wicked yellow talons.

Their secluded nest had been shredded by the attack, but the fisherman and his mate had painstakingly rebuilt it. Each night he left their home to seek more barbel and bream to feed himself and his family. It was while he was out fishing that he spied a new danger, Ingwe.

From the branch of a jackalberry, its bark as black as if it had been burned, he watched Ingwe. This was a young leopard, not long separated from its mother, and therefore not as stealthy as it moved through the undergrowth on the edge of the Sabie River. The fisherman's own remaining offspring should be ready to leave the nest soon; the sooner the better, as there was danger everywhere, especially now that Inkwazi knew their location. Fortunately for the fisherman's remaining chick, the fish eagle and his mate had lately been satisfied taking their fill from the river.

The fisherman turned his head to watch the cat, and instead of diving into the Sabie he flew through the cool night air to the next tree, shadowing Ingwe. From vantage point to vantage point they were moving closer to the sycamore fig where his family lived.

Ingwe paused, one paw still suspended in midair, at the sound of the owl chick's screech. The fisherman's youngster had seen its father and called in anticipation of the meal it expected. Ingwe looked up, tracking the noise with his night-vision eyes and his ears. His tail twitched as he lowered his body and crept silently to the base of the tree.

The fisherman gave his booming call and his mate, in the nest, responded with a whine that sounded like the high-pitched keening of the jackal. The fisherman left his branch and dive-bombed the leopard, swooping low over Ingwe's head. The cat looked up in annoyance. Other birds, creatures of the daylight hours, were roused from their sleep and a chorus of different calls echoed along the river.

Ingwe, to his eternal annoyance, was already used to this, to birds and even the ever watchful baboons and monkeys shrieking and hollering to give away his location to all and sundry in the bush. He was still a clumsy hunter of big game, of the wily bushbuck and the fleet impala, but since he'd been weaned he had been honing his killing skills on the littler things – hares, lizards, rodents and, occasionally, baby birds in nests in the trees where he and his mother had spent much of their time.

Ingwe hooked his fore claws into the bark of the fig and began to climb. The owl attacked him again, close enough to brush his rosette-covered coat, but the leopard ignored the pesky bird. He heard the chick's squeal again over the mother's alarm and climbed higher.

The fisherman hovered in plain view of Ingwe, keeping pace with the cat's climb. When it became clear that the leopard was heading for the branch with the nest, the fisherman played his final card: he dropped to the ground and whined out loud. In the clearing where he landed he crooked a wing and hopped about in a circle.

Ingwe stopped and looked down. The adult owl seemed to be injured. It thrashed about as though trying to fly, but could not leave the ground, and its call, like its size, dwarfed that of the chick in the tree and the female that flapped her wings and put herself between the leopard and the nest.

Ingwe had eaten baby birds that had fallen from nests, but he had never eaten a flying creature as big as the flailing owl on the ground. It was the size of a baby impala or a steenbok. Ingwe jumped to the nearest branch, turned around and retraced his path, running headlong down the trunk of the fig.

The fisherman watched the cat grow bigger with every bound as the leopard raced towards him, any thought of stealth now overtaken by the predator's youthful excitement. At the moment Ingwe's paws left the ground in what he thought would be his killing pounce, the fisherman's seemingly broken wing healed itself and the owl fluttered up into the air. Ingwe landed where the bird had been, but instead of stopping he bounced upwards, his right front paw clawing the air. He came close to the fisherman but the owl flew ten metres then dropped to the ground again.

Once more the fisherman feigned a broken wing and Ingwe, who was still too young to understand the ploy, followed his instincts to jump on any wounded creature that still moved.

The fisherman took flight again. Just when it seemed the leopard might finally wake up to the bird's deliberate attempts to draw him away from his chick, an eerie *wooo-ooop* checked Ingwe's pursuit. The leopard turned its head as the call came again.

As the fisherman left the ground for the comparative safety of a nearby branch he saw the pair of hyena lope into view, and Ingwe, the leopard, who was no match for these spotted beasts with their vice-like jaws, ran off into the darkness.

22

'I still can't believe we're doing this,' Kylie said the next morning as Cameron slowed to fifty kilometres an hour. He smiled and waved to the fat traffic cops leaning against the bonnet of their shiny Toyota as he approached the Komatipoort border post.

'You didn't have to come along,' Cameron said.

She folded her arms. 'Yes I did. Luis saved my life, too. Hell, everyone saved everyone's life underground, so why shouldn't we all do stupid things for each other now for the rest of our lives?'

He cracked a smile. 'You want Wellington out of business, permanently, as much as I do. This has become personal for you.'

He was right, though she hated to admit it. The events of the last few days felt completely surreal to her. She'd done the same stupid thing she'd told him not to do, from Australia. She had taken the law into her own hands and she had even killed a man. The first of the nightmares about the underground shooting had come to her last night, days after it had happened. She'd told Cameron about it, on the drive to the border, and he had told her the nightmares would never end. They would reduce in frequency, he assured her, but never end.

Cameron hit the electric window and Kylie felt the humidity wash in over them. It was hotter and stickier here than in Barberton or on the Sabie River. It must be like a furnace in the back, under the cover.

'Afternoon, how are you?' Cameron said to the security man.

'I am fine, boss, and you?' The man handed him a slip of white paper, a gate pass.

'Here we go,' Cameron said to her as he closed the window and drove up to the customs and immigration hall. 'Remember the plan?'

'If anyone finds Luis we act shocked and claim he stowed away in the back of the truck when we parked at the shopping mall at Mal–'

'Malelane.'

She practised saying the name. It sounded exotic, but this place where gold dealers met and billionaires played golf had seemed anything but as they had passed through from Nelspruit.

Cameron parked and Kylie forced herself not to look back at the truck. They walked to the entry door and Cameron slid the gate pass onto the counter in front of a bored-looking man in a SARS uniform. He barely looked up from his copy of the *Sowetan* as he reached for his stamp. Cameron greeted him in Tsonga and the man mumbled a reply.

'How many are you?'

'Two.'

The first lie, Kylie thought, her heart pounding and her mouth dry. The man wrote the numeral on the gate pass and thudded it home with his stamp.

Cameron had told her and Luis of his conversation with Colonel Radebe when a clearly unhappy Frankie had brought him back to Hippo Rock. Kylie had had the distinct impression that Frankie wanted them all gone as soon as possible.

'You cannot let that woman arrest me,' Luis had said when Cameron told him Radebe was on his trail. 'She is with Wellington – he bragged about having the police in his pocket, and his bed. She will have me killed on his orders.'

'I can try the Hawks again,' Cameron had said.

'No.' Luis had been adamant. 'Wellington has been arrested for breaking into Hippo Rock. You have seen him, first hand, trying to kill you underground. The police here have enough to put him in prison. Not even this Colonel Radebe can stop that. Please, Cameron, let me go home and bury my wife and see my son. If you can set up immunity for me, if you need my testimony, I will return from Mozambique to meet with the Hawks. You have my word. But first, I need to get home. I'm worried Radebe will have people watching the border for me, and in any case I have no passport.'

Cameron had offered to smuggle Luis across the border. Kylie had quietly objected, saying it was putting Cameron at risk. 'He won't be able to make Miriam's funeral any other way. If he walked through Kruger it would take him days.'

They had set out from Hippo Rock the next morning via Barberton, where Cameron had left Jess with her friend Mandy. He didn't trust Sindisiwe Radebe to see through Wellington's prosecution to a lengthy prison term, but at least he was behind bars for the time being so they could all sleep safe for a while. Why Kylie had decided to join Cameron on the trip, though, she still didn't quite know. Now, at the border, she was again wondering why she felt this loyalty to these two men, McMurtrie and Correia, and regretting her impulsive decision to be part of this. They had to wait a few minutes at immigration. The airconditioner was thrumming and struggling and only one officer, who took her time, was attending to people leaving South Africa. Four others faced long queues on the opposite side of the room, trying to keep pace with the seemingly endless parade of Mozambicans waiting, with varying degrees of patience, to enter the land of gold.

A woman with a baby on her back, the child tied to her in a blanket, was explaining something to the immigration officer in their language. The baby looked at Kylie and she smiled at it. She had yet to feel clucky, but she didn't dislike babies.

The woman moved and Kylie slid her passport over, remembering to greet the woman and ask how she was. The woman looked up and returned the greeting and said she was fine. The passport was stamped and that was it. Kylie exhaled on the way out of the door.

They got back in the *bakkie* and Cameron drove slowly towards the boom gate. A SARS man, a customs officer, just waved them on. Another security guard took the stamped gate pass and they were through.

'Phew.' Kylie ran a hand through her damp hair.

'It's not over yet. Now the fun begins.'

Once through the boom gate they left Komatipoort behind and entered Ressano Garcia – another world. Immediately, everything was different. It was more like transiting to another world, another culture, another time than just another country.

The SARS and home affairs officers on the South African side wore blue uniforms, starched and cut with an almost Aryan precision, but the officials she saw now on the Mozambican side looked like they'd been outfitted with surplus clothes from some failed South American dictatorship. Men wore berets set at jaunty angles, fitted tight with small black bows at the backs of their heads. AK-47s seemed the accessory of choice.

Unlike the South African side there were people milling around the car park. Young boys rushed the pickup as soon as Cameron pulled into a parking bay; they were waving wads of *meticais* notes and offering to escort them through the border. A man in jeans and body-hugging black lycra tank top and thick gold necklaces was passing something to a uniformed official.

In front of where they parked was a row of half-a-dozen or more offices, each set up in porta cabins, advertising insurance and customs clearance. 'Stay close, don't talk to any of them,' Cameron said as he got out of the truck.

Kylie followed him and was besieged by touts. 'No thank you, no thank you,' she said.

Cameron said nothing, and Kylie realised that even saying 'no thank you' was an encouragement to the chancers. Cameron pushed open the door of one of the porta cabins and held it for her.

'Yes, madam, I work for this company,' said one of the youngsters, trailing her closely. She squeezed past Cameron, eager to get inside. The airconditioning was almost as welcome as the relative silence.

Cameron greeted a man who rose from behind his desk. '*Bom dia,* Mr McMurtrie.'

'This is Freddy,' Cameron said. Kylie nodded to a young man in a white shirt who wore his mirror sunglasses inside.

'Did that boy say he worked for me?' Freddy asked, his Portuguese-accented English sounding strange to Kylie, coming as it did from a black African. He pointed at the nodding, smiling face of the last youth to tug on Kylie's sleeve.

'Yes,' she said.

Freddy turned to Cameron. 'Hit him if he says that again.'

'My pleasure.'

They sat down and Kylie soon gave up trying to keep track of the forms that were filled in and the monies paid to Freddy, and a runner who took all the paperwork across the car park while they waited in the refuge of Freddy's office.

'Customs?' Freddy asked, leaning back in his office chair and lighting a cigarette.

'We're in a hurry, Freddy. We don't want a thorough search.'

Freddy exhaled smoke through his nose. 'I understand. You can make a donation to the customs officers.'

'A hundred rand?' Cameron asked.

Freddy shrugged. 'It is up to you, but fifty would do.'

'I want to make sure we get away quickly.'

Freddy nodded. 'I understand.'

Kylie felt her anxiety levels rising. She was sure she would hear a shout from the car park as Freddy's runner escorted them across to the immigration hall where they had to present their passports for inspection and where Kylie, as an Australian, had to pay for her visa. The immigration officer had her stand in front of a blue background while he took her picture with a camera linked to a computer. Next she had to place her left and right index fingers on a scanner.

It all seemed a bit over the top, to her, for a border crossing in Africa teeming with people who mostly didn't seem to have a cent to their name.

While she waited for her visa to be produced her eyes were drawn to a flat-screen monitor showing a revolving series of advertisements and messages. *Do not become involved with illegal immigration*, said a message in Portuguese and English that seemed to be aimed directly at her. She swallowed her fear.

'Miss Kylie,' said the immigration officer at last. She took her passport and the runner escorted Cameron and her back outside. The advertising display was showing an Indian restaurant in Maputo which seemed to also do home-delivery pizzas.

Freddy and a short rotund woman in blue uniform slacks, shirt, tie and beret were standing an arm's length from the *bakkie*. Kylie saw Freddy palm her Cameron's hundred rand note. She slipped it into her pocket and placed her hand on the black vinyl covering the back of the pickup. Kylie imagined Luis in there, sweating under the cover. She and Cameron stopped. The woman was fiddling with the elastic cord that secured the cover to the hooks around the cargo bin.

'What's she doing?' Kylie whispered.

'*Sheesh*, no,' Cameron said.

Freddy was talking in rapid Portuguese to the customs officer, but she shook her head and unhooked the elastic.

Freddy looked across at them and rubbed his thumb and forefinger together, out of the woman's line of sight.

'I think she wants more money,' Kylie said.

'She could be suspicious because I told Freddy to give her twice the normal amount. Shit.'

'Change some rand, boss?' a young tout in a Blue Bulls baseball cap said.

'*Fokof*.'

'Madam?'

Kylie was as annoyed as Cameron by the invasive presence of the tout, who had no concept of personal space. The customs woman was unfastening another hook and shaking her head at Freddy's protestations. He looked to them, shrugging his shoulders. He probably figured they were just trying to get across the border with more tobacco or alcohol than was legally permissible. Kylie had a thought.

She reached into her pocket and then withdrew her hand. 'My purse!'

The tout took a step back, shocked at the volume and pitch of Kylie's scream. He looked puzzled.

'What?' Cameron looked at her.

Kylie pointed at the young scammer. 'I think he just pickpocketed me!'

Cameron reached for the man and grabbed his forearm, but the tout shook it off and backed away, his hands up. 'Not me, boss. I no take anything.'

'Officer!' Kylie shrieked at the customs lady. 'This man just robbed me.'

The portly woman let go of the elastic rope on the pickup's cover and started waddling towards them. Cameron lunged at the boy again and he broke into a sprint. The woman yelled in Portuguese to a man in green army uniform and beret who saw the running boy and unslung his AK-47.

'No!' Kylie ran after the tout and put herself between the fleeing boy and the man with the gun, who was starting to bring his rifle to bear. She didn't want the boy to be shot. The youth was looking over his shoulder, his eyes wide in panic, and didn't see the security guard in front of him who wrapped his arms around him and tackled him to the ground.

Cameron, Freddy and the customs officer caught up with them as Kylie went to the security guard, who had his knee on the tout's back, keeping the youth pinned on the ground.

'I'm sorry, I'm sorry,' Kylie said. She reached into another pocket and drew out her nylon travelling wallet. 'I've found my purse. I was mistaken. This man is innocent.'

Freddy translated for the benefit of the security guard and the customs lady stood there, hands on plump hips, shaking her head at the ruckus, which had by now drawn another half-dozen onlookers.

Kylie apologised again to the young tout, who just scowled at her. She pulled a hundred rand from her wallet and gave it to him. He turned his back, shaking a fist in the air, and walked away from them.

Freddy said something to the customs officer and she shrugged as she replied.

'Is everything all right with the truck?' Cameron asked.

'She says we are keeping her from her duties.'

'Tell her this is to compensate her for her lost time,' Kylie said, taking out another hundred and pressing it to Freddy. He slipped it into the custom's lady's hand as he shook it. She waved, dismissing them.

When they were back in the Toyota and passing through the security barrier, Kylie punched the air. 'Whoo!'

He looked at her and grinned as he changed gears. 'You enjoyed that?'

She laughed. 'In a funny way, I did. I've never consciously broken a law before.'

'Welcome to Africa.'

*

Cameron waited until they made it to Matola, on the outskirts of Maputo, before he turned off the EN4 onto a dirt road that led to a building site, a housing complex under construction.

More new housing estates, such as this one, were springing up every time he came to Mozambique, and old Portuguese villas and bungalows, once the homes of civil servants and businesspeople, were being renovated and repainted in Mediterranean pastels. Mozambique was still a desperately poor country, but it was moving forward. This was as good a place as any to release Luis from his stifling imprisonment.

Cameron got out of the truck and looked around. It was midday and he presumed the construction workers were having a siesta in the shade somewhere out of sight. He unhooked the elastic cord securing the vinyl cover of the cargo compartment. Luis raised his head and also checked around him before sitting up fully. His shirt was drenched in sweat and he blinked at the harsh sun. It always seemed hotter, brighter, here in Mozambique.

Cameron unlatched the tailgate and Luis swung his legs over the back and stood, taking a moment to straighten himself out before extending his hand. 'Thank you.'

'I'm sorry, again, for your loss, Luis. But Wellington is in custody and we will make sure he stays there, with your help.'

He nodded and Cameron saw the faraway stare. Grief, he knew from his time in the army, manifested itself in many forms. One of them was revenge.

Luis nodded again. 'Goodbye, madam.'

Kylie shook his hand, awkwardly mimicking the three-part African handshake that Luis and Cameron had just exchanged, and Luis forced a small smile in thanks for her effort.

'We're at Matola, where you asked to be dropped,' Cameron said. 'You're sure we can't take you further?'

'No. There may be roadblocks. I can get a *chapa* from here. I must get to the funeral home, and then to my son, and tell him what has happened to his mother.'

Kylie went to him and put her arms around him. Luis didn't cry, and seemed embarrassed to return the hug. He looked out over her shoulder and Cameron saw it again, the look he'd seen in the eyes of men who had killed, and men who wanted, needed, to kill again.

'I want Wellington to rot in prison as badly as you do,' he said to Luis.

Kylie took a step back and put her hands on her hips. She nodded in agreement. 'He's killed three of our people, too.'

Luis pushed his rimless spectacles up his nose, turned and walked up the dirt driveway to the EN4. Cameron waited until Luis had flagged down a minibus and then he and Kylie got back into the *bakkie*.

'What now?' she asked.

He exhaled and started the engine. 'I don't know about you, but I could use a drink.'

'You're driving a company vehicle, on company time.'

'I am.'

'We've got a crisis brewing back at Eureka and I have to read through my briefings on Zambia. We still have a flight to catch tomorrow.'

'I know.'

'Do you know somewhere nice?'

He smiled. 'I do.'

*

Kylie closed her eyes and stamped her foot into the footwell of the pickup as Cameron swerved to miss a minibus taxi that had slammed on its brakes in front of them.

Cameron laughed and she opened her eyes and looked at him.

'You have to laugh,' he shrugged.

'That's the first time I've heard you laugh. Ever.'

'This place,' he raised his right hand from the steering wheel and waved. 'It can get you down, cripple you with its tragedy and sorrow. Like poor Luis and his wife. But people have to carry on. They find a way to survive.'

Cameron found his way through the congested, chaotic, thumping, bumping traffic of downtown Maputo, dodging other cars and pedestrians who all jived to a set of rules Kylie could not begin to understand. That's if there were any road rules, she reflected. Maybe that was the secret to this place. Chaos reigned but, remarkably, she didn't see anyone lose their temper, or hear a horn tooted in anger.

Maputo's buildings were a mix of old Portuguese colonial grandeur and 1960s and 70s concrete monoliths. Everywhere there seemed to be construction or renovation happening and Cameron filled her in on the country's history. The country now known as Mozambique had been a trading port for the Dutch and British before the Portuguese had concreted their claim to its long stretch of Indian Ocean coastline. Even though the Portuguese had abandoned their former colonies in 1975 after going through their own domestic revolution, every sign Kylie saw and every snippet of conversation she overheard as they stopped for traffic jams and, occasionally, for red lights, was in Portuguese.

Cameron entered a grand square dominated by a whitewashed building topped with a domed cuppola. 'That's the train station,' he said. 'Designed by Gustave Eiffel, he of the tower in Paris fame.'

'Wow. What was he doing here?'

'I don't know that he ever made it here,' Cameron said, cruising slowly past the stately old station building.

She shook her head. 'To design something so beautiful and never see it in the flesh . . . This place is incredible, Cameron.'

'I know.'

He manoeuvred them out of town and onto what he explained was the Rua da Marginal, the coastal road that ran along the sand-fringed waters of Maputo Bay. Young boys splashed in the shallow water and one did cartwheels on a sand spit. Roadside traders sold beers and soft drinks from carts and when Cameron lowered his window she smelled chicken peri-peri sizzling on charcoal braziers. On their left, inland, was more construction – villas and shopping complexes.

Cameron indicated left and pulled into a car park in front of an art deco building washed in lime green and white. Tables were emptying on a sheltered verandah as patrons finished long or late lunches.

'This is us. For lunch. The Costa do Sol's been here since the 1930s and never stopped serving, even through the civil war.'

A waiter greeted them and ushered them to a prime outside table. Kylie put on her sunglasses to cut down the glare from the bay. 'This is a beautiful spot.' The waiter took their drinks order, with

Cameron asking for a Dois M beer and Kylie a glass of white wine and a sparkling mineral water.

'I love it here. I used to bring . . . I come here whenever I'm passing through Maputo.'

She looked at him over the top of her glasses, but he cast his eyes down to the menu. She was sure he had been going to say that he used to bring his wife here.

He had finally seemed to relax a little, which was odd given what they'd been through. Perhaps he was a man who thrived on risk and danger. She wondered why his wife had left; maybe it was his pig-headedness and inability to communicate his feelings.

'I was about to say, before, that I used to bring my wife here.'

Kylie was surprised. Before she had a chance to say anything the waiter was back with their drinks.

'That would have been not long after the civil war ended, right?' she said when the waiter had left.

He laughed. 'A few years after the fighting ended, yes. The country was in a terrible mess back then. Maputo was rundown, but it had existed as a kind of neutral safe zone during the war, with both sides agreeing not to shell it or shoot it up.'

'She must have been quite adventurous, your wife, back then.'

He looked at her for a moment as if trying to decide whether she was mocking him, but he rolled his shoulders and nodded. 'She was. I was. I wonder if she left because she just got bored, with me and my work.'

She saw the pain creeping back into his eyes. Her mother and her best friend said she worked too hard and that was why she didn't have a husband. She would angrily reply to both of them that she didn't have a husband because she hadn't met the right man, not because of some slavish commitment to her job. They painted her as a caricature of the hard-nosed career woman, which, in her mother's eyes at least, secretly translated to being less of a woman. They were wrong. At least she thought they were wrong. 'There's nothing wrong with being dedicated to your work.'

Cameron flipped through the menu, not reading it, but perhaps not wanting to meet her eyes, either. 'I wonder. You know, she left me for some guy on the internet, an American she'd never even seen in the flesh. What does that say about me?'

She felt a need to put her hand on his, on the table, but she checked herself. 'I think you need to ask what it says about her.'

He looked up at her now. 'I thought she was happy. I was wrong. I can't put all the blame on her for leaving us – me and Jessica. If I wasn't fulfilling her needs, then I've got to shoulder part of the blame, it's just that . . .'

Cameron shifted his gaze out over the bay. Kylie wasn't good at relationships. She hadn't had one that had lasted more than a couple of months, and had never lived with a man. A woman in human resources had hit on her at an office Christmas party a couple of years back. Kylie had politely declined the invitation to go back to the woman's flat, and on the way home, alone in a taxi, wondered how many more of her colleagues thought she was a lesbian. 'Don't beat yourself up too much.'

He waved his hand in front of his face. 'It's nothing. We need to talk about Wellington.'

She was glad he had changed the subject. While it was nice to see him open up a little, she knew she had no real advice to give a man whose wife had left him for a stranger. Oddly, though, she did feel this need to comfort Cameron. She had never felt this way about a work colleague. Perhaps it was because of what they had been through together – it had the effect of creating a bond. Or perhaps it was because she felt that he didn't really like her, so she had some basic need to make him like her or, at least, respect her.

The waiter returned and Kylie asked for a seafood platter. Cameron said it was a good choice and ordered the same.

Kylie sipped her wine, a Portuguese Lagosta vinho verde. It was cold and crisp. 'Wellington must still want Luis dead.'

Cameron nodded. 'Luis is a risk to him alive, because he knows too much.'

Kylie thought about Luis, and how he had behaved in the wake of his wife's murder. 'Luis is keeping something from us.'

'What makes you think that?' Cameron asked.

'I know men and different cultures handle grief in different ways, but Luis wasn't just bottling his emotions, he looked like he was planning something. The look in his eyes wasn't sad, it was cold.'

'You think maybe Luis will get word to Wellington somehow that he's in Mozambique?'

Kylie shrugged. 'Would he do that, to keep Wellington away from us?'

'He's a good guy, but that would be suicidal. Especially if Wellington gets out on bail. That could be what he wants, a showdown.'

'What *we* need,' Kylie said, 'is to go higher up the food chain in South Africa and find an honest cop we can brief about Wellington and his crimes.' Their food arrived and Kylie scooped the flesh from a butterflied prawn almost as long as her hand. It was succulent and tasted of garlic and lemon. 'You . . . we . . . can't keep carrying on like vigilantes.'

Cameron chewed a mouthful of seafood and chased it with beer. 'I only had to carry on like a *vigilante* because all you Australians in head office stopped me from running armed security operations underground two years ago. It was after that when Wellington's operations went from small scale to full production.'

Kylie ignored the criticism. She and Jan had agreed that the armed patrols should cease after a security guard had been wounded in the leg during a brief firefight with a *zama zama*. Their legal counsel had worried about possible actions against Global Resources. As Jan had said, Global Resources wasn't in the business of operating a paramilitary force, and the detection, pursuit and arrest of criminals was best left to the police. Kylie had now seen and heard first hand just how reluctant the police were when it came to enforcing the law of the land underground. She had to concede that as unorthodox as Cameron's previous policies were, and as out-of-step as they were with Global Resources' corporate culture, they had worked.

Three good company men and Luis's wife had been killed because Wellington had been allowed to expand his underground fiefdom to the point where Cameron had to go to war to stop him.

'I can see, now, that things are different here in Africa,' she conceded.

*

They chased the setting sun back to the South African border.

Kylie had drunk two more glasses of wine with her lunch, but Cameron had limited himself to two beers. There were only a few people queuing to get out of Mozambique so there was no need for fixers and bribes. They passed through the South African formalities with equal ease.

The alcohol had relaxed her at first, but now she felt a knot of tension in her chest as they raced back along the N4 and turned left to Barberton. They passed the spot where Sipho and Miriam had been killed and Kylie felt the hot sting of tears.

Cameron glanced at her as she sniffed and cuffed her eyes. She didn't want to appear weak. She looked over to him. 'I'm all right,' she said quietly.

'You said it yourself earlier today. People deal with grief in different ways. Your tears are a sign of respect.'

She swallowed hard. He reached over and put his hand on hers. There it was again, the touchy-feely thing. He moved it back to the gear stick to change down and overtake a truck, and then returned both hands to the wheel. She wouldn't have minded if he had put it back again. 'How do you deal with it, then? You were in the war, weren't you? In Angola?'

'How did you know that?'

'Jan told me. He said you were in special forces, like him.'

He nodded. 'I was working on a mine at Carltonville, near Johannesburg, and I got drunk the night after call-up came through for national service and decided that if I was going to go into uniform, instead of ending up as a clerk or cook or cannon fodder in the infantry, I'd go all the way and try out for the recce commandos. Jan and I never served together, but he was also on the mines and told me he thought the same way.'

'Brave.'

He shook his head. 'Stupid. I saw some things, did some things, in Angola that, well, I don't like to think about. But to answer your question, I dealt with the deaths of friends in different ways. Sometimes I drank, sometimes I cried and sometimes I went out looking for payback. The truth is that none of it really works. Time is the only thing that helps, and even then there are some things, some people, you can never forget.'

'Thanks.'

He looked at her, perhaps to see if she was being sarcastic, but she wasn't.

Darkness descended and they drove on in silence. 'I have to call Jess.'

'No worries,' she said.

Cameron dialled and used the phone's hands-free. 'Hello, my girl.'

'*Howzit*, Dad?'

'Fine. I'll be home in about half an hour.'

'Cool. I've been worried about you. Is Luis all right?'

'Yes, we saw him safely across the border.' He winked at Kylie. 'Do you want me to get a pizza for dinner?'

'I've made lasagne at Mandy's, Dad. Her mom's ready to take me home whenever.'

'That's *lekker*. Is there enough for three?' He glanced across at her.

Kylie was surprised. Caught off guard she returned his look with raised eyebrows and a shrug of her shoulders. Now that she thought about it, the idea of going back to the hotel and getting the lonely businesswoman's table for one seemed like a depressing prospect.

'Ja, I made enough for a couple of nights so there's plenty. Why? Are you bringing Kylie home?'

'I'll just ask her. Do you want to?'

'Sure. That'd be *lekker*. Is that the right word?'

273

Jess laughed. 'Yes, it is. I'll get a lift home now and get the table set and see you soon.'

About twenty minutes later they drove past Barberton prison, where Kylie hoped Wellington was safely under lock and key, and then left onto the winding dirt road that climbed up the steep mountainside. A car passed them in the opposite direction and Cameron waved and said it was Jess's best friend, Mandy, and her mother, Charmaine.

As they turned into the driveway Jessica flung open the front door. A dog barked somewhere nearby. Kylie wondered what sort of pets they had. The girl ran to her father, her arms reaching for him.

'Hey,' he said, hugging her. 'This is a surprise. We've only been gone a day. Are you all right?'

'Dad . . .' Jessica pulled her face from his chest and Kylie noticed her eyes were red from crying.

'What is it?'

'I didn't have time to call you. I only just got here myself a few minutes ago. I begged Mandy's mom to stay, but she said it would be best if I was alone, if it was just the three of us, but I don't want that. I don't want to be here.'

'Jess, calm down. What happened? Let's go inside so we can talk.'

Kylie smiled at the girl, but she was beginning to feel it was a mistake, her coming to dinner, as it appeared she had walked in on some breaking family crisis. A terrible thought chilled her from the outside in. She hoped Wellington hadn't escaped, or sent his goons to the house.

'Dad, I don't want to go inside the house. Can we just get in your truck, now, and maybe go out to dinner somewhere?'

'Maybe I should just get back to my hotel, Cameron?' Kylie said.

'No, come. We've invited you to dinner and Jess has made her famous lasagne and we're all going to sit down to a nice meal, just as soon as my daughter tells me why she's acting so crazy all of a sudden.'

'Dad, I'll tell you in the car. I can't go back in there.'

Cameron put his hands on his hips and turned to face Jessica. 'For heaven's sake, why not?'

Beyond him, Kylie could see movement and a woman with short-cropped peroxided hair and dark eyes appeared in the doorway.

Jessica sighed. 'Because Mom's back.'

23

I can't deal with this, I'm going to Mandy's. They only just left and I'm getting them to turn around and come get me. *You* deal with her.' Jessica had her cellphone to her ear as she ran down the driveway and onto the access road.

'Jessica!'

'Leave her, Cameron.' Tania came to him, then looked at Kylie. 'Found someone new already?'

'I . . .' She had no damn right to be snide with him. She had run away and left them. 'This is my boss from Australia, Dr Kylie Hamilton.'

'I should go,' Kylie said.

'No,' Cameron said, trying to gain control of his feelings and the situation.

'*Ag*, babe, please forgive me.' Tania sniffed and came to him, wrapping her arms around him.

He couldn't do the same. He stood there, arms by his side, trembling. She couldn't do this to Jessica, or to him.

'Please don't be so cold. Please don't reject me, Cameron. I'm begging you.'

Reject her? She had left with barely a word, and now her plan must have backfired on her. 'Please,' she sobbed into his chest.

He prised her away from him and looked at Kylie, who looked embarrassed. 'I'll take you back to the hotel.'

'I can manage. Perhaps I can call a driver.'

'No, I'll do it. This is South Africa, not Australia, you can't just whistle up a cab.'

He held Tania at arm's length. 'I'll be back.'

She sniffed and he looked briefly into her eyes. There were no tears. He turned his back on her and walked to the Toyota. Kylie followed in his footsteps.

Tania stood in the driveway of her empty house, arms folded. He slumped in the driver's seat and turned the ignition.

'I could take the truck,' Kylie said, 'and come back and pick you up tomorrow.'

He shook his head and reversed out, not looking at his wife. 'No, I need space . . . air. I feel like I'm drowning. I know how Jess feels. I'm sorry.'

'Don't be.'

As they set off, Cameron called Mandy's mother, Charmaine, on his cellphone.

'I've just turned around and picked up Jess halfway down the hill. What should I do, Cameron? Should I take her back to my place?' Charmaine asked.

'Yes, please. I don't have to tell you it's complicated. I'm still going on that business trip to Zambia I told you about, so if you're happy to look after her while I'm gone, maybe she can meet her mother on neutral ground somewhere.'

'I *don't* want to see her anywhere,' Cameron heard Jess say in the background.

'Shame. But, *ja*, OK,' Charmaine said. 'I'm still fine with looking after Jess while you're away.'

'*Baie dankie*, Charmaine.'

After that he drove in silence, down the winding access road, through the near empty streets of Barberton, out past the mines to the turn-off to the Consort mine and the Diggers' Retreat. He turned left into the hotel's driveway and down the long lane to the accommodation area and guests' car park. Kylie looked across at him.

'Thanks,' she said. 'It's been a hell of a day. What do you want to do about the trip to Zambia?'

His head drooped. 'Wellington's in prison, Jess is with her friend and I've got a wife at home I don't want to talk to. I'm still coming. I have to.'

'Look, Cameron, it's none of my business, but if your work contributed to the problems with your marriage, then you should stay here and sort things out with your wife. I can get one of the guys from the Johannesburg office or maybe Chris to come with me.'

'I could use another drink.'

She opened her door. 'Well, I can't tell you what to do, but if you want to come into the bar, it's my shout. My round, that is.'

He opened the driver's door and got out.

Kylie led the way through the hotel's empty lounge room and reception and into the Hangman's Tree bar.

A couple of locals who worked at Fairview mine nodded to him. That was the problem with this place: everyone knew him, and everyone knew his business. It wouldn't be long before they all knew that Tania was back. She would be the talk of the small town – again. 'Let's go out back,' he said.

Kylie nodded and they went outside and took a table under the thatched lapa by the side of the swimming pool. A waitress in her late teens came over. 'What'll it be?'

'Brandy and coke,' he said.

'Gin and tonic, please,' Kylie said.

He sat there, in silence, and nodded his thanks to the girl when she brought the drinks. He didn't know what to say to Kylie, or if he should say anything at all. Kylie was right, it was none of her business, but he had no one else he could talk to, no one else he could tell how he really felt, about Tania leaving and now coming back. He looked across the table at her and she gave a small smile, but said nothing, as if waiting for him to fill the void.

'I feel guilty,' he said at last.

'About her leaving you?'

'Yes.'

'No one's perfect, Cameron.' She sat her glass down on the table and smiled again. When she dropped the corporate routine she was very attractive. He knew she didn't understand what he meant, and wondered if he should explain further.

He was sure that she thought he was about to reveal all to her, and tell her what a lousy husband he had been, neglecting his wife in favour of the mine, perhaps having an affair with one of the girls in the office or sleeping with hookers when he was away at mining conferences.

'I do spend too much time at work. I know it. Tania didn't like it. She hated the hours, hated Barberton. She was brought up in Sandton, Johannesburg. Her parents are loaded; you saw the Hippo Rock house and that was just for weekends and holidays. We met when we were both on holiday in Thailand. I was an ex-soldier and a miner and she was a *kugel,* a rich Johannesburg princess. Back home she wouldn't have said hello to me, but we were two South Africans abroad and we had a holiday romance and Jess was the result of it. Tania thought having a child would define her spoiled existence, but the truth was she resented our daughter, and me, for taking her away from what would have been a life of luxury and parties and big houses.'

Kylie nodded, as though she understood the scenario.

He took a long sip of his drink. 'When she left, to go hook up with this *oke* from America she'd met on the computer, I couldn't believe it. I realised I'd been so neglectful of her, but how could she leave Jess?'

He exhaled and wrapped both hands around his glass, looking down into the liquor then up at her again. 'I know what a lot of people in town were saying. Tania could be the life of the party, and she was, well . . . flirty.'

'Did you suspect her of being unfaithful?'

He looked into her eyes and mulled over the question. 'For a while I did, but, no, I don't think she ever was unfaithful, before this business with the internet guy. I confronted her once and she said she had *wanted* to be, but she hadn't because she was worried that in such a small town people would talk and she couldn't keep it a secret.'

'Believe me, I know about mining towns and sexual gossip.'

He took another drink. 'So, finally, she meets this guy on the internet and decides the only way she can escape me, escape Barberton, and even poor Jessica, is to leave the country. It was crazy.'

He gripped the glass so hard he thought he might shatter it. She was watching him and he wondered what kind of a loser she thought he was. He had wanted to kill Wellington when he saw him, but he didn't feel the same way about the man who had taken his wife. 'I didn't . . .' He put his hand to his mouth and coughed, almost as though he was choking on the words that wouldn't come. He looked around him, but the bar was mercifully deserted. There was no one there who knew him and could report back on his near show of emotion.

He looked into her eyes and he could see that the truth had suddenly dawned on her. 'You didn't want her to come back, did you?' she said.

He stared at her, neither confirming nor denying, perhaps not able to bring himself to admit what he felt inside. She said nothing either, but held his stare.

He nodded his head slowly. 'You're right.' He lowered his eyelids, then opened them. 'I couldn't tell Jess, but after my initial shock, I was happy. For the first time in years. Jess and I get on really well and I was helping her get over her feeling of being betrayed by her mom.'

'What are you going to do now?' she asked.

He shrugged. 'This is hell for Jess. You can only imagine how the kids at her school have reacted to all this. It was the same for me at work. I know people were talking about Tania, and about me, behind my back, but I didn't give a damn. I was happy that she was gone, though I couldn't tell anyone that, and I didn't care what people thought were the reasons. The fact is that Tania's selfish and manipulative, a bitch to her daughter, venal, and totally obsessed with money and possessions.'

'Then divorce her. The courts would probably give you custody over Jess, given Tania's recent history of abandoning her family.'

Cameron drained his drink and called for the waitress. He ordered another and Kylie put her hand over the top of her glass, which was still half full. He took a slug of brandy and coke. 'I've got to think of Jess. Seeing her mom leave was a hell of a shock for her. I think it's probably better if I make up and we go back to pretending we're one big happy family.'

'That doesn't make sense. Jess seems like a smart girl. She'll know her mother can't fix the problems in her life simply by coming back because her internet fling didn't work out.'

Cameron put his hands out, palms up. 'Then what do I do, Dr Hamilton?'

She ignored the jibe. 'Don't come to Zambia if it's going to make matters worse. I'll take Chris.'

'So you're sidelining me from my new job as well as my old one?'

She folded her arms and sat back in her chair. 'You do what you want, Cameron.'

He downed his drink in two big swallows and called the girl over again. Kylie frowned. 'Drinking more isn't going to solve your problems.'

'Another, please,' he said to the waitress. She couldn't tell him what to do after hours.

'I'm going to bed, Cameron.'

'Fine.' He waved a hand in the air and burped.

*

Kylie got up and walked through the bar and lounge and out past Cameron's parked truck to her room. She slammed the door and sat down at the small writing desk. She wasn't drunk enough to fall easily into sleep, and she was too angry at Cameron's attitude to be able to relax. She got out her MacBook and connected to the internet. There were two dozen emails she could busy herself with while she tried to calm down.

She turned on the television and let BBC World news play in the background while she ploughed through the last of her messages. When she was finished she took out her Kindle and lay on the bed, still in her clothes, and tried to read.

It was hard for her to concentrate, so she turned off the e-reader and channel-surfed with the DSTV satellite television remote. As she flicked from program to program she became aware of a low, rhythmic noise somewhere. She turned the television volume down and strained to hear. There it was again. It was almost like someone or some creature was in pain somewhere.

Kylie hit the mute button on the television button and listened again. She heard the groan and felt her cheeks start to colour. It was next door. She thought of the rented four-by-four in the car park, the young couple with the heavy accents. They were having sex.

The girl, at least she assumed it was her by the pitch, started calling louder and faster. Kylie groaned herself, out of annoyance. She pushed the mute button again and tried to concentrate on the reality show. It was something to do with aircraft disasters. The calling changed to shrieking. She grabbed the second pillow and placed it over her head. The screams of pleasure pierced it. She thought of banging on the wall. She thought of Cameron. No doubt he would be coming to find her soon.

Kylie gave a small yelp when she heard thumping. It was coming from her door, though, not the bedhead next door.

'Kylie?'

'Shit,' she said.

She removed the pillow and got up, walking barefoot to the door. She opened it as far as the security chain would go. Cameron blinked at her through the gap. She smelled the brandy on his breath.

'Have you got my car keys?'

'You can't drive home this drunk, Cameron. I won't let you. Think of your daughter.'

He rubbed a hand down his face and swayed a little. 'I am. I just called her. Staying at Mandy's . . .'

He seemed to have forgotten the question he had asked her. 'You should get a room. The company will pay.'

'Not worried 'bout money,' he said, then hiccupped. 'Where're my keys?'

She hoped he wasn't a belligerent drunk. 'We'll have a good look for them in the morning.' They were in her handbag. She had taken them off the table when she left for her room. He was old enough to look after himself but she was worried that in his current state of mind he might do something stupid. 'Get a room, Cameron.'

He swayed back from her view, then forward again and she heard and felt his hand move to the door, pushing against it and her to steady himself. 'Tried. Full, tourist bus just arrived.' He hiccupped.

Kylie sighed. She hadn't expected that. 'Well, I'll give you a blanket and a pillow and you can sleep in the back of your truck.'

He shrugged and smiled. 'No keys. Give 'em to me.'

Kylie had almost been caught out. If she gave him his keys he would be stupid enough to try to drive home.

She closed the door on him, paused to think for a second, then realised she had no option. She unslid the security latch and opened the door. He was standing there, swaying still. 'Come in.'

He nodded and lurched into the room. He cocked an ear. 'Wha's that noise?'

The orgasm next door was reaching its crescendo. 'Stray cats.'

He smiled and hiccupped again. There was an awkward moment when his bloodshot eyes locked on hers and she felt her cheeks colour again. Then he passed out on the bed.

*

Cameron dreamed he was with a woman who loved him. She was smaller than Tania, slighter, her body toned and firm, her lips sweet and wet. She kissed him deep, but he couldn't open his eyes so he couldn't see her.

His hands roamed down over her body, and his mouth followed. He wanted to devour her, to kiss her all over. He drew on the nipples that came to life in his mouth, sampled his way over the smooth, flat paleness of her belly. As he roamed he had the vague sensation that he was dreaming, knowing it, but wishing it was real. It had been a long time since he and Tania had last had sex. He had tried to initiate it, but looking back she had probably already decided to leave him.

It didn't matter in the dream, though. His lover arched her back and opened herself to him. Tania didn't like that, being kissed down there, and used it as grounds for not reciprocating. He wondered, even in his delusional ecstasy, if she had let her American do that to her. Perhaps it wasn't the act she had hated, so much as Cameron. It didn't matter. He felt the woman's fingers in his hair, and the slickness of her on the tip of his tongue as he claimed her.

The next thing he knew she was in his arms and he held her tight, never wanting to let her go.

'Cameron!'

The shriek woke him and he sat bolt upright, unsure at first where he was.

Kylie, fully dressed, jumped up from the bed, clutching her arms across her chest. 'What were you doing?'

'I . . .'

'You had your arm around me.'

He rubbed his face and the action hurt his entire head. He coughed. 'Sorry, I must have been dreaming.'

He started to get up, then felt the erection in his underpants, a hangover from the dream. He felt his face start to colour. He wasn't wearing his jeans. He looked around the room and saw them strewn on the floor.

'What happened to your pants?' She looked away.

He blinked. 'I think I took them off when I got up to piss in the middle of the night.'

She shook her head and stormed to the bathroom and slammed the door.

Cameron burped and tasted stale brandy. With Kylie out of the room he sat up, and raised a hand to his forehead to try to slow the spinning. He reached out with his toe and hooked his jeans and dragged them to him. He wondered if they had done anything. The last thing he remembered was asking her where his car keys were. He heard the shower running and stood, unsteadily, and put his pants on.

He looked around the room and saw her handbag, half its contents spilling onto a chair. He spotted his car keys. Cameron found a pen and a bedside notepad and wrote: *See you at the airport.*

He left the room and got into his vehicle and drove out of the hotel car park. He turned on his phone and it beeped four times. There were three missed calls from his home number, and one from Jess's cellphone. He called his daughter first.

'Are you all right, Jess?'

She sounded sleepy. '*Ja* Dad.'

'Do you want to come home? I'm heading there now,' he said.

'No. I don't want to see her. And you're still going away again today, aren't you?'

His heart hurt as much as his head. He knew he should be with Jessica now, but he had made a point of telling Kylie he wanted to continue on with their plans to go to Zambia, where she was going to inspect another new project. Damn, he thought. He had backed himself into a corner. Jessica had planned on staying with Mandy while he was away and he asked her if she wanted to stick to that plan.

'Yes. I *told* you, I don't want to see her again.'

Cameron didn't know what to do. He wanted Jessica to have a normal, stable home life, with two parents, even if he, too, didn't want to be with Tania. He knew, however, that neither of them could continue avoiding Tania.

'OK. You take your time. I'll be back in a few days anyway and we'll all talk then.'

'All right, Dad. Love you.'

'I love you more than anything in the world. SMS me, OK?'

'*Ja*. Bye.' She ended the call and he hoped he wasn't losing her too. Cameron took a deep breath and called Tania at home.

'Cameron?' He heard the anger, but she seemed to be forcing herself to stay calm. 'I was worried about you, *engel*.'

He winced at the half-baked term of endearment. He was not the angel. 'I was busy last night.'

'Well, where are you now? Are you coming home?'

'I'm on my way, but I have to fly to Livingstone, and I'm going to be away for four days.'

'What? Your work, again, Cameron, I . . .' She paused to draw breath 'Maybe you can put it off, to stay with Jess and me?'

He gripped the steering wheel hard. His work *had* been a factor in her leaving, but she had run out on them and now she expected him to stay home and play happy families. No. He had no qualms about continuing on with the tour with Kylie. Jess was safe and happy at Mandy's and, as far as he was concerned, Tania could suffer. 'I'll be home in ten minutes.'

Cameron drove past the mine and longed for the days when he'd simply report for work there every morning. His marriage may have been a sham, but at least he'd had his work to focus on. He felt angry at Tania, at Kylie and Jan for trying to micromanage his mine, and at Wellington Shumba for wresting control of the mine and his life from him. Before he started feeling too maudlin, however, he thought of Luis Correia and the terrible tragedy he had been through. He could be much worse off.

This is it, he thought. If Jess didn't want to reconnect with her mother, then he would not waste time trying to reconcile things with her. He would give Tania her marching orders and file for divorce. He would embrace the new job Kylie had given him and he and Jess would leave Barberton and set up somewhere new. A fresh start would be good for them.

He wondered how Kylie was doing, and if he should call her. He thought better of it. He was sure nothing had happened between them, but flashes of the dream he'd been having popped into his mind. It had been too long since he'd had sex, or even the time to think about it. The mine had been occupying his thoughts, night and day.

Cameron checked his watch and accelerated, the tyres on his pickup scrabbling for grip on the steep gravel road to his home. He knew every bend and rut of the road. He would hate to leave it, but perhaps it really was time for him and Jess to move on. The dogs came bounding out as he turned into the driveway. He wondered what they thought of Tania being back.

He pulled up outside the garage and got out. There was no sign of her. He ruffled the dogs under their chins and walked in through the unlocked front door. The CD player was on and a slow Afrikaans rock song was playing. The heavy curtains were closed and he paused to allow his eyes to become accustomed to the dimness inside.

Cameron walked down the stone-tiled hallway to the master bedroom and saw the door was closed. It opened.

Tania stood in her cream satin dressing-gown. He looked at her, not with anger but with what he hoped was disdain. He saw her lower lip start to tremble and he felt his resolve weakening. Her big eyes glittered. There was dark makeup around them and her lips were cherry red, as full and inviting as the first time he'd met her on a balmy night in Thailand.

All he had wanted was for her to love him as he had loved her. He knew she hated their life, but he had also ultimately come to the conclusion that she hated him too, and perhaps even disliked their daughter. He had come prepared to send her on her way.

She smoothed imaginary wrinkles from the satin and his eyes followed her hands down over her full breasts, her still-flat tummy. It was only then that he noticed the stockings beneath the hem of the gown, and the strappy high heels she had bought on her last trip to Johannesburg.

Tania took a step towards him and he stopped in the hallway.

'Cameron, my love, I'm so sorry. Can you ever forgive me? I've been a total fool.'

He clenched his hands beside him and she came another step closer.

'I was an idiot to leave you and Jess. It's not about you and her, it's all about me, how selfish, how silly I've been. I should never have left home.'

He couldn't bring himself to tell her it was all right, that he wanted them to move on. He wanted to march past her and open her wardrobe and drawers and throw all of her stuff back into the open suitcase on the floor and toss it outside onto the grass. But he couldn't move.

She came to him and put her arms around him. He turned his face from her, but she persisted, kissing his cheek. She placed her hands on his chest, her fingers trailing as she moved down him. Tania moved her lips to his ear. 'Forgive me. Hold me.'

He moistened his lips to speak, but the words would not come.

Tania sank to her knees in front of him and looked up. 'I'm begging you, Cameron.'

He tried not to, but he couldn't help glancing down at her. She let a small smile play across her contrite face as she unbuckled his belt and reached for his zipper with glossy nails the colour of her lips.

24

K ylie checked her wristwatch for the fourth time in ten minutes. The boarding call had been made. There was no sign of Cameron.

She shouldn't have been surprised, she knew, or angry, but she was both. She felt a little silly for her outburst that morning, insinuating that Cameron had tried something with her in the bed. She felt a little guilty, too. She could have slept on the floor – or, better yet, rolled him out of bed so that he could. But she hadn't.

It had been a shock seeing him without his jeans on and to her horror she thought she had glimpsed a bulge in his underpants as she'd leapt from the bed, but she also had a vague recollection of half waking in the pre-dawn cool and feeling his arm around her. She hadn't stirred, she told herself, because she hadn't wanted to wake him. When she had woken, fully, she had jumped out of the bed.

She walked to the glass door of the small departures area at Kruger Mpumalanga International Airport and looked over her shoulder. Two security guards chatted by the single X-ray machine. He was not going to show.

She had called Chris and told him to get his arse on the next flight up to Johannesburg and then on to Livingstone, in Zambia.

He would miss the direct flight. Chris had tried to protest, but Kylie had been terse with him.

'I'm supposed to go and see Tertia again,' Chris had whined.

'Too bad. Besides, I'm not sure there's anything more to be gained by negotiating with that woman. I need someone with me and you're it.'

'I'm not feeling too *lekker*,' he had persisted.

'Then take a teaspoon of cement, Chris. If you're well enough to go see Tertia, you're well enough to fly to Zambia with me.' She had ended the call.

'Thank you, Dr Hamilton, enjoy your flight,' said the SA Airlink ground attendant as she tore off the stub of the boarding pass and handed it back.

Kylie hadn't called Cameron; she didn't want to appear to be chasing him up. He was an adult and he would make the best decision as far as his family and his career were concerned. Despite what Cameron thought, Kylie fully believed he would be a good fit for the special projects job Jan had created for him. He was too close to the mine and it had probably contributed to the breakdown of his marriage. His daughter seemed like a bright girl and Kylie was sure that while Jessica said she didn't want to leave Barberton she would eventually appreciate relocating to Johannesburg.

Kylie had been through a hell of a lot with Cameron in the short time she had been in South Africa. Nothing in Australia in her work or life experience could have prepared her for what she had seen and done in Africa. She realised, too, that Cameron had been trying to explain this to her and Jan for months, and that perhaps they should have let him persist with his efforts to winkle out the *zama zamas* by force, using hired guns. She had seen for herself the full extent of the violence underground; she squeezed her eyes tight for a moment to try and block out the memory of pulling a trigger herself, and the sickening, if justifiable, results. She opened her eyes again and forced herself to take a deep breath – good and bad memories of this place would stay with her for the rest of her life. As she moved to the departure gate door she heard an alarm beeping behind her.

'Wait! I'm coming!'

Cameron had set off the metal detector. He had gone back and was pulling off his steel-capped miner's boots and dumping them on the X-ray conveyor. He came through again and collected his boots, carry-on travel bag and his laptop. He hopped as he struggled to get his right boot back on.

'He's with me,' Kylie said, rolling her eyes at the ground attendant. The woman smiled and Kylie went back to Cameron and zipped his laptop into its bag and shouldered it.

'I can manage,' he said.

'Not from what I can see. I didn't think you were going to make it.' They walked briskly to the door and Cameron showed his boarding pass. They were the last of the queue of people walking across the tarmac to the Airlink jet.

'I got a seat next to you so we can talk on the aircraft,' he said as they climbed the stairs.

'I called Chris and told him to come in your place,' Kylie said. 'I'll try and text him before we take off.'

Cameron smiled. 'Relax. I called him already on my way to the airport. I knew you'd default to him.'

She didn't like being countermanded, but she was pleased, all the same, that he was here.

They found their seats and Cameron's phone chirped.

'Yes?' he said, cupping his hand over the phone and ducking his head below the level of the seat in front of him. Kylie saw the flight attendant's annoyed look.

'I can't talk. We're about to take off,' Cameron whispered into the phone. 'Jess is fine where she is. That was the plan – for her to stay with Mandy while I'm away.'

Kylie slid the in-flight magazine from the seat pocket in front of her and flipped through it, pretending not to listen.

'No. I can't tell you not to see her, Tania. Yes, you're right, she's your daughter, but . . . OK, OK. But it might take some time. I'll be home in four days, all right?'

'Cameron,' Kylie hissed. The flight attendant was eyeballing them and marching down the aisle of the aircraft.

'Sir, will you please switch off your cellphone now?'

He held up one finger. 'Got to go. Sheesh, you can use the mine *bakkie*, all right? I sold your car. Why? Do you have to ask *why*, Tania?'

'Sir . . .'

'*Ag*,' he fumed. He stabbed the end-call button with his thumb.

Cameron laid his head back against the headrest and closed his eyes. Kylie knew it was none of her business, but she was dying to ask him what had gone on between him and his wife that morning.

The jet took off and Kylie looked out at the patchwork of crops of green citrus and macadamia trees spread over rolling hills below. Off to their right was the uninterrupted wilderness of the Kruger National Park. Kylie thought about the animals down there, and remembered, with a tingle, the closeness of the elephants and lions on Tertia Venter's game reserve. Except, she reminded herself, it was no longer Tertia's farm. It belonged to the people who had lived on the land before the whites had arrived in South Africa. Didn't that give them the right to decide what was going to happen to the land? Wasn't it better to have a mine that would employ hundreds of locals directly, and benefit thousands in the community indirectly, than locking up the bush as the private domain of one crazy woman and her rich, mostly foreign clientele?

'Do white South Africans think animals are more important than people?' she said to Cameron as the flight levelled off.

He opened his eyes and looked at her. 'You're talking about the Lion Plains project.'

'Yes.'

He tried to rub the tiredness from his bloodshot eyes and yawned. 'Tourism is a big part of this country's economy, and so is mining. When the two collide you're going to upset people. Tertia's game farm isn't just about protecting animals and birds and the bush, it also provides employment for the local community.'

'But not as many as the mine will employ.'

He shrugged. 'There's a shortage of skills here, just as there is in your country. Who's to say Global Resources can find or train enough skilled people from Hazyview or Mkhulu or any of the other towns near Lion Plains to run a mine? We probably can't. If you talk about the wider community – South Africa – yes, then a mine will employ more people than a game farm, but you're also talking about our natural heritage here. That part of South Africa, the greater Kruger Park, is precious to many people.'

'You sound like you're not in favour of the Lion Plains mine,' she said.

The flight attendant handed them brown paper bags of food.

Cameron ignored his. 'No one's ever asked me if I'm in favour of it. I've been appointed head of new project development in Africa, but I wasn't part of the decision-making process for Lion Plains.'

He had a point. 'So, are you?'

'Does it matter?'

He was toying with her, but she hadn't really considered the ethics behind mining on Lion Plains. On paper, back in Australia, it had looked like a no-brainer. Every time they tried to develop a new mine, anywhere in the world, someone found an environmental reason to oppose it. In Australia it might be the remote possibility of the contamination of ground water; in South America it might be a threat to a rare type of mountain grass; in Papua New Guinea, the bird of paradise. They had known from the outset that Tertia would fight the mine, but the local people – the traditional owners – were practically begging for the mine. She'd thought that in a battle between people and animals, people would, should, always win. She needed to know, however, if Cameron was on board with their development strategy in Africa, and if he had the balls to stay the course. The fight with Tertia was far from over. 'Yes, it matters,' she said.

'Then no.'

'You don't think we should be mining on Lion Plains?'

'No.'

She opened her bag and took out a packet of potato chips and opened them. It wasn't healthy, but nor was being shot at by illegal miners underground. This country was driving her crazy. Cameron had made no secret of the fact that he didn't want to be moved into his new role and would rather stay in Barberton running his bloody mine. Was he being deliberately anti the coalmine in the hope that she or Jan would move him back to his old job? If that was the case, he was out of luck. Jan had told her, before she left Australia, that if Cameron didn't take the 'promotion', then they would have to let him go.

'You've been there, Kylie,' he said. 'You've seen the place.'

She knew what he was getting at, and she tried to tell herself to think like a businesswoman and not like a tourist.

He swivelled a little in his seat to make eye contact with her; she stared straight ahead. 'I saw your face when you saw your first elephant, your first lion. I know what this place, this country, the African bush, does to people. You have to be made of stone for it not to get to you.'

*

Colonel Sindisiwe Radebe took the key from the policeman who had accompanied her to the holding cells and then dismissed the man. When he was out of sight she opened the steel door. Wellington looked up at her smiled.

'In here? You might wake my neighbours in the next cell.'

'This is no time for joking,' she said. 'You were lucky I was able to get to you first. If you'd been taken into custody by those hicks at Mkhulu they would have beaten you to a pulp – they hate poachers there.'

'You're the only game I want to catch.'

She waved a hand at him and tried not to smile. 'Stop that. McMurtrie called me this morning. He was on his way to Livingstone with the woman. He wanted to know when you were appearing before the court and what I had charged you with.'

Wellington ran a hand over his scalp and yawned. 'What did you tell him?'

'The truth – that the business of the police is none of his business, but I can't hold him off forever. He will run to the National Prosecuting Authority, if he hasn't already. He is away for four days.'

Wellington was silent for a few seconds. He looked up at her from his hard prison bed. 'McMurtrie and Hamilton want revenge for the men who were killed. That is understandable, but the mine belongs to me now and I'm not going to give it back. Their testimony alone, even without Correia, is enough to put me away for a long time.'

Sindisiwe leaned against the concrete door frame. 'If something were to happen to them there would be no case against you, no witnesses. I am certain Correia is back in Mozambique now.'

He nodded. 'I agree. Mohammed will be eager for production to get back to full swing. We should be taking full advantage of the mine's closure. All I need is a couple of days, my baby, and things will be back to how they were.'

Sindisiwe shivered when she looked into his eyes, and couldn't tell if it was desire for this man and his promise of gold, or fear, or a mix of both. 'Come. Get your things.'

Wellington got up and followed her out of the cell.

*

The road heading north from Maputo, the EN 1, had been rebuilt with money from South Africa and was in good condition. Luis sat in the rear seat of the *chapa*, sandwiched between a woman with an ample posterior and a skinny young man who coughed continually into a soiled handkerchief.

Luis kept to himself and tried not to think about Miriam, whom he had buried yesterday. It was stifling inside the minibus taxi and opening the windows merely contributed to the heat; to do so was like opening the door on a blast furnace, so the sensible passengers kept the tinted glass closed.

When the taxi stopped in a petrol station for fuel and a break Luis took out his cellphone and dialled a man he had known from their shared time as illegal miners at Eureka. The man, a Swazi, answered and after the exchange of greetings Luis told him he needed some information.

'Anything, Luis. I still have not forgotten how you pulled me free of the rockfall. I might have died when the rest of the tunnel collapsed.'

'I need to know about Wellington. He was picked up by the police. Have you read anything in the newspapers or heard on the radio about him being charged?'

'No,' said the miner. 'In fact, the opposite. One of the guys told me he saw him in Barberton just this morning. Do you want me to get word to the Lion? We will need you in the mine, Luis.'

'No, no,' Luis said hurriedly. 'If you meant what you said, that you are grateful to me for saving your life, then you will please not mention this conversation to Wellington. Do you understand?'

'Of course, Luis. You can count on me keeping quiet.'

Luis ended the call. The Swazi was a good man, but most *zama zamas* would sell their sister to curry favour with Wellington or to earn a few extra rand, which was one and the same thing. Luis knew he should warn Cameron, if he hadn't already heard, that Wellington was on the loose again. He called the former mine manager, but his phone went through to a voicemail message advising he was in Zambia for four days. Luis was about to leave a message, but then his phone cut out and a message on the screen told him he had exceeded his available credit. The *chapa* driver beeped his horn and Luis climbed in as the side door was being slid shut.

The colours of his homeland were richer than the dull tones of South Africa. Here the sun burned brighter, the sea shone bluer and the fronds were the green of precious stones. After the months he had spent underground he still found it hard to be in the harsh light of day. He closed his eyes as the minibus resumed its journey, but sleep would not come to him.

The driver slowed once again, signifying they were approaching a village.

Luis looked out the window and saw the bare branches of dead trees festooned with plastic bags full of cashew nuts. This told him they were coming into Macia, a town famed for its cashew plantations. Luis focused his mind on Wellington, and how he would pay for the murder of Miriam. In the early afternoon the bus crossed the wide verdant floodplain of the Limpopo River on a raised bund and the bridge that led into the coastal town of Xai Xai.

The driver crawled through the crowded main street and turned into the bus station near the markets. Luis had further to go, to reach his son, but he had other business to deal with first. He left the *chapa* and walked to the police station.

Xai Xai was busier and more prosperous than he remembered. Indeed, the whole country seemed to be booming compared to his last visit five years earlier. When he'd held a legitimate job in the mines he would come and go to Mozambique every Christmas holiday, but when he had lost his job and his work permit and joined the ranks of the illegal miners he could no longer cross the border legally at will.

The old colonial buildings were freshly whitewashed and the streets swept. There were more stores than he remembered and people sipped coffee and smoked cigarettes outside sidewalk cafes. The cars that hooted and stopped and started were newer and the people looked better fed than they had in the years of privation during and after the civil war. A first-time visitor to this bustling town would have to search hard to find a bullet pockmark in one of the few unpainted buildings to prove there had ever been a war here, or that close to a million people had died.

Luis found the police station and walked in. A female officer sat behind the charge counter, reading a Portuguese gossip magazine. If she heard him enter, she didn't look up.

'*Bom dia,*' he said. She looked at him over the top of the page she was reading. 'I am looking for *Capitao* Alfredo Simango,' he continued in Portuguese.

'What business do you have with the *capitao*?'

'I am his cousin. It is family business.' He was pleased – at least Alfredo was here. In a letter, Miriam had mentioned that she had seen his cousin in their home town, Inhambane, when he was investigating a case. She had mentioned that Alfredo had told her that he was being moved from Vilanculos to Xai Xai, though he had given no dates.

The officer raised her eyebrows, asked him his name and picked up a telephone handset that might have weighed fifteen kilograms given the effort she exerted to call her superior. 'Sit,' she said to him after she finished the call, and pointed to a wooden bench by the wall.

Luis saw the grubby marks of sweaty heads on the fly-specked wall and kept his back straight. Alfredo emerged from a doorway down the corridor a few minutes later wiping greasy fingers on a paper serviette. The two cousins greeted each other, shook hands, and Alfredo invited him into his office.

'My cousin, I thought you were in South Africa working in the mines. The last time I saw your wife she told me how successful you were.'

Just the mention of Miriam brought back the pain. 'I was. But my wife, that is why I am here to see you, Alfredo. She is dead.'

'No!'

'Yes. Killed by a man in South Africa. I want this man.'

Alfredo rocked back in his chair and folded his hands across his policeman's belly. 'What do the South African police say of this matter?'

Luis thought his cousin was basically a good man, although Miriam had mentioned in her letter Alfredo was driving a new Land Cruiser and Luis knew such a vehicle would be beyond a police captain's honest wage. It had been said, when he had worked in Vilanculos, that he had turned a blind eye, if not actually participated in, the smuggling of goods into Mozambique that had been seized by pirates in the Indian Ocean. 'What do the South Africans care of the death of a poor woman from Mozambique?'

Alfredo nodded his understanding at the flimsy excuse.

'Besides,' Luis continued, 'I am sure the murderer is in Mozambique.'

'He is one of us?'

Luis shook his head. 'Zimbabwean.'

'Criminals, all of them.'

'I have a cellphone number for him, Alfredo. I was hoping you would have the resources to find the name and address of the owner. The government requires everyone who buys a phone or sim card to register their name and address.'

Alfredo nodded. Luis slid across a grubby corner of a piece of paper, with the number written on it. Alfredo studied it. 'It is irregular, if it is not part of a formal investigation, but it can be done. There will be costs – not for me, cousin, but for the people who will find this information for me. I hope you understand.'

Luis reached into his pocket and pulled out ten hundred-rand notes. He placed his palm down flat on the scratched desktop and Alfredo covered his hand. 'I am sorry for your loss, Luis. I will find the owner of this phone for you, but then what do you want me to do?'

Luis freed his hand from under his cousin's, but held his gaze. 'Nothing. I will do the rest.'

*

Wellington could have, at a pinch, contacted some people he knew in Lusaka, the Zambian capital, who, in turn, could have found someone local in Livingstone to do the job, but it was not in his nature to trust people he did not know, or to miss out on the chance of a kill.

He could not take the same flight as Hamilton and McMurtrie in case they recognised him. Instead, as he lay in the grass behind a granite boulder on the slope above Cameron McMurtrie's home, he used his iPhone to book a flight from Johannesburg to Victoria Falls, Zimbabwe, on South African Airways for later that day.

The wonders of modern communication, he mused. Next, he placed a call to his cousin, who had a farm south of Victoria Falls, on the edge of the Matetsi Safari Area, but lived in town. He hoped the man would answer his phone, as without him he would have to find the materials he needed from someone else. Not impossible, but he was working to a tight timeline.

'Hello?'

'*Kanjane*, cousin,' Wellington said down the line.

'Morrison, is that you?' the voice said.

'Please, no names, cousin. It's not businesslike.' Wellington didn't like his real name, Morrison, and hated others using it.

His cousin, Albert, laughed and asked after his health. Wellington raced through the required formalities and asked what he needed to know. 'Are you still fishing on that white settler's farm the way you told me you were last year, when we last met?'

It took a couple of seconds for Albert, who, Wellington recalled, was not the brightest member of the family, to see through the veiled speech. 'Ah, yes. I am, although the parks and wildlife dogs have tried to stop me, I move too fast for them, and I have a supply of *fishing* equipment from another friend who has been mining on his farm.'

Albert had, with the support of the local ZANU-PF chairman, occupied and subsequently been given a prospering cattle ranch during the farm invasions in 2002. The white farmer and his family had been hounded off by Albert and his mob of young supporters. Although they called themselves war veterans, not even Albert, the eldest of the occupiers, had been old enough to bear arms during the liberation struggle, which had ended with Robert Mugabe being elected to power in 1980.

Wellington was bitter about what had happened to his country. He felt no sympathy for the cattle rancher who had seen the family's dogs and his prize bull slaughtered and his children's lives threatened, but he resented the fact uneducated no-hopers like his cousin had become the beneficiaries of huge windfalls, while he had been forced across the border in search of work in the mining industry because of Zimbabwe's economic collapse. Albert had taken over a working farm with a big house and a workforce of fifty men and their families, and now he resorted to feeding himself and his wife and four whelps by fishing illegally in the rivers of the nearby safari area and Hwange National Park. He had tried to bully the farm labour into working for him, but the herd boys had left when he'd failed to pay them; he had stripped the grand farmhouse of its contents, including the copper water pipes and electrical wiring from the walls, and sold it all. When the money he made had run out he had lived off the white man's cattle until most of them perished in a foot-and-mouth outbreak. Those mangy beasts that had survived he had also sold. Albert was left with hundreds of acres of thorny bush and no means of income. So now he fished with dynamite.

'Good, good,' said Wellington to the dim-witted failure. 'I will be in the Falls this evening. We must drink some beer together and you must sell me some of your bait.'

'It will be a pleasure, cousin,' Albert replied. 'Times are very tough here in Zimbabwe and my family are hungry. It will be good to see you again, Morris – I mean, cousin.'

Wellington ended the call and rolled back onto his belly and picked up his small binoculars. There was movement at McMurtrie's house. The door opened and the man's thin white wife came out. She was wearing the dressing-gown she had been in when she had greeted McMurtrie earlier, but Wellington's keen eyes noted she had shed the high heels and stockings that had poked from beneath the gown. Her hair, coiffed before, was now in disarray. The mascara at her eyes was smudged. She looked like the whore that mine gossip said she was.

McMurtrie was a weak man who had let a woman make a mockery of him. Such a thing would never happen in Wellington's world. A wife who declared she wanted to leave for another man would not make it as far as the front door, let alone to another country, where this one had apparently gone, before slinking back with her tail between her soiled legs. Wellington was alternately repulsed and aroused by the thought of what McMurtrie's wife had done. McMurtrie was Wellington's enemy, yet he felt a strange kind of kinship with the man. Both he and his nemesis were warriors, now sworn to destroy each other. While Wellington would never have let a woman treat him the way McMurtrie's wife had, Wellington pitied his foe. This woman was an unwanted distraction for the mine manager.

Wellington watched the woman feed the dogs. Her moves were jerky, resentful, as she dropped the bowls of food in front of the hounds. She raised the back of her hand to a smudged eye.

'She is not good enough for you, Cameron, my friend,' Wellington whispered as he watched her through the binoculars.

McMurtrie and the Hamilton woman were on their way to Livingstone, as per the original plan, and Wellington would follow them there, via the twin town of Victoria Falls, just across the cascading Zambezi, and launch the final battle of this war between the empire below and Global Resources above.

The woman bent over to shift a bowl of food so a small dog could get its share. The satin of the gown slid up, revealing a long thigh. Wellington felt himself swell against the damp grass and cool earth beneath his loins.

This unfaithful whore needed to be taught a lesson. He wanted to move down the hillside, darting from cover to cover with the practised ease he'd learnt during the bush war. He had served in the struggle and had become disenchanted by the government's failure to deliver on the riches it had promised those who had sacrificed so much for Zimbabwe. He had been slaving in South Africa, for the whites, when the farms in Zimbabwe had been doled out to the well-connected and the party's thugs, such as Albert. He had turned to crime, and had made himself more money than his cousin's stupid ilk, but still he wanted more. It was not enough simply to win.

He rolled to one side and moved his hand to his belt. He wanted McMurtrie's wife, as well as his scalp, but if he took her now, used her and killed her, then word might reach McMurtrie before he boarded

302

his connecting flight for the wilds of Zambia. He needed McMurtrie to get on the flight to the copper belt for his plan to succeed.

He closed his eyes and imagined her, screaming, fighting, yielding. He let his imagination fulfil him as he bucked against the grass. The wife would die, soon enough, but it would appear an accident.

That would just leave McMurtrie's daughter.

25

Despite the best efforts of Kylie's personal assistant, Sandy, back in Australia, there was no way they could have connected to the charter flight in Livingstone in time to reach the remote Global Resources mine north of Kitwe in the copper belt on the same day they flew from Nelspruit.

Instead, they had to stay the night at Livingstone and Kylie had been happy to let their boss, Jan, recommend a hotel, which Sandy had booked. Kylie had not even bothered googling the hotel.

'I've heard it's a *lekker* place,' Cameron said as they exited customs from the small terminal and walked past the touts to the driver who held a sign saying, *Global Resource, Mr Cameron and Mrs Kylie.* 'That would be us.'

Kylie was glad they hadn't been able to make the connection. She wasn't here to sightsee, but after the horrendous few days they had endured she was looking forward to a quiet night.

The drive took them through the suburbs of Livingstone, mostly single-storey colonial-era houses with tin roofs, and then into the edge of the town, which seemed to be bustling with tourists and locals alike.

'Have you been here before?' she asked him. Cameron had slept through most of the flight.

'We drove up here on a family holiday a few years ago. Jess loved it. Tania hated it.'

'I didn't ask when you boarded – is your daughter all right?'

He nodded. 'She's staying with friends. I saw my wife this morning again.'

Kylie raised her eyebrows, waiting for him to supply more details, but he clammed up.

'I'll sort it when we get back.'

They travelled in an awkward silence for a few minutes.

'This place was a real dump when we were here last,' Cameron said, pointing out the window of the van. 'None of these shops were here. The place was rundown, businesses were closed and the roads were *kak*.'

'It seems pretty prosperous now.'

'Yes. But a lot of Zambia's prosperity has come at Zimbabwe's expense. A lot of tourist business from Zimbabwe, particularly the town of Victoria Falls just across the river, moved over to this side.'

'Last night . . .' Kylie began, changing the subject.

He held a hand up. 'I'm sorry. I don't know what happened. I didn't mean anything, Kylie, and I apologise if I offended you.'

'No, not at all. In fact, what I was going to say was that I apologise, for overreacting. I know you wouldn't have tried anything. Besides, you were too drunk.'

He laughed, though it was short-lived. He went back to gazing out the window, where the scenery changed from chaotic African cityscape to the dusty coloured bush. Through breaks in the vegetation, though, she started to catch glimpses of the river, its surface dark and rippled as it raced towards the sheer drop-off downstream. On its verges was a belt of thicker, greener trees and reeds.

'The Zambezi.'

Cameron had said it matter-of-factly, but the word was none-theless laden with exoticism. She felt a frisson of excitement at the prospect of seeing the Victoria Falls. A one-line addendum in Sandy's itinerary had mentioned that the hotel they were staying at was inside the Mosi oi Tunya National Park – the name meant 'smoke that thunders' – and that it would be possible to walk to the edge of the falls. She wasn't in Zambia for a holiday, but she couldn't come all this way, stay in Livingstone, and not see its famous natural wonder.

They passed a roadside picnic spot where people were drinking beers from cooler boxes and taking in the increasingly breathtaking view of the river.

'What are we going to do about Wellington?' Cameron asked.

'I called our government relations people in Johannesburg this morning and they put me in touch with the National Prosecuting Authority. They're sending someone to Barberton the day after we get back, so we can brief them on Wellington's crimes. I asked that the local police be left out and the agent I spoke to said that wouldn't be a problem.'

Cameron nodded in agreement. 'Our Colonel Sindisiwe Radebe is rotten to the core. We need to bring her down or, at worst, get her replaced.'

'I want him, Cameron.'

'You're talking like an African now,' he said.

*

Luis sat with his mother, on the sandy bluff overlooking the Indian Ocean. Behind them was the Ponta da Barra Lighthouse, which only worked for a couple of hours a night because its solar panel was faulty.

Lights were beginning to twinkle out on the greying waters, as the squid fishermen set out for their night's work. A young man in mismatching wetsuit top and pants carried his spear gun and flippers down to the water's edge. He would be hunting crayfish, bound for the *braais* of the South African tourists camped with their off-road trailers in the nearby campground.

'How is my son?'

'He is asleep,' his mother said. 'He will cry more tomorrow.'

'Jose is lucky to have you, Mother.'

'He would be luckier to have a father. He is growing up too fast. He keeps company with bad boys.'

Luis ploughed the sand with his toes. It was dirty beneath the fine, pale surface layer. The tourists thought of this place as paradise, but it had also seen sorrow and death during the bad years. He had fought and he had studied in order to escape the inevitability that he might end up out at sea rowing a flimsy *lula* boat made of driftwood and polystyrene foam, or diving for crayfish. His mother cleaned holiday lodges owned by foreigners. She barely earned enough to survive, yet she sent his son to school each morning in a freshly cleaned and pressed uniform.

'I only ever wanted the best for you, Luis.' She gestured out to the twinkling lights. 'You do not belong out there. You are an engineer, a geologist, a metallurgist.'

He nodded, but sighed. The letters after his name would not feed his son, or save his mother from the backbreaking work she would do until she could crawl on her knees no longer in a tourist's bathroom. A man with woolly, unkempt dreadlocks and dressed in layer upon layer of tattered rags walked along the beach waving his arms in the air. Snippets of his incoherent shouts reached Luis on the wind and spoiled the travel-brochure illusion of paradise spread out below him. He was envious, in a way, of the madman. He wanted to rant and shout and curse heaven and earth and cry out for the wife he'd lost, but he was tied to the real world by his memories, his dreams and his ambitions. Perhaps God had cursed him for being vain, for wanting more than he had a right to dream of. Luis had lusted for prestige and wealth and the trappings of a modern, peaceful society. It had almost been in his reach, in the early days in South Africa, but he had been dragged down into the hell of the country's deadly criminal underworld. He had been punished for his greed.

'You cannot go back to South Africa, can you?'

He looked at his mother. How could she know?

'Your wife, God rest her soul, believed you, Luis, because she wanted to. I know you. You would have come home to your family if you still had a proper job. You would have been like the others who come streaming home across the border at Christmas time if you had a job that paid for an annual vacation. Even when your father worked for the Boers, in the bad days, he was still allowed home for Christmas. If it was just that your papers were not legal you would have still come, like the *mahambane*, walking through the bush. Yet you stayed. Was the criminals' money worth it, Luis? Was it worth your son drifting into a life of crime, too, because he lacks a father's discipline?'

He looked at her and blinked. He felt the tears sting his eyes and turned away from his mother's gaze.

'Look at me, my son.'

He kept his gaze fixed on the lights on the water. Maybe he should use his money to buy a boat, and accept his fate. He could learn again the lessons of childhood. At least he could feed his son and his mother with honest work.

She grabbed his chin between her thumb and forefinger and turned his face to her. 'I have kept your school work, your papers from university, your thesis. I know you like no one else, my son. You are like your father. He went down into their mines and he came back and he fought for his country's freedom. He would not have been happy as a fisherman, Luis. He longed for more, but not for himself, for his children. For you. I want you to stay here and be a father to your boy.'

He looked into his mother's eyes and saw the strength of a woman who had endured so much loss – far more than he had. She did not question her fate. She cared only for her remaining son and her only grandchild.

Something she had said, just then, came back to him.

'You kept everything? My thesis?'

She nodded. As the realisation began to show on his own face she allowed herself a small smile of satisfaction.

*

Wellington Shumba smoked a cigar as he reclined on a sun lounge, in the dark, near the pool bar in the grounds of the Kingdom Hotel in the Zimbabwean holiday town of Victoria Falls.

His cousin wore his best clothes – a nylon shirt decorated with little balls of worn fibres, shiny grey slacks and scuffed vinyl shoes. Wellington's clothes all carried brand-name labels, none of them knock-offs. Wellington exhaled and regarded Albert through the fug of smoke and the perspective of success.

This man, and the other lazy, greedy idiots above him, had ruined Zimbabwe for all of them, but in a funny way they had spurred others on to greatness. Without the inmates who'd been given the key to the asylum, Wellington might still have been drilling holes in the ore seam beneath Bindura, earning his pay and blowing it on *chibuku* beer and whores. He would never have lost his job and he would have died without achieving very much.

But no, Albert, and his fearless leader, the comrade president, and every ZANU-PF fat cat and lackey in between had screwed his beautiful country and forced the hard workers to leave and set up somewhere else. The xenophobic resentment, official and unofficial, that Wellington had encountered in South Africa had pushed him into a life of crime and, eventually, the netherworld of the *zama zamas*. It was fate. It was a life he was destined for. There, he was able to combine the mining knowledge he had learned in Zimbabwe and the criminal skills he had developed on the streets of Alexandra and Soweto to deadly, lucrative effect.

'The fishing gear is in the bag,' Albert whispered conspiratorially.

Wellington looked down at the striped bag and nodded. He inhaled again, savouring the aromatic flavour, adding to it with the expensive cognac. He felt the warm, giddy head spin of victory, which danced enticingly in front of him through the smoke, personified in the ample bottom of the waitress who sashayed past them, caught his eye and smiled. 'Thank you, Albert.'

Albert raised his eyebrows. 'What are you going to do with it?'

Wellington raised his guard, as he would if he was anticipating the first blow in a shebeen fight. 'Why do you ask?'

Albert spread his hands wide and smiled. 'Just curious, cousin. Perhaps it is a task that you might need some assistance with. Things have been tough on the farm, and I am always looking to diversify.'

Wellington held back the laugh that rose in his throat. He didn't want to draw unnecessary attention to himself. '*Things have been tough on the farm.*' If Wellington had been given a mine he, even as a lowly miner, would have known how to run it and make a billion US dollars. Albert had been given a profitable cattle ranch and turned it into a useless sprawling patch of thorn trees.

Albert ran a finger around the collar of his shirt. 'The offices of our party were bombed in Gweru last month. It was said to be the work of reactionaries from the opposition Movement for Democratic Change. These lapdogs of the British will do anything to undermine the revolution.'

Wellington laid his cigar in the ashtray and fixed his cousin with his eyes. The man was a moron. Wellington raised his right hand in a clenched fist. '*Pamberi ne* revolution, comrade.'

'*Pamberi,*' his cousin smiled with relief, also raising his hand in the black power salute.

The idiot thinks I'm serious, Wellington thought. 'It is late, cousin, and I have work to do.'

Albert winked and nodded. 'I understand. It was good seeing you again, cousin.'

Wellington stood and clapped him on the shoulder. 'You too. *Fambai zvakanaka.*' *Go well, my arse,* Wellington thought as his cousin shook his hand. 'I will take care of the bill.'

Wellington took a final puff of his cigar before he stubbed it out, drained the last of his cognac and left a fistful of greenbacks on the bar for the barman. He did, indeed, have work to do in the privacy of his room.

*

Cameron sent Jessica an SMS from his room in the Royal Livingstone. He had been chauffeured there in a golf buggy driven by an

African man in white shorts and safari jacket and a matching pith helmet. The luxurious room overlooked a manicured lawn that rolled gently to the Zambezi River. He could see the spray rising from the falls, just beyond the bar. *You would love this place.*

Gee, thanks, she messaged back.

At least she hadn't lost her sense of humour. *Heard from Mom?*

The reply pinged back a few moments later. She was faster with her slender, nimble fingers than he was with his miner's stubs. *Hectic, Dad. She phoned all afternoon. I'm meeting her for coffee after school.*

Cameron shook his head. What had happened to their family that mother and daughter had to schedule an appointment for coffee? He wished Tania had never come back and, at the same time, suddenly felt guilty for running away and leaving them to sort things out. His room phone chirped.

'Hello?'

'It's Kylie. I'm going for a drink before dinner. Do you want to come along?'

He had hardly slept the night before – apart from lying all over her – and he had been sick as a dog that morning. What he should do was have a shower and go to bed, but right now it seemed like a cold beer was the only thing that would save him. 'Sure, thanks.'

'OK. See you at the bar.' She hung up, abrupt as ever.

Cameron checked himself in the mirror. His face was stubbled and his shirt creased from the flight, but he couldn't be bothered changing and assumed Kylie wouldn't either. He walked out and hailed a passing golf buggy. The driver took him back to reception. Off to his right was a colonial-themed bar: slow-turning overhead fans, dark wooden panelling and matching furnishing. The long, polished bar looked inviting, but even more so was the view he glimpsed outside, beyond the lawn. He walked past the pool, where a couple of blonde European tourists were treading water in each other's arms, and down to another bar set on a wide wooden deck overhanging the Zambezi. An African man was playing show tunes on a flute, but not even that could distract from the magnificence of the Zambezi and the curtain of spray that hung over the point where the river disappeared into the gorge.

'Mosi, please,' he said to the waiter as he sat down in a deep armchair. He'd beaten Kylie to the bar. A dark-haired woman walked past him and smiled. He smiled back. He hadn't even had time to think of himself as single before his wife had come back into his life. Self-consciously, he looked over his shoulder, checking to see if Kylie was in sight yet. She wasn't, and he wondered why he'd felt strangely guilty making eye contact with the brunette. The waiter brought his chilled Mosi lager, named after the waterfall.

The sun was melting into a haze of oranges and reds beyond the spray and the Mosi worked its soothing magic. For a minute it was almost possible to forget Tania, the mine, Wellington and the horrors they had been through. He wondered if Kylie would ever bother to come back here once she returned to the safety of predictable Australia.

'God, it's beautiful, isn't it?'

He turned and saw Kylie, her skin bathed in the reflected glow of the sunset. She had changed into a black cocktail dress that ended above her knees. She smiled and her teeth shone like polished ivory. For the first time he noticed, really noticed, how attractive she was. Even her business clothes had been mannish and the mine overalls she'd worn underground had cloaked her figure. He stood. She smiled, a little self-consciously.

'You look . . .'

She waved a hand. 'Forget it. It's the last clean stuff in my bag.'

'Drink?'

'Gin and tonic, please.'

He beckoned to the waiter and moved an armchair for her to sit in. She had high heels on and smelled of soap and perfume. She had showered. Her hair was straighter than he remembered from the flight.

'Thanks.' She lowered herself into her chair and crossed her legs. The waiter brought her drink and they raised their glasses. 'What shall we drink to?'

He shrugged. 'Africa.'

She smiled. 'Crazy fucked-up beautiful place that it is.'

He laughed. His boss was a stunner and he hadn't noticed. 'That it is.'

'I walked down to the falls just after we arrived. Pretty spectacular,' she said.

He set his beer down. 'I'll have to take you to the Zimbabwean side some time. The view's different over there. On this side you're on the edge, looking down; on the Zimbabwean side you can see the breadth of the falls. It's spectacular from both sides.'

'That might be nice,' she said. She took the swizzle stick from the glass and sucked it dry.

Cameron ordered another beer. He felt unsettled suddenly and craved the relaxation the alcohol would bring. Only natural, he thought, given what they'd been through lately. He caught her perfume again, on the slight breeze.

He looked out at the view, not knowing what to say. He wanted to try again, to compliment her on how she looked, but it seemed the moment had past. He was hopeless with women. No wonder Tania had left him.

'We got off on the wrong foot, you and I,' she said.

He looked at her but stayed quiet.

'Even in the video conferences I was always talking over the top of you. I thought, Jan thought – we all thought – we knew better than you when it came to the *zama zamas*.'

'I can understand you people in head office not wanting to authorise an underground war.'

She shook her head. 'We were wrong. We should have trusted you, Cameron. It's only now that I see that.'

He nodded. 'We were making headway. The armed security guys were only part of the strategy I was working on. With that crooked Sindisiwe Radebe in charge of the local police I knew we had to go around her. I was briefing the prosecutors and the Department of Mineral Resources on the problem and we were bypassing the police. My guys and I were filling out the charge dockets for the *zama zamas* that we would arrest from time to time, and we would work direct with the prosecutors to get them into court. It was working, although on several occasions Colonel Radebe arranged for the prisoners to "escape" or walk on so-called technicalities with the paperwork. It was two steps forward, one step back, but we were making some slow headway. When you guys in Australia stopped us using armed security we lost our ability to take the criminal miners into custody, and the prosecutions stopped.'

'I can see that,' she said. 'We all thought you should leave it to the police, but the police were working against you.'

Finally, he thought, she was beginning to understand.

'We arranged an amnesty,' he said, and explained how his men had posted leaflets around the mine and handed them to *zama zamas* in person when they passed them in the tunnels, as some-times happened. 'But only half-a-dozen illegals took advantage of it. We found out that Wellington was threatening to kill the families of anyone who deserted him. These men were single and desperate to get out. In the end, we would have had to go down there with the armed security. It would have been the only way to bust Wellington's hold on the mine and his men.'

She sat there, taking it in, saying nothing for a while.

'What are you thinking?' he asked.

'Oh, nothing. Well, not something I want to talk about. It's just strange, the whole sequence of events.'

He didn't press her for more clues as to what she was processing in that sharp mind of hers. She really was the whole package, he thought: brains, beauty, balls.

'What are you smiling at?'

'My own joke,' he said and looked over his shoulder, across the lawn to the terrace restaurant. 'Looks like they're ready for dinner.'

The sun had set, turning the Zambezi from molten gold to rippling lead. They finished their drinks and walked across the lawn to where tables had been laid out on the verandah of the hotel.

A waiter in a black tie showed them to a table for two lit by a paraffin lantern, whose light danced on the cutlery.

'The company's paying, but you'll know the wines better than me,' she said, indicating for the waiter to give him the wine list.

Cameron scanned the list and ordered his favourite red, a Zandvliet shiraz from the Cape, as well as another beer and gin and tonic.

*

Tania McMurtrie lit another cigarette and finished the bottle of wine. She went to the fridge, hoping she'd missed a spare bottle the last time she had looked. There was none in the linen cupboard, which had served as their cellar.

She wanted another drink. She *needed* another drink to keep the despair from rising up inside her again. She looked around the home where she had lived for fifteen years and she knew she had been wrong to come back.

Cameron was away. His work was everything to him. Her daughter was away – her mother meant nothing to her. Tania drew back her arm and threw the empty glass at the wall. It shattered. She felt the tears roll down her cheeks.

Chuck – she'd thought his name manly when they'd first met online and now it reminded her of vomit – had emailed her, pleading with her to come back. The perversions they'd shared via cyberspace had been exciting, at a distance, but ridiculous in the flesh. He was an overweight, overbearing, balding bully with no money. She had been mad to think her life could be better with him.

She had come home with good intentions and full of contrition. She would make her marriage work. She would not complain about life in the small *dorpie* of Barberton. She would try and make her daughter like her. She would be faithful this time. She would be sober.

Tania wiped her eyes with the back of her hand. To hell with them all. She picked up her phone, opened a new SMS and scrolled through her contacts until she came to Barend, the plumber. She tapped in the letters. *Back in town. Are you free?*

She wondered if he was in the pub. He was divorced, and swore he would never marry again. It only took three minutes for her phone to buzz. *For you, always. Free and hard.*

Tania didn't smile. She felt no shame, as she stood, a little unsteadily, and rummaged in her handbag for her keys. Then she remembered there was no car parked behind their home. Cameron had sold it. He didn't want her back. They hated her. She remembered him saying she should use his mine *bakkie*. Ordinarily there was no way she would have been seen parking the mine vehicle outside a hotel. That was just too obvious in a small town. Now she didn't care. She had told Cameron, when he'd asked her if she had cheated on him, that she hadn't. That had been a lie.

She found his keys in the wooden bowl by the front door. She didn't bother changing. It was only Barend, and he would most likely rip a few buttons off when she walked through the hotel room door. It was the way he liked it, the way she liked it. Fast. Uncaring. Exciting. She hiccupped as she bounced off the doorframe and walked out into the night.

When she sat in the Toyota and started the engine she did have a pang of guilt. She took her phone out of her handbag and scrolled through the recent calls until she came to Cameron's number. She sniffed. She wanted so much to be good, and for them to be happy, but she never had been. Why had he left her, when she had come home to him? Her thumb hovered over the call button, but then she thought of Barend's hard body and the way he did her from behind so she wouldn't have to look into his eyes. She tossed the phone on the passenger seat.

Tania released the handbrake, reversed, then let the car roll down the drive in neutral. She knew every centimetre of the winding gravel road and how fast she could take each bend, regardless of her level of sobriety. Sometimes, coming back from an afternoon of drinking and fucking, when she could barely speak, it had felt like the car had driven itself home. She had always allowed enough time for a short nap, to sober up a little before Cameron came home from work and Jess came back from whatever friend she preferred to her mother.

She accelerated into the first bend and took it with ease, although the Toyota's rock-hard rear suspension made it bounce a couple of times through the corner. She liked the loss of control. It made her shriek with excitement. She pushed the pedal harder as the next bend approached.

A genet darted into the beam of her headlights and Tania swerved to miss the spotted catlike creature. The rear of the *bakkie* drifted and Tania yanked the wheel back the other way, overcorrecting.

'Shit!'

She put her left foot on the clutch and stabbed the brake pedal with her right. There was plenty of room to stop, but the car didn't respond. There was a squishy feeling and her right foot went to the floor. The Toyota didn't slow. The edge of the cliff raced towards her.

Too late, she remembered the handbrake, but as she yanked on it the front wheels went off the edge. This couldn't be happening, she thought, and it felt like the end of her life was coming, not in a rush but in slow motion.

Then the truck stopped.

Tania screamed, then forced herself to think. The Hilux teetered on the edge of the precipice. The drop, almost sheer, was two hundred metres and the steep hillside was studded with boulders. The truck creaked as she breathed. She reached behind her for the seatbelt and fastened it. She never wore a belt on the drive from their house down to the main road, and if she thought the police weren't patrolling she didn't bother at all. She didn't know if the seatbelt would save her if the truck tipped over the edge, but without it she would surely die. Even the tiny movement of fastening the belt made the vehicle rock. It settled.

Slowly, carefully, she leaned towards the passenger seat, but her phone was just out of reach.

'Damn it.'

She unclipped the belt again. She needed to call for help. As she leaned, the car creaked again. Tania pressed the dial button, then tossed the phone into the foot well as the vehicle started to slide. This was it, it was going over the edge.

Tania reached for where the door handle would be on her little car, but the Toyota was different. By the time she had found it the *bakkie* was bouncing down the slope, rocks and trees racing towards her.

'Cameron! Jess!'

She must get out, she thought, or she would die in the truck as soon as it ended its fall.

Just as she opened the door, the nose of the Hilux slammed into a tree. The airbag exploded in front of her, hitting her side on and pinning her. The engine had smashed through the firewall and her legs were numb. Tania breathed and screamed. Her ribs, she guessed, were shattered, but at least she was alive. The phone was out of reach.

She heard a voice, somewhere.

'Tania?'

Then the spark of the shorting battery lead caught a dribble of petrol and the Toyota exploded.

26

Cameron saw Tania's name flash on the screen of his phone and cursed inwardly.

It had, surprisingly, been a fantastic night. The food had been excellent and they had ordered a second bottle of wine.

A band had been playing, a female singer crooning jazz and slow songs from the fifties and sixties. Three couples had got up from dinner to dance on the wide verandah.

'That's something I've always wanted to do but have never learned,' Kylie had said.

'My wife made me learn to dance for our wedding. I actually enjoyed it and we went to lessons regularly for a while.'

'I'm hopeless,' she said. 'When I have to dance, at weddings and things like that, I end up stepping on my partner's toes. But I love all those shows on television, you know, where the minor celebrities you've never heard of try to dance.'

He watched her, leaning over the back of her chair, watching the couples. They were into the second bottle and the candlelight made her exposed arm shine like a seam of free gold. 'Come, let's dance.'

She looked back at him. 'Is that how you ask a girl for a dance in South Africa?'

'*Ja*.' He stood and held out his hand.

Kylie looked nervous, almost scared. He liked her on the back foot, but this wasn't about a power exchange. He wanted to dance with her. He bowed at the waist. 'Please, Dr Hamilton, may I have the pleasure?'

She smiled, still unsure, and for a second he thought he would have to resume his seat, looking like a fool. 'OK.'

He led her by the hand, the skin smooth but warm with uncertainty, to the fringe of where the other couples were gliding by. She gripped his hand as he laid his other on her hip. She felt stiff and tense as he started to move. He moved closer to the band, but she fought him and tried to steer back to the outer area.

He moved his mouth closer to her ear and felt her body go even more rigid. 'You have to let me lead.'

'Oh. Sorry. It doesn't come naturally.'

'I know. Relax.'

She exhaled and he felt her start to ease into the music a little more. A stiletto heel stabbed his right foot and he tried to hide the grimace.

'Sorry.'

'You're doing fine.'

'I'm rubbish.'

'Let me lead you.'

'OK,' she said.

He held her tighter and she let him draw her into him, finally giving in as he took her deeper into the rhythm. He twirled her and she gave a small shriek, causing another couple to titter, but her face was flushed with joy when he brought her back into his arms.

'Phew.'

'You're a natural.'

She threw back her head and laughed. 'Liar.'

As the song ended he went for broke and dipped her. Kylie's body initially stiffened, but then she trusted him and arched her back in his arms. The other dancers applauded and they went back to the table.

'Gosh, that was fun.'

'We could do it again . . .' He refilled their glasses.

'It's a slow song this time.'

'Less risk of injury in the workplace.'

They each took a big sip and he led her back out onto the terrace. The other couples were moving slowly, dancing closer. He drew her to him again and this time she didn't fight it. He and Tania hadn't danced like this for years. He thought he should feel guilty, but he didn't. That morning, as she'd tried to take him in her mouth, on her knees in the hallway, he had almost succumbed. He had moved her hands from him and walked past her, into the shower, and locked the bathroom door. He hadn't told Kylie and he hadn't told Jess, but it was over between them. He had been a fool to think that Jess would be better off with two parents locked in a loveless relationship than with just one who really loved her.

Kylie looked up at him. 'What are you thinking?'

'That I like this song.'

She rested her head on his chest. 'Me too.'

'I'm sorry, for being so stubborn,' he said.

'Me too.'

The band stopped and the singer said they were taking a break. Terrible timing, Cameron thought, as they went back to their table.

'It's late,' Kylie said, looking at her watch.

He called the waiter over as they finished the last of their wine. They sky was clear, and the moon laid a silvery trail on the Zambezi. 'I was thinking I'd walk back to my room, rather than take the golf buggy.'

'I had the same thought,' she said.

'I can drop you on the way,' Cameron said.

They started to walk along the grass and Kylie stopped to take off her high heels. 'Damn impractical footwear.'

'Nice, though.'

'Thanks.'

They walked side by side, in silence for a while, on the lawns in front of the accommodation units, which each housed four suites. 'Ouch,' she said.

Cameron stopped. Kylie lifted a foot and rocked on one leg. He put out a hand to steady her and she grabbed it. 'It's a thorn.'

'Maybe you'd better put your shoes back on. We can walk on the pathway.'

Kylie slipped one shoe on and then, still holding his hand, put on the other. She was still a little unsteady, as her heels slid into the irrigated lawn and the wine started to take effect. He held on to her hand and when they reached the pathway he didn't let go. She looked down at their entwined hands, then up into his eyes. He raised his eyebrows in a question. She said nothing, but just started walking, so they continued like that, holding hands.

When they got to her block she led the way upstairs and let go of his hand to fetch the key card out of her handbag. Cameron's heart was beating fast. He couldn't remember feeling this nervous, this out of control, this excited in a long time. She produced the key and turned to him. She said nothing.

His phone rang in his pocket and he took it out.

*

Kylie sat on the end of her bed and slipped off her shoes and ran both hands through her hair. 'Jeez, girl, what were you *thinking?*'

She had been a hair's breadth from asking him in for coffee. The dancing had done it. She had felt the heat building in the pit of her belly and wondered if he could sense it as she had. Her face felt flushed. The phone had saved them.

'No, no, no!' She slapped the bed. This was not what she needed. She was not falling for a big South African mining oaf. She was just feeling sorry for him, but then his bloody wife had called on his phone and he had turned tail and scurried off to his room. She was stupid for almost inviting him in, and he was still in love with Tania, despite what she had done to him. Stupid prick. They had probably had sex that morning when he'd gone home to her, and now he thought he could get his end away with her on a business trip. She had lived and worked around miners long enough to know how men acted. 'Bastard.'

Kylie stood and grabbed the hem of her dress and lifted it over her head and tossed it on the bed. 'Dickhead.'

She walked to the bathroom and opened the taps on the spa bath. Next, she pulled down her pants and hopped on one leg as she took them off, then opened a small bottle of bubble bath and tipped it in. 'Arsehole.'

The doorbell rang.

'Shit.' She went back into the room and leaned over and grabbed her dress from the bed and pulled it back on again. It was probably the bloody butler, who came with each room, coming to ask if she wanted her bed turned down and a bloody chocolate on her pillow. She flung open the door.

Cameron stood there.

'Can I help you with something?'

'Yes.'

He stepped into her room and took her in his arms and kissed her.

It was like when they were dancing. He picked her up off her feet and turned her, so her back was against the wall of the hotel room. She registered him kicking the door closed behind him. He was bloody sure of himself, but she preferred that to him moping.

Their tongues met. She was hungry for him, and as much as she'd told herself that she didn't want this, she knew that she really did, so she put her arms around the back of his neck and held him tight. She hooked a leg around him, wanting the feeling of weightlessness to continue. To hell with work and to hell with his wife, she thought. She remembered the whoosh as he'd dipped her in his arms on the dance floor. That's what she wanted, for the rug to be pulled out from under her; to fall and know she would be caught.

She loved the feel of his big hands, the weight of him pinning her to the wall like a butterfly under glass, the bulge below his waist, pressing into her. She lowered a hand from his neck, down between them, and felt him.

He set her down and she leaned against the wall, catching her breath. He lowered his face as he freed one of her breasts from her bra and dress. She ran her fingers through his thick hair as he took her nipple into his mouth and drew on it.

Kylie brought his face to hers again and kissed him. He picked her up, this time cradling her in his big arms, and carried her to the bed, where he dropped her. She bounced and giggled.

He stood over her and started unbuttoning his shirt as he smiled down at her. Suddenly he stopped. She saw the look of consternation wipe the moment from his face.

'What is it?' Not his bloody wife, she hoped.

'I didn't think . . . it's been so long since I was single. I don't have . . .'

'Oh, is that all?' She rolled over on the bed and reached for her handbag on the side table. She had to rummage all the way to the bottom but, mercifully, the little foil three-pack was still there. She had waited a hell of a long time for this rainy day. She was about to toss the condoms to him, then had a better idea. She beckoned to him with a crooked finger. 'Come here.'

'*Yebo*, boss.'

He walked to her. She swung her legs over the bed and reached for his zipper, sliding it down. Kylie looked up at him and licked her lips lasciviously. She put a hand in his pants and felt the glorious weight and length of him. She freed him and could see he was more than ready for her. She massaged the head of him, then up and down the shaft a couple of times, revelling in the way his eyes were locked on hers. She had never had the opportunity to try something that she and some girlfriends had laughed about over a glass of wine years earlier. She ripped open the foil packet with her teeth and placed the condom flat, between her upper and lower lips and teeth. Kylie lowered her face to his erect penis, positioned the folded rubber over him, then used her teeth to roll the latex onto him. It must have worked, because she heard him groan.

Grinning, she looked back up at him and rolled the condom the rest of the way down. 'Can't have you going to work without the correct personal protective equipment.'

'I want you, now.'

'Shit!' She got up, suddenly remembering something, and ducked around him and ran to the bathroom.

'What is it?'

'The bloody bathtub!'

He followed her in and grabbed the towel rail to stop from falling as his feet slipped on the floor, which was awash with hot soapy water. He had to laugh as he watched her get down on her knees and fish for the plug. She found it, and the water gurgled.

Still on her knees she looked over her shoulder. 'What's so funny?'

He shook his head, slowly. 'Nothing.' Her dress was wet from where she had leaned into the tub, and the hem had ridden up her thighs. She was bare underneath. He undid his belt. 'Put the plug back in.'

She did as he asked and stood and pulled off her sopping dress and unclipped her bra. He was naked by the time she was, tossing his clothes about the wet floor. She climbed into the spa bath and slid so her back was against the wall, her breasts bobbing on the waterline, shrouded with bubbles. He climbed in after her and pulled her to him. Kylie sat astride him. They kissed again, steam rising around them. He brushed a plastered strand of hair from her face so he could look at her. His gaze sent a shiver down her back. The arms that held her were hard and muscled, the skin above the tan line pale.

Kylie rose up on her knees and pressed her soapy breasts against his chest, the wiry hair teasing her nipples. She reached between them and rubbed the head of his penis against herself. She lowered herself down on him, slowly. God, she thought, as the momentary discomfort gave way to pleasure, it had been too long. She lay her cheek on his shoulder, savouring the fullness.

'No,' he whispered. She felt his hands on her cheeks, rocking her back. 'I want to see your face.'

She nodded, her lower lip between her teeth as she started to move on him. Greedy for her, he raised his pelvis to meet her rocking. He reached out an arm on the side of the tub to steady himself and felt the button. He pushed it. Her eyes widened at the first shock of the bubbles then the smile played across her face as she adjusted their position to take full advantage of the new sensation.

Kylie gave herself over to the sheer unadulterated lust of the moment and rode him harder and faster. More water slopped over the rim of the tub, but she didn't care. He had his hands on her breasts, his thumbs and forefingers, slick with the suds, alternately pinching and slipping from her nipples.

He stared into her eyes as she came. She threw back her head and cried out with the sheer bloody joy of release.

Her vision blurred and she felt light-headed from the steam coming off the water and the after-effects of her orgasm. He was still moving inside her. 'What do you want, Cameron? Anything . . .' she breathed.

She would do it, she told herself, anything he wanted, to please him. She had an overwhelming urge to tell him to take the condom off and fuck her bare. She didn't know if he had told the truth about never cheating on his wife, but you could never trust a miner.

'Just you.' She felt her second orgasm coming as he began to shake beneath her.

*

The next morning after breakfast on the same terrace where they had first danced, they took one of the hotel's courtesy cars to the airport. They sat side by side in the back of the limousine, holding hands.

Kylie tried to find interest in the Livingstone streetscape as they skirted the town, but couldn't. 'Is it just me, or is this, like, totally weird?'

'Totally.'

She laughed. 'We sound like a couple of teenagers.'

He squeezed her hand. 'I feel like one. It's not all bad.'

'You don't . . .'

'What?' he asked.

'You know, regret it, or anything? I mean, these things happen on work trips, right?'

He leaned back from her and gave a disapproving look. 'They do? Maybe to you, but not to me.'

Kylie punched him in the arm. 'You know what I mean.'

He shook his head. 'No. It feels right to me. Is it right for you?'

She leaned over and kissed him as the driver stopped to take a ticket from the car park security guard. He drove through to the general aviation area, separate from the main terminal. There were no customs or immigration formalities as they weren't leaving Zambia. A pilot wearing a short-sleeved white shirt, mirror sunglasses and, somewhat incongruously, khaki cargo shorts and sandals, strode through the heat haze shimmering up from the runway in front of a parked twin-engine Cessna.

'Dougal Geddes. Welcome,' he said, and shook both their hands.

They boarded and it was baking inside the aircraft. The blue vinyl of the seat was hot on the backs of Kylie's thighs beneath the hem of the cotton dress she was glad she had packed. She didn't feel like wearing jeans today; she remembered the feel of his fingers on her.

Dougal pointed out the emergency exits, did his checks, and they were airborne within a few minutes. As they climbed Cameron leaned over and put his cheek close to hers, perhaps on the pretext of looking out the window. She loved the feel of him so close. She knew she was blushing, but didn't care. It had been too long since she had allowed herself to fall for someone. It was crazy.

Ten minutes into the flight Dougal asked them, via the headsets they wore, if anyone would mind if he took a detour over Kafue National Park. It was, he said, a massive area, bigger even than the Kruger National Park in South Africa, which itself was the size of Israel.

Cameron looked at her and shrugged, as if to say, 'What do you think?' Kylie thought that if she had been her old self, the one to whom work mattered more than anything else, she would have judged the pilot's suggestion that they delay arrival at the copper belt mine to go joyriding as a frivolous waste of company money.

'Sounds great to me,' she said into the headset's boom microphone. Cameron smiled and she saw again how handsome he was when he was happy.

Dougal peeled off their flight path and dropped down so that they were just a few hundred feet above the ground. The countryside below changed from a disorderly patchwork of small maize farms and wonky roads cut into the blood-red dirt of Zambia to wide open floodplains carpeted with swaying golden grass.

'Look, Lichtenstein's hartebeest,' Dougal said as he turned to follow the course of a wide vlei.

'Where?' she asked. Cameron pointed them out for her and she spotted the tan-coloured antelope. There were about twenty of them in the herd, including babies.

Kylie slid across the seat a little so that her thigh was touching Cameron's. Sunlight was streaming into the fuselage. He put his arm around her and kissed her, first on the cheek and then on the mouth.

He kept her in his embrace as they both looked out the window again. Dougal continued over the countryside as it opened into a series of wide plains, delineated here and there by glittering streams. Cameron spotted a couple of elephant and it was almost as exciting seeing them from the air, raising their faces and trunks to inspect them, as it had been from the safari vehicle at Lion Plains.

'This place is wild,' Cameron said into her headphone.

'Wild, and beautiful,' she said. She wanted to kiss him again; all day, in fact, and all night.

Then the aircraft exploded.

PART FOUR

27

The wind shook the sycamore fig and rippled the normally smooth waters of the Sabie River. The fisherman puffed up his feathers at the chill and huddled next to his chick and his partner in the hollow of the tree.

At their feet was the almost picked-clean bones of what had been a fat barbel. The fisherman and his family were temporarily sated by the fat oily flesh of the catfish. The fluffy down that had covered the chick since birth had now given way to feathers, and in recent days the fisherman's surviving offspring had clearly been itching to leave the nest. The little bird had begun flapping his wings and jumping higher and higher in the nest and onto the branch of the fig.

The chick had survived the deadly attack by Inkwazi, the fish eagle, which had taken its weaker sibling, and had narrowly avoided being gulped down as an appetiser by Ingwe, the leopard, thanks to the fisherman's faking of an injury.

Now, as the gusting wind heralded the closing of winter and the storms which would soon follow from Mozambique, it seemed the chick might be blown from the tree if it decided to venture out onto the branch, as it was doing more frequently these days. The youngster was keen to take its next and most momentous step of its life.

A lion called in the night, as if reminding them all of the dangers that lurked in and along the river of fear, but in those same churning waters a tigerfish jumped, its silvery flank and stripes visible for a split second in the glint of the moonlight, reminding them of the riches that awaited the chick as he learned to hunt.

The fisherman perched on the branch and rotated his head to scan for danger. All was quiet, save for the rustle of the leaves. Even the lion had finished his talking. His partner turned to look at their chick. It was time.

The little one flapped his wings and screeched; his parents watched him closely. Unsteadily at first he hopped from the nest, lost then regained his balance, and in a blur of madly beating feathers he was gone. The fisherman left his perch and followed his youngster's erratic first flight to the ground. But the chick landed safely and within a few seconds, after seeming to gather his wits, he was off.

A booming call from his mate made the fisherman turn back. At that moment a powerful gust of wind tore through the sycamore tree. The bough in which they had made their home snapped with an almighty crack.

The branch tumbled into the swirling waters of the Sabie below and the pair and their chick watched as it drifted away. Now they would need to find a new home.

28

Jessica and Mandy were listening to Elvis Blue on Mandy's iPod with one ear bud each as they sat on Mandy's bed. Her father had SMSed her from Zambia in the morning, saying he was on a charter aircraft to Kitwe, but she hadn't heard from him since. Perhaps, she thought, the phone signal wasn't good where he had been heading.

They had been home from school for an hour. Jess liked school, but it was home she was dreading. She was meeting her mother for coffee at the Wimpy in half an hour. 'I don't want to go.'

'*Sheesh*, man, I know what she did was hectic, but she's still, like, your mom,' Mandy said, pulling the bud out of her ear.

'Jess?' called Mandy's mother. 'There's someone here to see you.'

'Oh my god, I hope she hasn't come to collect me. I don't want your mom having to talk to her,' Jessica said. 'How embarrassing.'

Mandy's mother, Charmaine, was at the doorway. 'Jess, are you expecting someone from the mine to come and fetch you?'

'No, Mandy and I were just going to walk to the Wimpy, why?' It was only a short walk, and Mandy's mother would need her car to go pick up Mandy's younger brother, Gareth, from rugby practice.

'The dominee's here, with a guy from the mine. Please come to the door, Jess.'

Mandy's mother had gone pale. She looked at Mandy, who put her hand over her mouth and looked at her mother. Jessica felt a sudden pang of terror. She remembered Mandy talking about the day her dad died, in an accident at the mine, and how the local clergyman, the dominee from the NG Kerk, the Dutch Reformed Church, had come with Jess's father to deliver the news. Jess's dad had come home afterwards and cried.

'No.'

'Please, Jess. Come see what they want.'

Jess felt her legs turn to jelly as she tried to stand. Mandy's mother put an arm around her and Mandy followed close behind as they walked to the door. The dominee was a tall thin man, with grey hair and a long, skinny face. 'Jessica, I have news. This is Solomon, he is a driver at the mine. He was sent to fetch me.'

The man behind the dominee bobbed his head. Jess recognised the Global Resources uniform but not the driver. But she remembered the dominee. She'd stopped going to church about a year earlier, when her mother had overheard some of the other parishioners saying something about her after a service and vowed never to go again.

'I'm very sorry, Jessica . . .' said the dominee.

'No. I don't want to hear if something's happened to him.'

She started to turn, but Mandy's mother held her in a tight embrace.

'There has been a plane crash, in Zambia, the flight your father was taking with the Australian woman, on business. Solomon was sent on the orders of Mr Coetzee, the new mine manager, to fetch me. I checked on my computer, on News24, just before I left home. The reports are that there were no survivors, Jessica.'

'No! He can't be dead. They must check the bodies. He's alive!'

'The reports are there were no survivors,' the dominee said again. 'I am so sorry for your loss, but we must be strong.'

The man in the mining company shirt shuffled forward a pace. 'Mr Coetzee says you must come to the mine, miss,' he said to Jess. 'Your mother is coming there now. She knows we are coming to get you.'

'We must go there,' the dominee said, nodding his head. 'We will get more facts, do some more investigating.'

'You're sure her mother knows about this?' Mandy's mother said.

'Yes, madam,' said the mine man. 'She was crying. She said she didn't know if she could come for Jessica now. She wanted to go to the mine to find out more from Mr Coetzee.'

Mandy's mother harrumphed as if, Jess thought, she would have expected nothing less from Jess's mother. Jess felt a prickle of defensiveness. 'I need to see her now. I'll get my things.'

She walked back to Mandy's room and grabbed her bag. Her vision started to blur at the edges and she choked as the tears rose in her throat. Not her dad. It couldn't be. Not him.

The dominee put his bony arm around her and she cringed, but she let the men lead her to the mine *bakkie*. Jess turned and waved to Mandy and her mother.

'I'll come as soon as I've collected Gareth. We'll all come and you can stay here tonight if you don't want to go home, Jess. For as long as you like.' Mandy was crying too now and Jess turned away from the window as the *bakkie* pulled away.

The dominee sat in the front passenger seat, and Jess was all alone in the back of the double cab. She sniffed and tried to dry her eyes. It had to be a mistake. Solomon was driving very fast. Her dad would have told him off, as he always did anyone who broke the speed limit in a company vehicle.

She leaned forward, between the two front seats. 'How long have you worked at the mine, Solomon?'

'I am only new, miss. I am very sorry to hear about your father. I know he was a good man. Everyone said so.'

'Amen,' said the dominee.

Jess saw a glint of metal as Solomon depressed the clutch to change gear. He wore a company shirt, and jeans, like many of the guys who worked above ground, but his shoes were soft polished leather with little chains across the top of them. They looked expensive.

The driver glanced back at her and saw her looking down at his shoes.

'Nice shoes,' she said.

'Thank you, miss.' He licked his lips and Jessica felt the car start to move faster. They were through Barberton now, on the road to the mine. She knew the turn-off was coming up soon. It was funny, then, that he was speeding up.

'I feel sick,' she said.

The dominee swivelled in his seat. 'What's wrong, my child? Is it the shock?'

She nodded. 'Please, pull over, Solomon, I think I need to be ill.'

He glanced back at her again. 'Nearly at the mine, miss. We will find somewhere for you to lie down there.'

'Solomon, if the child is going to be ill, better it not be in the vehicle. Pull over, man.'

The turn-off to Eureka was in sight. Solomon changed gears again and Jess knew there was something wrong.

'His shoes, Dominee, his shoes!'

'What, my child?' the old man looked confused.

'They're not safety shoes – he doesn't work for the mine!'

Solomon glared at her. The needle on the speedometer climbed above a hundred and thirty.

'That was the turn-off, man,' the dominee said, craning his head to look back. 'Turn around, Solomon, you stupid . . .'

Solomon leaned forward, one hand on the wheel, and reached under his seat. When he sat up again he was pointing a black pistol at the dominee. 'Shut up, you old fool, or I'll kill you and the girl.'

Jessica grabbed Solomon's arm with both her hands and bit it.

'Ow!' The gun boomed and Jessica screamed. She cowered back into the seat. 'You stupid little bitch.'

'Please, please, don't hurt me,' the dominee whined. He held up his hands in surrender. The bullet had passed him and gone out the open window.

They passed the turn-off to the Diggers' Retreat Hotel. After that, Jess knew, it was just the Sheba mine and Sheba siding, where a lot of the illegal miners lived. She guessed he was one of them. From then on, it was just bush until the R38 joined the N4. No one would find them if he stopped out here.

Jessica moved to the door and saw Solomon check her out in the rear-view mirror. He stamped on the brakes and Jess was thrown into the back of the dominee's seat as the car skidded and stopped on the gravel verge. 'Get out,' Solomon said to the dominee.

Jess saw her chance and fumbled open the back door, stumbled and fell to the dirt, then got up and started running.

'Stop!' Solomon called behind her.

She ran into the thornbushes on the roadside, not caring about the barbs that scratched her all over. 'I'm going to kill him if you don't come back, Jessica!'

Jess slowed her pace, then stopped.

'Come out, come out wherever you are,' he called.

Jessica was panting, her arms and legs criss-crossed with blood from the thorny branches. She was confused and terrified.

'I'm going to count backwards from ten and then the churchman dies if you don't come out, Jessica.'

Jess screwed her hands into her eyes. She didn't even like the dominee. She thought he was creepy. But she slowly retraced her steps, until she came to a tree big enough to hide behind. She peered around the trunk and saw the old man, kneeling with his hands behind his head. He had cried like a girl, she thought, begging Solomon in the *bakkie* not to hurt him. What about her, she wondered.

'Seven, six, five, four, three, two . . .'

Solomon's arm was out straight and she could see, even from this distance, his finger curling around the trigger. She wished she had just kept running. She didn't know what this man wanted with her and the minister but she couldn't let him be killed.

'Wait.' She walked out from behind the tree with her hands up in the air.

'No . . . my child,' the dominee said through his sobs. There were tears running down his cheeks. 'You should have run.'

'Come closer,' Solomon said, 'or I will kill him.'

She walked towards him, trying not to show how scared she was. 'Kneel down.'

She did as she was told.

The dominee sniffed back his tears. 'And you, with a name from the Bible. You will burn in hell if you don't release us now.'

The man laughed. 'My name isn't Solomon, it is Wellington Shumba. I am a general and a lion, and I take no orders from you.'

'You're Wellington?' Jess said. It was a name she'd heard her father speak often.

He smiled down at her. 'You should have listened to the preacher man, little girl.'

Wellington pulled the trigger and the dominee pitched forward.

*

A cellphone beeped and buzzed and Chris Loubser opened his eyes, momentarily disorientated by the sea of fluffy pillows he seemed to be drowning in.

Tertia Venter put her phone down on the bedside table, lit a cigarette, drew on it, then passed it to Chris, who struggled to shrug his way up to a sitting position and escape his prison of Egyptian cotton.

'You fell asleep. Did I tire you out, my poor baby?'

'Yes,' he grinned. Chris took a puff, coughed and handed the vile cigarette back. He hadn't smoked since he was sixteen, and he had hated it back then too. There were some things she couldn't make him do, but, he reflected, not many. 'That will kill you.'

'I don't care. I'll die happy knowing I saved this place.'

He rolled onto his side and propped himself on his elbow. He was enchanted by her; not just her body, but by her toughness and her supreme confidence. She feared nothing. 'What makes you so sure you have? It's not over yet.'

She blew a stream of smoke towards the ceiling. 'The mine's closed, pending the review of the air quality samples, and we know how that's going to turn out; the unions are threatening to stop work in Global Resources' other operations; the government's ordered an inquiry into the company's fitness to mine coal here; and, I'm almost sorry to say, we're not likely to be hearing from Dr Hamilton or Mr McMurtrie again.' Tertia lifted the duvet and swung her legs over the side of the bed and stood.

Chris yawned and scratched his head, then down below. He was sore. She had been insatiable, as always. They'd had a bottle of wine and some spirits before lunch and retired to her house for an afternoon of making love, golden sunlight bathing her pale body as they sated each other. He had fallen into a deep postcoital nap. He watched her walk across the room to a desk, where her laptop was open. She was full-figured, womanly, sexy, not like the younger girls who sometimes threw themselves at him. Tertia knew more than any of them; how to please him, what she wanted. He felt himself stirring as she sat and turned on the computer.

'A friend of mine just SMSed me. Told me I must check News24.' She tapped at the keys, opening her internet browser. 'Yes, here it is. Dr Kylie Hamilton and Cameron McMurtrie have been killed in a plane crash in Zambia.'

'What?' Chris threw off the covers and jumped off the bed. He darted to her side. 'Let me see. Oh no. My God, Tertia, no.'

She looked up at him. 'Yes.'

How could she grin? he wondered. He knew how much she hated the company, but these were people he knew – Cameron especially. He read the story online over her shoulder, twice. 'He has a daughter.'

'Yes, well I'm sorry about that, of course. But McMurtrie was going to head up their new mines division. He would have overseen the destruction of our beautiful paradise, Chris.'

She took his hand. He gripped it, out of grief rather than sympathy with her cause. Cameron was a good man and Chris couldn't find anything to celebrate in his death, no matter what it meant for Lion Plains or Tertia.

'He was just doing as he was told, Tertia. I got the feeling his heart wasn't in this project at all, or in his new job. He never wanted to leave the mine.'

She let go of his hand. 'Just following orders? Grow up, Christiaan. That's what the Nazis used to say. He would have happily turned this place into a pit of coal dust.'

He didn't like being spoken to as a child, or admonished. He hated it when his mother called him Christiaan, and it had the same effect when Tertia used it. 'He was a good man, Tertia.'

She shrugged. 'Well, I can't say I will miss him, or that woman. She was a cold fish. The company's in chaos and their CEO from Australia, Jan Stein, is flying out to try and prop things up out here, but there's nothing he'll be able to do. Their share price has collapsed.'

She put an arm around his naked body and reached for his semi-tumescent member. 'Things will work out fine, and you can leave the mine and come and run this place with me. It's what you want, isn't it, baby?'

He stared at the screen. It had been what they had talked about so often, but Cameron's and Kylie's deaths had taken the shine off things. It wasn't how it was supposed to happen.

Her hand closed around him. It didn't seem right, given the news. He stared at the words on the screen and felt her hand move up and down his length. Looking down at her he saw her shift on the office chair, opening her legs. Her right hand moved to her pubis. She started stroking herself, not looking up at him, and the sight of her doing that made him harder. She leaned her body against him as her fingers moved faster, on him and herself, bringing them both close to the edge.

Tertia threw her head back, gasping as she arched her back. Chris was worried he might come over her computer, but she pushed him aside, gripped her desk and pulled herself to her feet. She bent across the screen and led him to her. 'Fuck me.'

He exploded as soon as he entered her.

They stayed there for a little while, panting, as she lay under him, across the machine. 'We need to shower,' she said at last.

They never used condoms. She was forty, eleven years older than he, but she told him she wanted a child, with him. It was, she said, proof of her love for him. He could have been some young stud just fucking her for sport, he thought, but she seemed to know how she had captivated him. It was why it hadn't scared him off, the idea of them having a child together. It had made things, he'd thought, somehow honest, as though they were doing what they did to ensure the future of Lion Plains for the next generation.

He followed her to the shower and she turned on the water and stepped in. 'What's to stop the community simply doing a deal with another mining company, even if the Global Resources coalmine doesn't go ahead?'

She massaged shampoo into her sopping red locks and grinned at him. 'Two things . . . money and a little something I'm going to show you after we're finished in here.'

He stepped into the shower, still annoyed at the way she had been before: her glee over Cameron's death and her treating him like a child. But when she said turn, he did, and she scrubbed his back.

'Tell me more,' he said.

'When we're outside, on the game viewer. Away from prying ears. And we have to wait until it's dark outside.'

She must have sensed his hostility towards her, because she dropped to her knees, in order to finish washing him.

Dried and changed, he followed her outside to her game viewer. Night had fallen. A scops owl called to its mate. Tertia stopped by her office to pick up her rifle in its protective sleeve, a heavy Pelican waterproof plastic camera case which she gave him to carry, and a pair of bulky-looking binoculars, which she slung over her shoulder. It was only six o'clock and the other vehicles were out, taking the lodge's few guests on their evening game drives. They wouldn't be back until seven-thirty, for dinner.

'So, are you going to tell me why you're so sure you're out of the woods?' The movement of the open-topped vehicle produced an instant breeze that ruffled her drying hair.

'You know the property behind us, Kilarney?'

'Yes.' He'd studied maps of the area many times and the company had researched the neighbouring properties. Kilarney was a game farm that had once made its income from trophy hunting, but it had been mismanaged, and pilloried in the press for offering canned hunts. Stoffel Berger, the intransigent old man who ran it, had successfully fought the land claim on his property and, such were the vagaries of the land commission, he had won where Tertia had failed. Tertia suspected the community and its lawyers had put more effort into winning Lion Plains because it was bigger earning, through tourism, than Stoffel's rundown, shot-out wildlife butchery. The coal discovery had been the icing on the cake. 'It's almost valueless. There's no game, the fences are falling down, and no one will buy it as it's going to have a coalmine between it and the Sabi Sand Game Reserve.'

'I'm going to buy it. For a song,' she said.

'You're mad.'

She shot a look at him, before returning her attention to the rutted road. 'Am I? When the mine is cancelled I'll have my own land, which no one can take from me. The community will have no mine, and never will. I'll tell them I'll drop the fences between Kilarney and Lion Plains so the game can repopulate Stoffel's place, and their reserve will in effect double in size. I'll offer them a deal where I'll still manage the lodge on Lion Plains but I'll have my own place as well. Stoffel always resisted joining up with the rest of the Sabi Sand Game Reserve because he still wanted to hunt, and they wouldn't allow that. I'll merge Kilarney with the game reserve and the community will continue to get an income stream, and more jobs from my new lodge, which is what they care about, and no one will ever be able to try and mine on Lion Plains again, because the property will now be enclosed by the game reserve as opposed to being on the edge of it.'

'I can understand all that, in an ideal world, but first you'll have to ensure that the Global Resources deal is dead and buried and, even before that, buy Stoffel's place while it's still virtually valueless on paper. I don't know how one woman can do that.'

'One woman can't, but with the help of a little fisherman, she can.'

'I don't understand.'

'Patience, my boy, patience.'

They passed the dam where Kylie has seen her first lions, and it saddened Chris, again, to think of the tough Australian dead. He'd found her sexy, in the same way he was aroused by Tertia's confidence and directness. But now she was dead. As much as he hated the idea of the Lion Plains mine, and even though he had done all he could behind the scenes to stop it from going ahead, it seemed somehow unfair now that Kylie and Cameron were gone. Selfishly, though, he was glad Cameron would never find out where Chris's allegiances had really lain. In his dreams, Chris would be Tertia's husband and the ranger in charge of her game reserve. This was what he wanted in life, not to spend his days overseeing the health and safety of miners so that they would be fit and strong enough to rape the earth.

Tertia took a turning that Chris knew ended in a cul-de-sac. She stopped at the end of the track and they got out of the Land Rover. Tertia reached behind the seats and pulled out the gun case. From it she took her .458 hunting rifle. She loaded five rounds from the pocket of her shorts into the breech. The sight of the firearm made Chris nervous and reminded him of the terrible din of the under-ground gun battle, and bodies bleeding in the dark. He swallowed his nausea and followed her down the pathway.

'Bring the camera case.'

A raised wooden walkway led to a bird hide, but Tertia went past that and carried on into the thick bush along the river that fed the dam, following what appeared to be a well-worn game trail.

'Watch out for buffalo.' She patted the worn and pitted wooden stock of her hunting rifle. 'That's why I've got this. I've come across dagga boys here a few times.'

He nodded. Dagga boys, lone male buffaloes who took their name from the slang for the mud that plastered their hides, were probably the most dangerous animals to encounter on foot. Tertia stopped, sniffed the air, and cocked her head. 'Elephant.'

He could hear the snap of branches and the crunch of vegetation being chewed. Chris sniffed the air, and finally picked up their earthy scent.

'They've moved away from the river. They won't bother us.'

The path led them to the water's edge and Chris took a step back in fright when he heard something rustling in the reeds beside him, followed by a splash. Tertia grinned at his face. 'Crocodile.'

She knew the reserve intimately, but still Chris felt nervous. He wondered if she had changed since he had first met her, or if he was simply getting to know her better. She was certainly very animated when she was in the bush, but when she grinned at him like that he saw something else in her eyes. She was like another predator out here, and he thought that if it ever did come to bulldozers arriving on site, she might try to go out fighting. He loved her passion, but sometimes, as now, it frightened him.

A bird made a loud booming call, which also caused Chris to start, and he was surprised when Tertia pointed to the tiny black crake wading at the water's edge. It made a hell of a racket for something so small.

A chorus of frogs tuned up for their evening concert and Chris slapped at a mosquito that buzzed in his ear. The sun was almost gone. 'Tertia, shouldn't we get back to the vehicle before it gets totally dark?'

'The guy we're looking for only comes out at night. Relax, I've got a light.' She unclipped a small LED torch from the belt on her skirt and turned it on. Like the crake's call, the powerful beam belied the size of its source. Chris still didn't know what use it would be against a charging buffalo or, even worse, a hippo out on its nightly foraging expedition. One of the behemoths grunted and laughed ahead, confirming his fears were justified.

'What guy?'

'Shush.'

She led on and Chris closed the gap between them. He'd never walked in the bush at night. It wasn't as terrifying as being underground, but he was out of his depth and he would rather be back in bed with her. Tertia said she had something important to show him, but as he stumbled on he wished she had forgone the dramatics and just told him what it was.

Tertia stopped and leaned her rifle against a green fever tree. She unslung the bulky binoculars from her shoulder and pressed a button on top of them.

'Night vision,' she said as she lifted them and scanned the riverbank opposite. She handed the binoculars to him.

Through the eerie lime green wash of the night vision he tracked a pair of Egyptian geese, late home to bed, that squawked and honked as they flew low up the river, the beat of their wings rippling the steely surface. Around him the night birds were starting a new shift. He heard the shrill chirp of a scops owl, and a moment later the reply of its mate further away from the river.

'Sit.' Tertia said. 'We may have a little while to wait. He's shy.'

Chris handed the binoculars back to Tertia. He looked behind him and kicked leaves and imaginary scorpions away from a patch of trodden earth and eased himself down. If a buffalo, hippo or elephant came now they would be well and truly finished. Far off a lion roared, its throaty wheeze rolling across the bushveld. Chris shivered.

'Get the camera out of the case,' she commanded.

He did as she asked and checked out her Nikon and the unfamiliar lens.

'It's also night vision,' she said, lowering the binoculars and noticing him fiddling.

He sat the camera down in the foam of the open case. 'Do you think it was an accident, what happened to Kylie and Cameron?'

She resumed raking the far bank with the glasses, too preoccupied to lower them. 'What? Oh, that. It's Africa. Shush.'

Admonished, again, he plucked stems of grass. They were her enemies, but still he couldn't understand her callousness. Cameron had been civil with her and even though she had rejected the compromise, of her setting up a wildlife research place near the mine, Chris thought she might have had some lingering respect for the way Cameron had handled himself. Cameron had risked his life, as had Kylie, to save him from Wellington. Chris felt his rising tide of nausea intensify, the more he thought about the loss of his colleagues.

'There!' Tertia snapped her fingers and pointed. 'The camera. Now!'

He passed the Nikon to her, in exchange for the binoculars.

'See that tree, the big jackalberry on the other side of the water?'

He blinked at the green glare in the viewfinders, then quickly became used to the bright but one-dimensional picture. He lowered the binoculars to sight the tree in the dark first, then found it through the gadget's lenses. 'Yes.'

'The low branch, the one that hangs out over the river. Follow it from the trunk halfway. See him?'

Chris followed her directions, slowly moving the binoculars. At first he thought it was just a stubby offshoot from the main branch, but then it moved, ever so slightly. 'An owl.'

Tertia's Nikon clicked away on auto wind. 'This is brilliant, Chris. I'm getting him. Yes, it's an owl, but tell me what kind.'

He was no *fundi*, no expert on birds, but he knew most of the bigger raptors and the brightest coloured, most attractive birds of the lowveld. 'Giant eagle owl, I suppose.'

'Look again,' she said over the whirring of her camera.

He studied it. 'It's odd. It doesn't have ear tufts, but it's helluva big.'

'You're getting close. Look, look . . .'

The bird swooped from its perch, but instead of flying off, or heading to the bank to take a mouse or a snake, it plunged into the water of the river, splashed about for a split second, then took off again. It returned to its perch with a shimmering, struggling fish in its talons.

'My goodness, it isn't . . .'

She lowered the camera and in the dark he could see her teeth glowing brightly as she grinned and nodded. 'It is.'

He drew a sharp breath. 'A pel's fishing owl?'

*

Jessica stumbled and fell to her knees. Wellington grabbed her pony-tail and yanked her hair to drag her back to her feet. She screamed into the gaffer tape that gagged her. It was dark and the bush had closed in on either side of the winding path that led up into the mountains.

He slapped her again. 'You silly little bitch. Do you think I am stupid? Do you think that I don't know you are trying to slow me down. It makes no difference. No one is coming to look for you.'

She didn't believe him. Mandy and her mother would have gone to the mine after they'd picked up Mandy's brother and they would know by now that Mr Coetzee hadn't sent anyone. They would be looking for her everywhere, all over town and in the mountains.

'You think your friends will raise the alarm. They will not.' He glared at her with his yellow, bloodshot eyes, and their tiny pupils. She wondered if he was on some sort of drugs. 'Coetzee did order someone from the mine to come and fetch you and the dominee, but he was my man. I paid him well for the information he gave me. He has gone into hiding. The hyenas who live in the nature reserve will take care of the holy man.' Wellington laughed. He reached into his pocket and pulled out Jessica's BlackBerry. 'If you don't believe me, have a look at this.'

He switched it on and held the glowing screen in front of her. 'See, this is from you to your friend Mandy, the pretty girl with the pretty mother. *Sorry Mandy, I can't take this. I'm catching a bus to Joburg to go stay with friends there. Luv u.'*

Jessica shook her head with anger. The creep had even copied the way she signed off her messages to Mandy. He must have checked her message log.

He looked back at the screen, scrolling down. 'And this reply from your friend: *Come back soon babe.*' Wellington laughed again.

'Nothing from your mother, though.' He shut the phone down. 'That is because she is dead, like your father.'

Wellington prodded her in the back with his gun and she stumbled on. He moved alongside her, grabbing her by the arm, and they came to what looked like a dead end, a bush in the middle of the track. Wellington pushed her to her knees and put his gun in his jeans. He used both hands to grab the tree and shifted it to one side. It wasn't living, but rather the camouflage for a black hole that opened in the side of the mountain.

Jessica screamed again and felt more tears springing from her eyes and rolling down her cheeks. This couldn't be happening. Her whole family was gone. What did he want from her? Her dad couldn't be dead. Suddenly she missed her mother as well. What had they done to anger this man so much that he would destroy all of them? Sooner or later Mr Coetzee would track down the man who had actually been sent to fetch her; someone would notice the dominee missing tonight. Someone would come. The nightmare would end.

29

L uis's cellphone rang. '*Ola?*'

'*Ola,* cousin, how are you?'

It was Alfredo, the police captain. They exchanged pleasantries and then Alfredo said, 'I have news for you, Luis. I have an address, in Maputo, for the cellphone number you gave me. Do you want me to get the local guys to send some officers around?'

Luis thought about that. It would be best to let the law deal with Wellington. That would be the sensible thing to do. 'No.'

'You're sure? If this is the man who murdered Miriam I will see that he is arrested and never released.'

Luis reconsidered, but only for a minute. Despite his cousin's machismo, Luis knew that the police in Mozambique could be bribed, and that the case against Wellington, even in a recognised court of law free from corruption, would be hard to prove. It would be impossible, too, for Luis to return to South Africa and get the police to open a docket on a man with a nom de guerre living in Mozambique. More likely, he thought, they would want to question him over the body of the gunman that had been left at the scene and the other thug, if his corpse had been discovered. Luis knew that Wellington had the local police commander, Sindisiwe Radebe, in his pocket. Indeed, he had bragged that he had the colonel is his bed. No, there was only one way to handle this matter. 'I'm sure. But you can help me with something else. Two things, in fact.'

When Luis explained what he wanted his cousin took a deep breath down the line and told him to come to Xai Xai.

Luis bade farewell to his mother and his son. Jose seemed withdrawn, the shock of his mother's death still not fully registering. The father he barely knew was leaving him again. He had ruined their lives and could only hope that he might make it up to them, in time. 'I will be back.'

Luis took a small daypack and walked from his village to the main road and boarded a *chapa* bound for Xai Xai. He whiled away the cramped, hot hours in the back of the minibus by reading the fading typed pages of his thesis. It seemed like a century ago that he had been a student, thirsting for knowledge and full of hope for his battered, shattered country.

As arranged, Luis called Alfredo on his cellphone when the *chapa* was a few kilometres from Xai Xai. Alfredo gave him the name of a cafe opposite the park a few blocks past the KFC. The minibus slowed to walking pace once they entered the clogged main street of the busy coastal town and Luis told the driver he wanted to get off. It was good to squeeze through the crush of bodies on board and breathe fresh, if somewhat exhaust-tainted, air. He walked through the crowds, envying these simple people with their simple lives. He turned his face from the throng to the clear blue sky, relishing its warmth on his face. He would be happy if he never went underground again. He longed to turn his back on crime and to provide a safe future for Jose. He was so close, but he was under no illusion that the hundred thousand rand that bulged in the pocket of his trousers would be enough to set him up for life.

He found the cafe and took a seat outside and ordered an espresso. Alfredo, who had changed from his uniform into civilian clothes, waved to him from across the street and came to him. They shook hands. His cousin carried a plastic shopping bag with something

350

wrapped in newspaper inside it. He placed the parcel at his feet as he sat opposite Luis.

Like every policeman in Mozambique, Alfredo's wealth was evidenced in the rounded belly that protruded over his jeans, his chubby cheeks and his mirrored Ray Ban aviator sunglasses, which might, depending on how many bribes Alfredo had taken recently, be real or fake. Luis did not doubt that Alfredo was a good policeman. Serious crimes, such as murder and armed robbery, were rare in Mozambique compared to South Africa, and Alfredo had a good network of informants in the villages around Xai Xai and the town itself. If his cousin did not have a hand or a controlling interest in a local racket, then it was soon shut down.

They sipped the short, bitter coffee the waiter brought them. Alfredo used his foot to shift the shopping bag across the pavement so that it touched Luis's ankle. Luis leaned back, so he could see under the table, and peered into the bag. He could tell by the shape it was the pistol he had asked for. 'Ammunition?'

'Two magazines,' Alfredo said softly. 'It's a Russian Tokarev. You'll remember it from the old days.'

'Sadly, yes. Thank you, cousin.'

Alfredo slid a piece of paper across the table to Luis.

Luis checked it and saw an address in Maputo. It would be the registered address of the owner of the cellphone that Wellington had used to call the young men who assassinated his wife. Even if Wellington was not there now it would be a lead. Perhaps he would come back there, in time, to find Luis waiting for him. Luis savoured the small fantasy. But he had other things to do first. Revenge, the English said, was a dish best served cold. He could wait for Wellington, but his hundred thousand rand would not last long – Alfredo would require some of it now – so he needed a new source of income.

'You know I am only charging you for my out-of-pocket expenses, cousin,' Alfredo said.

'Of course. How much?'

'Five thousand rand, cousin, for the gun and for the woman at the telephone registration office. She did not come cheap.'

Luis counted the cash out beneath the table, out of the view of passers-by who might be tempted, or those who might recognise their rotund police captain in mufti. He passed the money to his cousin, who swiftly pocketed it.

Alfredo nodded his thanks. 'The other information you asked for, about drilling rigs in the local area, comes free of charge. There is an NGO drilling for water at a village southwest of here, on the road to Massangir and the Limpopo Transfrontier Park. It is out of my *distrito*, but the Swedish man doing the drilling came here to report an accident. He hit a boy of fifteen with his pickup truck and the boy broke his leg. I am afraid that some of the youngsters around here may be deliberately throwing themselves in the path of cars driven by foreigners as they know that the drivers will pay them compensation in order to avoid prosecution. The boy's family asked him for money, but the Swede insisted on coming to me. Naturally I am only here to see that justice is done. In the end the aid worker saw it was more sensible to pay the family some compensation rather than to risk prosecution for negligent driving.'

'Do you have the Swede's cellphone number?' Luis asked.

'Back in my office. He left it when he made his report. I can get it for you if you want it. Should I ask why you wanted this information about a drilling rig?'

'Perhaps not,' Luis said. They finished their coffee and ordered a second as Luis treated his overfed cousin and himself to omelettes. Luis was eager to get on the road, but manners insisted he stay a while and chat, now that the business was concluded. His cousin had done well out of him, but Luis could not complain. He was on the path to salvaging what remained of his life.

When they had finished Luis took his package in its innocuous shopping bag and boarded another *chapa*, which took him south, across the broad floodplain of the Limpopo River.

At Macia, he left the *chapa* and crossed the EN 1 and joined a throng of people waiting under a sign that pointed to the Limpopo Transfrontier Park. The park was an extension of South Africa's Kruger National Park, and the road led back to the country that Luis had for so long dreamed of escaping.

Soon enough a minibus taxi arrived and Luis was jammed into the *chapa* with too many other passengers. The road inland took them through vast sugarcane fields, irrigated with a canal built by the Portuguese. Here and there white-painted farm villas with asbestos roof tiles painted to look like terracotta harked back to a colonial era that had not existed for nearly forty years but whose presence was still pervasive.

The commercial farms gave way to bush and small villages. It was dry, inhospitable country where people eked out a meagre subsistence. He opened the map Alfredo had drawn for him and saw they were approaching the village where the Swede and his team were drilling a new well. He got out in the village, outside a cellphone tower surrounded by a fence topped with razor wire.

Luis took out his cellphone, marvelling that he could pick up a four-bar cellphone signal in a place where people could barely feed themselves or find enough clean water to drink. He dialled the number Alfredo had given him.

'Hello, Anders speaking!'

'Good morning, sir, how are you?' Luis said in English. 'You do not know me, but I would like to enquire about hiring your drilling rig for three days.'

'What?'

'Your drilling rig, sir. I would like to rent it from you.'

'What? You want to rent the rig. No, of course not. This is for the village water project, not for anyone to come along and use for his own purpose. This rig has been paid for by the people of Sweden.'

'I see,' said Luis. It was the answer he was expecting. 'Thank you for your time.'

Luis walked across the street to a small roadside *spaza* store and looked inside, greeting the skinny female proprietor. There was not much produce – some warm bottles of coke, Sunlight Soap, packets of biscuits, tinned pilchards and some brightly patterned cloth wraps. To the surprise of the woman, he bought one of the wraps. '*Mama*, where are the white people drilling for water?' he asked in Tsonga.

She gestured with her hand to a track that ran from the road, behind her, into the bush. 'One kilometre.'

Luis thanked her and as he walked down the road he bit into the seam of the wrap, snapping the fibres, and then tore off a long strip. He tossed the remainder of the cloth into the bush. Luis had rarely seen television in his life, usually only when passing the front of an Incredible Connection or Dion store in South Africa when he had been a legal mine worker. He had never owned a television. When he had studied, in Russia, he had been befriended by a female engineering student from the Ukraine. As well as taking him to her bed, the blonde-haired, blue-eyed girl liked to take him to see illegal American movies. She was not as committed to socialism as he was back then, but he had been too entranced by the things she did under the heavy bedcovers, keeping both of them more than warm in the process, to object to being exposed to decadent imperialist images. One of the films they had seen was a western and he remembered it now as he tied the remnant of the wrap around his neck and adjusted it so that it covered his mouth and nose, like a stagecoach robber.

He heard the *tucker-tucker* of the generator, the whine of the compressor and the shriek of the drill as he walked down the dusty track between the thornbushes. He reached into the plastic bag and took out the pistol and a magazine of bullets. He stuffed the spare ammunition into the pocket of his jeans and pulled back the Tokarev's slide. The brass casing of the first of the bullets in the full magazine glinted in the sunlight and Luis released the slide to chamber the round. He held the pistol loose at his side, remembering the scenes of the cowboys drawing their guns for a shootout at the end of the film.

Luis's feet sent up puffs of dust as he walked into the clearing. A tall fair-skinned man in a yellow hard hat and ear muffs sat on a seat on the drill rig, operating it. Mozambican labourers carried lengths of drill rods.

One of the local men saw the strange figure emerging from the heat haze, face masked, pistol rising. He yelled to the white man, who shook his head, unable to understand what the man was saying, and too intent on the job at hand.

The din roused Luis. As much as he'd hated his time underground as a *zama zama* he missed the noises of the mine, the ceaseless exploration and harvesting of the earth that had defined his life. He knew economies, businesses, governments and people depended on what men dug from the ground. Some opposed it, others lived for it and by it, but no one on earth could exist without the rocks and minerals people like him brought to the surface.

Luis walked up to the rig and finally the Swede saw him. He took off his clear protective glasses, as if that might change what he was seeing. Luis pointed the Tokarev at the man's face, not three metres away. The noise of the rig was almost deafening this close, without ear protection, and the sudden silence, when the Swede shut it down, also seemed to make his eardrums throb.

'What do you want?' asked the big white man in singsong accented English. His labourers were edging away from the confrontation. Luis doubted they would interfere.

'Good morning, sir. I would like to hire your drill rig.'

The man's face creased in concentration. 'Ah, you are the one who called me on the telephone.'

'I need your drill rig.'

The man climbed down from his machine. He towered over Luis and seemed unafraid of the gun. Luis wondered if his appearance, with his brightly patterned mask, was not threatening enough.

'I told you, this has been paid for by the people of Sweden. It is not for you to go drilling for your own water. Put the gun down and we can negotiate.'

Luis lowered the pistol and the man took another step towards him, sensing he had won his way. Luis squeezed the trigger twice and put two bullets into the dirt less than a metre in front of the man. The blond giant stopped as if on the edge of a precipice. 'On your knees and put your hands on your head, please.'

The man complied and Luis called to one of the labourers, who he had glimpsed hiding behind a stout tree. 'Come here or I will kill your boss!'

Both men in overalls emerged from hiding. 'Tie his hands and feet.'

The men found some rope on the rig and did as Luis ordered. 'Now get the rig ready for transport. Quickly.' While the men worked, Luis stood guard over the Swede. He checked the bonds and made sure they were secure.

'What do you want with my drill rig? There will be water for all once we are finished. Please do not hurt my men.'

Luis ignored the question but was pleased the white man cared for his labourers. Luis grabbed the collar of the man's shirt and eased him forwards. 'I will send someone from the village to find you. Do not try and follow me, or I will kill these two men, understand?'

The man nodded his head. Luis kept him covered, in the sparse shade of a denuded thorn tree, while the rig was packed, then he motioned the men to get into the cab of the truck and told one to start the engine and drive. They left the Swede covered in a layer of dust, but otherwise unharmed.

'Where are we going, *baba*?' the driver asked.

'A place I know. A place I have not been for many years. There are ghosts there. Do not force me to make you join them.'

*

Chris Loubser waited on a bench under the high-vaulted thatched roof of the Kruger Mpumalanga International Airport terminal. He had seen the SA Airlink Embraer land and watched the doors for the appearance of a man he had only met once, but whose name was instantly known to anyone in mining circles. Jan Stein had left South Africa for Australia, like so many of his countrymen, and had worked his way to the top of Global Resources. Like Cameron McMurtrie he had served in the elite recces during the bush war, but whereas Cameron ruled by engendering respect, Jan ran his company through a mix of fear and force. He had sacked senior managers on the spot for failing to perform and stared down angry strikers underground. His aggressive, take-no-prisoner style of expansion had earned him criticism from environmental groups and would, Chris thought, be his demise.

Tertia had wanted to open a bottle of champagne over breakfast, but Chris had told her he could not leave his CEO stranded at the airport. Coetzee had ordered him to collect Jan. 'Besides, I need to tell him your news, about the owl,' he had said to her.

'I'd like to give the story to the media first,' she had said.

Chris had disagreed. 'Let's give him the chance to voluntarily withdraw the Lion Plains project first. If he refuses, or tries something drastic like maybe sending someone in to shoot the owls, then we'll be able to publicly destroy him in the media. I'll know what he's up to. I'm still part of the inner circle there.'

She had reluctantly agreed with him, and sent him on his way with a kiss and a promise that she would be waiting for him, whenever he was ready to finally show his true colours and leave the company.

Chris wiped his palms on his pants as the swing doors to the arrivals area opened and Stein strode out wheeling his carry-on bag.

'Loubser?'

The man still had the bearing of the special forces officer he'd once been: tall, straight-backed, steel grey short hair and hard dark eyes. '*Ja*. Yes, sir. *Howzit?*' Chris didn't really know how to address him.

'You want me to say *lekker* after a fourteen-hour flight to Joburg and then a two-hour delay waiting to fly out here?' Chris offered to take his bag, but the man shook his head. 'Let's just get to the mine, OK?'

'Yes, boss.'

Chris opened the door to the mine *bakkie* and Jan put his bag in the rear and got into the front passenger seat. For the first fifteen minutes of the drive back through White River then along the R40 to Nelspruit the CEO was silent, checking his BlackBerry for emails and sending replies.

When Jan put away his phone Chris knew he had to summon up the courage to tell him the news. 'I've been to see Tertia Venter again.'

'Hmph. What does that woman want to have us executed for now?'

He wanted to tell him, there and then, that he quit and that he could stick his earth-raping company up his corporate arse. But Tertia had told him to stay silent about their relationship a little longer. 'There's been a discovery at Lion Plains.'

Jan looked out the window. 'What do you mean "a discovery"?'

Chris swallowed. 'A pel's fishing owl, boss. Three of them, in fact.'

Jan waved a hand. '*Ag*, you're being taken for a fool. There are none of those birds on that property. They've only ever been spotted along the Sabie River, and Lion Plains doesn't have any river frontage, only tributaries. Venter lists all the birds seen on Lion Plains on her website and there's no mention of a pel's. If there was she'd have said so. Twitchers from around the world would come to see them.'

'I know,' Chris nodded, 'but they're there. She showed me, boss, last night. The birds must have just moved in.'

Jan closed his eyes and leaned back against the headrest. '*Fok*. What are you going to do about it?'

'Do? The only thing I can do. She's going to put a submission in to the department and she is going to say that I also witnessed the breeding pair and their chick. I can't lie, boss.'

'I'm not asking you to.'

Chris glanced across at Stein every now and then, but it appeared the man had drifted off to sleep. He was surprised. He wondered if the CEO even grasped the significance of the birds.

Stein opened his eyes and rubbed his face and looked around them as they crossed the N4 and began the climb into the pass that led to Barberton on the other side of the mountains.

'Boss, you do know the significance of finding a breeding pair of pel's fishing owls and a chick on Lion Plains?'

'I'm not an idiot. The pel's is on the International Union for the Conservation of Nature's red list. Finding them on the site of our mine puts an end to the project, assuming it's true.'

'Yes, boss. Sorry, boss.'

'We can't fight the law and this will sink us once Tertia takes it to the media, as she undoubtedly will. Besides, I've got bigger things to worry about. Are there any updates from the Zambian police about Cameron's and Kylie's deaths?'

'No, boss. The last I heard was that the bodies of the pilot and the passengers, two males and one female, had been flown by helicopter to Lusaka. They're apparently burned beyond recognition so the identities will have to be confirmed by dental records.'

'And the mine's still closed?'

'Yes, boss. The department of minerals and resources is getting an independent firm in to do another round of monitoring. The union is saying it's too dangerous for its members to go underground, and they've also pointed out that the *zama zamas* have returned to the mine and are spreading the word around Barberton that they own Eureka now and that any miner who does report for work is liable to be killed. There was blasting going on last night.'

'It sounds totally lawless,' Jan said.

Chris didn't know what to say. The CEO was right. They had lost control of Eureka and Coetzee was not the man to take it back. Chris almost felt sorry for the company. Its African operations and plans for expansion were falling like a straw house in the wind. And the big bad lion, Wellington Shumba, had been released by the police and was reportedly back underground, back in charge of his subterranean fiefdom.

'Have you spoken to Cameron's wife? I heard she was back in town.'

Chris licked his lips. So much had been happening he had forgotten to brief Jan on the latest news. 'The local police found

Cameron's *bakkie* at the bottom of a gorge below their house in the mountains. Tania was killed. There was reportedly an empty bottle of gin in the car. His daughter's run off to Johannesburg.'

Jan pinched the bridge of his nose with his thumb and his forefinger. 'How did it ever end up like this?' He looked up and across at Chris. 'Have you got any more bad news for me?'

To hell with it, Chris thought. It was time for him to start acting like a man, and to stop taking orders from Tertia. If they were going to live together as man and wife then he needed to start making some decisions for himself. He had hated his time in the mine, the working underground, being part of something that degraded the environment, the criminal intent of a company that wanted to destroy a piece of the finest wildlife reserve in Africa.

Nature had provided Tertia with the trump card she needed. There had been no need, after all, for the lying and deceit and his double dealing with Global Resources. He felt sullied by the way he'd gone about things. He should have had the courage to resign when he first learned the company had been granted a lease to mine on Lion Plains. He should have joined Tertia then, publicly, and fought a clean, open fight. God had surely been on their side, placing a family of the endangered pel's fishing owl on the very spot where Global Resources wanted to start blasting.

'I quit.'

30

L uis kept to the back roads, heading north again. He knew he would have to rejoin the EN 1 at some stage, to take him back towards his hometown of Inhambane. By then the Swede would have been released by someone from the village.

His cellphone rang. Keeping his pistol pointed at the driver, he pulled the phone from his pocket. '*Ola?*'

'Hello, cousin, how are you?' Alfredo asked.

'Fine, and you? Do you have news for me?'

'I had a call from that Swedish man I told you about. He reported that his drilling rig was stolen by an armed bandit. You wouldn't know anything about that, would you, Luis?'

'Ah, no.'

'I thought not. I have taken his complaint and will have to notify all of the traffic police in the province to keep an eye out for this drilling rig, but the radios are not working too well today, and it is a miracle that I can get a line even now to talk to you, cousin.'

'How long, Alfredo, do you think these poor communications will keep you from reporting the theft of this drill rig?'

'A day, perhaps two.'

'Two would be better,' Luis said.

'Two it is, then, cousin. Please let me know if you see this drill rig. The people of the village do need their water.'

'They will have it soon.'

Luis ended the call as they reached the tarmac road. After the bumping of corrugations on the gravel road the smooth black surface of the national highway was soothing. Luis told the driver to watch his speed when they came to each village, as he knew there was a good chance they would pass traffic policemen and their speed cameras. 'You will not be harmed if you do as I say,' he reassured his two press-ganged workers.

As they cruised north, making good time on the tar road, Luis's thoughts drifted back twenty-six years earlier, to the day when he had fled from the advancing Renamo rebels and failed to kill the man with the crucifix.

*

When Luis came to he blinked at the strong sunlight.

The glare was momentarily blocked by a face. Around the man's neck was the silver cross. It was the Renamo soldier whose life Luis had spared. Luis tried to speak, but his mouth was parched.

The man with the cross shot out a hand and slapped Luis hard across the face. Luis put his hand to his cheek and it came away wet and sticky. His head throbbed and as he gingerly touched his scalp he felt a furrow creased along his temple. His neck and the collar of his shirt were also soaked in blood. The young man, eyes wide with bravado now, yelled out to a colleague. 'Come, I have shot the dog who was fleeing.'

Whistles were blowing in the bush around him. An armed party of four men strode up to them. Luis could tell by the age and bearing of the shortest of the men that he was a leader. 'Good work, but why were you so far behind the assault line?' he asked the man with the cross.

'I heard this man running and I doubled back, sir.'

There were occasional gunshots, but Luis could tell the battle was over. It seemed the commander was deliberating what to do with him. 'Tie his hands, bring him. He can march with the civilians he was trying to defend.'

The command party walked off, and as the young man rolled Luis over and tied his wrists with twine, Luis heard a new sound, like the mooing of a herd of cattle. But he knew, immediately, they were not beasts. When his captor pulled him to his feet, by his collar, Luis saw the head of the forlorn column. They were the women, children, babies and old people of the village of Homoine, the people he and his hopelessly outnumbered colleagues had been detailed to protect. The noise he heard was the wailing of the womenfolk, the screaming of the infants. He had failed them, and now Renamo were taking them away from their homes, though to where he had no idea.

'Where are we going?'

The young man with the cross prodded him in the back with the muzzle of his AK-47. 'Shut up, dog. That is not for you to know.'

'I saved your life, boy,' Luis hissed.

'Then you are a fool.'

Now and then a Renamo soldier would fire a shot into the air to keep the ragged parade moving deeper into the bush. Some carried hastily gathered bundles on their heads; a basket or woven bags. Most had nothing but the clothes on their backs. A woman with a baby in her arms, its mouth fastened to her bare breast, glared at him as she walked past. He turned away from the accusation of failure. The Frelimo command had thought the village of Homoine was safe. Most of the Renamo offensive of July 1987 had been taking place in the north, in Manica and Sofala provinces. The attack at Homoine, instead of the coastal town of Inhambane and much further south of the action, was, Luis thought, either a diversion designed to siphon off Frelimo troops from the main battles in the north, or the opening of a new front. Either way, they had been taken by surprise.

Luis had seen his share of fighting further north and his commander had rewarded his numerous instances of bravery with a redeployment closer to his home in Inhambane. He had taken a *chapa* every couple of days from the coastal capital to Homoine, commuting to and from his military post. It was almost like having a regular job, and until that day's attack there had been no action. His new girlfriend, Miriam, would be worried when rumours of the attack reached her. He supposed they were being taken deep into the west, into a Renamo bush camp, where he would be kept as a prisoner, perhaps in a work gang. He feared more for the civilians, especially the young women and girls. Why the rebels were taking the old as well, he had no idea.

'What do you want with the old people?'

'I said, *shut up*,' the soldier said, and prodded him along again.

He doesn't know, Luis thought. The Christian soldier obviously regarded Luis as his personal prize, as he kept him close by, walking him in parallel to the throng of civilians. The heat of the day took its toll on the villagers, many of whom carried wounds of some kind from the assault on Homoine. An elderly woman was being supported by two girls, her arms across their shoulders. Luis wanted to help, but the boy refused to untie his hands.

It was hard to tell how many noncombatants there were in the march, but Luis thought it must be at least four hundred. Bound as he was, he could not brush the branches of thorn trees out his path as they moved through the bush. His face and chest were scored with scratches and wait-a-minute bushes snagged at his blood-soaked uniform and exposed skin. His head still ached and he guessed he had suffered a concussion from the bullet that had, luckily, only grazed the side of his head. How fortunate he was, though, remained to be seen.

They came to a grassy vlei and the bright sun burned them as the soldiers halted the crowd and condensed them into the centre of the open floodplain. Men with RPDs, light machine guns fitted with drum magazines containing belts of bullets, were posted around the group, but only on two sides. Other soldiers lined the same two sides of what was becoming a rough open square.

Luis forgot the pain in his head and his raging thirst. He felt his heart start to pound faster as more troops were brought to the flanks. This was far more men than was needed to guard a gaggle of unarmed civilians. The commander he had seen before called for his men's attention. Those soldiers whose weapons weren't already cocked readied them for action. Instinctively some of the civilians, mostly the old men, started jostling deeper into the crowd for protection.

'No!' Luis said.

'Get on your knees,' whispered the young soldier behind him.

'They're going to kill them all,' Luis said, reluctantly easing himself to his knees and bracing himself for what was to come.

And then the commander gave the order to open fire. The volleys were ragged at first, but as more of the villagers screamed and some of the soldiers emptied their first magazines, so the madness took hold. All of the Renamo men were firing, some of them laughing as terrified civilians climbed over each other to get away from the storm of lead. Some civilians, predictably, ran from the open sides of the square towards the tree line on the far side of the vlei.

But the commander had chosen his killing field well. As the first of the youngest and fittest of the villagers reached the bush the explosions began. Landmines planted at the edge of the clearing blasted feet and limbs from children, yet still others ran blindly into the garden of death the rebels had sown.

Luis watched, horrified and hopeless as the lines of soldiers, on an order from the commander, advanced through the vlei and finished off those who were screaming and crying. Occasionally a villager who had played dead or hidden under a body got up and started to run. The soldiers joked with each other and competed to put the fleeing human down.

'Kill him,' yelled the commander, pointing to Luis.

Luis glanced back over his shoulder. The young soldier's mouth was slack and his eyes glistened with tears.

'I said kill him!'

'May God have mercy on your soul,' Luis said, and turned his eyes to the ground in front of him.

Luis gave a start as the bullet from the AK-47 exploded from the barrel just inches behind his head. He felt the projectile whizz past his left ear, close enough for the displaced air to buffet his head slightly. He saw, clearly, the bullet bury itself in the ground in front of him. Amazingly, though, he was still alive. The boy could not have missed at this range and Luis pitched himself forward, face-first in the grass, and lay as still as he could.

Above and behind him he heard a sniff and a stifled sob, and the swish of the young soldier's footsteps through the grass as he walked away.

Luis lay in silence, trying to ignore the ants that crawled over him and the flies that buzzed and ferreted at the graze wound on the side of his head. He had deliberately twisted his head as he fell so that he could play his part in the boy's ruse, and that a casual observer would see the blood and assume he was dead. He heard more voices and movement. Among the noise he identified the deep voice of the short commander who had ordered the killing.

'Dry your eyes, boy. You are a coward. This is the way we will beat these communists, by striking fear into their hearts. None will dare support Frelimo when word of what happened here gets out.'

Luis was amazed by the commander's cruelty and stupidity. The words stopped, however, at the sound of an approaching helicopter. The *whop* of the blades and the whine of the engines increased and Luis was aware of a shadow passing over him. The helicopter landed and Luis was blasted with grit and grass from the downwash.

'Go help them unload,' the commander said, presumably to the young soldier.

Luis held his breath as he heard footsteps getting close to him. Around the clearing sporadic shots told of the last of the civilians being given the coup de grâce. Further away explosions began occurring. Luis wondered if they were tossing grenades in among the bodies to make identification harder.

Luis had his eyes slitted and could tell when the shadow of a man settled over him. 'No, that one is dead,' said the commander. The commander walked away and called a greeting in Portuguese: '*Ola, Captitao* Lotz.'

'*Ola*, you have followed your orders well,' replied another man. 'When news of this reaches Frelimo they will divert hundreds of troops from the north to find you and your men. You must disappear now, deep into the bush.' The voice was not Mozambican, and the Portuguese was spoken in a guttural accent. The man who spoke it, Luis was sure, was white and probably an Afrikaner. It might have been kept secret in South Africa, but it was well known in Mozambique that Renamo was covertly supported with arms and ammunition and advisers from the apartheid regime across the border and this Lotz must be one of them.

The commander stepped over Luis, who dared not move a muscle, apparently taking the visitor from the helicopter on a tour of the scene of the massacre.

When they were thirty or more metres away, in the clearing amid the bodies, Luis widened his eyes a little. The man was white, and he wore the uniform of the South African military. He was tall and dark-haired, broad-shouldered with a sun-tanned face and forearms. His nose was crooked, as though it been broken at some time. The man laughed at something the commander said and slapped the shorter African on the back.

Luis smelled the acrid smoke of the explosives, from the landmines and the grenades. The white man dropped to his knees and scooped a handful of dirt and inspected it. He let the black powder filter through his fingers, then wiped his hand on the side of his fatigues. Luis saw how the man's hand and trousers remained stained, and he knew what it was, in the ground.

*

Luis was jolted back to reality as the driver braked. A portly traffic policeman strode out into the middle of the EN 1 and was waving at them to pull over.

Luis grabbed a jacket of the one of the workers and draped it over his gun hand. 'Nice and cool and no one gets killed, all right?'

'Yes, *baba*,' said the driver. The other worker looked terrified.

'Driver's licence,' the policeman said.

The man fumbled in his back pocket for his wallet. '*Bom dia,* how are you?' Luis asked the policeman.

'Fine. Where are you going?'

'Inhassoro, sir, to drill for water at the holiday home of a government minister.'

'Ah,' the policeman's eyes widened in understanding. He took a cursory look at the licence and decided he did not want to raise the ire of a wealthy politician. 'You may proceed.'

The driver whistled through his teeth as he put the truck in gear and drove off, careful to stick to the speed limit. Just past the turnoff to Inhambane, they took a left following the sign for the R43, to Homoine. As they came to the village Luis saw the spot where he and Joao had failed to stop the Renamo advance in 1987, and where Joao had been killed and Luis had made his suicidal dash through the enemy lines into the bush. Beyond the palm trees, deep in the thorns, was the clearing where four hundred and twenty-four people had been murdered.

'Turn left here.'

He had been back to this place, after Renamo had been beaten back, to show the cadres from Frelimo the decomposing bodies, mangled by the hand grenades. Later, he had returned again to help with the burial of the bodies. After that he had turned his back on his shattered, eviscerated homeland and gone in search of money in South Africa. Politics meant nothing to him any more, such was his disillusionment over the civil war.

'Turn on to this gravel road, into the vlei,' he told the driver. 'Stop here.'

Luis got out of the truck, lost in his memories, not even bothering to keep the two workers covered with the pistol that he held loose by his side. He lifted the Tokarev and looked at it. How he wished he hadn't ever had to hold such a thing again in his life; how he cursed the men who made such things and turned Africa's soil redder still in the name of their irrelevant, long-dead ideologies; how he wished he would never have to kill again.

He heard the springs on the drill rig truck creak, and turned towards it. The workers were getting down, not running, but moving tentatively through the long grass to where he stood.

'Is this where you want us to drill, *baba*?'

He looked out over the vlei and remembered the screams of the women and the children, the blasts as the young ones ran for the shelter of the trees only to meet their agonising deaths in the minefield soon to contain the massacre. He heard the crump of the hand grenades scattering flesh and bone. He saw the white man who had come off the helicopter, the swaggering bravado of the little commander, the tears of his young guard.

'*Baba?*'

Luis looked back at the driver. 'No, not here.'

'This is the place you mentioned, the place of ghosts?'

He nodded his head. No doves cooed here, no cicadas screeched, no kingfishers chirped. Perhaps, at night, there was the plaintive cry of the jackal, or the supernatural whoop of the hyena through this field of ghosts. 'You can feel it.'

'This is Homoine,' the younger of the two said. 'We learned about this in school. This is where the Renamo dogs murdered the innocents.'

We were all dogs, in our way, Luis thought, *none of us truly innocent.* Civil war brought out the animal in men. Except that, unlike men, animals killed for a reason.

'We will not drill here, but we will find somewhere close by, away from this graveyard.' If it was here, so close to the surface, then it would be nearby as well. He remembered the powder running through the white man's hands.

Luis led the workers back to the rig, not even bothering any more to cover them with the gun. If they ran, then so be it. He knew the basics of how the rig worked and could pay or press-gang more labourers if needs be. He heard them whispering behind him. Luis opened the door of the truck, climbed up and looked down at them.

'We will come with you, *baba*. You are not drilling for water, are you?'

'No.'

'You are not disturbing the spirits are you, *baba*?' asked the older of the two. 'We want no part in disturbing ghosts.'

Luis shook his head. 'No more ghosts. And do not worry, I will be paying you.'

They both smiled and climbed into the truck. Luis surveyed the land as they drove. When he found the spot he was looking for he told them to stop and to begin unloading the drilling gear.

It was hot, hard, noisy work that cloaked them in dust. The sun came out from behind the clouds and burned down on them mercilessly as they pierced the earth, driving ever deeper.

The rig was shut down and Luis extracted a sample and studied it. He had to rely on knowledge he had not put into use since his university studies, but the indicators he was looking for were plainly there.

'What is it, *baba*?' asked the younger of the two. The older probably knew it was better to refrain from asking too many questions of a man who had hijacked their valuable equipment at gunpoint.

Luis allowed himself a small smile. 'Pack up the rig. It is time for you to go back to the Swedish man. He will be worried about you.'

Luis reached into the pouch hanging around his neck, beneath his sweat- and dust-stained shirt. He opened the envelope containing the money Cameron McMurtrie had given him. He counted out five thousand rand for each of the men and handed it to them. The older man nodded his thanks, while the younger man's face broke into a wide grin. To the elder, Luis said: 'I am giving you ten thousand for the Swede, as compensation for the loss of his equipment. Tell him it is a donation to whatever charity funds him. I am sending him an SMS, advising him of this, so don't cheat me.'

'I will do as you ask, *baba*.'

'What did you find?' asked the young one again.

'A way home.'

31

Wellington parked his Audi out the front of the Hub, the central entrance to the Riverside Mall shopping centre on the R40 between Nelspruit and White River.

The security guard offered to look after his vehicle and Wellington ignored him. He lifted his Ray Ban sunglasses onto his head as he went through the revolving door. There was the usual mix of shoppers: bleached blonde Afrikaner housewives, black diamonds dripping with bling, and swarthy Portuguese on a day's shopping trip from Maputo in designer beach wear. He turned right and went into the Spur restaurant.

The waitress asked if he wanted smoking or nonsmoking, indoors or outdoors. He chose outdoors for this meeting. He was afraid of no one. Few knew his face and if, by chance, one of them saw him here with his guest, they would be too scared to report him. Besides, who would they report him to?

He stood as he saw police Colonel Sindisiwe Radebe enter the restaurant. She was in sexy mufti: platform shoes and a miniskirt stretched over her ample behind. In her hands she clutched a brace of shopping bags. 'Sindisiwe, sister, how are you?'

'I am fine, and you?'

'Fine, fine.'

'I got here early, so I did some shopping. I saw you pull up. You make quite an entrance.'

He made a show of pulling out her chair for her. She set her bags down on the spare seat. 'Johnny Walker Blue Label, on ice, times two,' he said to the skinny Afrikaner girl who would be their waitress.

'You remembered my drink.' She smiled coquettishly.

He had ordered it for room service, after he had bedded her the first time, in a room in the Southern Sun hotel on the other side of the mall complex, near the casino where they had played afterwards. He glanced at the shopping bags and saw one was from a lingerie shop. She saw what had caught his eye. 'Do you have to get back to work this afternoon?'

She batted her fake eyelashes. 'At the station in Barberton they think I am at a conference with the provincial chief in Nelspruit. I have the afternoon free.'

The girl brought their drinks. He swirled his, enjoying the tinkling of the ice cubes. Sindisiwe ordered the ladies' fillet and he chose the ribs. 'I wonder what we can do to help you while away the hours?'

She leaned forward, elbows on the table. 'Business first. McMurtrie's daughter has disappeared.' She waited for him to say something.

He shrugged and spread his hands. 'It's not surprising his daughter has run off. The news media reported her father has died in a plane crash and then, I heard, the mother drove herself off a cliff.'

'Hmm, yes. Coetzee at the mine said he sent one of his drivers to collect the dominee and the girl after he heard about the deaths of McMurtrie and the Australian woman. The dominee is missing, as is the driver. How did you hear the girl had run away?'

He sipped his Scotch. He didn't like the seriousness that creased her face. The sex was better for the colonel than it was for him, but he needed her in his pocket if he was to ramp up production at the mine. He had already sent word to his network of *zama zamas*, and those he had not been holding against their will, his hard men and enforcers, had started moving back underground. A small team had already begun blasting the night before. With the legal mining operations halted due to the enquiry into pollution, his small band had free rein underground. They had even bribed a Global Resources man on caretaking duty to start up the compressors for them, so they could use the power drills left underground by the company. With Global Resources in chaos, the time was right for him to bring his workforce back to what it had been, and potentially double it. 'I have my sources, just as you do.'

She leaned closer to him, lowering her voice. 'The mine worker Coetzee sent, Timothy Nyati, was known to us. He had a record for assault. Your kind of man. Was he one of yours, Wellington?'

The waitress brought their food, forcing Sindisiwe to suspend her interrogation and sit back in her seat. He wished she would shut up and eat her food so he could fuck her and be on his way back to his mine. When the white girl was gone he said: 'I have many men in my pay.'

'As I said, he's gone missing as well. Wellington, we have a golden opportunity,' she let out a little snort at her pun, 'to make some serious coin out of the mine now. But a missing girl and a missing churchman is already drawing the media to me. It will only be a matter of time before the Hawks descend on me if I cannot solve this case. I will have to do something.'

She folded her arms over her bosom. He cut his ribs up and began chewing. He preferred traditional food, *sadza* as they called the maize meal starch in Zimbabwe, and the rich relish of meat and gravy. But coming here to this wild-west cowboy-themed restaurant, and taking a room at the hotel afterwards, was about status. He chose the time and place of their meetings, and always made them in public, so that Sindisiwe would know who called the shots. If she wanted her share of the money she had to take her share of the risks.

He finished a second rib and licked his fingers. She glared at him over her untouched steak. He took another sip of Scotch and caught the waitress's eye and pointed at his glass. 'What if I told you the girl was alive?'

Sindisiwe was a big woman who needed plenty of fuel. Her hunger got the better of her. She cut into the rare steak, and seemed to be forcing herself to play it cool. 'And the dominee?'

He shook his head and picked up another rib.

She ate a small mouthful. When the waitress returned Sindisiwe asked for a glass of red wine. 'And this man Nyati? Do you know where he is, Wellington? Look at me when I talk to you, this is important.'

He felt the rage shoot to boiling temperature inside him. How dare she. If she had been his wife, in Zimbabwe, she would have felt the back of his hand for such a remark. 'You're not going to get the girl back.'

Sindisiwe shook her head. 'If she has been with you or your men I don't want her. Her story will go front page. We will all be finished. They will send the recces underground to kill every last one of you.'

'She is unharmed. For now.'

Sindisiwe put down her knife and fork and put her hands over her ears. 'I don't want to know, but I want this resolved.'

He sucked a rib, grazing the last of the tender meat off with his teeth on either side of the bone. He licked his lips when he was finished and savoured some more Scotch. 'I want to hear you say it. Tell me you want the girl dead.'

'Keep your voice down.'

'Say it.'

She looked nervously around the restaurant at the gossiping housewives, the fat child's birthday party, the shopkeepers and busi-nessmen taking their lunch breaks.

'Say it,' he said again, leaning in.

Her eyelids narrowed and her lips parted a little. He saw her big breasts heaving. Something had changed in her. She had dropped the façade of integrity and concern for a moment and he could see into her dark soul through her limpid, almost hidden eyes. 'Tell me what you have planned for her,' she whispered.

'Mohammed wants to sell her.'

A smile played across the colonel's painted, glossy lips. 'So she will make us much money.'

He nodded. 'A golden-haired child is worth almost as much as gold.'
'Finish your drink. It is time for us to go to the hotel.'

*

After they had showered and Sindisiwe had reapplied her makeup, they both drove back to Barberton in separate cars. Wellington passed her early on, his Audi hugging the twisting turns of the pass as though it was on railway tracks. He waved at her and thought he would not see her again for some time, but her big black BMW loomed large in his rear-view mirror.

She accelerated hard and passed him at a hundred and fifty kilometres an hour. Fuelled by the Scotch and the memory of her screams in the hotel room, he geared down and revelled in the surge of power he felt vibrate up through his body from the engine. He was doing a hundred and sixty when he edged alongside her and they stayed like that for a few seconds. She had been better in bed this time than on any of their liaisons. The talk of the child had done it for her. She was sick.

He gunned the Audi's engine and left her in his wake. He had work to do. In the mirror he could see her easing back to the speed limit, as befitted a senior officer of the South African Police Service. She was getting back to her patch now and had to be careful.

Wellington took his phone out and dialled Timothy Nyathi's number while he drove. At Wellington's instructions Nyathi had stayed away from work, in hiding, since the news of McMurtrie's and Hamilton's deaths. As one of Wellington's paid spies Nyathi had dutifully called Wellington and told him the news as soon as he'd heard it, and relayed Coetzee's orders to him to go and pick up the dominee and McMurtrie's daughter. This had given Wellington the opportunity to kidnap the girl and eliminate the minister, though he had not told Timothy of his plans, merely that it was time for him to lay low in preparation for an important, lucrative job.

'Hello, boss, how are you?' said Timothy Nyati.
'Fine. Are you still in Emjindini?'

'Yes, boss. The newspapers, the radio, they are full of talk about the dominee and the girl, I . . .'

'Relax, my brother. It will all be fine. I need to collect you, now, as I have another job for you.'

'Boss, I –'

'I will be in the township in ten minutes.'

He pulled up outside the pastel blue house and waited, the engine running. Nyati emerged from the modest backyard, where Wellington knew he had been staying in a shack. A legal miner lived in the house, but he was also on Wellington's payroll.

Timothy was looking behind and all around him as he darted out to the road and slid into the low-slung car. Wellington spun the wheels as he took off. 'Boss, I am worried.'

Wellington reached under the driver's seat and pulled out a brown paper bag. 'Open that, take a sip.'

Nyati opened the bag and broke the seal on a half-jack bottle of Johnny Walker Blue. 'Hey, this is the good stuff, boss.' He took a swig and passed the bottle to Wellington, who made as if he was taking a long draft, but in fact swallowed very little.

'Have more,' Wellington said. 'Open the ashtray. There is a *zol* in there. I want to thank you for what you did, my brother.'

Nyati found the joint and lit it. Sweet marijuana smoke filled the cab. Again, when he passed it to Wellington, the general held it to his lips for a while but inhaled only a little.

Nyati coughed. 'Boss, about the girl . . .'

'Chill, my brother. Have some more of my weed.'

Wellington drove into Barberton and turned left at the Toyota dealership and headed out towards the mine. 'Like I said, all will be fine. I have been talking to the police, Timothy. We have come up with a way to make it look like someone killed the dominee and the girl and then killed himself. But I need your help again. Don't worry, you will be paid, just as I have always paid you for your information.'

Nyati nodded. The drink and the drug seemed to have eased his worries. 'I have never killed anyone, boss.'

'I know, Timothy, and I'm not going to ask you to. But I do need you to be my backup. Have you ever fired a gun?'

He shook his head and drank some more. 'No, boss. But I have seen it done, on television.'

Wellington passed Fairview Mine and the turn-off to the Diggers' Retreat and Sheba. He checked the Audi's odometer and when he had gone far enough he indicated left and turned onto a narrow farm road. He stopped the car and got out. 'Come, Timothy, let's have some fun. Bring the bottle.'

Wellington started walking into the bush, careful not to let the thorns snag on his tailored shirt and designer jeans. When Timothy said, '*Eish*, boss, what is that smell?' Wellington knew he had come back to the right place.

'Some dead animal. Finish the Scotch and give me the bottle.' Wellington waited while Timothy, already unsteady as he tipped back the bottle, finished the liquor and handed it over. Wellington then walked twenty paces and rested the bottle in the fork of a thorn tree. He went back to Timothy, took the unlicensed Sig Sauer nine-millimetre pistol from the waistband of his jeans, cocked it and handed it to the other man. 'See if you can hit it.'

Timothy grinned like a boy and nodded. He held up the pistol and it wavered as the target swam in his vision. When he pulled the trigger the noise of the gunshot and the recoil took him by surprise. His hand jerked up and he closed his eyes instinctively. When he opened his eyes a look of dismay clouded his face. The bottle was still in the crook of the branch.

Wellington came up behind him. Timothy flinched away when Wellington put his hand on his shoulder. 'It's OK. Let me show you, brother.'

He placed his right hand over the younger man's hand and used his left to show him how to steady the pistol. 'Squeeze.'

Wellington eased his grip on Timothy's hands and he fired again. The bottle shattered. 'Yes!'

'That is good, my brother. Now we have work to do, but first let us see what is smelling so bad.'

'All right.' Timothy handed the pistol back to him.

Wellington led them through the wait-a-bit bush, in between the trees. The stench became stronger and Wellington's eyes started to water. 'Look, there he is.'

'He?' Timothy moved up from behind him to get a look. Timothy retched and put his hand over his mouth and nose. 'Ah! It is a human. Who is this, boss?'

'It's the dominee.'

Timothy gasped as he stared at the bloated body. 'Who killed him, boss?'

Wellington raised the pistol and put it against Timothy's right temple. 'You did.' He pulled the trigger.

*

The men sat around the meeting table in the mine manager's office. Pictures of Coetzee's wife and daughter had been placed on Cameron's old desk.

This office would always remind Chris of Cameron, and now that he knew for sure he would never see the old mine manager again, he felt the sadness drag him down. Cameron had been a good man, respected by the whole workforce. He had been hard on men who broke the rules, but only because ignoring or flouting the regulations made for an unsafe workplace. He'd had a true commitment to the environment and pollution control and Chris thought this had gone deeper than just complying with the company's rigorous standards. He was sure Cameron had been against the plan to mine Lion Plains, and that was a turning point for Chris. Chris had argued against the development, even as he was forced to tick the boxes of the development application as part of his duties as the environmental manager. Cameron had not stood up to the company, so Chris had done what had to be done. All the same, he would never have wished for Cameron, or Kylie for that matter, to be killed. He suddenly felt sick to his stomach and his peripheral vision started to blur.

He was barely aware of what the other men on the executive team were discussing. Jan had ordered him to attend the meeting; even though he had verbally tendered his resignation he would have to work out his notice and hand over to a new environmental manager.

'Chris?'

'Yes. Sorry?' he looked at Jan and realised he had not heard the question.

'I asked if you have any news about the independent review of air quality in the mine.'

'Oh, right. Sorry, boss. The team hasn't been able to take samples yet.'

'Why not?'

Chris looked at Coetzee, who remained impassive. 'The *zama zamas*. They've come back to the mine. The monitoring guys bumped into two men yesterday, one armed with a pistol and the other with an AK-47 and the criminal miners told them to *voetsek*. The guys are too scared to go back down without an armed guard now.'

Jan looked to Coetzee, who coughed, clearing his voice. 'I had to reprimand two of our guys this morning. I was doing a walk around and saw the compressors were running. I asked them why and one guy said one of the *zama zamas* had come to him, in the township, and pulled a gun on him. He said if he didn't come into work and start the compressor, then the guy would kill his wife and child.'

'*Bliksem*.' Jan ran a hand through his hair.

Chris could see the big boss was stressed. He wondered if Jan's lapse into the local vernacular was intentional, to make it seem like he was still one of them.

'Do we get the armed security guys to come back?' Casper, the geologist, chimed in.

Jan shook his head. 'Not for now. We've been in the news too much in the last two weeks. I don't want the media crawling all over us again. We'll wait until things die down and then send some teams down.' He looked to Chris. 'But we've got to get the independent monitors down there. Chris, you were with the illegals for quite a while; you know where they were mining.'

Chris held his breath. He felt the fear-induced adrenaline surge through his bowels. 'No.'

Jan held up a hand. 'Hear me out. This mess with the samples happened on your watch. You can't explain how the pollutant readings were so high and you kept telling Cameron and Kylie and me that we were compliant, then all of a sudden it goes off the Richter scale. You know where they were operating and you can take the monitoring team to somewhere else underground.'

'No. I told you, I quit. I'm not going underground again.' He fought but couldn't contain the panic in his voice.

'We'd send armed security down there with you. Just to protect you and keep the *zama zamas* at bay, not to take them on like last time.'

Chris placed his palms down on the table to steady himself. 'That didn't work last time. Paulo Barrica and Themba Tshabalala were killed.'

Coetzee coughed again. 'Ag, he did have a rough time down there, boss.'

Jan fixed him with a stare for a few seconds and Coetzee coughed again and looked away. 'It's a mine,' Jan said. 'It's supposed to be rough.'

Chris pushed back his chair. 'I'm sorry, I can't take any more of this. I told you in the car, I *quit*!'

'Sit down.'

Chris felt dizzy, and there was something about the quiet way that Jan had spoken that made the words sound more like a threat than an order. He lowered himself back into his chair and hated himself for being such a damned coward. Hein, Casper and Roelf were all sitting silently, watching him and the boss.

Jan stared at him across the table. 'You know where those elevated contaminant samples came from, and you know how and when they were taken, don't you?'

Chris swallowed back the stinging bile that was rising up the back of his throat. The room swam and his heart started pounding. 'No, I . . . I mean, yes, they were part of the normal testing regime in the mine and they came from level eleven and . . .'

'Bullshit.'

The others looked at him accusingly. Chris felt the perspiration beading his forehead. Even the eyes of the black miner on the wall, the painting that had been given to Cameron as a gift by the mining union, of all organisations, glared at him in accusation and disgust.

'No . . .' He choked on the rest of his flimsy protest and coughed.

'Yes. You were carrying monitoring pumps when you and Tshabalala were ambushed by the *zama zamas*. You were with the criminal miners, underground, for a week before Cameron rescued you. We know the *zama zamas* care nothing for safety. You got the illegals to wear your pumps and you had the samples hidden on you when you were brought up to the surface.'

'You don't know what it was like . . .' Chris began, although his heart wasn't in his defence. He couldn't continue the lie and, as sickening as it was, he knew he would never be completely right with himself. This would cleanse him, like a bitter, purgative drug.

'I don't care, you fucking wimp. You brought those highly contaminated samples back from where your *zama zama boeties* were working and you substituted them for the regular samples taken from the Global Resources workers. Either those bastards at the monitoring company went behind our backs to leak the information to the press because they *told* you about the elevated readings and you did nothing, or you organised the leak yourself. *Jissus*, Chris, you've nearly bankrupted this company because of your dishonesty, but that was what you intended all along, wasn't it?' Jan was red in the face, his fist bunched above the table as if he was about to jump across it and pummel him.

Chris took a deep breath. 'No. I didn't want to bring down the company. I just wanted to stop the mine going ahead at Lion Plains.'

Coetzee whistled through his teeth. Casper balled his fists on the table and Roelf shook his head in disgust.

Jan simply nodded, as though his words had confirmed what he thought. But how, Chris wondered, had he guessed? Perhaps someone had noticed the chemistry between him and Tertia. It had been her idea to submit the contaminated samples. After he was rescued she had asked him what he had done when he was underground with the *zama zamas* and he had told her about the air testing and the fact he had the samples with him.

Jan put his elbows on the table and his fingertips together. He lowered his eyes, almost as if he was about to start praying. 'Leave us, gentlemen. I want some time alone with Chris.'

The other three stood, their chairs scraping on the floor in their haste to be gone from the poisoned atmosphere in the room. Coetzee shot Chris a look of pure loathing as he and the others filed out of the manager's office.

'How did you know it was me who switched the samples?' Chris asked. He would keep Tertia out of this, at all costs.

Jan reached into the top pocket of his shirt and pulled out a packet of cigarettes, printed, Australian-style, with a picture of a dead cancer sufferer. He offered the pack to Chris, who shook his head.

'Smoking's not allowed indoors.'

'You'd do well in Australia.' Jan shook a cigarette from the pack, put it in his mouth and lit it with a silver zippo and exhaled to the ceiling. 'It's good to be back here, despite all this *kak*. Life was simpler in the old days. Everyone smoked everywhere, we *moered* the blacks when they didn't do what we told them, and if someone like you did what you've done, your body would have been dumped in a *madala* side.'

Chris gulped. Jan blew his second stream of smoke in his direction and he coughed.

'There's nowhere in Eureka's legal operations where the level of dust contaminants is above the legally mandated minimum, is there?' Jan asked.

Chris shook his head.

'No, because Cameron ran this mine properly. So those samples had to come from somewhere else. It was ironic, but clever, for you to be involved, because you could have lost your job over this. If the independent review proved, as it would, that there were no unsafe areas underground, then the only person who would have done wrong in this whole fucked-up mess, apart from whoever it was at the lab who leaked the result, was you. You didn't tell Cameron about the elevated findings. If you had, we could have gone proactive and launched our own investigation rather than have the government and the union shut us down.'

'I thought I was doing the right thing. And it wasn't the lab. I leaked the letter they sent to the mine.'

Jan reached across the table with a speed that left Chris no chance to duck out of reach. He grabbed Chris's shirt front and hauled him across the table until their faces were just inches apart. Smoke leaked from Jan's mouth as he spoke, making Chris's eyes water. 'Don't lie to me, boy. I've cut the throats of better men than you.'

Chris tried to struggle free, but Jan held him, effortlessly, for a few more seconds, before letting him go. Chris slumped back into his chair. 'You made no secret of the fact that you were not in favour of the Lion Plains mine, but like a good little drone you still filled in all the forms in the environmental impact assessment that said there was nothing inherently wrong with our application. I admired your work ethic – viewing the project objectively, and concluding that we met all the requirements, but I also thought you were a gutless *moffie*.'

Chris shrank in his chair. He most certainly was not a homosexual. Indeed, it was his love of a woman that was partially responsible for his predicament.

'If you were a real man you would have resigned in protest and fought the Lion Plains mine fair, but no, you decided to sabotage the company from the inside.'

It was true. He knew that if he could release damning evidence of Global Resources flouting the government's environmental standards the public outcry over mining on a game reserve – already strong and gaining momentum thanks to Tertia's relentless PR campaign – would force the government to stall, if not cancel, approval for Lion Plains.

Jan sat back in his chair and drew on his cigarette again. 'So,' he waved his free hand in the air, 'what do I do with you now, you two-faced piece of shit?'

Chris glanced over his shoulder.

'Don't think about making a run for the door. I'll beat you to it.'

Chris wanted to stand up to this bully, to call his bluff and assert that there was no way the CEO of a globally listed company would physically assault one of his staff members. But then, Chris reasoned, Global Resources was going down the toilet and it was possible the members of the board, not to mention the company's many shareholders, might already be planning Jan's retirement.

'Yes, better you say nothing for now. I'll tell you what's going to happen. You're going to go back down my mine, with a couple of armed security guys and the independent monitoring guys, and you're going to make sure they take their samples in a clean area so that we come up smelling like roses. You're then going to work with our resident spin doctor, Musa Mabunda, to come up with a little fairytale about how you inadvertently mixed up some samples. You can say you had monitoring pumps set up near the ore face to record contaminant levels at the time of blasting and you mistakenly sent these to the lab as samples recorded by workers. When the mistake was brought to your attention you covered it up to try to save your skin.'

Chris shook his head. '*Ag*, no ways, man. No one will believe it. Why would I do such a thing if it was just an honest mistake?'

'Because you're a lying little snake. You'll resign again, in public this time, and I'll accept your resignation. But first you have to go down there and get the new samples.'

Chris felt his lower lip start to tremble. 'I . . . I can't.'

'You can, and you will. Looking at you I can't believe how you had the balls to set this up in the first place. Cameron told me how scared you were every time you went underground. No, my boy, I think someone else was pulling your strings.'

'No!'

'Oh, very forceful. Quite the tough man all of a sudden, aren't we? Who was it? Some other tree-hugging greenie? Greenpeace? World Wildlife Fund? No, they wouldn't be involved in something illegal. Who else wants my company bankrupted and the Lion Plains project cancelled?'

Chris said nothing.

'Who was in on it with you?' Jan persisted. 'Was it that crazy bunny-hugging bitch, Tertia Venter? Is that it? Is she pulling more than your strings, boy?'

He looked up. 'No! I acted alone. But, please –'

Jan silenced him with a stare and stubbed out his cigarette. 'You'll go down the mine. This little scheme, whoever cooked it up, has backfired. You can leave here quietly, after you've done the testing, or I'll call in the cops. If they won't charge you with anything, then the company lawyers will sue you for loss of production.' He stood and leaned across the table. 'I'll fucking crush you, do you hear me, boy?'

32

'Yes, the body of a white male, aged fifty-four, was found at the scene of the shooting,' Colonel Sindisiwe Radebe said into the telephone, 'and it appeared this male had been killed several days ago. A note was found next to the body of the deceased gunman expressing remorse for two crimes he said he had committed.'

'Thanks, Colonel,' said the reporter from MPower FM. 'That's great, but can you give me a little more off the record? My sources told me the old dead white guy was the dominee who went missing the same time as Cameron McMurtrie's daughter.'

'Ah, there has been too much tragedy in this little town of ours,' Sindisiwe said, not answering the question. She had been interviewed by the media many times in her rapidly advancing career. She knew how to avoid questions, and she knew that nothing, truly, was ever off the record.

'Colonel?'

'Off the record, yes, I saw the deceased male's body and I am sure it is the missing dominee. The note left by the man, who was a worker in the office at Eureka, said he committed suicide over his remorse for killing the church man, and for raping and killing

386

Jessica McMurtrie, whom he had admired from afar for a long time.'

'Wow. I mean, thanks, Colonel. How much of that can I use?'

'I will trust you to use this information in a way that does not compromise our ongoing working relationship,' Sindisiwe said, then hung up. She smiled to herself and thought of the afternoon of lovemaking yesterday. Wellington was becoming too big for his boots, but if things could return to normal at Eureka, with the pirate miners earning just enough money to keep her in designer clothes and a new car every two years, without becoming so greedy that they sparked another underground war, then all would be well.

Sindisiwe picked up the copy of *Lowveld Living* she had been reading when the reporter had called. It was the latest edition of the glossy lifestyle magazine, delivered to her straight from the presses. She had ten copies on her desk, waiting to be mailed to family and friends. She opened it again to the feature on '*LOWVELD WOMEN CRASHING THROUGH THE GLASS CEILING*'. There she was, in her field uniform, leaning on the bonnet of a police car, her right hand on her holstered Z88 pistol, giving the photographer her best Dirty Harry stare. On the next page she was in a figure-hugging black sequinned evening dress, in killer platform heels, leaning across the top of a piano in the casino next door to where she had met Wellington. '*Just because I'm a cop doesn't mean that I can't be a sensitive and sensual woman*' she was quoted as saying under the second picture. She couldn't wait to show Wellington. She wanted to remind him just how powerful she was.

Her phone rang. 'Colonel Radebe.' She never tired of how fine that combination of words sounded.

'Ma'am,' said Moses, the desk sergeant, 'there are some guys here from the Hawks to see you. It's about the dominee and the McMurtrie girl.'

Sindisiwe dropped the magazine on the edge of the desk and it fell to the floor.

*

Jessica had experienced the total darkness of the world where her father worked twice before. Once she had gone down in the cage with him on a day when all of the kids in school had had to go to work with one of their parents. The other was as part of a school excursion to Eureka, and she had felt proud because when the other girls shrieked and the boys chattered nervously, she kept her cool because she was ready for the blackness when the miner switched off his lamp.

It was black.

More than that, it was impenetrable. When her dad had signalled the cage operator to stop it halfway down, and told her to switch off her miner's lamp, she had been unprepared for the darkness. She hadn't been able to see the fingers of her hand, no matter how close she held them to her face and how much she strained her eyes.

But her father had been next to her, and although she couldn't see him either, she could feel him, and that made everything fine. It had been kind of fun, as well.

When they had switched their lamps back on and reached the level where the men were working, she had been amazed at how much was going on. Compressors hummed, an LHD – a low-slung load, haul, dumper – rumbled by, and sweating men leaned into screaming drills that probed the rock face.

And she had loved it.

Her mother had hated the mine and resented her father for working in it and making them stay in Barberton. When Jessica had announced, after attending a careers day, that she wanted to study engineering at university, her father had looked proud as a peacock. Her mother had suggested she study something less manly. Jessica had pointed out that there was a shortage of engineers in South Africa and that there were programs to encourage girls to study. Her father had said that she wouldn't be restricted to working in the mines, but her mother had accused him of brainwashing her. 'It's no place for a girl,' her mother had said.

Jessica sniffed and coughed again. Her throat was raw from the dust she had inhaled. It was warm and it was pitch black, but it was not a nice place where she was.

He had put her on a steel-framed bed that had squeaked when he had dropped her. The thin foam mattress smelled of the acrid sweat of miners who had slept there, and other odours that she didn't want to try to place. Her tears had flown for a long time, soaking into the rancid sponge.

Her hands were bound behind her back with a cable tie, but he had removed the gag. She had screamed until her throat hurt, but it was no good. If anyone could hear her in the darkness, none of them cared about her, or they were too scared of the man to come and save her. The blindfold was gone, but that meant nothing, because here she was again, in the impenetrable blackness. Instead of comforting her, the darkness had begun to freak her out. But she had calmed herself.

She had wondered if he had left her here alone, thinking her a defenceless child; if she could free herself she could perhaps find a lamp of some kind and find her way out of the mine. More than most kids she had an idea of how a mine worked and where the tunnels might lead. Her need to find out who, if anyone, was beyond the door of this chamber had made her think about what to scream next. 'I need to go to the toilet! I am going to piss all over this mattress!'

She had waited and a key had scratched in the door lock a few minutes later. He had entered.

He had stood, close to her, not speaking, for what seemed like an age. Her heart had thumped in her chest, the myriad imaginings of what he would do to her torturing her. When he had reached out in the dark and touched her thigh she had screamed and scrambled, as best as she could, away from him. The side walls, however, had blocked her. When she had felt his touch again she had kicked as hard as she could, but he had just laughed at her.

'I'm going to take your pants off. So you can go to the toilet. No hands, though.'

She had sobbed and kicked and writhed, but in the end she had succumbed to his touch. He hadn't touched her, down there, but what made it almost as bad was that he had taken control over her. He knew she couldn't bear to wet her pants, and he had helped her. She wanted to kill him.

'I'm not going to hurt you,' he had said quietly as she'd scrunched herself up to try to protect herself from him, burrowing into the corner on the stinking foam. She had tried not to cry. 'You're going to help me, Jessica.'

And then he had left her, in the all-encompassing, impenetrable darkness.

33

The next morning Colonel Sindisiwe Radebe drove to Eureka in her BMW, tailing the two know-it-all agents from the Hawks who had had the temerity to question her the day before about the killings of the dominee and the girl.

The Hawks, an elite investigative unit, were the successors to the ill-fated Scorpions, who had been crushed like the insects they were when they had tried to smear the president with corruption allegations. Sindisiwe had been a member of the ANC all her adult life and had been active in student politics in the dying days of the apartheid regime. She thought the government was doing a good job, trying to right the many wrongs of the past and offering plenty of opportunities for bright, hard-working members like herself to rise through the ranks and to prosper on the way.

There were two of them, both men in their thirties, one white and one black, although the latter was more coconut than a brother. He was brown on the outside but white on the inside. They may have fancied themselves the squeaky clean face of the new South Africa, but to her they were an oppressor and a sell-out. There was something repugnant, Sindisiwe thought, about law enforcement officers questioning other officers and insinuating they were corrupt. The white one, Pretorius, had asked her how it was that thirteen alleged *zama zamas* had managed to escape from the holding cells in the police station in one night.

Sindisiwe had retorted that she was the station commander, not the policeman on duty. The man had been counselled against leaving his key in the lock of one of the cell doors, but he was an otherwise good police officer with a spotless record as, she reminded the smarmy agents, was she.

They had probed her about her investigations into the death of the dominee and the disappearance of the McMurtrie girl and she had told them the case was all but solved. The mine's driver, Timothy Nyati, had left a written confession.

'Have you spoken to his wife?' Pretorius had asked.

The man was a fool. As if she, a colonel, would go to the home of a murderer to inform the man's wife her criminal husband was dead. 'One of my men did.'

'Was she shown the alleged suicide note?' the African sidekick asked.

'You cannot come to Barberton and tell me how to run my investigations,' Sindisiwe said.

'Are there plans to search for the missing girl's body?' Pretorius asked.

She snorted. 'You really do not know where you are, do you? Men have been digging holes in these mountains for more than a hundred and thirty years. There are hundreds, maybe thousands of places to throw a body. We would never know where to start looking. The girl is gone, and her mother and father were both recently killed. It is a blessing, in a way.'

Pretorius had squared up to her, as if he could intimidate her like some old-regime policeman. 'We have information, Colonel, that the abduction and alleged killing of Jessica McMurtrie, and the death of her mother, may be the result of a payback operation by Wellington Shumba, the man who is believed to be the ringleader of the illegal miners at Eureka and was last seen in your custody, after being arrested on the edge of the Kruger Park.'

She had wondered where his information had come from.

'Unfortunately, Shumba escaped from custody before he could be charged. The same officer who allowed the others to get away on his watch has been counselled further.'

But they had stayed and, worse still, another team of police officers had arrived from Johannesburg shortly after the pair of pied Hawks. Sindisiwe felt professionally insulted that the commissioner in Joburg had sent a team from a new specialist mine-security unit to go underground in search of the missing girl. It was all for PR, she knew. There was no way they would find Jessica McMurtrie, certainly not by making a full-frontal assault down into the mine via the cage. Wellington would have the girl well hidden in his labyrinth. Even though she had deliberately not agreed to any requests from Eureka for police operations to be mounted underground, she still felt slighted that the commissioner had sent his own team.

They all pulled up at the security checkpoint at Eureka and showed their IDs. The Hawks led the way, followed by a double-cab *bakkie* groaning under the weight of four spectacularly built Zulu policemen and their arsenal of weapons and kit in the back. Sindisiwe couldn't help but admire them again as they got out of the vehicle and began readying themselves for battle.

A photographer and journalist Sindisiwe knew from the *Lowvelder* had also arrived. The commissioner might have sent these warriors, to try to prove the force was taking the problems in Barberton seriously, but Sindisiwe was determined to ensure that if there was any positive PR from this pointless operation then she would benefit from it. The photographers took mock candid pictures of her talking to the underground assault team members.

A Global Resources *bakkie* pulled up at the entrance to the headgear and Chris Loubser got out. He was wearing blue overalls, gumboots and a hard hat with a miner's lamp attached. She was surprised to see him here.

Sindisiwe went back to her car as the men moved into the cages. There was nothing she could do, and the journalist and photographer had packed their gear and left. Sindisiwe decided she would

393

do the same, and perhaps invent a meeting in Nelspruit so that she could go shopping at i'Langa Mall.

*

Chris closed his eyes and prayed as the rope, as miners called the cable connected to the cage, spooled and whined. His stomach lurched as the cage dropped and he felt the dread and the darkness engulf him.

The four policemen accompanying him had been full of bravado as they had done their final checks, tapping magazines on their helmets to ensure the springs inside weren't jammed and then ramming them into their rifles. They yanked on the cocking handles of their R5s and bumped fists. They'd been bristling with attitude, but now, as they descended, all of them were quiet. The cops would have had experience underground, perhaps as former miners, but none of them was boasting now.

Chris fought to control his breathing as the rock face of the shaft whizzed by, just inches from him. He wrapped his arms around his body and squeezed, imagining Tertia holding him. He was doing this for her, for them, and for Lion Plains and its helpless wildlife. He had to be brave for all of them.

Two of the policemen were talking softly, discussing tactics for when the cage stopped. Chris hoped the crooked Colonel Radebe had tipped off the *zama zamas* and they'd be hidden deep within the mine. This was a show raid, put on to make it look like the force was doing something, and no doubt provoked by the front-page outrage in the media. It had even made the national papers, the killing of the dominee and Cameron's daughter. Chris prayed the criminal miners were not stupid enough to take on a police team.

The cage started to slow. It jerked to a halt and Chris, who was acting as the onsetter, operated the door to open it after the all-clear bells had rung. The first officer switched on his lamp and stepped onto the level, his rifle raised to his shoulder, as if he was expecting someone to emerge from the gloom.

'Clear!'

He took two steps forward and a single shot rang out. Sparks flew off the rock side wall and the policeman fell back, screaming. He must have had his finger on the trigger because a burst of bullets ricocheted off the wall.

A second officer provided cover, firing blindly into the darkness, while a third dragged the injured man towards the cage. The fourth was futilely trying his radio. Chris rang the bell furiously to signal the hoist driver to bring them up immediately. Another two shots erupted from the darkness and the officer who had been firing fell backwards onto the floor of the cage. Chris put his hands over his ears and started screaming. Two of the police were down, a third was still giving first aid, trying to slow the bleeding of his fallen comrades' wounds. Three shots were all it had taken. The fourth policeman had given up trying to make his radio work and held his R5 above his head in surrender and emptied the rest of his magazine. When the breech locked open he ejected the magazine and fumbled in a pouch of his bulletproof vest for a fresh one.

Chris felt the hot gush of urine down his leg. Again and again he rang the bell and he finally felt the cage jerk as the winding gear was engaged. The officer giving first aid had his head lamp on and as his eyes moved from one injured man to another the beam of his light bounced off the tunnel walls. The fourth policeman's rifle was jammed and he was frantically trying to clear the obstruction.

Chris looked up towards heaven and the surface of the earth, unseen in the darkness. 'Come on, come on!'

The cage jolted and started to move upwards at last. The policeman who had been firing had gone back to his radio and was speaking rapidly into it in Zulu.

Chris glanced at the tunnel and saw a man emerge from a cubby, an alcove in the side wall where he had been hiding. He was wearing a black balaclava, but his height and posture gave him away immediately. He had on night-vision binoculars. 'No!'

Wellington raised his AK-47 and pressed the button on the night-aiming device attached to the fore grip. Chris looked down in horror at the pinprick of red light resting on his chest. The Lion shifted his aim slightly to the right so that the glowing dot was over Chris's heart.

A shot echoed up the shaft. Chris fell to the floor of the cage. The last thing he saw in life was a bright light far above as he felt himself being carried up.

*

The helicopter came up the valley, low and fast, and circled the mine once before the pilot began his descent. Jan Stein looked up, shielding his eyes from the hot African sun. The noise of the aircraft and the smell of the fresh blood brought back memories.

He peeled the sticky latex gloves from his hands and turned his back to avoid the rotor wash as the aircraft settled onto Eureka's emergency helipad. Eight of his own men, four to a stretcher, carried two wounded policemen to the helicopter. A crewman stepped out, connected to the machine by an umbilical radio cable. He waved the stretcher bearers forward.

Jan nodded to the surviving officers and they waved their thanks. He had assisted with stabilising the shot officers, drawing on skills he hadn't used in twenty-five years. They were brave men, fighting back the pain, and Jan knew that the police would not be hurrying back to try to shut down the *zama zamas*.

He walked to the mine *bakkie* and looked into the load area. He pulled back the plastic tarpaulin and saw Chris Loubser's white face, drained of life. His eyes were wide open, still showing the shock of the realisation that he was about to die. Jan had seen that look too many times. He reached down and closed the boy's eyes.

'Go with God.'

He wondered if it was all worth it; the things men did to crush these comparatively miniscule amounts of yellow particles from the grip of the earth. It was over now, he realised. Wellington was firmly in control of Eureka and there seemed little chance the independent monitors would be allowed underground any time soon. Without their report the government and the unions would still assume that Cameron McMurtrie had been neglectful of the safety of his men, and that Eureka was a deathtrap. Following the ambush of the police officers, the board in Australia would countenance no more paramilitary action to root out the criminal miners.

On top of all that, Tertia had discovered a rare bird and that had apparently scuttled Global Resources' bid to enter the coal market in South Africa. Things couldn't be worse for the company.

He pulled the plastic sheet up over Chris's body. Looking down the hill from the helipad he saw an undertaker's van coming through the security checkpoint. He took out his cigarettes and lit one as the helicopter lifted off, taking the wounded policemen to the Nelspruit Mediclinic. At least they would live.

Coetzee came out of the office block and walked down the stairs and over to him. Jan offered him his packet of cigarettes, but the mine manager shook his head. 'No thanks, I gave up.' He glanced down into the back of the pickup, then averted his eyes to watch the fast disappearing helicopter. 'So, what do we do now, boss?'

Jan kept staring out over the valley. The fading whine of the helo's engines took him back in time, again. 'I don't know.'

'I was just online. The company's share price in Australia has gone into freefall. A lot of the boys here are worried. Most of them don't want to go on strike. It's only the union bosses who are whipping up this pollution thing. The guys know the mine's safe and some of them are talking about going underground and taking on the *zama zamas* themselves. There's a rumour going around that Global Resources might try and sell Eureka. There's speculation on the internet that there's a Chinese company that's going to try and buy it. Do you think that would happen?'

Jan exhaled a stream of smoke and didn't make eye contact with Coetzee. 'The way things are going the company might pull out of Africa altogether. The Chinese might pick up all our operations for a song.'

'You can bring us back, boss. You can sort this mess out. Shit, man, I'll go and find that *bladdy* owl at Lion Plains and shoot it if you want me to. We're miners, boss, we've got to work, we've got to keep the country going.'

Jan shook his head. 'No. Leave the birds alone. I can't sort this out. I'm going to have to resign before the board sacks me.'

'You can't, boss.'

Jan walked slowly back to the office block, leaving Coetzee with the *bakkie* to greet the undertakers. He knew it was weak of him, but he couldn't watch them load Loubser into the back of the van like a side of beef.

*

Jessica heard the echo of the far-off gunshots and tried again to sit up on the stinking bed. The muscles in her arms were on fire, thanks to her hands being tied behind her and her constant efforts to break out of the cable ties.

She had failed and, unlike in the movies and books, there was no jagged piece of metal or broken glass for her to saw through her bindings. Instead, her wrists also burned and felt sticky where the plastic had cut into skin. She heard footsteps running down the tunnel. The door to the refuge chamber opened and Wellington's mining lamp illuminated the room. He held a rifle in one hand and a balaclava and night-vision binoculars in the other. He grinned.

'They came looking for you, but they're not coming back.'

She prayed it wasn't her father that Wellington had been shooting at. She still refused to believe he was dead.

'I have good news for you.'

She tried to be defiant, glaring up at him, but the truth was she was terrified he was going to rape her before he killed her. He couldn't ransom her, as a kidnapper would, because he would know that her father would catch him and kill him. The thought that her father might still be – no, the thought that he *was* – alive was the only thing that kept her from bursting into tears.

He reached for her and she screamed.

'Shush, my precious girl.'

She wriggled away from him as far as she could, her back against the warm rock wall.

'What are you going to do with me?'

He smiled and sat on the bed, which squeaked under his weight. She tried to burrow into the rock. 'I'm taking you away from here. To somewhere nice. You will be cared for.'

She couldn't allow herself to believe him. 'Where's my father?'

'He's dead. I killed him. I put a bomb on the plane he and the Australian woman were flying on in Zambia.'

'No! You're lying.'

He shrugged. 'Why would I lie? And why would I confess a murder to you?'

Jessica swallowed back her tears. She thought it was because he was going to kill her, but she didn't want to play his games.

'I'll tell you why. You are valuable to me.'

She felt the tears welling and sniffed them back. 'What do you mean?'

'You can die, or you can live. There is a man I know who has offered to buy you. You will leave Africa with him and live as his woman. You will be prevented from escaping, but you will live, probably in luxury.'

Jessica thought she would rather die than become some foreigner's slave. There had been stories about this kind of thing in the media every now and then, but she had never known how true they were. Being sold into the slave trade was something that happened to poor black kids, not to her. Her world had descended into a nightmare.

She blinked into the light on his head. All she could see was his maniacal eyes. He was enjoying teasing her, torturing her. 'You're sick.'

'No, the man who wants to buy you is sick. I am a businessman. You are a virgin, yes? I have told him you are, but it will have to be verified. He won't want you otherwise.'

She thought him the most revolting creature she had ever seen. She shivered, then nodded, slightly. 'I want to live.' She had to stay alive long enough for her father to find her.

And long enough for him to kill this prick.

34

The horizon spun crazily, making her feel sick. She glimpsed a dry grassy plain and shimmering pools of water. The vista was studded with black dots. When she focused on them, not without pain, she recognised them as antelope, a long way off.

The sky was marbled with grey clouds, hiding the sun, but it was hot. She felt a sheen of sweat all over her body. Her head throbbed with pain, the blood pooling in her cranium because, she vaguely realised, she was very nearly upside down. Her leg hurt too.

She passed out.

When she awoke again she was lying down. She blinked her eyes. A fly buzzed around her and she felt a sharp sting on her arm. 'Ow!'

She had no idea where she was. Her vision was blurred, but she could make out leaves. The ground was damp under her, soaking up through the back of her shirt and her skirt. She tried to sit up and felt nauseous, so lay back down again.

'Hey.'

She turned her head a little and saw a man. He knelt beside her and mopped her brow with a damp cloth. He pursed his lips. He looked worried. 'Do you know your name?'

She coughed on the first attempt. Her mouth was so dry. 'Kylie,' she croaked.

He smiled again. 'And my name?'

'George Clooney?'

'No, you're not dead. This isn't heaven.'

Kylie coughed again. 'What happened?'

He sat and put his arm under her as she tried to sit up again. 'No,' she said, 'I feel woozy.'

'Rest.' He laid her back down, her head supported by a backpack that smelled of smoke.

'Fire. I remember fire.'

Cameron nodded. 'We crashed, Kylie. We were blown out of the sky.'

'Blown . . . bomb?'

He reached for a water bottle and tipped it to her lips. She slurped the warm water greedily and it ran out the side of her mouth. She tried to wipe it away, feeling strangely self-conscious. He mopped her mouth for her and put a finger on her lips. 'Don't exert yourself.'

She felt the tenderness of his touch, heard it in his words. They had made love. She remembered. But where were they? What had happened? She closed her eyes and felt his hand on her cheek in response. She opened them again and saw the relief wash over his face.

'There was a bomb, Kylie. The blast came from underneath, in the aircraft's cargo compartment. The fuel tanks are in the wings, so it wasn't a problem there. It was something stored with the bags.'

Kylie looked from side to side. 'The pilot . . . Dougal. The others?'

Cameron shook his head, then closed his eyes to try to blot out a memory. 'They're dead. It's just you and me.'

She recalled the deafening bang, the smoke, the screams of the couple seated in front of her. The smell of old smoke brought back an image in a flash. 'They burned.' He wrapped both his arms around her as the sobs rose up from deep inside her. 'They were on fire, Cameron.'

'Yes. But you're alive, Kylie. I was so worried about you. You were knocked out. Your leg was badly cut as well.'

She sniffed back her tears and felt for the source of the pain in her head. She felt the padding of a bandage. Kylie raised her head a little and looked down at her right leg. The calf was bandaged.

It flooded back now, swamping her with visions of horror as she screwed her eyes shut. The flash of light, the terrible noise, the smoke filling the cabin. Dougal, the pilot, kept looking back at the couple behind him as he fought to control the stricken aircraft. Cameron managed to find a fire extinguisher and sprayed it on the young man and the woman.

Their screams.

The terrible sound stayed with them until Dougal spotted a clearing and brought the Cessna down. All the way, though, the young couple, burned black, screamed and screamed. She tried to put the memory of the smell out of her mind.

Cameron had made sure she was strapped in tight and he'd returned to his seat, just seconds before the belly of the plane bumped the ground. Kylie had thought the pilot would make it, but he had hit something on the second bounce and the nose of the aircraft had crumpled in on Dougal and they had flipped upside down. Kylie had hit her head and passed out.

She looked up at Cameron.

'Dougal almost made it, but we hit a termite mound,' he said. 'You were out cold and I carried you about thirty metres from the aircraft. I went back, but a fresh fire had started. Dougal was killed outright. The others . . .'

She felt his hold on her relax and she gripped him with her hand as the faces of the other passengers, the couple who were already on the aircraft when they boarded, came back to her. 'No, Cameron. There was nothing you could have done for them. I remember. They must have been nearly dead by the time we crashed.'

He looked away from her. 'They were still screaming when the aircraft exploded.'

She saw the raw skin on his hand and his forearms now, the singed eyebrows and hair. His face was blackened and there was dried blood crusted on the side of his face. He slapped at his leg. She looked at his eyes. They were red, and there were streaks leading from them over his cheeks as though he'd been crying. She wondered if his wounds were worse than she could see, if he was in pain. She hadn't thought him the crying kind.

Kylie closed her eyes and thought about the young couple. It was the pilot's brother and his girlfriend. She thought hard for a moment to remember their names. Paul and Julia. He was an ex-Zimbabwean living in New Zealand and she was a Kiwi. They were already on the aircraft when Kylie and Cameron boarded. She had been under the impression they were going to be the only two passengers, and she wondered if Dougal had slipped his brother and girlfriend on board without the owners of the aircraft knowing. She and Cameron had had taken the bench seat at the rear of the aircraft. She remembered the hot blue vinyl on the backs of her legs, and wondered if being at the rear of the Cessna, just a little further away from where the bomb had gone off, had saved her and Cameron.

She opened her eyes again as her mind processed the scenario. 'It was Wellington.' Another fly landed on her. It was big and brown, with scissor-like wings that folded over one another. She slapped at it, hit it, but it just shook itself and flew away. 'What are these bloody monsters?'

'Tsetse fly,' Cameron said. 'And yes, I think you're right about Wellington. Our testimony about him trying to kill us in the mine could have put him behind bars for a long time.'

'Well, he's added three people to his murder tally.'

Kylie sat up slowly, with Cameron still supporting her. She looked around. 'Where the hell are we, Cameron?'

'About ten kilometres east of the crash site.'

'You carried me *ten* kays?'

He shrugged.

'Look, I'm no expert in survival, but one thing they always tell us when we're travelling long distances by road to mines in the outback is that if you have a breakdown to stay with the vehicle. I know Dougal was probably off course, but surely it won't take the local authorities too long to find the crash site.'

He nodded. 'They've already found it. A helicopter flew over yesterday. It must have landed because it was quite a while before it tracked back over us and . . .'

'A helicopter! Are you bloody concussed too? Cameron! Why didn't you wait, and why didn't you try and signal it?'

He looked at her and she checked his eyes again. They were different from those that had seen into her soul when he was holding her. These were the eyes of an animal, a predator of some kind, devoid of emotion.

'I couldn't get to Julia and Paul. The fire had taken hold, but I grabbed Dougal's backpack from the rear of the aircraft, and yours. In his bag was a satellite phone. I called my home first, and there was no answer. I called Jess's cellphone and it was switched off. That's not like her. That thing's an extension of her body.' He sniffed.

'Cameron, what is it?' She saw something else in the red glistening eyes now. Pain.

'I called Charmaine, Jessica's friend's mom, at her florist shop. She started crying when she recognised my voice.'

'Cameron.'

He gritted his teeth and his face contorted in barely suppressed rage. 'She said Jess was raped and killed, Kylie.'

She reached for him and hugged him, but he was rigid in her embrace. Kylie held him at arm's length and looked into his eyes.

'Charmaine said there was no body, although they found the dominee, our local pastor, who was killed by the same man. She said the guy who did it killed himself; he was one of my drivers, Timothy, but I know it couldn't have been him. He's no rapist or murderer, though Barrica had suspected him of being one of Wellington's stooges.'

Kylie's head throbbed and she was having trouble absorbing all this news. She thought of pretty Jessica and she wanted to believe she was still alive. 'What about your wife?'

Cameron took a deep breath to steady himself. 'Dead. They found her body in my *bakkie*, at the bottom of our hill.'

'My God, Cameron.' His whole family was gone.

'I told Charmaine not to tell anyone that I had called her.'

She was injured and they were lost in the African bush. Kylie thought that perhaps Cameron really was concussed. 'Why, exactly?'

'Everyone thinks we're dead,' he said, 'including Wellington and the people he works for. I've got to get back to South Africa. I won't believe Jess is dead until I find her. I don't accept that Timothy killed her or the dominee. Wellington's behind this and if he killed Jess and wanted people to believe Timothy killed her, he would have left her body for the police to find.'

'But what would he want with her alive?' Kylie asked.

'You don't want to know.'

'And if you can't find her?'

'Then I'm going to find Wellington and kill him.'

She wondered if the suppressed grief was making him crazy. 'But he's in the police lockup, in Barberton.'

'He escaped,' Cameron said. 'Like we feared.'

Kylie put her fingers to her forehead and gingerly touched the bandage. The pain was a constant throb. 'My parents. They'll be going out of their minds. I've got to call them and tell them I'm alive.'

Cameron nodded. 'I've thought about that. You must. We'll get to Lusaka and you can fly from there to Johannesburg and then on to Australia. All I ask is that you don't contact anyone from Global Resources, or the South African police, for as long as you can. Every day you give me is another day for me to find Jess and Wellington.'

'Cameron –'

'I sent an SMS to email from the satphone and contacted an old army friend who works for a geological survey company in Lusaka. He called me back and he's coming to get us. He should be here in a couple of hours. There's not a lot of battery life left on the satphone, but you should call your parents. Just ask them not to tell anyone.'

'All right, but I'm coming with you to South Africa.'

35

Cameron couldn't help but fall into a deep sleep after he had showered at his room at the Southern Sun Hotel in Lusaka. His phone's ringtone woke him. Dry-mouthed and disorientated, he fumbled for his Nokia and answered. Kylie stirred beside him on the bed and rolled over and blinked a couple of times. A doctor had stitched and rebandaged her leg wound, and the gash on her head had stopped bleeding and was now covered with just a small dressing.

'Cameron, *howzit?* How are you two doing?' It was his old army comrade, Attie, who had rescued them.

'Better, thanks Attie,' Cameron said. 'Have you got any news for me?'

Cameron and Kylie had slowly continued to head east through the wilds of Kafue National Park after Cameron had contacted Attie. Kylie had called her parents, whose relief was audible to Cameron standing nearby. They had questioned the wisdom of not telling anyone they were alive, but the beeping of the phone's dying battery had silenced their argument. They saved the last of the phone's power to SMS Attie the GPS coordinates of their location once they reached a road running north–south. There Cameron sat them down in the shade of a leadwood tree and they tried to sleep. Attie, who was already on his way from Lusaka and waiting for another coordinate, used the GPS in his Land Cruiser to find them, two hours later. He had brought them to Lusaka where a friend who managed the Southern Sun had found them rooms.

'*Ja*, Cameron. That's why I'm calling. I don't know how you guys feel about flying right now, but we've got a charter going back to Johannesburg in an hour's time. We've got four geologists on board, but there are two spare seats. It'll be landing at Lanseria.'

'That sounds good.' Cameron ran a hand through his hair. Lanseria was Johannesburg's second airport and from there they might be able to charter a light aircraft to Barberton. 'But it will just be me on the aircraft.'

Kylie grabbed the phone from him. 'Attie, it's Kylie. Thank you, thank you, again. But please make that two of us on the charter.'

Cameron took the phone back. 'I'll confirm that later, Attie, but thanks again. I'm heading to the airport now.'

'You don't get to make decisions for me just because we've slept together.'

He stood and looked down at her. 'OK. But you can understand me not wanting anything to happen to you.'

'Damn it, Cameron. Can't you *tell* that I feel the same way about you? Whatever crazy plan you've got for when we get to South Africa, I'm going to be a part of it.' She got off the bed and walked to him. She put her arms around him and pressed her naked body against his. 'I want to help you find Jessica,' she said, her tone softer and quieter, 'but you have to prepare yourself for the worst. Whatever happens, though, we'll get him.'

'Yes. We will.'

*

Luis ended the call to an impatient Coetzee, who clearly had no desire to give him more than the barest details about the deaths of Kylie Hamilton and Cameron McMurtrie. Luis had lost family and friends and was still coming to terms with the loss of his wife, but the news about the two people who had helped him so much was like salt poured in fresh wounds.

At an internet cafe in Inhambane, where he had returned after finishing his business with the drill rig, he had found a string of news reports but he could not believe the aircraft crash was an isolated accident. Cameron's wife and daughter had also been killed. Luis, better than most, knew how the Zimbabwean thought and operated. 'Wellington,' he said to himself.

'Who, Father?' Jose asked him from the next computer. He was researching something for a school assignment.

'Nothing,' Luis said to his son. 'I am finished here.' In every sense of the word, he thought as he paid the woman at the counter for the use of her machines. He and Jose walked out onto the street, dodging South African tourists, a woman hawking peanuts and locals going about their business. Luis felt his spirits flag.

'It's good to have you back, *Pai*,' Jose said, using the familiar term for father.

He smiled at the boy. Luis's cellphone rang and he took it from the pocket of his trousers. He couldn't believe the name that flashed up on the screen.

'Cameron!'

Jose looked at him as Luis told the mine manager he had just been reading about his death. Cameron filled him in on what had happened, assuring him that Kylie, too, was alive.

'I am so happy to hear from you,' Luis said. He knew there was an element of self-interest in his words, but it seemed a gift from God that Kylie and Cameron had survived.

Cameron's voice was calm to the point of coldness as he told Luis that he was on his way back to South Africa and would be flying to Barberton, in secret. He wanted to find Wellington, and he believed his daughter was still alive, underground. Luis wanted to believe Jessica was unharmed, but he knew Wellington's modus operandi: he exterminated witnesses and anyone who was not of use to him. Luis doubted the girl had been kidnapped, but he, too, wanted Wellington, and Cameron and Kylie were probably the best chance he had of making something of his life again and providing his son with a future.

'I will come to Barberton as soon as I can,' Luis said.

'You weren't so keen when we left you in Mozambique,' Cameron said. 'Can I count on you? You know the illegal workings at Eureka better than anyone.'

'I will come. You have my word. Things have changed here.' Luis ended the call. He needed to move fast but almost had second thoughts when he saw Jose's eyes as he told him of his plan.

'*Why* do you have to leave again, *Pai?*' Jose asked him when he told him he had to return to South Africa. Father and son walked the pavement outside the Mercado Central, the main market in a fetching but dilapidated building in the *baixa*, the lower part of town.

'There is business I must finish. Important business. I want you to behave well for your grandmother, stay away from the boys she says have been leading you astray, and study hard. Your exams are close.'

Jose looked down as they walked. 'You have only just come back. My *mae* was wrong to go looking for you.'

Luis stopped and his son carried on another three paces before he stopped and looked back. Tears began to well as he thought of his cherished wife and Jose's *mae*, mother. 'Nothing *your mae* ever did was wrong. I wish I could say the same for myself.' He swallowed hard. 'You are old enough to know the truth. Come, let us get coffee and I will tell you.'

And he did, of his work in the mines in South Africa as a legal miner and, later, after circumstances changed, as a *zama zama*. 'Nothing good comes from crime, Jose. Remember that. Even though the money is appealing, and I fell for that, in the long run it cost me a price too terrible to bear.'

'Are you going to commit more crime now?'

Luis thought about the question. 'I am going to right a wrong, and to stop further crime. Hopefully, too, I will make a deal that will help all of us, you, me and your grandmother, to live honestly and well for the rest of our lives. If anything happens to me, though, you must go to your second cousin Alfredo, the policeman in Xai Xai. I have been doing some business with him and I have asked him to ensure you are taken care of. Your grandmother has some money I brought with me from South Africa, enough to see you through your next year at school.'

Jose looked at him with wide eyes that started to blink. 'You're not coming back, are you?'

Luis felt his own tears forming and knew he must leave. 'I have to do this.' He paid the bill, hugged his son, and walked to the bus depot. He couldn't look back at the boy.

*

Jan drove back to the mine from the guesthouse in Barberton where he had been staying. 'Get one of the armed security men to come to the manager's office. Now,' he said to the guard on duty.

Eureka's administrative offices were empty. A skeleton maintenance staff was keeping the mine running and, probably, Jan thought, keeping the *zama zamas* supplied with anything they needed while they ramped up their operations underground.

Even as he waited in the office he felt a tremor rise up from the earth below. Wellington was blasting. There was a knock at the door. 'Come in.'

'Yes, boss,' said the security guard.

'Get me an R5 and five magazines of ammunition, and a set of camouflage overalls.'

'But boss –'

'Do as I *fokken* say or you'll be out of a job like the rest of the stupid bloody miners who've gone on strike.'

'Yes, boss.'

*

Colonel Sindisiwe Radebe closed her eyes as she lay on the massage table in the spa treatment room at Cybele Forest Lodge, nestled in the hills between White River and Hazyview.

She had decided to treat herself to an afternoon off and was feeling pleasingly mellow as a result of the wine she had drunk at lunchtime while having business negotiations with her cousin, a builder, who was about to get the contract to repaint the police station.

Sindisiwe was face down, just a towel draped over her buttocks. She heard the girl enter the room and sighed in anticipation of the warmth of the hot stones that would soothe the tension from her knotted muscles. She felt feminine hands on her shoulders.

'Be gentle with me.'

'Of course, Colonel.'

Sindisiwe opened her eyes. She hadn't introduced herself by her rank and she had been in civilian clothes over lunch. Perhaps the girl recognised her from the recent spread in *Lowveld Living*, but she sounded foreign and white, with a strange accent. She twisted her neck to try to see the masseuse, but her movement was checked by cold steel.

'Don't move. It's a gun and it's in the side of your head.'

'Do you know who I am? If you do, then you must know you are already dead, and if you don't, well, let me tell you, you are already dead.'

'You're cool, I'll give you that.'

'What do you want?' Sindisiwe asked. 'My keys and credit cards are in my purse on the sideboard. But you already know that.'

'You can't buy your way out of this. It's information I want.'

Sindisiwe nodded into the sheet. She could pick the accent now, and she had seen the woman on television. *Wellington, what have you done*, she thought. *Or, rather, what have you failed to do?* 'All right, I will tell you what you want to know. Just don't hurt me.'

'That's a long way from "you're already dead".'

'What do you want?'

'Get dressed. We're going for a drive in the forest. If you try anything, I'll shoot you.'

Sindisiwe rolled over and swung her legs over the side of the massage table. It was the Australian woman, all right. Hamilton.

The one who was supposed to be dead. She was holding a Sig Sauer. 'You're not from here; you won't shoot me.'

'I killed a man underground, and this time a girl's life is at stake. You're going to take us to where she is.'

'She's dead. The murderer confessed before he killed himself.'

Kylie shook her head. 'We don't think so.'

'This is preposterous. How dare you insinuate that I, a police commander, would have inside knowledge of the commission of a crime?' Sindisiwe put on her pants and fastened her bra. She would fix this meddling bitch, in time. Sindisiwe was worried for Wellington, but more so for herself. The fact that the girl was alive worked in Sindisiwe's favour. If she could somehow wrest her back from Wellington and his master Mohammed and produce her live, it might save her own skin, if not Wellington's. 'Listen to me. I am a law enforcement officer. I am not a criminal. Perhaps together we can find McMurtrie's daughter, if you truly believe she is still alive. If you have information, you must share it with me and together we can save the girl. I will even forget about you pulling a gun on me; we all have the child's safety as our number one priority.'

'That's just what I thought. She *is* alive, you know where she is, and you're going to bargain your way out. That suits us just fine.'

'Us?'

'Finish zipping your skirt and put your Jimmy Choos on, Cinderella. Time for you to go to the fucking ball.'

Kylie Hamilton draped a towel over her gun and dug it into the small of Sindisiwe's back. Sindisiwe heard the resolve in the Australian woman's voice and doubted she would be able to talk her into handing over the gun. It was ignominious, being taken like this, but she could negotiate with them. As much as she had enjoyed the money and the sex that Wellington provided, it looked like it was time to cut her losses.

Cybele was set in a sprawling forest of eucalypt trees. The Australian motioned towards a Corolla sedan. The rear door was opened from inside and when she climbed in she saw Cameron McMurtrie, dressed in miner's overalls.

'Colonel.'

'Cameron.'

'It's time for you to start talking, Sindisiwe, or we're going into the woods and you're not coming back.'

'So I've been told.'

'What happened to Wellington?'

'He escaped from custody.'

'That happens a lot from your holding cells.'

She shrugged her shoulders. 'You won't escape once I have you arrested and charged.'

'Spare me the defiance and the righteous indignation. Is my daughter alive?'

Sindisiwe looked into the mine manager's eyes and she shivered. 'You daughter's killer confessed in a note before taking his own life.'

'Bullshit. I knew Timothy well. He was crooked, but he was no killer or rapist. Wellington set him up,' Cameron said.

For all Sindisiwe knew, Wellington had reneged on his part of the deal and raped and killed the girl himself. She loved his strength and his impetuosity, but she had no doubt about the evil he was capable of.

'Give me the gun,' Cameron said.

Kylie passed the weapon to him and Sindisiwe, a trained inter-rogator, saw the change in the woman's expression. It went from cocksure to horrified surprise. The Australian was reading Cameron's face and both women saw the same thing in his eyes as he raised the pistol and rested the end of the barrel against Sindisiwe's right temple. 'Get out of the car, Kylie. You don't want her blood and brains all over you.'

'Cameron, no . . .' Kylie said.

'Get out of the car. We can't let her live; she'll have us arrested and locked up. I'll make it look like a suicide, just as Wellington must have done with Timothy.'

Kylie opened the car door, hesitated a moment and got out.

'Wait,' Sindisiwe said. 'She was alive, last I heard.'

Kylie slid back into the seat beside Sindisiwe, and she allowed herself a couple of breaths.

'What did you have planned for her?' Cameron asked.

'*I* had nothing planned. I have a confidential informant who told me that Wellington is holding the girl somewhere in the mine. He has given orders that she is not to be touched or harmed in any way. Perhaps . . . perhaps he has someone interested in her.'

'Jesus,' Kylie said.

'That's all bullshit, about the informant,' Cameron said. Sindisiwe felt the gun dig into her skin.

'So what,' she said, looking sideways at his crazy eyes. 'Do you want to try and get your daughter back or not?'

'I'm listening.'

'She's in the mine. That is all I know. You'll have to find her. I'm not sending any of my men down there.'

'You don't have to. You're coming with us.'

*

Jan opened the doors of the cage when the lift stopped at level fourteen. He raised his R5 assault rifle and started moving down the tunnel. Candles flickered in alcoves in the wall. He heard *zama zamas* talking further down and smelled marijuana smoke.

Already, he could see, the criminal miners had been blasting out the support pillars. They had turned this viable working into a deathtrap. Even if Eureka was reopened to the legitimate mining company it would never be safe to work this area.

Jan turned off to the right down a side tunnel and it became darker the further he moved away from the illegal workings. He was a world away from his corner office on the thirtieth floor overlooking Sydney Harbour. He was back in his native Africa where the strong survived by killing the weak. It was time for Wellington Shumba to die.

A wave of air washed over him, nearly knocking him down, followed a split second later by a deafening boom. Dust rushed up the tunnel behind him. Jan coughed and spat. The fools were blasting too close to where they were still trying to work. It was no wonder so many of them died. Jan carried on through the fog of grit and smoke.

Ahead of him he saw a light flaying across the side wall. He flattened himself against the rock and raised the R5 to his shoulder. A *zama zama* walked around a bend, an AK-47 held loose in his right hand. Jan knew that an armed man would be a guard or a sentry, not a worker, and this told him he had taken the right turn. Wellington would be close.

Jan stepped into the middle of the tunnel and levelled his rifle at the man. 'Make a noise and I'll kill you,' he whispered.

The man laid down his AK and followed Jan's gesticulations with his rifle to kneel. 'Put your hands on your head.' Standing behind him, Jan slung his rifle over his shoulder and took a Leatherman from its pouch on his belt. He unfolded the serrated blade, reached around the man, put his hand over his mouth and cut his throat.

He held the man as the life thrashed from him, then silently lowered the body to the ground. Jan wiped his hands on his camouflage fatigues and moved on into the darkness. *I haven't felt this alive for decades*, he thought.

*

Cameron stopped the Corolla on the road between Komatipoort and Malelane at the place he and Luis had discussed.

'You must let me go,' Sindisiwe Radebe said again. 'I have no idea where the girl is underground.'

'Shut up or I'll gag you,' Cameron said.

Luis emerged from the bush at the side of the road, looked left and right and climbed into the car, in the front passenger seat. His eyes widened when he greeted Kylie and Cameron and saw Kylie pointing a gun at the Barberton police commander.

'Thank you for coming back, Luis,' Cameron said.

'When I heard about your daughter, I had to come. This man has caused too much sorrow and it is time to end it for good.'

Cameron nodded and turned the car around and drove back towards Barberton and Eureka. They said little on the drive, though after fifteen minutes Luis said: 'If it is all right, Dr Hamilton, there is something I would like to discuss with you, once this business is done.'

'I'm sorry,' Kylie said, 'you know we can't offer you a job here in South Africa. I checked the company's share price today and to tell you the truth, the way it's heading, we'll be lucky to keep most of our people on the payroll.'

'I understand. This is not about me asking you for work,' Luis said.

Luis directed them to turn off onto a dirt road about five kilometres short of the mine. Cameron followed the track, which looked like a fire trail. They started to climb into the hills that rose behind Eureka and rolled back to Swaziland and the Mozambican border. This was wild country.

'Where are you taking me?' Sindisiwe asked from the back seat.

'Relax,' said Cameron. 'We're going to a disused mine shaft the *zama zamas* sometimes use to enter and leave the mine. You've got some exercise ahead of you.'

On Luis's instructions Cameron stopped the car and they got out. Kylie opened the boot and took out a pair of overalls, boots and helmet with a miner's lamp and gave them to Sindisiwe. 'Change into these. Your stilettos won't cut it underground.' Reluctantly, the police colonel pulled on the trousers then slid off her skirt and swapped her expensive shoes for the boots.

Cameron had stopped by his empty house before kidnapping Sindisiwe from the spa and had once again loaded his shotgun and combat vest. He shrugged on his gear and chambered a round in the shotgun. He handed Luis his spare pistol and ammunition. The Mozambican checked and loaded the weapon with practised ease.

Cameron respected the man. He was recovering from a gunshot wound from their last encounter with Wellington and he had lost his wife. But the coldness in Luis's eyes told Cameron they were both on the same frequency for this mission.

As Luis led them through the bush and into the hole, which had been hacked into the side of the mountain perhaps a hundred years ago or more, the earth beneath them shimmied with the muffled report of an explosion far underground.

Luis started climbing down a rope ladder and Kylie motioned for Colonel Radebe to follow him.

*

Jan stepped into the arc of light cast by a paraffin lantern and Wellington Shumba looked up from his laptop. The glow from the computer's screen was reflected in round reading glasses, which the pirate miner took off.

'Mr Stein. Welcome to my mine.' Wellington laughed at his rhyme. 'We meet at last.'

Jan held the R5 tight into his shoulder and kept his aim steady on Wellington's heart. 'Your security could be better.'

Wellington nodded. 'If you killed the man who should have been watching the entrance to this tunnel, then I am better off without him. I wondered how long it would take you to come down here. You sit in your office in Australia dictating orders and you send a woman to do your dirty work; I wondered if you would ever visit my mine.'

It irked him, the way the Zimbabwean referred to Eureka as 'his'. 'Where is the girl? You shouldn't have taken McMurtrie's daughter. Global Resources is finished; you have control of the workings, and there are bodies from here to Zambia except for Jessica McMurtrie's. I couldn't leave South Africa knowing she might be alive. Where is she?'

'Read the newspapers. She was raped and killed by one of your workers, who took his own life because he couldn't live with the shame.'

'Rubbish, man. If you'd killed her you would have left her body with the dominee's, or somewhere else where it would be found, so that no one would come looking for you. I've come for her.'

'She's dead.'

Jan shrugged. 'Fine. Then we have nothing more to talk about.' Jan curled his finger around the rifle's trigger and started to squeeze.

36

The explosions were happening more frequently, but they didn't scare Jessica nearly as much as the waking and sleeping nightmares she had of the future life Wellington had tormented her with. She would rather die than let him sell her to some old pervert.

It if was true, that her mother and father were dead, then there was no one looking for her. But she couldn't believe that was the case. She twisted her wrist in the cable ties and felt blood. Still she tried. Every time the ground shook beneath her she rattled on the metal-framed bed, trying to shake something loose, but when she stopped to rest she always seemed as tightly restrained as when he had first put her here.

There was a rumbling noise, unlike the far explosives going off. This came from deep within the rock around her and reminded Jessica of the low growlings she had heard elephants use to communicate with each other in the Kruger Park. It was as though the earth was not happy with the people who drilled and blasted and tortured her, and she was venting her feelings.

A crack appeared above the bed where Jess lay. She screamed. From somewhere outside along the tunnel there was a report of a gunshot, then the roof groaned and lumps of rock as big as television sets started raining down.

*

Jan cursed. The roof of the tunnel had started to collapse a split second before he pulled the trigger. Wellington was lost in a cloud of dust that rolled back over Jan. A rock pillar had collapsed, just as he expected. Wellington's greed had, hopefully, cost the pirate miner his life.

Jan moved back out into the tunnel, which was half-filled with rock debris. 'Jessica?' He coughed and spluttered and in the dying echoes of the rockfall he heard the girl's scream again.

'Help!' came the return voice.

Jan set down the R5 and started shifting rocks by hand, pausing every few seconds to listen for her voice. 'Come get me. I'm in the refuge chamber,' he heard her call.

Jan moved the fallen ore as quickly as he could, but he kept peering through the curtain of dust that hung in the air in case Wellington Shumba, the Lion, had survived and was waiting somewhere further up the tunnel to kill him. More likely, Jan thought, if Wellington had survived the fall he would be on his way to the nearest escape route.

'Help me! Who's there?' the girl called.

'It's Jan Stein,' he called. 'Remember me?'

There was a moment's hesitation. '*Oom* Jan. Yes, I remember you.'

He smiled at her calling him uncle. They had only met a couple of times and she'd still been in pigtails the last time he had seen her. 'I'm coming, Jessica,' he called back. 'Are you all right?'

'Yes . . . I think so.'

Jan could hear voices behind him and in front of him, on the other side of the rockfall. He heard orders barked in an African language; Swazi he thought. His grasp of it wasn't good. He continued toiling. He had to get to Cameron's daughter.

*

Cameron saw through the green glow of the night-vision goggles a figure moving towards them through the dust. He recognised the broad shoulders and the bald, unhelmeted head. He raised his shotgun to his shoulder and fired.

The blast echoed down the tunnel and was answered with a burst of AK-47 fire. *Damn it,* Cameron said to himself. He had missed. He should have waited, but he was seething with rage at the sight of the man who had tried to wipe out his family and had killed so many others.

'Come on,' Cameron said to the others behind him, not caring about the danger. Wellington had turned back and they heard his footsteps echoing back from the way he had come.

'You're going to get us all killed,' Sindisiwe Radebe spat.

'The way he's heading, the only way for him to get out of here is back up through the main shaft,' Luis said. 'We have him bottled up, Cameron.'

'Listen to him, Cameron,' Kylie said. 'He's like a cornered rat now. He'll be even more dangerous, but he won't get away this time.'

Cameron took a breath, but he couldn't calm himself. 'Jess is here somewhere. We have to get to her before that bastard does.' He looked at the police colonel. 'You, go ahead.'

Sindisiwe shook her head. 'Me? No way, white man. This is your crusade.'

He pointed the shotgun at her. 'It's my daughter or you. If we find her and she's . . . she's not alive, then I'm going to kill you.'

'You're bluffing.'

'He's not,' Kylie interjected. 'You know this man Wellington, don't you?'

The colonel said nothing. 'Reach out to him,' Kylie said. 'Tell him the game's up. Reason with him. We won't drag you down if you help us.'

'Pah. You make offers you cannot deliver. And you don't know this man. He is ruthless.'

'Then help us kill him.' Cameron raised his free hand to stop Kylie from interrupting. 'If we take him alive he'll implicate you. All

421

I want now is two things: my daughter, and Wellington. Dead or alive. It's up to you.'

Sindisiwe looked to Kylie, but she was stone-faced in the glare of the miner's lamp. Cameron silently thanked her, but also felt a pang of guilt for what he'd put her through, and how her high-minded morals had been dashed against the hard rock of Africa.

Sindisiwe glared at Cameron with undisguised hatred, then moved forward, the beam of her miner's lamp playing on the walls. Cameron switched off his night-vision goggles. He felt no sympathy for her. She was a disgrace to her uniform, and if she wasn't complicit in Jessica's kidnapping, she had helped cover it up by doing nothing.

'Wellington,' she called into the darkness as she moved gingerly forward. 'Wellington, it is Sindisiwe. You must give yourself up.'

*

Wellington was trapped, with Jan Stein between him and the main shaft and McMurtrie and the others blocking his way to his emergency exit. There was no way he would be able to escape via the cage up the shaft, even if he could kill Stein. Stein or McMurtrie would have shut the hoist down.

He crouched behind a mound of fallen rock, put down his AK-47 and drew his pistol.

Sindisiwe reached the pile of ore and gingerly began making her way around the obstruction. 'Wellington? Are you there?' As she passed him he reached up and wrapped his hand over her mouth and drew her to him.

'Hush. You will help me get out of this. We'll run away together,' he whispered.

She tried to mumble something in reply but he just clamped his hand harder then stepped out from behind the rocks. The light on Sindisiwe's helmet illuminated the others; there was McMurtrie, Kylie Hamilton and that traitorous bastard Correia. Wellington fumed; Sindisiwe struggled in his grasp but he held her tight.

McMurtrie pointed his shotgun at him. If the former mine manager had brought a pistol or an assault rifle, then at this range he might have got off a shot into Wellington's head and perhaps saved Sindisiwe, but McMurtrie would be realising now that if he pulled the trigger on his shotgun Sindisiwe would be peppered with pellets, whether or not he hit his intended target.

'Move against the side wall. All of you. I'm coming through,' Wellington said. He smiled at the frustration on McMurtrie's face. 'Lower your weapons as I pass, unless you want the colonel to end up like your environmental man, Loubser. She and I are leaving.'

McMurtrie moved to shelter the woman with his body. Very noble, Wellington thought. He couldn't believe they had survived the aircraft crash, but here they were. He wanted to put a bullet through McMurtrie's forehead, and Correia's, but the Mozambican had a pistol levelled at him. He might get one of them, but the other would finish him off. It was time to cut his losses, but Wellington hated that he was leaving the mine, and Stein, McMurtrie and Hamilton were all back here. This was *his* kingdom. He would find a way to reclaim it.

Correia flattened himself against the wall. He followed Wellington with the weapon in his hand, but Wellington couldn't help but notice how the barrel shook with the man's rage. All the same, he made sure Sindisiwe's ample curves were covering as much of him as possible as he backed his way down the opposite side of the tunnel. 'I'm going to kill you as soon as I get the chance,' he said to the Mozambican.

'You took the words right out of my mouth,' Correia said.

Further down the tunnel there was the echoing report of a gunshot. McMurtrie and the others instinctively looked towards the sound and Wellington used this as his cue to force Sindisiwe into a run. They fled into the darkness.

*

Jessica flinched at the noise of the shot. The door to her underground cell flew open and she screwed her eyes against the glare of the light that played into them. Beyond the glare she made out the form of a man. Smoke curled from the barrel of the rifle in his hands.

'*Oom* Jan?'

'Jessica.' He had shot the lock off the door.

'Oh my god, thank you.'

'Jessica!' yelled a voice from behind Jan that made her want to shriek and cry all at once.

'Dad!'

Stein turned then stepped out of the doorway into the room as her father, Kylie Hamilton and Luis all rushed in.

PART FIVE

37

The fisherman and his partner peered from the hollow of the new tree they called home and watched the lioness feeding her cubs below them.

Their own chick had left them now, after they had given it some lessons in fishing. Where their youngster had gone they had no way of knowing. The fisherman had lately spied a genet in a neighbouring tree and the catlike predator would be watching their nest closely. The future for he and his partner, and any more young they might raise, was never certain.

Danger and death still lurked nearby.

38

C ameron lowered the copy of the *Citizen* newspaper and looked across at Kylie, seated opposite him in the lounge at Pretoria railway station reserved for passengers boarding the luxurious Blue Train. 'I can't believe it.'

'What?' She sipped her coffee.

He wanted to kiss her. They might have been out of immediate physical danger, although he would never feel truly relaxed about their safety until Wellington was caught or killed, but their fight wasn't quite over yet. So much was riding on what would happen during this twenty-seven-hour train journey to Cape Town, yet he still had thoughts about making love to Kylie again. Love, and lust, had been absent from his life for so long.

'What are you talking about?' she asked again, then lowered her voice. 'And are you undressing me with your eyes?'

'Yes. But what I can't believe is this story about Sindisiwe Radebe. And I quote: "*Colonel Radebe is to be awarded the South African Police Service's highest decoration for valour, posthumously, for her part in the rescue of Barberton teenager Jessica McMurtrie last week, after being shot by a wanted man known to the police after negotiating with him for the girl's release.*"'

'What's that?' Jessica asked. She carried a glass of orange juice in her hand and sat down next to Cameron.

'Nothing.'

'You can't shield me from everything, Dad. I was there, remember. Anyway, I heard what you said about the policewoman. She's the one who let Wellington out of jail, wasn't she?'

'Yes.'

'Then we're better off without her,' Jessica said.

'Jess, you can't talk that way. But one thing's for sure, I'm not letting you out of my sight any time soon.'

'Cool. The Blue Train's better than school any day.'

Jessica wandered off to inspect the array of croissants and other pastries on the buffet table.

'I spoke to Chris Loubser's father yesterday,' Cameron said. 'The family's engaged a lawyer and they're going to allege we failed in our duty of care, sending Chris down the mine when we knew there were armed men down there.'

'The first time or the second time?' Kylie asked.

'Both, I suppose. I know he tried to ruin the company, but I liked him.'

Kylie nodded. 'I would have liked him more if he'd fought the Lion Plains mine in public, maybe used his credentials as a miner to state his case, rather than going behind our backs. Jan can be tough, that's for sure, the way he sent him back down.'

'He did have a police escort, not that it did him or them much good.'

'Here's the Chinese delegation,' Kylie said.

Cameron looked around and saw the troop of suited businessmen, eight of them, enter the lounge. Jan was with them, laughing at something one of the men had said via an interpreter, the only woman in the group. Cameron grimaced to Kylie, who scolded him with her eyes. Jess moved back to them and the three of them stood and braced themselves for the introductions. The names of the men from China Dynamic Mining rolled over him. Their female interpreter, who was introduced as Miss Li, asked if Jessica worked for Global Resources as well.

'Jessica is Cameron's daughter,' Jan interjected. 'Cameron is paying for her to come on this trip out of his own pocket.'

'I meant no disrespect,' Miss Li said.

'None taken,' Cameron said as Jan escorted the posse to the other side of the lounge where the four male and one female member of the Global Resources board, all Australians, were seated.

'You should be over there with them,' Cameron said to Kylie.

She sat back down. 'To be honest, I'd rather dip my nose in a bowl of hot cockie kak.'

'That doesn't sound nice.'

Jessica laughed.

'It's an old Australianism for "no",' Kylie said. 'I hate what's going on. I know our share price is still falling, but I can't stand the thought of us selling out to China Dynamite.'

Cameron nodded. China Dynamic's nickname had come through ongoing criticism of its environmental and workplace safety record. It was ironic, Cameron thought, that Global Resources had been sent into a spiral because of its inability to proceed with the Lion Plains project because of an endangered species and perceived weaknesses in its mine safety, and here it was about to be bought out by a company that couldn't care less about such things.

'Don't get me wrong,' Jessica said, setting down her juice, 'I'm not complaining about going on a luxury train, but if Global Resources is in such financial trouble, why is Uncle Jan spending so much money taking you all to Cape Town this way? Why not just fly there for the meeting, or have it in Joburg or Barberton?'

'It's all about perceptions,' Kylie said, unable to hide her bitterness. 'Jan knows the Chinese are fully aware of how tough things are for us at the moment, but he wants to give the impression that the drop in the share price is just a temporary glitch. I've seen our South African figures. The truth is we can't afford a junket like this – at least not while there are miners laid off until we can get Eureka operational again. It's all about saving face and posturing.'

Cameron looked across the lounge filled with well-heeled travellers – foreigners in safari wear and locals dripping in designer labels and bling. Jan was blustering away for the sake of the Chinese, who would probably pick up a mining conglomerate for a song. The Australian government's foreign investment review board had given a merger – they didn't want to call it a sale – the go-ahead to protect Australian jobs and to keep Global Resources' Australian operations as a locally-run independent business unit. That meant the South African and Zambian mines would become Chinese.

Cameron's phone beeped. He took it out of the inside pocket of his blue blazer and checked the screen.

'Is it from Luis?' Kylie asked.

He shook his head. 'No, it's Coetzee. The *zama zamas* are blasting again.'

'Geez,' she said. 'We can't catch a break, can we?'

Cameron saw the change in Jessica's face. She'd gone from being the self-conscious teenager trying to act mature beyond her years, excited at the prospect of the five-star train trip, to a frightened little girl again. He saw her lip tremble and put his hand on hers to reassure her. 'Don't worry. We're a long way from Barberton now. Funnily enough, killing Colonel Radebe, his partner in crime, has finally put Wellington on the most wanted list. Luis is certain he's in Mozambique. The criminal miners in Eureka are probably just locals. The company will sort them out once this financial business is done. The Chinese won't take any prisoners if they do end up buying us, that's for sure.'

'Where is Luis?' Kylie said testily. 'He should be here by now. He was so insistent that he meet Jan and the board while they were all together, and now he hasn't shown. We're boarding soon.'

On cue, the train manager turned on his microphone and welcomed them all to the Blue Train and explained the boarding procedures.

*

431

Luis was supposed to be in Pretoria, waiting to join the Blue Train, ostensibly as another well-off paying guest, but instead he was sitting in a darkened room in the Cardoso Hotel in Maputo holding the pistol Alfredo had given him.

Wellington's clothes and possessions were littered around the room. It was odd, Luis thought, looking at the dirty socks on the floor, a shirt hanging over the back of the chair at the writing desk, toiletries in the bathroom through the open door, how ordinary everything looked. There was nothing that screamed pathological killer or criminal. The labels on the clothes were reputable, not flashy, and his luggage was likewise functional.

Luis had been watching the hotel since midnight and it was now seven-thirty in the morning. The Lion was at breakfast. The smell of the prostitute's perfume, and their sex on the rumpled bed linen, hung in the air. Wellington had sent the girl away half an hour earlier and Luis had let himself into the room using one of the hotel's skeleton key cards. The door opened.

Wellington stood in the doorway, perhaps registering that the curtains had been closed. He glanced at one of the pillows on the bed.

Luis raised his own pistol, and Wellington's, which he held in his left hand. 'It was easy to find under the pillow; not very original. Sit down.'

Wellington smiled. 'Professor. Good to see you, my old friend. I was worried for you. I heard what happened to your wife and wondered if you were safe.'

Luis gritted his teeth. 'Sit. Down.'

Wellington held up both hands, pale palms out. 'Chill, my brother.'

'I am not your brother.'

Wellington moved the chair from the desk and turned it around. 'Close the door.'

Wellington kicked it shut, not taking his eyes off Luis, then sat down, facing him. 'You have come to kill me?'

Luis shrugged. 'I would like to, but no, I am here to talk business.'

Wellington raised his eyebrows but said nothing.

'You gave orders to take me alive when your men killed my wife.'

'Yes, but her death was a mistake. She was not meant to die. If anything, I wanted her alive so that I could use the threat of harming her to get you to come back to work for me. I know how much the woman meant to you.'

Luis exhaled through his nose. 'I don't admire your honesty, but I respect your cunning.'

'I am sorry for your wife, believe me.'

Luis didn't, but if he stopped to think about Miriam now he would become too emotional. This was about business. 'You tried to kill McMurtrie and Hamilton. Why?'

Wellington shrugged.

'Answer my question. Was it revenge?'

Wellington swatted away the question with a wave of his hand. 'Orders. Plus they could identify me from the gunfight when they rescued Loubser.'

'And the girl – why did you kidnap her instead of killing her?'

'Mohammed didn't want her killed, said we could sell her instead to some rich sheikh. It wasn't my first preference. Why are you here, Luis?'

'I have a son to raise, and no prospects of a job here in Mozambique. I need money.'

'I don't carry much cash with me, but you are welcome to what I have in my wallet.'

'Keep your hands where I can see them. No, I don't want your petty cash; I want to go back to work, but not as one of your underground slaves.'

'You want a cut of the business?'

Luis nodded. 'You can't go back to South Africa just now. They want you for the kidnapping of the McMurtrie girl and the killing of the police colonel. The Hawks will connect the dots and realise you killed the dominee as well. I can get across the border and into Eureka and bring production back up to where it was, or higher.'

Wellington shrugged. 'So what? Why should I cut you in on anything?'

'Because you are no use to Mohammed if you cannot produce gold. You are hiding here with your whores, but your money will not last forever. My plan is that I will go back and run the mine and you will stay here, in Mozambique, as the middleman. I know the mine and I can run it, better than you did.'

'So what do you want from me, a signed contract?'

'A meeting with Mohammed. A guarantee from you, and from Mohammed, that my son will not be harmed if I come back to you voluntarily, and that I will get a share of the profits, linked to increases in productivity in the mine. I believe I can boost production by twenty per cent, at least.' Luis could see the Lion was doing the sums in his head.

Wellington shook his head. 'I owe you nothing. You can come back to work for me for the same money. I'll review your pay in six months and we can talk about a profit share then. I can find a metallurgist and engineer anywhere.'

'Then I'll go to the South African police.'

'*Pah.* You're a *zama zama*, and a foreigner, like me. You'll never get citizenship and a job with a South African mining company, and if you could have found a position with a Mozambican company you wouldn't be here now.'

'What you say is true. So that leaves me no option.' Luis raised the pistol in his right hand until it was pointed between Wellington's eyes.

'Wait, wait!' The pitch of the Zimbabwean's voice had risen an octave. 'Don't shoot. We can negotiate.'

'Who is Mohammed? What is his full name? Where do I find him?'

Wellington shook his head again. 'I cannot tell you that. I would be killed. Please, Luis, my friend, my *partner*, we can structure this deal without Mohammed being involved. What you want will come from my share. Mohammed need never know and I will give you this in exchange for my life.'

'No. With you gone, Mohammed will find me, in the mine, when he wants his next shipment of gold. You owned me for too long, Wellington. It is time for me to send you to hell.'

'No! Please!'

He looked piteous, almost, Luis thought. He took up the pressure on the trigger.

'I'll tell you who Mohammed is. Just put the gun down, please, my brother.'

*

Capitao Alfredo Simango and three detectives waited in the hallway of the hotel, outside Wellington's room. Alfredo checked his watch. If he didn't get the signal from his cousin in the next five minutes, he would go in. They had been in there too long.

Luis should have been in South Africa, meeting with the mining people, but instead he had begged to be in on the operation to entrap Wellington. He was wearing a wiretap under his shirt. The South Africans had put pressure on the Mozambican police to find the killer, but Alfredo had played his cards close to his chest. He had Wellington's cellphone number, courtesy of his cousin, and that was how they had tracked him to the hotel, by tracing the phone's signal. Now it was he, Alfredo, who would catch the wanted Zimbabwean.

He was worried about Luis. He had been in there too long with Wellington and had not called them. He worried the Zimbabwean had got the drop on his cousin. Using a keycard to enter the room would give advance warning to Wellington – he would surely hear the buzz of the lock being freed. Alfredo nodded to the detective next to him, who had a sledgehammer for just such an eventuality. The other two men, like Alfredo, had Makarovs drawn and ready.

'On three,' Alfredo whispered in Portuguese. 'One, two . . .'

The gunshot made them start and the man with the sledge-hammer swung his muscular arms.

Alfredo had his pistol raised, ready to fire, as he entered the room. 'Police!'

435

'Don't shoot, cousin.' Luis held out his two pistols, dangling from his fingers through the trigger guards. Wellington was sprawled backwards, a neat hole drilled between his eyes and blood rapidly pooling on the carpet.

'What happened?'

Luis shrugged. 'He went for his gun; it was hidden under the pillow on his bed.'

'That gun you have in your left hand?'

'Yes.'

'Give it to me.' Alfredo took the pistol from Luis, pulled out the tail of his shirt and wiped the weapon clean of prints. 'Wait outside,' he said to the other men. When the trio had moved to the corridor Alfredo took Wellington's pistol, wrapped it in the dead man's right hand, aimed to the right of where Luis still sat, and fired. Luis flinched.

'It is done. All will be fine,' Alfredo said. A siren blared from the street below and someone was yelling from a neighbouring room.

Luis checked his watch and pushed his glasses back up his nose. 'I hope so. I have a plane to catch.'

*

In the Blue Train lounge the train manager read out their names and suite numbers, confirming Kylie, Cameron and Jessica would be in consecutive rooms on the train. They picked up their hand luggage and had started moving towards the platform when Kylie heard an annoyingly familiar voice.

'The name is Venter. V-e-n-t-e-r.'

Kylie looked back and was shocked to see she had heard correctly. 'Tertia!'

Cameron turned and swore softly. 'What's *she* doing here?'

Even more surprisingly, Kylie saw Jan get up from his chair and walk over to her, and take her hand.

'Madam, sir?' the carriage butler said to them. 'We must board now.'

'I'll catch up with you,' Kylie said. Jan was steering Tertia towards the members of the Global Resources board. She walked to where Tertia was now being introduced to the Chinese delegation. 'Jan. Can I have a private word, please?'

'In a moment, Kylie.'

Kylie fumed. She was his number two and he was acting as though she wasn't there. 'What are you doing here?' she said to Tertia once the introductions were complete. Miss Li, the interpreter, translated the question for the Chinese businessmen.

'I heard about this little powwow on the grapevine. I came here because I wanted to meet your board and to get an assurance from them that they weren't secretly negotiating with the Chinese for them to move onto my land once the sale is done.'

'That's all out of our hands,' Jan said, trying to defuse things. 'Tertia, this is a public train so we can't stop you coming on board, but while our meetings will be confidential, you know that the discovery of the owls on Lion Plains means that no coalmine will go ahead there.'

Tertia glared at him. 'And if the birds move off? What then? What's to stop you or your new Chinese owners going back to the government with a new claim?'

The board members glanced at each other uneasily, none of them wanting to buy into what was fast becoming a public spectacle.

'I want your Chinese buyers to also know how you've been poisoning your workers underground. Translate that,' Tertia said to the interpreter.

The train manager called a cabin number for the third time and Tertia glanced at her boarding pass. 'That's me. I'm going now, but I'll be going to the media the minute we get off this train in Cape Town if I catch one whiff of you plotting some way to come back onto Lion Plains.'

Tertia stormed off and Jan took Kylie gently by the elbow. 'She's insane,' he said out of the side of his mouth. 'But I decided to be as cordial to her as possible. I don't want her to upset the Chinese any more than necessary. We *need* this sale to go through. So please don't pick a fight with her again.'

'I did not pick a fight with her. I just asked her what she was doing here.'

'Well, just don't goad her. She can't stop the sale from going through. I won't let her.'

Kylie bridled at the tone he was using with her, but she imagined he was under considerable stress. 'What would happen if we got offered another coalfield, maybe in Mozambique?'

Jan shook his head. 'Too late, and we've been losing so much to the *zama zamas* we don't have the liquidity to buy another concession. There'll be some compensation from the South African government but that could take months or years to get back from the local community that owns Lion Plains. The best thing for Global Resources now is to at least sell the African operations and, if possible, hold on to Australia. That's what we're discussing here on the train, Kylie.'

'I *know* what we're discussing, but –'

'We have to board.' He walked away from her and she headed after him, onto the platform.

Musa Mabunda, dressed in a grey suit and maroon tie and carrying his laptop bag, caught up with her on the platform. 'You look like you're having a bad day already.'

'It's getting worse by the minute,' she said.

'Cheer up,' Musa said. 'You'll probably still have a job by the end of this train trip, but I don't think China Dynamic has much time for PR. From what I've read of them online, their idea of public relations is to say no comment to the media and pay off whoever needs to be paid off to make their problems go away.'

'How's your cousin Tumi?' Kylie asked. 'Happy that she's still going to be working as a safari guide instead of a mine forklift driver?'

'Very, I'm sure. In fact, that reminds me, I got a voicemail from her saying she wanted to speak to me urgently, but I was too busy organising champagne and orange juice and brandy for the Chinese. Those people can drink.'

'I'll see you on the train, Musa.'

'We may as well enjoy it while it lasts.'

Kylie found her way to her carriage and the butler was waiting for her in her suite. She only half-listened to the instructions about the television, the airconditioning and the times for meals. She felt as though the situation, like the company she had once been so proud to work for, was slipping away from her. When the butler left she went to the next suite and knocked on the door.

'Come in,' Cameron said.

She opened the door. He had his laptop open and was checking his phone. 'Luis tried to call me a little while ago, but the call kept cutting out.'

'We can't go to the board without details of this offer he wants to make to us. And in any case, Jan seems to have given up hope. He sees the Chinese buyout, of Africa at least, as a foregone conclusion.'

Cameron patted the couch next to where he sat. 'Perhaps it is.'

'You don't look so worried.' She sat down and he took her hand in his.

'I'm not. I thought that running a goldmine was the most important thing in the world to me, but it turns out it's not. It cost me my marriage, and while I'm desperately sad about what happened to Tania, particularly for Jess, I know that pretending our relationship was fine for so long was no good for any of us – not me, not her, not Jessica. I came close to losing Jess and I don't want that to happen. When she finishes matric, if she wants to stay living with me, then I'll do what's best for her. She says she likes the idea of moving to Mozambique.'

'Seriously? You're going to buy a charter boat and take tourists out snorkelling?'

'Why not? I think I've had enough of living underground. I want to enjoy the sun a little, and spend some time with my daughter before she runs off with someone who I won't think is good enough for her. What about you?'

'What about me?'

Cameron drew her to him, and she slid over and sat on his lap. He brushed a strand of hair away from her face and kissed her, long and deep. She felt safe in his arms. When they broke the kiss he said: 'I meant, what about us?'

She frowned. She wasn't ready to give up work and be a beach bum. Not yet, anyway. Kylie didn't know if she would be kept on in the company if the Chinese took over, and it was likely the succession plan she had envisaged, with her taking over from Jan one day, was just a half-baked dream now. 'You could move to Australia. There are heaps of South Africans working for our mining companies. Jess could study there.'

'I'm African, Kylie. I was born here. I just can't leave this place.'

He reached around her and ran his fingers down the back of her neck, then down her spine. She shivered. Their time together had been torrid, at loggerheads at the beginning, and now making love with the urgency of people who had been denied too long. There was important business to be discussed with the Chinese, and who knew what, if anything, Luis would bring to the table if he ever contacted them again. And there was Jan, who was freezing her out of the last days, perhaps hours, of the company. There was so much to do that she didn't have time to have sex with Cameron. His hand moved to her bottom, grabbing it as he kissed her again, then to the hem of her skirt.

She *really* didn't have time for this. 'What about Jess?' she whispered in his ear. 'She might walk in on us.'

'I've ordered her to do at least an hour's study in her suite. She brought her books with her.'

He pushed her pants to one side and she felt the delicious touch of his fingers on her again. 'Anyone would have thought you had this all planned.' Kylie reached for his zipper and straddled him on the couch. 'Really,' she mumbled through a kiss, 'this is not what I need.'

'Well it's exactly what I need.' He reached across to the table under the cabin window and slid a foil-wrapped condom from a pocket of his laptop bag.

'You dog,' she said as she leaned back so he could roll it on. The train started to pull away from the station as Kylie lowered herself on to him, kissing him deeply as she rode him to the clickety-clack rhythm.

Kylie hugged him tight as she came and felt him pulse inside her. The warmth flowed through her body and she wished, right then, she could have it all: career, man, love, lust, work, play. Cameron. Hell, maybe even a child of their own. She sighed against him. It was all a dream. She was going back to Australia in a few days, possibly onto the unemployment line. The mining industry was still booming, and she was sure she would find a lesser position somewhere else – Global Resources would be a toxic brand for some time – but what were the chances a new job would bring her back to Africa any time soon?

Cameron shifted under her, but she held him tight. She wanted to stay connected to him for as long as she could.

39

Cameron was coming to the end of his presentation on Global Resources' new business projects in Africa. The Chinese executives and Mary Li were seated on one side of the long polished-wood table in the Blue Train's conference car, and Jan, Kylie and the Australian board members were on the other.

With the Lion Plains coalmine off the books, Cameron's Power-Point brief, projected on the screen at the end of the carriage, was exactly that – brief. He had trouble padding it out to the allocated forty-five minutes. Even Miss Li, who also had a role to play in the presentation, was covering a yawn with her hand.

To exacerbate the risk of lethargy, they had all eaten lunch. Cameron had noticed the Chinese businessmen quaffing back wine with their meal, while the Australians pointedly stuck to sparkling water. China Dynamic, it seemed, was already celebrating their next acquisition. All that was left to negotiate was how much of a steal they would get the African mines for.

He scanned his audience and Kylie winked at him.

There was a knock on the door and Musa Mabunda walked in. He coughed. 'Cameron, I need to speak with you for a minute. It's urgent.'

'I'm nearly finished, Musa. Are there any questions?'

'Cameron,' Musa said quietly but urgently.

If there was a word that summed up the PR man, Cameron thought, it was polite, so this intrusion during a presentation was completely out of character for him. Jan stood and said, 'Cameron, I'm sure you've covered everything. We'll be arriving at our scheduled stop in Kimberley shortly and I'm sure everyone would appreciate the chance to freshen up before we get off the train for the tour.'

Miss Li translated rapidly and there were enthusiastic nods from the Chinese delegation, some of whom had been showing drowsy eyes. 'Very good, Cameron,' said Hilary Hann, the sole woman on the Global Resources board.

Cameron excused himself and followed Musa out into the corridor of the gently swaying carriage. 'Cameron, I'm sorry but I just got off the phone to my cousin at Lion Plains. I have to tell you what she told me.'

'OK.'

Kylie joined them and Musa looked at her.

'You can say whatever it is you need to say in front of Kylie,' Cameron said.

'Very well, but I suggest we go back to my suite.'

They followed Musa to the next carriage and the three of them found space in his cabin to sit. 'My cousin just told me that a Chinese woman by the name of Mary Li visited Lion Plains yesterday.'

'Mary? *Our* Mary Li, the translator?' Kylie said.

Musa nodded. 'Seems she's more than an interpreter. Anyway, Tumi was checking a fault in an electric fence and heard Mary Li and Tertia talking in one of the lodge's birding hides. Tertia told Miss Li she had just put in an offer on Kilarney, the farm neighbouring Lion Plains, and that old man Berger, the owner, had accepted.'

'Stoffel Berger, the guy who vowed he would never sell to anyone?' Kylie asked.

'The very one. Tertia boasted to Li that he had agreed to sell to her because she had done such a good job protecting Lion Plains.

He was worried the government would take it off him eventually, to give it to the local community, and Tertia told him that with the mine plan cancelled she would roll it into Lion Plains and restock it with game.'

'That does make sense for her, now that she's got some security, but what would this have to do with someone from China Dynamic?' Cameron asked.

Musa took a deep breath. 'Tumi said that the Chinese woman then said, "Good, as soon as the sale of Global Resources goes through you can sell Kilarney to China Dynamic." Tumi didn't really know what to make of that, but she was amazed to hear Tertia and this woman doing business together. Tumi googled China Dynamic afterwards and found out they are a mining company.'

Kylie thumped the polished timber carriage wall beside her. 'She's been playing us and her local community all along.'

'So it wasn't about "her" wildlife at all,' Cameron said.

'No,' said Kylie. 'It was about good old-fashioned greed. She had nothing to gain and everything to lose if the local community was successful in getting us to mine on Lion Plains. If it had still been her land she would have made a fortune had we bought the rights from her. As it was, her game lodge concession on the community land would be put out of business. I almost feel sorry for her, but she organised the public campaign that accused us of being environmental rapists, while the whole time she was sweet-talking old man Berger into selling her his place so she could sell the mining rights to the Chinese. She doesn't care if a future mine affects business at Lion Plains because it's not hers anyway. She'll probably be able to buy half-a-dozen game farms with the profit she'll make on Kilarney, and at the same time her publicity campaign was cruelling our share price, which makes us an even softer target for China Dynamic.'

'We've got to go to Jan with this,' Cameron said.

Kylie looked to him, then Musa.

'What?' Cameron asked.

'Nothing. I don't know. You're right, we should tell him. If she's come here to do a deal on the quiet with the Chinese, maybe we can get in first.'

Cameron shook his head. 'They'll just outbid us and, besides, there's the problem of our cash flow. Jan still needs to know.'

The train started to slow and the manager announced over the PA system that they would soon be arriving in Kimberley. Outside the light was fading and a bloody sunset soaked the open landscape.

*

Luis was in the air, on an Airlink flight from Johannesburg's OR Tambo Airport to Kimberley. He checked his cheap digital watch again. He was late. From his online research he knew the Blue Train would only be in Kimberley for a little more than an hour and if the train was on time, then it was already there.

The captain advised his passengers they were beginning their descent. Luis felt the knot grow in his stomach. He would have to organise a car or taxi from the airport. He didn't know if he could make it in time, but he had to get to Cameron and Kylie and give them the information he had extracted from Wellington before he had killed him. Even if he was allowed to use his cellphone from the aircraft, which he wasn't, it wouldn't work as he had run out of credit.

His future and that of his son might be lost because he had been in too much of a rush to board his flight in Maputo to recharge his phone. He had only been late for the flight because he had killed a man – albeit a bad man – in cold blood. Perhaps the Lord had decided his fate long ago, when Luis had first cast his lot in with the criminal miners. He bunched his hands into impotent fists.

'*Ja*, I get nervous at landing time too,' the grey-haired Afrikaner matron next to him said. She reached over and patted his arm. 'You'll be fine, man.' He smiled at her and her unexpected charity. Perhaps all was not lost.

*

Tertia followed the delegates from the mining companies into the cinema where they were to view the short film that was part of the Kimberley tour. She'd been here before and knew that afterwards they would all inspect the Big Hole, the remains of a huge open-cut diamond mine. She knew the Australians thought of her as a vindictive leech, hanging off the dying corpse of their company, and they were not far wrong. She couldn't care less.

Mary Li hung back, pretending, no doubt, to defer to her male colleagues, and Tertia took the seat next to her as the cinema lights went down. The big screen was filled with the image of a small boy running through brittle, dry farmlands, and the story began of how diamonds were first discovered.

'My chairman will see you this evening, after we get on the train but before dinner. There is a break in the interminable presentations,' Mary Li whispered without preamble.

'Good. You've passed on the amount we discussed?'

'I have. We're Chinese; we'll want to negotiate. But you will do well out of this sale.'

'They understand the need for absolute secrecy? If the man selling me the farm gets a whiff of this deal he will pull out,' Tertia said.

'I have told my board this,' Mary said. 'We, too, want this kept quiet until the purchase goes through.'

Tertia glanced along the row of seating. The Australian contingent was beyond the Chinese and Jan Stein was watching the screen. Just an hour or more to go, she told herself, until the beginning of a new, perfect life. It had been a long time coming and she did regret some of the things she had done to get here, especially what she had put Chris through.

He had loved her like a puppy, with boundless enthusiasm and without the need for her to match him. And he had been a beautiful boy. But he was a means to an end and nothing could have come of their relationship. It was always bound to end, and at least he had died in love and not with a broken heart.

Tertia looked back at the rows of seats behind her. Cameron McMurtrie and Kylie Hamilton were not there. She had watched them on the train, at brunch, and had seen how close they were sitting in the departure lounge. They had become more than business colleagues, she thought. She wondered if they had skipped the tour in order to stay on the train and fuck.

She remembered Chris's touch, and his lips, as soft as a girl's. Yes, she missed him, but it would all be worth it. She had saved Lion Plains, even if it would forever exist next to an open-cut mine, and she was about to reclaim her family's fortune.

*

Kylie and Cameron looked out over the Big Hole. It was more than two hundred metres deep and four hundred wide, Kylie had read. It was a fitting monument, she thought, to endeavour and greed.

'We can sink Tertia,' Cameron said.

'By calling old man Berger and ratting her out, you mean?' Kylie said.

'Yes.'

Kylie sighed and leaned against the railing, staring down, literally, into the abyss. 'She's doing something immoral, but not illegal. I wonder how many people have levelled the same criticism at our industry over the centuries.'

'I know what you mean,' he said. 'I was never happy about us mining in a wildlife area, but I guess when you think of it, everywhere there's a mine now was once a pristine piece of wilderness.'

'I still believe in what we do,' she said. 'I know of communities in Australia and other countries where mining is their lifeblood. We can do it well, better than the likes of China Dynamic, and still give something back to the environment.'

Cameron shrugged. 'Well, Global Resources looks set to pass into history, whether Tertia gets rich out of it or not, and –'

'Luis!' Kylie pointed to the man jogging up the walkway.

Cameron walked to meet him and they shook hands, then Luis took Kylie's hand. 'I'm so glad I have found you both.'

'It's good to see you, Luis,' Kylie said, 'but I think you may be too late to help us. Tertia Venter, the woman who runs the Lion Plains Lodge, has secured a neighbouring property and is about to sell the rights to mine on it to the Chinese company that's in the process of buying Global Resources.'

'She can't do that.'

'Well,' Cameron said, spreading his palms, 'there's nothing we can do to stop her.'

'No, but the law can.'

'How so?' Kylie asked.

'She is guilty of murder, of arranging and paying for murders at least. Of your man Chris Loubser, of the security guard and Loubser's assistant, and of the attempted killing of you two.'

'But Wellington was behind all those,' Kylie said.

Luis shook his head. 'Wellington had a boss.'

'This Mohammed whom he supposedly reported to, but no one knows anything about,' Cameron said.

'Mohammed was in South Africa all along,' Luis said. 'Wellington told me, just now, in Maputo. And Mohammed was not a "he", but rather a "she".'

'Tertia Venter?' Cameron said.

'I can't believe it,' Kylie said.

'Yes,' said Luis. 'She wasn't just trying to save Lion Plains. She had been bankrolling Wellington by buying his gold for the last few years. By bringing down Global Resources she could stop the coalmine and increase illegal production at Eureka while your legal operations were shut down. Wellington told me she paid him to kidnap Chris Loubser and to get him to take contaminated air samples. She thought you two were getting close to discovering the truth, so she sent Wellington to sabotage your aircraft in Zambia. Wellington was ruthless, for sure, but this woman is evil. Even he seemed scared of her.'

'And my daughter?' Cameron asked.

'Wellington wanted to kill her, but Mohammed – Tertia – wanted her kept alive. Apparently she dealt with gold buyers from the United

Arab Emirates who would visit Lion Plains to negotiate, and one of them had expressed an interest in buying a white girl.'

'I'll kill her,' Cameron said.

Kylie put a hand on his arm. 'Cameron, be calm. We have to think this through. We need proof. Did Wellington sign a confession? Where is he? Do the Mozambican police have him locked up?'

Luis looked at the walkway for a second, then into Kylie's eyes. 'I was wearing a wiretap when I met with Wellington. He confesses to everything on the tape and names Tertia Venter, but my cousin, a policeman, took it from me and said he was going to erase it.'

'For God's sake, why?' Kylie said.

'Killing my wife was Wellington's idea, so I didn't think it fair that he live out his days in a prison. The recording makes it clear Wellington was begging for his life when I shot him. I am sorry, not for what I did, but for you not having your proof about Tertia.'

'Shit,' Kylie said. She rubbed her temples as she thought. 'We've got to get Jan in on this. There's no way Tertia can profit from all this killing. We've got to get the South African police onto the case. There must be phone records or bank details or something that can link her to Wellington and these gold buyers. We won't let up until we've got her, but first we've got to put her out of business.'

'I will testify, in court, as to what Wellington told me, but it will be the word of a former *zama zama* against a wealthy white woman,' Luis said.

'I'll SMS Jan. He's in the museum now. You have to tell him every-thing you've told us, Luis.'

He nodded. 'Of course. And I need to talk to your Mr Stein, with you two present. I have found a coal seam in Mozambique, near my home town, which dwarfs the concession you bid for at Lion Plains, but we can negotiate a very good deal for Global Resources.'

'Who's "we"?' Kylie asked.

'My cousin, Alfredo Simango, is a police captain and his wife's uncle is the governor of the province. While Alfredo and I cannot buy this land and sell it to you, we have already spoken to the right people. Mozambique needs more investment and employment and this will give you a presence in a different African country. People there will welcome a new mine and not care about Lion Plains and your problems here in South Africa, and the coal seam I have discovered is on land not being used for anything else.'

'And what do you want out of this?' she asked.

'A job. Any job in a future joint-venture mine between Global Resources and the Mozambican government. I don't care if I am a humble miner or the driver of a truck. I want an honest start, in my own country, in the industry I love.'

Kylie swallowed. They had gone out on a limb for Luis and he was repaying them with a find potentially worth millions of dollars. Jan had to hear about this. They would find a way to make this deal happen and Tertia would get her comeuppance, according to the letter of the law.

'Here he comes now,' Cameron said.

Kylie looked down the walkway and saw the tall figure of Jan Stein striding towards them.

'Cameron, Kylie. I hope this is important. I had to leave the board with the Chinese and I don't want them talking with me away from them.'

'Jan,' Kylie said, 'this is Luis Domingues Correia. He helped us when Cameron went to rescue Chris. He's got a deal for Global Resources – a new coal find in Mozambique.'

Jan gave a pained look but extended his hand to Luis. 'So what is this deal you have for us? I really don't have time to waste on a wild goose chase.'

'No,' Luis shook his head. 'I will not waste your time. There is no deal.'

*

The Blue Train passengers were filing back onto the bus, their brief visit to Kimberley over. Luis showed the train manager his booking and agreed that, while it was highly unusual for a passenger to board the train halfway to Cape Town, there was nothing stopping him from doing so.

Luis had walked away from Jan Stein without another word and Cameron and Kylie had followed him. 'I'll tell you on the train,' was all he had said to Cameron.

Cameron got up from his seat on the bus and walked to the rear, where Tertia was sitting by herself. He slid into the seat next to her. His rational side knew he should gather more evidence and get the police involved before he confronted Tertia, but quiet rage over what she had done consumed him. 'I know who you are.'

'I should think you should by now,' she said to him.

'Mohammed.'

She didn't flinch. 'I have no idea what you're talking about.'

'You were going to sell my daughter into slavery. You had good people killed. Wellington was your attack dog. You're going to jail, Tertia, for a very long time.'

She turned to him and fixed him with her narrowed eyes. 'Prove it. I heard today Wellington was killed in a police raid in Maputo. Shoddy work, as now he couldn't testify even if he wanted to.'

Cameron got up and went back to his seat, his fists balled by his side. When they got off, he and Kylie followed Luis and a carriage butler onto the train and waited impatiently for the suite briefing to be done with, then crowded into Luis's suite. Cameron closed the door behind them. 'You came all this way to make a deal and now you won't even talk to Stein? Why not?'

'His name's not Stein. It's Lotz.'

'What are you talking about?' Kylie asked.

'I've seen him before, back in 1987, during the Mozambican civil war. He was a South African military adviser to the Renamo anti-government rebels. He was with the Renamo commander who ordered a massacre of civilians at the town of Homoine, near my home.'

Cameron ran a hand through his hair. 'Are you sure it's the same man?'

'He had a moustache and sideburns then, and he's put on a little weight, but it's him – I could also tell by his crooked nose. I was pretending to be dead, lying in the grass, wounded. He was working with the Renamo commander and was as guilty as any of the rebels. Also, as soon he spoke I recognised his voice. I cannot deal with a war criminal.'

Cameron took out his cellphone and scrolled through his contacts until he found the number for Gert Cronje. He called it.

While he was waiting for the connection to come through Kylie asked him who he was calling.

'I've got an old army friend, Gert, who wrote a book about the recces. I never remembered a Jan Stein – or anyone called Lotz for that matter – but on the odd occasions Jan and I talked about days on the border I could tell he'd been to the places he talked about and done the things he said he'd done. You get some guys who pretend they've been part of special forces and you know they're faking it, but I could tell Jan was genuine – even if his name isn't.'

'It's all falling into place, now,' Kylie said, while Cameron dialled Gert's number and waited. 'Jan – Lotz – always avoided interviews with South African newspapers and magazines whenever they contacted Musa. He never visited here and he was grooming me to handle all the media in Africa. He was worried about someone recognising him.'

Cronje answered. After the initial pleasantries, Cameron said: 'Gert, did you ever come across a guy called Lotz – first name unknown – in the recces? A shade under two metres, grey eyes, fair hair, bent nose?'

'Lotz? *Ja*, I knew a Karl Lotz. He was a captain. I went to his wedding, in fact.'

'Could he have served in Mozambique? In a covert role in support of Renamo, late eighties?'

'Why do you ask, Cameron? You know some *okes* are still pretty sensitive about that sort of thing?'

'It's important.'

'Well, all I know for sure is that Karl left the recces; he was seconded to another government department and you know what that means. The old government could have had him running covert support to Renamo, political assassinations, who knows? He dropped out of sight for a few years and the last time I saw him was in '94, just after the elections. I saw him at Jan Smuts airport and he told me he had split up with his wife and was off to live in the bush in Botswana. But I thought you would have had plenty of background on Karl Lotz.'

Cameron was confused. 'Me? No. Why would I know about him? That's why I'm calling you.'

Gert laughed. 'Man, I thought you big mining company *okes* would have done your homework better than that. Karl Lotz's ex-wife has been running rings around you in the newspapers every day.'

Cameron was speechless.

'You there?' Gert asked. 'You did know that Karl Lotz used to be married to Tertia Venter, didn't you?'

40

The train started moving again and Kylie, Luis and Cameron left Luis's cabin to confront Jan Stein.

'Wait a minute. Just let me check on Jess.' Cameron knocked on his daughter's cabin. There was no answer. 'Jess?' He felt the panic rising inside him.

The automatic door at the end of the carriage shushed open. 'You're looking for Jessica?' Jan said.

Cameron looked at him. 'Yes.'

'She's in the lounge car, studying. I just had a quick coffee with her.'

'We need to talk to you,' Cameron said.

'I'm busy. I've got another meeting with the board before dinner.'

'We can do this in public, in the corridor, or in my cabin,' Cameron said.

Jan looked to Luis. 'I don't want *him* in there.'

'Luis is going to be in on this. He has made some serious allegations against you, Captain Lotz. We're going to hear your side of the story and you're going to tell us what's going on between you and your ex-wife.'

Jan licked his lips and Cameron could see he knew he was cornered. 'All right.'

It was close in the suite, as the beds had been made up. 'Sit,' said Cameron. He wanted to be standing over the CEO. Cameron folded his arms. 'Your name is Karl Lotz.'

'My name is Jan Stein. I've got an Australian passport to prove it.'

'You killed innocent people,' Luis said.

Kylie laid a hand on Luis's forearm. 'Let him speak, Luis.'

Jan seemed to crumple. He put his elbows on his knees and his head in his hands. 'I was a soldier.' He looked up at Cameron. 'You know what it was like.'

'I never murdered civilians.'

Jan shook his head. 'Neither did I, but I witnessed some things. Terrible things. I was seconded from the recces to work for the intelligence service. I was a patriot. I did as I was ordered.'

Luis looked away, out the darkened window. A passing train blared its horn.

'What happened between you and Tertia?'

Jan sighed. 'When the old government started to unravel, when de Klerk surrendered to the blacks, a few of us knew we would be in trouble. There was already talk of a truth and reconciliation commission, but some of the things I did, under orders, Cameron, I knew I would not be pardoned for. Tertia and I were having troubles at home; I was drinking too much to try and forget the things I'd done and I was sure she was sleeping around when I was away on missions. We were going to split up, but as much as she disliked me, and what I had been involved in, she didn't want to see me rot in prison. Some contacts arranged to get me out of the country and set me up in Australia with a new identity. I went back to mining and Tertia put it about that I'd run off with one of her female safari guides, to Botswana. I tried to keep my face out of the press as much as I could, but I supposed I always knew that when I became CEO someone here would eventually recognise me.'

'Are we supposed to feel *sorry* for you?' Luis asked. 'You need to be tried for your part in the massacre at Homoine.'

Jan glared at him. 'Do you know how many innocents Frelimo killed? It was a civil war; such things bring out the animal in men. I was an adviser to Renamo, but I never killed any civilians.'

'For all we know you *advised* them to carry out the massacre. Innocent civilians were killed; the rebels even cleared out the medical centre, slaughtering the ill, pregnant mothers . . . everyone. It was a *strategic* move, designed to draw Frelimo forces from the north,' Luis said.

Jan shrugged. 'I did no such thing, and I won't be going to Mozambique to face any trial. As soon as this deal is done with the Chinese I'm resigning. I'll cash in some shares, for what they're worth, and disappear.'

'You passed up earlier opportunities to invest in coalfields in Mozambique,' Kylie interjected. 'I saw the proposals, but you always argued against them and convinced the board to bid for the Lion Plains concession instead. Was that because you were too scared to set foot in Mozambique in case you were exposed, or because you wanted to get back at your ex-wife?'

'I don't know; a little of both, perhaps. The thought of dealing with some Frelimo fat cat turned my stomach, and yes, Tertia had made it plain to me a few years ago that she was not interested in reconciling and moving to Australia when she lost her game farm to the local community. She accused me of ruining her life, when she was the one who had cheated on me. When the opportunity came up to bid for the coal reserves on Lion Plains I was attracted to the idea of hurting her.'

Kylie shook her head. 'And she relished the challenge. And she won.'

'Yes, she did. Fair and square as it turns out, even if she and Loubser were in bed together – perhaps literally – and set us up with the contaminated samples. In the end it doesn't matter what dirty tricks she used because the presence of those bloody owls has finished Lion Plains as a mine for good.'

'We've got more news about your ex-wife, *Karl*,' Cameron said. 'Wellington told Luis in Maputo this morning that Tertia was also a partner in the illegal mining operation in Eureka. She set up Chris Loubser to be kidnapped. Wellington knew when and where he and the others would be going underground and that Chris would have the monitoring pumps with him. If Kylie and I hadn't rescued Chris, then Wellington would have eventually ransomed him back to us and smuggled out the samples to Tertia. As it was, Chris had the samples on him, which just made it easier for Tertia to set us up. Wellington also claimed it was she who ordered the killings of Barrica, Tshabalala, Sipho and Kylie and me.'

Jan's eyes widened. 'I knew she could be a vindictive bitch, but an organised crime boss? Murderess? Well, unless you can prove all you've said, it looks like she might get away scot-free.'

'And she's bought Kilarney and is going to sell it to the Chinese as soon as they take over Global Resources,' Kylie said. 'We can't let her win, and we have to get the police involved as soon as possible.'

'I agree,' said Jan. 'Let me take all this to the board, along with my letter of resignation. They've known it was coming for some time. I'll tell the Chinese that Tertia can expect to be met by the police in Cape Town. That should deter even China Dynamite from doing a deal with her.' He got up to leave.

'That's it?' Luis said. 'He's just going to walk out of here, away from all this?'

Jan moved until his face was just inches from Luis's. 'You want to try and stop me now? My life is over. You have a coalfield; sell it to the Chinese and watch your natural resources and your money drain away from your *kak* country.'

Cameron stepped between the two men and Jan let himself out of the cabin. Luis sat down on the bed where Jan had been. 'So that is it? This war criminal will go free?'

'No, Luis,' Kylie said. 'It's up to you what happens to him. You need to go to the authorities and make a complaint against him. Perhaps to the International Criminal Court.'

Luis sagged. 'My first priority must be to my son, and to the memory of my wife. I cannot let evil people like Wellington and this Tertia triumph. But Lotz is right; I fear that if I deal with this Chinese company it will not be in the best interests of my country or my people.'

'We need to go direct to the board,' Kylie said. 'With the truth.'

Cameron opened the small closet in his cabin and checked inside his travel bag.

Kylie saw the look on his face. 'What's wrong?'

'My pistol,' he said. 'I packed it, and it's gone. I'm worried about Jessica, Kylie. I'm going to look for her.'

'I'll come with you.'

'What about going to the board?'

'That can wait.'

'I'll come with you,' Luis said.

'Wait a minute,' Kylie said as they started walking towards the lounge car at the rear of the train.

Cameron looked back, his impatience showing.

'Cameron, did you tell anyone, anyone at all, that we were going to your wife's parents' house at Hippo Rock with Luis and Jessica?'

'No. Of course not. It was supposed to be a secret. Did you?'

*

Jan closed the cabin door behind him and gazed into the eyes of the woman he had loved with all his heart since he had first met her in high school.

Tertia came to him, her eyes misting, and he folded her in his arms. She pressed her face into his chest. 'My God, I have missed you, Karl.' She looked up at him. 'What's wrong? Kiss me.'

He swallowed hard. They had waited years for this moment, forced to live apart, and quietly, via the internet, plotting a future where he would be able to return to South Africa and the pair of them would have money and property to last them the rest of their lives.

The blacks had taken Tertia's beloved game reserve and wanted to sell it off as a coalmine. It had seemed a gift from heaven when he, as the CEO of a mining company, had been given the opportunity to bid for the rights for Lion Plains. He had made sure Global Resources won the tender – offering over the odds for the actual price and a small fortune to greedy hands behind closed doors. Their plan, for the project to then fail and for Global Resources to be left as an empty shell which the Chinese would pick up for a song, had been going perfectly.

'It's all within our grasp, lover,' Tertia said to him. 'Talk to me, you're scaring me. Are the Chinese getting cold feet?'

He shook his head. 'No, they'll stick to their word.' He had sought out China Dynamic five years ago when they had tried unsuccessfully to buy Global Resources. He'd been on his way up in the mining industry in Australia, working under his assumed name, but it had seemed that as much as he made and as hard as he worked he would never be able to give him and Tertia the life they deserved, especially after Lion Plains was taken from her. He needed to make a quantum leap.

He had read an article about corporate moles – people who wormed their way into the senior ranks of companies, often the African offshoots of foreign companies where oversight was less rigorous and the talent pool smaller than in the home countries. Global Resources was at the time a mid-sized company looking to expand in Africa and he was African born and heading up through the ranks of a competitor. When the CEO's job became vacant Jan approached China Dynamic and laid out a plan for them. If he, Jan Stein, could run Global Resources, build its portfolio of African mines and then systematically erode the company from within, to the point where it was in need of a fire sale, would China Dynamic guarantee him a five million dollar bonus if he could deliver it to them?

The Chinese had agreed.

The Lion Plains affair had just added sweetness to the deal. Tertia had given up on the idea of running a game farm – she just wanted revenge against the people who had taken it from her, and an even bigger windfall from the purchase and subsequent sale of Kilarney to China Dynamic. They would both walk away from Africa, from the bush, from mining, and from their continent's politics. Rio was shaping up as their preferred retirement destination, and their life would be one of unending opulence until they died.

'They know about you,' he said.

'There's no way they can prove any of it.'

'Your trained lion, Wellington, squealed before the Mozambican shot him. Kylie Hamilton and Cameron McMurtrie are going to the board right now. They know that you are the mythical "Mohammed".'

'You should have shot Wellington when you had the chance underground,' she said, and her tone irked him.

'I wouldn't have been underground if you hadn't let McMurtrie's daughter live. That was a mistake. We could have finished off Wellington at our leisure.'

'I'll deny it all. It's hearsay,' Tertia said.

'There's going to be enough publicity about all this for the Hawks to move on you. They'll trace your movements, bank accounts; we have to face reality, my love.'

'No. Wait, let me think.'

She broke from him and sat on the made-up bed in the suite. Her chest was rising and falling.

'Do they know about you yet?' she asked him.

He shook his head. 'They know we were – are – husband and wife, but they bought my story that I had Global Resources bid for Lion Plains to get back at you, because I hated you. I told them you also hated me but didn't want to see me arrested and paraded before the courts here or in Mozambique.'

Tertia frowned and nodded. 'So you're in the clear, but that doesn't help me.'

'Berger won't sell Kilarney once your plans are exposed, but the Chinese will still buy Global Resources. I'll get my bonus from Mary Li, and we can sell all the shares we've been buying through the front companies as soon the Chinese get the mines back up and running and the share price rises again. With Wellington dead and us out of the *zama zama* business, Eureka will be back in the black in days. All this will be forgotten.'

'And I'll be in prison.'

He shook his head. 'No, you must disappear now. You have the fake passports and IDs that I arranged for you, in the lockers at Johannesburg and Cape Town airports?'

Tertia nodded. 'Yes, our escape plan. But I want you to come with me. I've waited so long to be with you. I can't bear being away from you any longer. Come, run with me, Karl.'

'No. I can get through this. I'll be in Rio with you in a month, with more money than we need.'

She looked up at him and blinked her eyes. After all she had done, all the killings and theft and lies, she was the same big-eyed, adoring, spoiled rich girl he had fallen for all those years ago. He had agreed to, perhaps even been slightly aroused by, her plan to seduce Chris Loubser and use him as their pawn to help undermine the company and the Lion Plains project, and he wondered, often, if she slept with Wellington when they met, for her to take the gold for sale to the Arab buyers. But she *had* changed; he knew it. It seemed the more crimes she committed, the more perversions she indulged in, the more wicked she became. He had disagreed with her decision to sell McMurtrie's daughter; to him, killing the girl seemed kinder, given that the rest of her family was supposed to be dead.

'How shall we do it?' she asked.

'Put on your jeans and boots and your overcoat, tie a scarf, or better yet a towel around your head to protect you. I'll hit the emergency stop button and as the train starts to slow, jump for it. Tuck your arms in and keep your chin on your chest, roll when you hit the ground.'

'Karl . . .'

'Do you want to meet the police at the next station?'

'No.'

He passed her the clothes she needed while she changed out of the cocktail dress she had been going to wear to dinner. He couldn't help but notice the expensive lingerie she was wearing; perhaps she'd had a plan to sneak him into her room in the middle of the night. They had been so close.

When she was ready, her head encased in the towel, he took from his suit jacket pocket a small hammer that he had found at an emergency exit, the kind that would shatter reinforced glass. 'The train's windows don't open. We will have to do this quickly.' He kissed her, long and deep, and thought his heart must surely break.

'I love you,' Tertia said.

'I love you too. Always.' He smashed the picture window in the cabin with the hammer and the glass fell away like a thousand diamonds being scattered into the night. The wind rushed into the cabin. He knocked the remaining shards from the bottom of the window frame. 'Sit up here.'

He scooped her in his arms and lifted her so that her legs were dangling out of the window. 'Mind your head, my love,' he said. He placed a hand on the top of her head, to shield it from the sill, then moved his palm to the base of her cranium. His other arm he wrapped around her neck, then started to squeeze.

Too late, she felt her airway being constricted and her spine protesting. She tried to look back at him, but he couldn't bear to see those eyes again. There was no way she would escape South Africa if she survived the fall. It was regrettable, to lose her now, but with Tertia dead he could create a new life for himself, in her honour.

'Goodbye, my love.' Her neck snapped and, gently, he pushed her out the window.

Karl Lotz sat in his wife's cabin, breathing in her scent for the first time in years and the last time in his life.

*

Lotz entered the dining car and shot the starched white cuffs from his suit jacket then smoothed down his hair. He saw McMurtrie, his daughter, Hamilton and Correia all look up at him as he walked through the carriage.

'Has anyone seen Tertia?' Lotz asked them.

Kylie shook her head then put down her knife and fork, halfway through her starter. 'No. Have you?'

'No, I was tendering my resignation. Hilary Hann accepted it on behalf of the board,' he said. He looked at Luis. 'So, are you going to sell your coal to the Chinese? From what I could gather from Hilary, the sale is still going ahead.'

'It is none of your business,' Luis said quietly. 'And I will not rest until I see you in prison.'

Lotz snorted. 'Well, good luck with that.'

'I hate that the company can't put off the sale and do a deal with Luis now that he's resigned,' McMurtrie said, loud enough for Lotz to hear as he passed them and took a table by himself. Lotz smiled.

As the waiter was taking his order the train started to slow. He wondered if one of the carriage butlers had discovered Tertia missing and raised the alarm. He rested his forehead against the cool glass of the window and saw the modest outskirts of a Karoo farming town trundling into view. Ahead was the station. A blue light flashed. Lotz felt sweat prick under his armpits. He had to stay cool. Probably Tertia's broken window and absence from the train had been noticed and the train management were hoping to start a search without alarming the other passengers.

Lotz had ordered the springbok for his main course and the waiter set a weighty steak knife down on the side of his place setting.

Lotz looked behind him and saw McMurtrie easing himself out of his seat. Lotz slid the steak knife from the table and into the cuff of his shirt. Hamilton was getting up too.

'Jan, Karl, whatever you want to call yourself. Please get up and come with me,' Cameron said.

Kylie stood behind him, arms folded, trying to look menacing.

'Why should I?'

'The police are waiting for you, and in the interests of the other passengers I told the manager I'd escort you off the train and onto the platform.'

'And what crime have I committed? None. I changed my name by deed poll in Australia, legally. I failed to report a conflict of interest to the board and for that oversight I have just resigned.'

Kylie moved closer to him, also keeping her voice low to avoid making a scene. 'You were in on it with Tertia all along.'

'Rubbish. I told you, I was working against her.'

'Bullshit,' Kylie said. 'You were working against *us*. It was you who called a halt to the use of armed security against the *zama zamas* and you who pushed for the Lion Plains mine when the board favoured an early investment in Mozambique. You've been working to bring us down for years.'

'Prove it.'

'She doesn't need to,' Cameron said.

'I asked Cameron if he had told anyone that we were taking Luis to Hippo Rock after his wife died,' Kylie said. 'He didn't tell a soul, but I did. You. I told you in my daily update that we were going to a holiday house Cameron's in-laws owned. I just remembered and Cameron told me that he had talked to you about Hippo Rock in the past and emailed you pictures of the house, and that you liked the sound of buying a place there one day. That was the only way Wellington could have known where to find us. Where's your wife now?'

Lotz shifted his eyes left and right. Most of the other diners were oblivious of their conversation, but some were pointing out the window at the approaching flashing lights.

He looked pointedly out into the darkness and smirked, sure they could see his reflection.

'Don't look away from me when I ask you a question, you bastard,' the Australian woman said.

'Kylie . . .'

Lotz saw the movement he had hoped for, in the reflections in the carriage window. Kylie had moved past Cameron and was between him and McMurtrie. Lotz sprang from his seat and raised his elbow up and into her, catching her under the chin so that her head snapped back. Before she fell he caught her, then slid the sharpened steak knife from his sleeve. He had it at her throat before she recovered from his first blow. McMurtrie, fists balled in impotent anger, took a step back.

Wine glasses spilled, women shrieked and men stampeded for the exits at either end of the carriage. At the same time, he saw Cameron's kid – the girl – enter the carriage.

'I'm getting off the train, with Kylie, and she stays with me until I get what I want.'

'Dad?' Jess shouted.

Cameron looked back at his daughter. 'Jess, get out of here. Go back to your cabin.'

'No, Dad, I'm not leaving you.'

Cameron shook his head and turned back to Lotz. 'You're being ridiculous, Karl. You know how it will end. There are a dozen heavily armed police on the station. You know they'll end up shooting you dead. Do you want to take Kylie with you?'

'Maybe.' He pushed the knife into the soft skin of Kylie's neck. 'Maybe I'll just kill her now anyway and let the cops finish me off. My wife's gone and so is yours, Cameron. I've been watching you and this one. I think you're sweet on each other. If I can't have the happy ending, then why the fuck should you?'

Lotz backed towards the rear of the dining car. 'But for now I'll keep her alive until I can get a helicopter. I see you haven't pulled a gun on me yet, Cameron. Guess you must have thought you were safe.' The train juddered and the brakes squealed. 'Sit down, Cameron, Luis. We're going to be here for some time while the negotiations play out. Or you can leave if you want.'

'I'm staying,' Cameron said. 'Jess – go.'

'Good advice. Listen to your father,' Lotz said.

'No, Dad. I'm staying.' She glared at Lotz. 'I'm not going anywhere. You weren't coming to save me, were you? You were working with Wellington. Did you come underground to kill me?'

'Clever girl.'

'For God's sake, Jess, get under the table,' Cameron said. 'If the cops come in shooting there'll be bullets everywhere.'

'More good advice from dear old dad,' Lotz said. Jessica lowered herself to the ground, next to her bag of schoolbooks. Correia, the coward, got down on the floor next to the girl, on his belly. Karl wondered, briefly, what kind of child he and Tertia might have had if they had been given a chance.

'*Karl Lotz. This is the South African Police,*' blared a voice through a loudhailer. '*Release your hostage and lay down your weapon. Come out with your hands high.*'

'They'll have a sniper taking a sight picture on you by now,' Cameron said.

Lotz laughed. 'In this *dorpie*? No, that will be hours away. I don't really think I can wait that long and of course I know you're right. This will never end with me being flown to Cape Town airport in a helicopter with Kylie as my hostage, and me boarding a plane to Rio. It just doesn't work that way, does it? There are no happy endings. You lost your marriage; I lost my country and my wife. Be thankful you got your daughter back. Kylie wanted my job, but now she won't get that because the Chinese will put their own person in, so I think she and I will make our exit now.'

He started to push the knife into Kylie's neck as she kicked and writhed against him.

Then his world went black, as impenetrable as a darkened mine.

EPILOGUE

Musa Mabunda watched in silence as his cousin, Tumi, swept the far bank of the stream with her spotlight, searching for the telltale glow of the owls' eyes.

They had left the other two passengers in the Land Rover, parked a short distance back, where they had stopped for sundowners. They had arrived at Lion Plains that morning and it was the first time Musa had seen Tumi in person since they had spoken by phone, on the Blue Train.

'Is it true what they said in the newspapers, that McMurtrie's daughter helped kill Jan Stein?' Tumi asked him in a soft voice.

'Yes. She had Cameron's gun with her; she feared for her safety after being kidnapped by Wellington. She passed the pistol to the Mozambican, Luis Correia, and he shot Stein – Karl Lotz – between the eyes.'

Tumi shook her head. '*Eish*. I'm safer here in the bush with all the lions and the leopards.'

Musa laughed quietly. They had come to Lion Plains not just to visit his cousin and spend a night in the lodge, but also to see the owls that had turned the coalmining project on its head. 'Are you enjoying being the lodge manager now?'

Tumi sighed. 'Acting manager. And it's hard work, but the good news is the community leaders have given up thinking about mining and they are committed to making Lion Plains the best game reserve in the area.'

'That's good,' Musa said.

'We need to find these owls soon as you have to get back and have dinner. It will be ironic if they have left. But even if they have, I won't tell the local community.' She looked back and winked at Musa.

'We've got an early start now. We have to go see our new Mozambican project manager, Luis Correia, in Maputo tomorrow.'

'Sshh! Musa, look!'

Tumi shone her spotlight and Musa could see the glowing orange eyes staring at him. The owl blinked, but a second later it flew away.

'Damn, that was the pel's fishing owl!' Tumi said. 'He's gone. But look at that hollow in the tree trunk, near where the big branch joins it. I'm going to have a look.'

'But, Tumi, it's dark, and it's dangerous out here at night.'

'Man up, Musa! The researchers I spoke to need as much information as they can get, especially about nesting sites. I'm going to have a look.'

Musa stood disapprovingly with his hands on his hips as his crazy cousin waded into the stream below the bank and scrambled up onto the other side. He shook his head as he watched her climb the tree they had been watching, as agile and sure-footed as a leopard. She hoisted herself up onto the branch and peered into the hollow near where they had seen the owl.

Tumi screamed, and Musa feared for a heartbeat she had been bitten by a black mamba or some other deadly snake. Then he saw the startled blur of wings and feathers as the owl burst from the hollow. Tumi lost her grip on the branch and dropped to the ground.

'Tumi, are you all right?' he called.

She stood, laughed, and brushed herself down. When she forded the stream back to the other side she was grinning wide. 'That gave me a fright. It must have been the female. Musa, you'll never guess – there were two eggs in the hollow!'

They retraced their steps through the bush, Tumi shining the light ahead of them. 'Kylie will be so excited. She said she really wanted to see the owls,' Tumi said.

'And so did Jess,' Musa said, pushing a branch out of his way. 'It's a shame she had to stay in Barberton, studying with her friends.'

'She is a clever girl, that one.'

'You know,' Musa said, 'I'm glad the mine never went ahead here. I'm pleased for you, and pleased for the company that Luis has found us a coal field in Mozambique where the local people are happy to have a mine and the income it will bring.'

He looked up at the rising moon and breathed in the rich scents of the bush around him. Musa wondered why Cameron and Kylie hadn't come with them on the walk but had decided instead to wait with the Land Rover whilst Tumi tried to find the owls and, if she could, follow them back to their nest.

He and Kylie had spent an hour that afternoon working on a draft media release for the Global Resources board about their search for a new CEO. Kylie had been acting in the role since the incident on the Blue Train and Musa had assumed she would end up with the top job on a permanent basis. The Eureka mine was open and back up to full production, and mine security was winkling out the last of the *zama zamas*. Cameron had decided to stay with the company as head of new projects and, as the next big one would be the coalmine, he and Jess would relocate across the border to Mozambique once she finished school. The company's share price was recovering and all was looking good for a change. Musa had been surprised, then, when Kylie had told him to write that she was not putting her hat in the ring to be considered for the permanent CEO's position. She would be staying as the head of health, environment, safety and community, across the company, and the board also wanted her to oversee its African operations, particularly during negotiation and development of the new Mozambican coalmine. She had always struck him as a particularly ambitious and motivated woman, and while it was clear from their short stay at Lion Plains that her love affair with the African bush was continuing, he still couldn't understand why she would want to spend more time in Africa instead of in the company's headquarters in Sydney.

They reached the clearing where Tumi had left the Land Rover. Tumi put her hand up and Musa stopped behind her. He hoped Kylie and Cameron hadn't been eaten.

When he peered around his cousin's shoulder, however, he saw what the matter was, and a few things fell into place. Cameron McMurtrie and Kylie Hamilton were still in the back seat of the Land Rover where Tumi had left them, and they were kissing.

Acknowledgements

O ne of the many things I like about writing novels is that my job gives me a chance to explore – not just new places, but parts of life I would otherwise never have been exposed to.

However, when I started writing a book about mining I soon learned that this was a whole other world with a language of its own. I would never have been able to attempt to negotiate the literal labyrinth of the world of mining without some excellent guides. First and foremost I'd like to thank Casper Strydom, General Manager of Barberton Mines, in the historic gold mining town of Barberton, South Africa. Casper and his equally helpful Chief Geologist, Roelf le Roux, patiently explained the workings of a gold mine and the history of their town, and took me underground for a first hand look at the Fairview Goldmine, including sites where criminal miners had been working. Casper and Roelf read the manuscript for *The Prey*, as did Steve Smith and Scotney Moore, who also work in the mining industry. All provided much appreciated corrections and valuable feedback; needless to say, any technical mistakes that remain are my doing alone. Thanks to you all for your help, time and patience.

Thanks, too, to James Rickards for his insights into the corporate side of the mining world; to Annelien Oberholzer for her patient and ongoing correction of my Afrikaans; to Wayne Hamilton from swagmantours.com.au for his input into the tourism related scenes; to John Roberts for his in depth knowledge of Mozambique and its history.

Lianne Kelly-Maartens from the Sun International hotel group organised for me to stay at the excellent Royal Livingstone Hotel in Zambia while was researching the book and I thank her and the staff there for a lovely stay.

Hippo Rock Private Nature Reserve and Lion Plains private game lodge mentioned in this book are fictitious, but bear strong similarities to real places. Nicola and I now own a house (as well as our trusty Land Rover) in a place similar to Hippo Rock and were generously hosted by people in several lodges in the Sabi Sand game reserve while researching this book. Thanks to our new neighbours for welcoming us and making us feel at home in Africa.

Deep thanks, too, go to Cameron and Tania McMurtrie, who made a generous donation to the Mother Africa Foundation to ship a container of books from Australia to schools in Zimbabwe. Cameron, I hope you enjoyed being the hero of the story; Tania, sorry!

As always my unpaid and forthright family of editors, wife Nicola, mum Kathy, and mother in law Sheila helped get the book to print and for that, I thank them. Thanks, too, to my agent, Isobel Dixon, and my publisher and editor at Quercus Books, Jane Wood and Katie Gordon. Words can hardly express how lucky I am to be spending half my life in Africa doing what I love most.

And thank you – I couldn't do it without you.